The Adventures of Pinocchio
皮諾丘
木偶奇遇記裡的真相
—小木偶教我們的12堂誠實人生課—

卡洛・柯洛迪 Carlo Collodi ―― 著　　盛世教育 ―― 譯

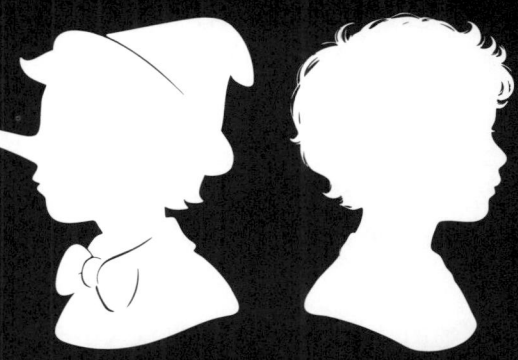

笛藤出版

作者簡介

卡洛・科洛迪 Carlo Collodi
（1826 年 11 月 24 日 — 1890 年 10 月 26 日）

卡洛・柯洛迪，原名洛倫佐・洛倫奇尼（Lorenzo Lorenzini），1826 年 11 月 24 日出生於義大利托斯卡納區的佛羅倫斯，成長於一個普通但熱愛文化的家庭。他的筆名「Collodi」，取自母親的家鄉——一座風景如畫的小鎮，也成為他日後在文壇上的身分象徵。

早年他曾進入神學院學習，但因對政治與文學充滿熱情，選擇投身新聞與寫作工作。他在 19 世紀中葉積極參與義大利的民族統一運動，曾親自上戰場參與解放戰爭，筆鋒亦常見於政治諷刺與社會批評。

卡洛・柯洛迪的文學生涯起初多以成人小說與諷刺文為主，但他最廣為人知的作品《木偶奇遇記》（Le Avventure di Pinocchio）則是在他中年後轉向兒童文學領域時創作的。該書自

1881 年於《兒童雜誌》連載起即引發熱烈迴響，於 1883 年集結出版後迅速風靡義大利乃至世界，成為兒童文學的永恆經典。

《皮諾丘──木偶奇遇記裡的真相：小木偶教我們的 12 堂誠實人生課》透過頑皮木偶皮諾丘的成長歷程，傳遞誠實、悔改、勇氣與責任的重要，寓教於樂，被譽為「給孩子的道德指南」，並被翻譯超過三百種語言，是歷史上義大利被翻譯最多的文學作品之一。

卡洛・科洛迪於 1890 年 10 月 26 日辭世，長眠於佛羅倫斯的聖米尼亞托大殿（San Miniato al Monte）。他的故鄉 Collodi 小鎮今日設有皮諾丘主題公園，紀念這位創造了不朽童話角色的作家。即使在他離世一百多年後，皮諾丘的故事仍持續感動著全世界的讀者。

生平年表

- 1826.11.24
  生於義大利托斯卡納一個叫科洛迪(Collodi)的小鎮,這也是作者筆名的由來。

- 1848
  積極參加義大利民族解放運動並參加了義大利解放戰爭。

- 1876
  發表作品《小手杖》。

- 1878
  發表作品《小木片》。

- 1881
  開始在《兒童雜誌》上分期連載〈一個木偶的故事〉（第二年改名為〈木偶奇遇記〉）直到1883年才連載完畢。

- 1887
  代表作品《快樂的故事》

- 1890.10.26
  在佛羅倫斯去世,被埋葬在聖米尼亞托大殿。

- 1892
  發表最後兩部作品《愉快的符號》、《諷刺雜談》。

皮諾丘主題公園

卡洛‧科洛迪的筆名來自於他熱愛的家鄉科洛迪 (Collodi)，一座保存了他童年美好回憶的幽靜小鎮。《木偶奇遇記》發表後，受到全世界讀者的喜愛，科洛迪小鎮的每個角落裡都陳列著與《木偶奇遇記》相關的雕像和圖畫，主要的街道和小巷全部都是用《木偶奇遇記》中的人物和動物命名.

1956 年，科洛迪小鎮專門建造了一個皮諾丘主題公園 (Parco di Pinocchio)，用來紀念作者和這個長鼻子的玩偶。公園裡有皮諾丘的銅像，有馬賽克藝術和雕刻展示了木偶歷險的經過，還有迷宮、遊樂場和兒童餐廳等設施。

皮諾丘
木偶奇遇記裡的真相

目　錄

第 1 章 …………… *014*	第 19 章 …………… *096*
第 2 章 …………… *018*	第 20 章 …………… *100*
第 3 章 …………… *023*	第 21 章 …………… *104*
第 4 章 …………… *028*	第 22 章 …………… *107*
第 5 章 …………… *032*	第 23 章 …………… *112*
第 6 章 …………… *035*	第 24 章 …………… *119*
第 7 章 …………… *038*	第 25 章 …………… *126*
第 8 章 …………… *043*	第 26 章 …………… *131*
第 9 章 …………… *047*	第 27 章 …………… *135*
第 10 章 …………… *051*	第 28 章 …………… *143*
第 11 章 …………… *054*	第 29 章 …………… *149*
第 12 章 …………… *059*	第 30 章 …………… *158*
第 13 章 …………… *066*	第 31 章 …………… *166*
第 14 章 …………… *071*	第 32 章 …………… *174*
第 15 章 …………… *075*	第 33 章 …………… *182*
第 16 章 …………… *079*	第 34 章 …………… *191*
第 17 章 …………… *083*	第 35 章 …………… *200*
第 18 章 …………… *090*	第 36 章 …………… *206*

The Adventure of Pinocchio

CONTENTS

Chapter 1	222		Chapter 19	311
Chapter 2	226		Chapter 20	316
Chapter 3	231		Chapter 21	320
Chapter 4	237		Chapter 22	324
Chapter 5	241		Chapter 23	329
Chapter 6	245		Chapter 24	336
Chapter 7	248		Chapter 25	344
Chapter 8	253		Chapter 26	349
Chapter 9	257		Chapter 27	353
Chapter 10	261		Chapter 28	362
Chapter 11	265		Chapter 29	369
Chapter 12	270		Chapter 30	379
Chapter 13	277		Chapter 31	387
Chapter 14	282		Chapter 32	396
Chapter 15	287		Chapter 33	405
Chapter 16	291		Chapter 34	415
Chapter 17	296		Chapter 35	425
Chapter 18	304		Chapter 36	432

卡洛・齊奧斯特里 (Cario Chiostri,1863-1939),義大利插畫家,他創作了第一版大號字體《木偶奇遇記》的插畫。

The Pigeon took flight, and in a few minutes had soared so high that they almost touched the clouds.

鴿子扇著翅膀往上飛,幾分鐘之內就貼近了天邊的雲彩。

Pinocchio, standing on the top of a high rock, kept calling to his father by name.

皮諾丘站到一塊高高的岩石上面,不斷地叫著他父親的名字。

查理斯・詹姆斯・福卡德（Charles James Folkard，1878-1963），英國插畫家。

Don't listen to the advice of bad companions.

不要聽壞朋友的意見。

If you don't want to tire yourself, then my boy, amuse yourself with yawning, and much good may it do you.

假若不想累著你自己，那麼，孩子，你就打著哈欠自娛自樂吧！希望它會給你帶來很多好處。

What species of fish is this?

這是什麼品種的魚？

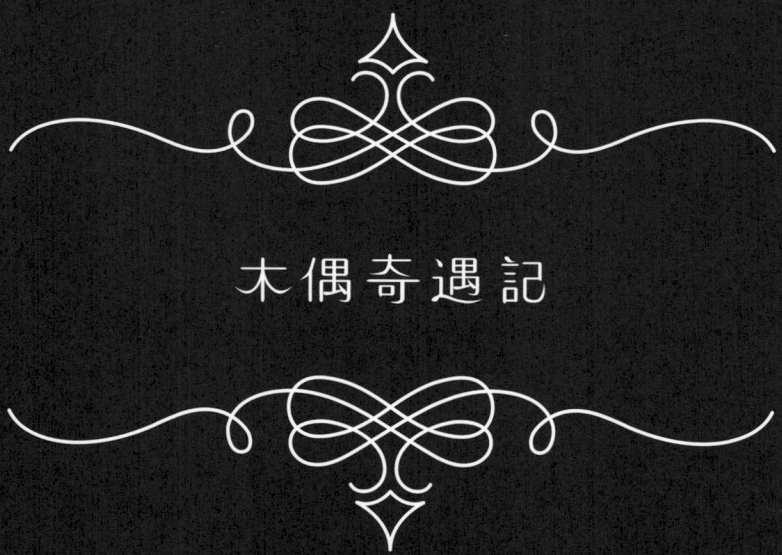

木偶奇遇記

皮諾丘──木偶奇遇記裡的真相

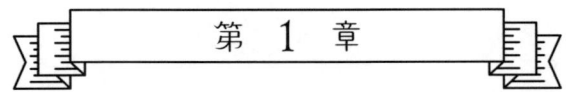

老木匠櫻桃師傅是如何發現一塊像個孩子般會哭又會笑的木頭。

很久很久以前有……。

「一位國王！」我的小讀者們會立刻接著這麼說。

不,孩子們,你們錯了。在很久很久以前有一‧塊‧木‧頭。

這塊木頭並不怎麼值錢,它就是一塊很普通的木頭,是那種在寒冬裡放到火爐和壁爐裡生火和溫暖房間用的。

事情究竟如何發生的很難詳述,但經過是這樣的:在某個美好的一天,這塊木頭就出現在一位老木匠的店鋪裡。老木匠的名字是安東尼奧,但大家都稱他為櫻桃老師傅,因為他的鼻頭就像熟透了的櫻桃,又紅又亮的。

櫻桃老師傅一看見這塊木頭,臉上就顯露出很開心的表情,他心情愉悅地摩拳擦掌,自言自語:「這塊木頭來得正是時候,剛好可以用來做一張小桌子的一條腿。」

這一說完,他便立刻拿出一把鋒利的斧頭,準備把樹皮和木頭粗糙的表面砍掉。但是,就在他正打算砍下第一刀的時候,手卻舉在半空中停住了,因為他聽到一個細若游絲的聲音哀求著他說:「不要那麼用力打我!」

讀者們可以想見,善良的櫻桃老師傅有多麼驚嚇啊!

他轉了轉那雙害怕的眼睛,細思極恐地滿屋子上上下下地尋覓,想要找出那微弱的聲音是從哪裡傳出來。可是,他並沒有看見任何人啊!他看一看長椅底下,沒有人;他再看了看那個經常關著的壁櫥,沒有人;他又看了裝著刨花和鋸末的籃子內,還是沒有人;甚至,他打開了店鋪的大門,瞥了一眼大街上,依舊沒·有·人!那麼,究竟是誰呢?

「我知道怎麼回事了。」,突然櫻桃師傅笑了出來,然後抓了抓頭上的假髮說,「那微弱的聲音肯定是我幻聽了。還是繼續做事吧。」

於是,他再次拿起斧頭往那塊木頭用力地砍了下去。

「喔!喔!你弄痛我啦!」那個細微的聲音再次哀淒的叫了起來。

櫻桃老師傅當下真是嚇呆了。他因恐懼而張大了眼睛,嘴巴也嚇到大大地張開，吐出的舌頭都快垂到下巴了，就好像是聳立在噴水池裡的雕像。直到稍微恢復平靜能再次開口說話時，他不停地顫抖然後結結巴巴的說：「那個微弱的『喔～喔～』的聲音到底是從哪兒來的呢？……這裡肯定沒有活生生的靈魂啊！難不成是這塊木頭，還學會了像個孩子一樣哭哭鬧鬧的？我無法相信。這塊木頭，就是在這裡的這塊木頭；就和其他大多數的木頭一樣的，不過是一截可以生火的木材，把它丟進火裡，應該能煮熟一鍋豆子……

那麼，那麼怎麼會發出聲音呢？難道有人藏在這木頭裡面嗎？如果真有人躲在裡面，那他可慘了，我會馬上解決掉他的！」

他一邊這麼說的同時，一邊抓起了那塊倒楣的木頭，毫不憐憫地將它朝牆上丟過去。

然後，他停下手中的動作，聽聽還有沒有那個小小的哭鬧聲響起。兩分鐘～沒有；五分鐘～沒有；十分鐘～還是沒有！

「我知道了。」他再次抓了抓假髮，笑著自言自語地說，「那微弱的『喔～喔～』聲，應該是我的幻覺！我還是繼續手頭的工作吧。」

但是他還是提心吊膽的，於是試著用唱歌來給自己壯膽。

他決定收起了斧頭、拿起鉋刀準備把木頭刨光，就在他來來回回刨著的時候，他又聽見那個小小的聲音笑著說：「停下來！這可癢死我了！」

這當下啊！可憐的櫻桃老師傅就像被雷劈到一樣，整個人嚇到都癱軟了。等到他終於清醒時，發現自己已經坐在地上了。

他不但臉色大變，連那向來紅通通的鼻頭都嚇得發青了。

皮諾丘——木偶奇遇記裡的真相

第 2 章

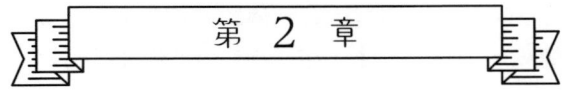

櫻桃老師傅將那塊木頭送給了他的朋友傑佩托，傑佩托用來製作了一個會跳舞、擊劍，以及翻跟斗的神奇木偶。

正在那個時候，有人咚咚咚地敲門了。

「請進。」老木匠說，但是他已經震驚到無法站起。

一位精力充沛的小老頭很快走進了店鋪。他名叫傑佩托·葛派特，可是附近的孩子們老愛作弄他，總是喊他的綽號「玉米糊」，這是因為他的黃色假髮實在是太像印第安玉米做成的麵糊。

傑佩托非常的憤怒。只要誰敢叫他「玉米糊」，他就會暴怒，到時可是沒有人能控制住他的脾氣的。

「日安,安東尼奧師傅。」葛派特‧傑佩托說,「您為什麼坐在地上啊?」

「我啊,正在教螞蟻識字。」

「希望您玩得開心。」

「是什麼事讓您大駕光臨,我的鄰居傑佩托師傅?」

「當然是我的腳啊。不過說真的,安東尼奧師傅,我過來是有事求您幫忙。」

「我隨時準備著為您服務。」老木匠說著說著就跪了下來。

「今天早上,我腦海裡冒出了一個想法。」

「說來聽聽。」

「我想做一個美麗的木偶;不僅僅是一個完美的木偶而已,它還要會跳舞、擊劍、翻跟斗。我想和這個木偶一起環遊世界來賺錢好買點麵包吃,買杯酒喝。您覺得這個主意如何呢?」

「棒呆了,玉米糊!」那個微弱的小聲音又驚呼了,不知來自何方的聲音。

一聽到有人叫他玉米糊,傑佩托氣到像一隻發怒的火雞脹紅了臉,轉頭衝著老木匠怒氣狂飆地說:「您為什麼要侮辱我?」

「誰侮辱您啦?」

「您叫我玉米糊!」

皮諾丘──木偶奇遇記裡的真相

「那不是我說的！」

「不是你說的，難不成是我自己？我說，就是你。」

「我沒喊！」

「你喊了！」

「我沒喊！」

「你喊了！」

兩個人越吵越生氣，最後竟然拳腳相向打起架了。只見他們抱成一團扭打起來，又是咬又是抓的，野蠻極了。

這一架打完之後，安東尼奧師傅手中正抓著傑佩托黃色的假髮，傑佩托發現自己嘴裡還咬著老木匠灰白的假髮。

「把假髮還給我」安東尼奧師傅喊道。

「那你，也把我的假髮還來，我們還是講和吧。」

兩位老頭兒分別戴回自己的假髮，然後握著對方的手，發誓說餘生還是要繼續做好朋友。

「那麼，老鄰居傑佩托先生。」老木匠說，為了表示誠意：「您需要我幫什麼忙呢？」

「我需要一塊木頭做我的木偶，您可以送給我一些嗎？」

聽到這句話，安東尼奧師傅真是不禁大喜，飛快地跑去長椅下撿起那塊讓他驚恐不已的木頭。就在他正打算把木頭給朋友的時候，木頭蠕動了一下，接著用力地從他手中掙脫出來，然後不偏不倚地就打中了～那可憐的傑佩托乾乾瘦瘦的小腿骨上。

「啊！安東尼奧師傅，您禮數還真多，有這麼送禮的嗎？您差點兒就要把我的腿給弄殘廢了。」

「我發誓，真的不是我做的！」

「那麼，您是說是我自己做的不成？」

「都要怪這塊木頭啦！」

「我知道是木頭打了我的腿，但把它打在我腿上的是您！」

「我沒有用它打您！」

「騙子！」

「傑佩托，您別罵我，否則我就要喊您玉米糊喔！」

「笨驢！」

「玉米糊！」

「笨猴！」

「玉米糊！」

「笨狒狒！」

「玉米糊！」

傑佩托聽到這第三聲玉米糊時，憤怒讓他失去理智了，猛然將老木匠撲倒在地,兩個人又拚了命地打了一架。

　　這場戰鬥結束後,安東尼奧師傅的鼻子上多了兩道抓痕,而傑佩托的馬甲背心上掉了兩顆鈕扣。當他們扯平後,再次緊握著對方的雙手,發著誓說後半輩子還會是好朋友。

　　然後,傑佩托帶著那塊很棒的木頭,辭謝了安東尼奧師傅,一瘸一拐走回家去了。

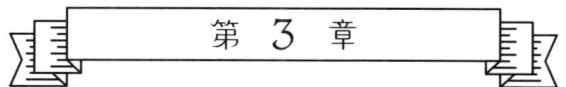

傑佩托回到家後就開始製作木偶,並取名為皮諾丘。皮諾丘第一次就闖了大禍。

　　傑佩托住在一間狹小的地下室裡,只有些微的光亮從樓梯那邊透露出來。就連傢俱也非常簡陋,一把破爛的椅子,一張廢舊的床,一張跛腳的桌子。房間的盡頭有個生火的壁爐,不過那火是畫出來的,火上面畫著一個燉鍋,鍋裡咕咚咕咚熱氣騰騰的地冒著煙。當然,那些熱氣也一樣是畫出來的,但畫的也算十分逼真了。

　　傑佩托一進門,馬上就拿起工具動手雕刻他的木偶。

　　「該為他取什麼名字呢?」他自言自語道,「叫他皮諾丘好了。這個名字可以給他帶來福氣。曾聽說有個家庭,全家人都叫這個名字:父親、母親、幾個孩子都是皮諾丘,而且他們

皮諾丘──木偶奇遇記裡的真相

都過得很好。其中最富有的一個還是乞丐。」

為木偶取好名字之後，傑佩托就專心地工作了。先是做出了他的頭髮，然後是他的前額，接著是他的眼睛。

雙眼一完成，傑佩托發現它們居然動起來了，然後，兩隻眼睛直愣愣地盯著他看。想想看，傑佩托有多驚嚇啊！

傑佩托看著直盯著自己的那兩隻木頭眼睛，開始有點後悔了，然後氣呼呼地說：「壞木頭眼睛，你盯著我幹嗎？」

沒有人回應。

於是，他繼續刻出鼻子。然而，鼻子剛完成，它自個兒就開始長了起來。它長啊～長啊～長啊，就幾分鐘的時間，已經長成了一個巨大的鼻子，似乎還要長個沒完沒了似的。

可憐的傑佩托盡全力想把鼻子砍短，但是他越是砍掉，這個鼻子就變本加厲地變得越長！

接下來是還未成形的嘴巴，竟然發出聲音嘲笑傑佩托。

「不要笑！」傑佩托生氣地說。不過，他這話就像是對著牆壁說的，毫不起作用。

「我說，你不要笑了！」他用威脅的語氣，開始咆哮起來。

這下，嘴巴是止住了笑，但是整個舌頭卻吐了出來。

為了不破壞手藝，傑佩托裝作沒有看見這些怪事，繼續做他的工作。嘴巴完成之後，他開始刻下巴、脖子、雙肩、腹部、胳膊和手。

就在手即將完成的同時，傑佩托的假髮被扯下來了。他四處看看，猜猜看他見到什麼啦？只見他那黃色假髮正被木偶抓在手中。

「皮諾丘！⋯⋯把假髮還給我，馬上！」但是，皮諾丘沒有把假髮還他，而是把它套在了自己頭上，差點兒就把自己給悶死了。

木偶這種粗野無禮的舉動，讓傑佩托感到了前所未有的悲傷和難過。他轉身對著皮諾丘說：「你這個小淘氣鬼！我還沒有把你完成，你就已經開始不尊重父親了！你真壞，我的孩子，你簡直壞透了！」

然後，他擦乾了眼淚。

但是，腿和腳還沒有做好呢！

傑佩托剛把腳完成，鼻尖上就被踢了一下。

「我這是自作孽啊！」他自言自語道，「起初我就該想到這一點！現在一切都晚了！」

然後，他把木偶放到了腋下，然後再放到地面上教他走路。

起初皮諾丘雙腿僵硬，幾乎不能行動，於是傑佩托慢慢教著他，告訴他一步一步地邁出去。

當他的腿靈活起來，皮諾丘就開始自己走路，然後圍著房間跑，最後竟然溜出了房外，還逃跑到大街上了。

皮諾丘──木偶奇遇記裡的真相

可憐的傑佩托跟在他後面追,可是怎麼也追不上。皮諾丘那個搗蛋鬼在他前面蹦蹦跳跳的,就像隻野兔。那雙木頭腳劈哩啪啦地敲在地面上,像是有二十位農民穿了木屐走路的響聲。

「攔住他!攔住他!」傑佩托大聲喊道。可是大街上的人們看到那跑得像匹小馬的木偶,都只顧驚奇地停下腳步,看著他笑了又笑,笑了又笑,笑到都無法用言語形容。

所幸,最後有警察出現了,他聽到人聲喧嘩,還以為是一匹小馬從他主人手裡掙脫了。那員警勇敢地站在馬路當中,叉開雙腿,下定決心要把馬攔在路上,以免造成更大的禍患。

當皮諾丘遠遠地就看到警察把整條街都給擋住了,他出其不意地衝過去,就從警察的兩腿之間溜了過去。不過顯然的他失敗了。

警察似乎沒有太費力的就敏捷地抓住了他的鼻子(因為那個鼻子出乎意料地長,像是特意做出來方便給員警抓的),然後把他交付給傑佩托。當傑佩托想馬上揪住他的耳朵,好好教訓他一番時。卻發現他找不到木偶的耳朵,一時之間他的心情還真是難以言喻。讀者知道原因嗎?原來,當時他急急忙忙地刻啊~刻啊,居然忘記了要做一對耳朵。

於是,傑佩托只好揪著木偶的後頸把他往回帶,一邊搖晃著他的頭威脅地說:「我們現在立刻回家,等到了家再算這筆帳,我說到做到!」

皮諾丘一聽到他放狠話,直接就倒在地上,再也不動了。

正在這時,那些遊手好閒又愛打聽的人瞬間就聚過來,圍成了一圈。人群中開始你一言我一語地紛紛議論起來了。

「可憐的木偶!」一些人說話了,「他不願意回去是對的!誰知道傑佩托那個壞老頭要怎麼收拾他呢!」

接著,有其他人不懷好意地瞎起鬨:「傑佩托看著像個好人,可是他對孩子很凶呢!如果那個可憐的木偶栽在他手裡,肯定會被他剁成碎木片。」

結果,就在眾人七嘴八舌、添油加醋、你一言我一句下,竟讓那位警察把皮諾丘放了,反倒把傑佩托關進了監獄。可憐的人哭得像個孩子,他都還來不及為自己辯護呢!在送往監獄的路上,傑佩托抽泣著說:「壞小孩!我辛辛苦苦要把他做成一個好木偶!結果竟然落得如此下場!我一開始就該想到這一點的……」

以後發生的故事簡直超出了想像,在接下來的章節中將陸續為大家講述。

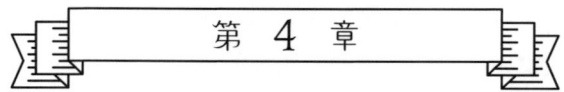

這章是關於皮諾丘和會說話的蟋蟀先生的故事。從這個故事中，我們將可見到一個無禮無知的孩子總是不肯接受見多識廣者善意的勸說。

接下來，孩子們，我要告訴你當可憐的傑佩托無辜地被關進監獄時，皮諾丘眼見自己逃脫了警察的控制，立刻全力衝刺地跑走。為了能早點到家，他抄近路穿過了田野，瘋了似的往前狂奔。他翻過高聳的田間，越過帶刺的樹籬，跳過滿水的溝渠，就像一隻被獵人窮追猛捕的小山羊或者小野兔那樣的逃命。

他發現街上的某間民宅大門半開著，於是走到門前開門進去，接著鎖上門閂後，他就地一坐，長長地吐了一氣，一臉志得意滿的樣子。

不過,他的好心情並沒有維持很長的時間,就被屋子裡面「唧唧—唧唧—唧唧」的聲音給打斷了。

「誰在叫我?」皮諾丘驚恐地問。

「是我!」

皮諾丘轉過身,見到了一隻大蟋蟀,正慢悠悠地沿著牆壁往上爬。

「告訴我,蟋蟀,你是誰?」

「我是會說話的蟋蟀先生,已經在這房子裡生活了百年以上。」

「不過,這房子現在是我的了。」木偶說,「不介意的話,請你頭也不回地,馬上離開這裡。」

「我不會走的。」蟋蟀先生回答,「直到我告訴你重要的真相。」

「那麼,你說吧,快說完吧!」

「那些反叛對抗父母、任性逃家的孩子,終究是絕不會有好下場,遲早他們都會悔不當初。」

「蟋蟀先生,你盡情地自吹自擂吧!至於我,已經下定決心,明天天一亮就逃離這裡,要是繼續留在這兒,肯定也無法逃避和其他孩子一樣的命運。我將會被送去學校,然後被逼著學習。告訴你實話吧,我一點都不想學習,還不如去追追蝴蝶

皮諾丘——木偶奇遇記裡的真相

或爬樹掏鳥窩、抓小鳥來得更有趣呢！」

「可憐的小笨蛋！難道你不知道嗎？那樣的話，你會變成一頭十足的大蠢驢，每個人都會嘲笑玩弄你的。」

「管好你的嘴，你這個既可惡又不吉利的傢伙！」皮諾丘叫道。

耐心又有智慧的蟋蟀先生，儘管遭遇了皮諾丘無禮的對待，依然心平氣和地說著：「你要是真的不想上學，那為什麼不去學門手藝，至少能活的堂堂正正！」

「你想聽聽我的想法嗎？」皮諾丘開始不耐煩地回應說，「在這個世界所有的手藝中，我真正感興趣的只有一樣。」

「那門手藝是什麼呢？」

「就是吃喝、睡覺、玩樂，以及從早到晚無所事事地遊蕩。」

「通常來說～」會說話的蟋蟀先生依舊平心靜氣地說，「真要有那麼做的人，他的結局不是進了醫院，就是去了監獄。」

「小心點，你這個不吉利的壞蟋蟀！要是惹惱我，你就要倒大楣啦！」

「可憐的皮諾丘！我真的同情你！」

「你為什麼同情我？」

「首先，你是一個木偶，更糟的是，你還有一個木頭腦袋。」

聽到最後這句話，皮諾丘生氣地跳了起來，拿起長椅上的木錘，狠狠地朝著會說話的蟋蟀先生砸了過去。

或許，皮諾丘其實沒有真的想要攻擊他，但不幸的是，木錘不偏不倚地就擊中了會說話的蟋蟀先生的腦袋，所以最後只聽見—唧—唧一聲，那隻可憐的蟋蟀就這樣黏貼在牆上，一命嗚呼。

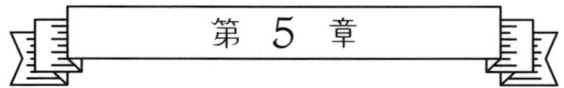

皮諾丘餓了，他找到一顆雞蛋準備煎蛋，但是，戲劇性的事情發生了，那顆蛋居然從窗戶裡飛出去了。

　　黑夜漸漸來臨，皮諾丘想起已經一整天都沒有進食，他開始覺得有想吃東西的慾望，因為胃開始咕嚕咕嚕地在抗議了。

　　這食欲來得非常的快，事實上幾分鐘之後，食欲就變成了一種饑餓感。不久之後越來越強烈了，皮諾丘簡直餓極了，已經到了無法忍受的地步。

　　可憐的皮諾丘立刻朝壁爐跑去，爐上有個冒著熱氣的燉鍋，他伸手剛要揭開鍋蓋看看有什麼吃的，才發現那僅是牆上的一幅畫，他有多失望可想而知，而且，那原本已經夠長的鼻子又變長了至少三根手指頭。

他開始繞著滿屋子跑,翻遍了每個抽屜,找遍了每個角落,只希望能找到一些麵包。無論是一片乾麵包、一點麵包屑、一塊被狗啃過的骨頭、一些發霉的玉米糊、一根魚骨頭、一個櫻桃核也好,總之,任何能夠吃的東西都可以。但是,最終什麼也沒找到,一些些殘羹菜餚都沒有。

與此同時,他的肚子卻越來越餓了。可憐的皮諾丘除了打哈欠,找不到任何可以消除饑餓的方法。就連打哈欠的樣子也都很誇張,每一次嘴巴都要張開到耳朵那裡去了。在打完哈欠後開始嘔吐,吐到都快氣力虛脫了。

他絕望地邊哭邊說:「會說話的蟋蟀先生是對的。我做錯了,我不應該反抗爸爸、還逃家……如果爸爸現在這裡,我就不會因為打哈欠難過到要死了。唉!肚子餓是多麼可怕的疾病啊!」於此同時,他覺得好像在垃圾堆裡看到什麼圓圓白白的東西,很像是雞蛋。他迅雷不及掩耳地跳過去抓住那個東西。它真的是一顆雞蛋。

皮諾丘的興奮真是難以描述啊;一切就像是做夢一般,他把雞蛋捧在手心裡轉過來倒過去,又摸又吻的欣賞。最後他親吻著說:「現在,我要怎麼吃它呢?做個蛋捲?不,更好的烹調方式還是放在碟子裡煮!……或者,用煎鍋不是更美味嗎?還是,簡單煮一煮就好了?最快的方式還是放在碟子裡煮;總之,我迫不及待想吃它了!」

毫不浪費時間地,他將瓷盤放在一個裝滿燒紅木炭的火爐上,然後用了些水來代替油或奶油來煮,當水開始加熱冒煙發出嘶嘶作響時……他用盤邊敲開蛋殼準備煮蛋了。但是，此時從雞蛋裡倒出來的不是蛋清和蛋黃，而是一隻充滿活力又有禮貌的小雞。那隻小雞優雅地向他致敬，接著說道：「萬分感謝，皮諾丘先生，由於您幫忙弄破蛋殼，讓我省了很多麻煩！後會有期了，請多保重，代我向您的家人問好！」

小雞一說完就拍拍翅膀，然後從開著的窗戶飛出去了，就這樣消失在皮諾丘的視野裡。

可憐的木偶愣在那兒像被施了魔法一樣，眼睛瞪的大大地，嘴巴張得開開地，手裡還拿著蛋殼。不過，他就呆站了那麼一會兒，馬上就清醒過來，隨後又哭又鬧，絕望得一直跳腳，哭喊著說：「啊！會說話的蟋蟀先生是正確的！要是我沒有逃家，要是爸爸在家，我現在就不會被餓死了！啊，飢餓是多麼可怕的疾病啊！」

他的胃哭得更大聲了，但皮諾丘還是沒辦法讓它停止。於是，他想到不如還是離開家裡到附近去轉一轉，希望能遇到善心人士肯施捨點麵包給他。

第 6 章

皮諾丘把腳放在火爐上睡著了,次日早上醒來時發現雙腳都被烤焦了。

　　這是一個可怕的冬夜,暴雨大作,雷聲轟隆,電閃如晝,天空似乎著火了一般。刺骨的寒風在怒吼、在咆哮,還捲起田野裡的陣陣塵灰,吹得樹木嘎吱嘎吱作響。

　　皮諾丘雖然非常害怕閃電雷鳴,但此刻飢餓遠超過對閃電雷鳴的恐懼。因此他關上了房門奔向村子,一路狂奔後終於來到目的地。他像隻玩瘋後的狗,跑得上氣不接下氣,連舌頭都吐出來了。

　　但是,村莊裡一片漆黑,沒有半個人影;店鋪也都門窗緊閉,街道上連一隻狗都看不到,整個村子似乎陷入一片死寂。

皮諾丘在沮喪及饑餓的驅使下，抓著某戶人家的門鈴死命地搖個不停，他心裡想著說：「總會有人聽到的！」

不出所料，一個頭上戴著一頂睡帽的小老頭出現在窗邊，生氣地對著他嚷嚷：「這麼晚了你想要幹嘛？」

「請您行行好，給我點麵包好嗎？」

「那你先等會兒，我馬上就回來。」那個小老頭回答著，他暗想著肯定是遇上小無賴了，才會三更半夜來戲弄別人，拉著別人家的門鈴不放，吵醒本來安安靜靜睡覺的居民，老頭準備要好好教訓他。

過了半分鐘後，那扇窗戶又打開了，同一個小老頭對著皮諾丘大喊道：「到這下面來，用你的帽子接著。」

皮諾丘摘下帽子並伸到窗下，突然一盆水從天而降傾瀉在他身上。全身從上到下都被淋濕透了，如同一盆乾枯的天竺葵。

像隻落湯雞般地，皮諾丘回到家中，又累又餓，精疲力竭，連站著的力氣都沒有了，只好坐下來將那兩隻濕透的、滿是泥漿的腳，放在燒著木炭的火爐上烘乾。

他就這麼睡著了。此時，他那雙木頭腳也燃燒起來，一點一點地燒著，終於燒成了灰燼。

皮諾丘繼續呼呼大睡，還打著呼嚕，彷彿那兩隻腳不是他的，而是旁邊不相干的人的。終於，在天剛破曉的時候，他被一陣敲門聲吵醒了。

「誰在外面呀?」他打著哈欠、揉揉眼睛問道。

「是我!」一個聲音回答。

這是傑佩托的聲音。

第 7 章

傑佩托回家了,他替木偶做了兩隻新腳。這個可憐的老人,還把自己的早餐給了木偶。

可憐的皮諾丘在睡夢中半睜開了眼睛,但他還沒有發現雙腳已經燒掉了。所以一聽到父親的聲音,馬上從椅子上跳下來要跑去開門。但是他的身體在兩三次的搖晃之後,整個人都摔倒在地上。

他倒地發出的聲響,就像是裝了一麻袋的木勺子,從五層樓上被扔下來的聲音。

「開門!」這時在外面街上的傑佩托喊道。

「親愛的爸爸,我沒辦法開門。」木偶在地上滾來滾去,邊哭邊說。

「怎麼會沒辦法開門？」

「因為我的兩隻腳被吃掉了。」

「誰吃了你的腳？」

「貓。」皮諾丘說。因為他看到一隻貓正在用前爪自娛自樂。

「我告訴你，給我把門打開！」傑佩托又說了一遍，「否則，等我進屋了，我給你隻『貓』！」

「我沒法兒站起來，是真的。喔，我好可憐～我好可憐～後半輩子我都要用膝蓋走路啦！」

傑佩托認定這不過是木偶的另一個藉口罷了，想著還不如直接點，於是他就爬過牆從窗口翻進了房間。

傑佩托非常生氣地罵個不停。然而，當看到皮諾丘真的失去雙腳而躺在地上時，他的心立刻軟化了。他立刻把匹諾丘摟在懷裡，親吻他，撫摸他，一遍遍地安撫他，斗大斗大的眼淚從臉上流下來，嗚咽著說：「我的小皮諾丘！你怎麼把腿給燒掉啦？」

「我不清楚，爸爸，可是您要相信我。我經歷了一個恐怖的冬夜，我一生都會記得。晚上電閃雷鳴，肚子又飢餓難耐，然後有一位會說話的蟋蟀先生對我說：『你是自作自受，你太壞了，這都是罪有應得。』我對他說：『你當心點，蟋蟀。』他說：『你是個木偶，有著僵硬的木頭腦子。』所以，我拿起木錘子朝他扔過去，結果他就死了，這都是他的錯，原先我可一點都不想打死他的。接著，我把陶瓷盤放在火爐上，可是小雞卻鑽出來說：「後會有期，替我向您家人問好。」但是我實在太餓了，因此那個戴著睡帽的小老頭打開窗戶對我說：「站到下面來，拿你的帽子接著。」然後一盆水就從我頭上淋了下來，討點麵包吃並不羞恥，不是嗎？後來，我就回家了，因為一直很餓，便想在火爐邊暖暖腳。然後您也回家了，我卻發現雙腳給燒毀了。到現在我還是很餓，而我的腳也再也不會有了！哇！哇！哇！哇！」可憐的皮諾丘開始放聲大哭，悲戚的哭聲連五英里以外都可以聽到。

傑佩托聽完小木偶雜亂無章地說了一大堆後，只聽懂了一件事，那就是皮諾丘快要餓扁了。於是他從衣服裡拿出三個梨，遞給木偶說：「這三個梨本來是我的早餐，不過我很高興把它讓給你吃。吃吧！希望你吃完就不餓了。」

「如果你想要我吃掉它們，就好人做到底，幫我削皮吧。」

「削皮？」傑佩托反問道，顯得十分詫異，「我的孩子，你太出乎我的意料，嘴居然那麼挑剔。這可太糟糕了！活在這個世界上，就要從小養成好習慣，什麼都喜歡，什麼都吃。在世上會遇上什麼事情，實在是說不準的，因為凡事皆有可能發生！」

「您的話毫無疑問是對的。」皮諾丘打斷他說，「但是我絕不吃沒有削皮的水果，我不喜歡水果皮。」

於是，善良的傑佩托拿起一把小刀，耐心地把三個梨削好，然後把梨皮堆在桌子的一角。

皮諾丘兩口就把第一個梨吃完了,正打算把梨核扔掉時,傑佩托擋住他的手說:「不要扔掉。在這個世界上,所有的事物都自有其用途。」

「可是我敢保證,我是不會吃梨核的。」木偶像蛇一般扭來扭去地叫道。

「誰知道呢!萬事皆有可能!⋯⋯」傑佩托沒有生氣,只是重覆說了一遍。於是,三個梨核沒被扔出窗外,而是和梨皮一樣都堆放在桌子一角。

皮諾丘吃完三個梨,或者說囫圇吞了三個梨後,打了個大大的哈欠,接著又煩躁地說:「我肚子又餓了!」

「但是,我可憐的孩子,我再也沒有其他東西可以給你了。」

「沒了,真的沒有了嗎?」

「我就只剩下這些梨皮和三個梨核了。」

「那只好將就一下吧!」皮諾丘說,「如果真沒有別的吃的了,那我就吃塊梨皮吧。」

於是,他嚼了一塊梨皮。起先他還皺著一張臉,不過後來一塊接一塊,眨眼間他吃光了所有的梨皮;吃完梨皮還不夠,他又吃起梨核,等到所有東西都吃完,才滿心歡喜地用手拍拍肚子,心滿意足地說:「哈!現在我感覺舒服極了!」

「現在,你明白了吧!」傑佩托再次教育他,「我剛才說的話是對的吧！不要把自己的口味養得太講究，太挑剔。親愛的孩子，我們永遠不知道將來會遇上什麼事情。凡事皆有可能發生啊！」

第 8 章

傑佩托替皮諾丘做了一雙新腳,又賣掉了自己的外套給他買了識字課本。

木偶剛填飽肚子後,就為了吵著要一雙新腿,而開始哭鬧了。

但是,傑佩托為了懲罰他的頑皮搗蛋,就任由他鬧脾氣半天,然後才開口說:「我為什麼要替你再做一雙腳呢?難不成是為了讓你能夠再次逃家嗎?」

「我向您保證!」木偶哭著說,「從今以後,我一定好好做人。」

「所有孩子,每當想得到什麼的時候,他們都會說這樣的話。」傑佩托回答。

「我向您保證,我會去學校讀書,學習做一個品格優良的人。」

「所有孩子想得到什麼時,都會說同樣的話。」

「但是我和別的孩子不一樣!我比他們都要好,我從來都說真話,爸爸,我向您保證,我會學會一門手藝,等您年紀大會孝順奉養您的。」

傑佩托雖然面無表情,但是實則他眼裡含著淚水,心裡充滿悲傷,看著可憐的皮諾丘一副可憐兮兮的樣子,他什麼話也沒說,只是拿起工具和兩塊風乾的木片,一心一意地做事。

不到一個小時,一雙木腳已經完成了。這是兩隻靈巧的小腳,結構良好,精雕細琢,這是傑佩脫勤奮用心的傑作。

之後,傑佩托對木偶說:「閉上你的眼睛,睡覺吧!」

皮諾丘閉上雙眼,假裝睡著了。

在他假睡的同時,傑佩托用了一點裝在蛋殼中的溶膠,把兩隻腳和他的身體黏著在一起,表面看不出一點痕跡,簡直天衣無縫。

木偶發現自己又有了新腳,立刻從原先躺著的桌子上跳了下來,狂喜得像發瘋了似地,滿屋子上躥下跳、翻了上千個跟斗。

「為了回報您替我做的這一切。」皮諾丘對他父親說:「我馬上就去學校上課。」

「真是好孩子！」

「不過，去上學總得穿衣服啊！」傑佩托很窮，口袋裡一塊錢也沒有，於是他只好用印花紙裁剪了一套小衣服，用樹皮做了一雙鞋，用麵包碎屑捏了一頂帽子。

皮諾丘馬上跑到水缸那裏看看自己的倒影，他對自己的這身打扮十分滿意，像一隻自得意滿的孔雀說：「我看上去真像一位小紳士！」

「是的，確實啊！」傑佩托回答說，「不過你要銘記在心，讓人成為紳士，靠的不是華而不實的衣服，而是整齊清潔的衣服。」

「順道一提……」木偶想到什麼加了一句話，「我上學還缺少一件東西，一件不可或缺的東西。」

「哦，是什麼東西？」

「我沒有識字課本。」

「你說得對，不過我們要怎麼弄到課本呢？」

「很簡單啊。我們去書店買一本就行了。」

「那錢呢？」

「我沒錢。」

「我也沒錢。」好心的老頭很傷心地說。

雖然皮諾丘是個樂觀的孩子，這會兒也開始感到悲傷。說到貧窮，身無分文時的無奈，想必每個人都能同理，哪怕他是個孩子。

　　「好的，耐心的等一下吧！」傑佩托大聲說道。他猛然站起來，穿上那件綴滿補丁的粗布舊上衣，從房間裡面衝了出去。

　　他很快就回來了，手裡拿著給皮諾丘準備的識字課本，但是身上的舊衣服卻不見了。當時外面正在飄著雪，而這個可憐的老人只穿著件薄襯衫。

　　「你的外套呢，爸爸？」

　　「我賣了。」

　　「你怎麼把它給賣了？」

　　「因為我太熱。」

　　皮諾丘瞬間就理解這句話的意思，內心的感動像潮水一般湧了上來，他張開雙臂一把抱住傑佩托的脖子，一遍又一遍地親吻他。

第 9 章

皮諾丘為了去看一場木偶表演而賣掉了識字課本。

在雪停後,皮諾丘就把他的第一本識字課本夾在腋下上學去了。他一路地走著,但小腦袋瓜裡面停不住地幻想連連,在心中描繪了上千座空中樓閣,一座比一座精美。

他自言自語:「今天在學校,我就能馬上學會讀書,到了明天我便會書寫,後天我要學習算術;然後憑藉真才實學,我將會賺很多很多的錢。當我的第一桶金到手,就立刻給爸爸買一件好看的衣服。嗯……我剛剛說到哪兒了?哦,布,對的!要用金絲銀線織成的布,用寶石做的鈕扣,可憐的爸爸配得上穿這樣的衣服。他為了給我買書,賣掉了外套供我上學,只給自己留了件襯衫……更何況天氣如此寒冷!只有身為父親的人才能作出如此大的犧牲！」

就在他情緒亢奮地自言自語時，突然聽到遠處有聲音傳來，像是吹橫笛和打鼓的聲音，嗚嗚嗚，嗚嗚嗚……，咚，咚，咚，咚。

他停下腳步仔細聆聽。那個聲音……似乎是從通往海邊小村莊的一條岔路的盡頭傳來。

「這音樂是做什麼的呢？真遺憾，我還要去學校，要不然……」

他躊躇不定，但是無論如何總得作個決定。他是應該去學校呢？還是去聽吹橫笛？

「今天我就去聽吹橫笛，等明天再去學校吧！」最終，這個小傢伙還是聳聳肩地做了決定，。

當他越往前跑，橫笛和打鼓的聲音就越清晰，嗚嗚嗚，咚咚，咚，咚。

最後他發現自己竟跑到了人潮洶湧的廣場中央，那裡，人們全都圍繞著一座用木頭和帆布搭成且色彩斑斕的大帳棚。

「那個大帳棚是做什麼的啊？」皮諾丘轉身問當地的一個小孩子。

「你看佈告啊！上面都寫著呢，看了你就明白了。」

「我也很想看，不過今天我恰好還看不懂。」

真是大笨蛋！那我來讀給你聽。佈告上面那幾個火紅色的大字寫的是：

「偶戲大劇院。」

「戲開演很久了嗎？」

「剛剛開演。」

「進場要多少錢？」

「兩便士。」

皮諾丘實在是太好奇木偶戲了，失去了自制力，失去了羞恥心的跟剛才說話的小孩子說：「你可以借給我兩個便士嗎？明天還你。」

「我本來很願意借給你的……」那孩子嘲弄地回答他說，「不過，今天我剛好沒辦法借你。」

「你給我兩便士，我把外套給你！」之後木偶對他說。

「你覺得我拿著件紙做的外套可以用來幹嗎？一旦下雨天就被淋濕了，就有可能脫都脫不下來。」

「你想買我的鞋子嗎？」

「那個只能用來生火。」

「這頂帽子你可以出多少錢？」

「那可真是有用極了！一頂用麵包碎屑做的帽子！我要是戴著它，看來老鼠就要爬到頭上吃帽子了！」

皮諾丘左右為難，他想到還有最後一樣東西可以賣，但是卻沒有勇氣說出來。他遲疑不定，猶豫不決，內心鬥爭激烈。後來，他還是忍不住說了：「我這本全新的識字課本兩便士賣給你，可以嗎？」

「我還是個孩子，不會從一個孩子手中買東西。」跟他說話的孩子這樣回答他，這可比他聰明多了。

「我可以用兩便士買這本識字課本。」一個賣二手衣的小販大喊道。因為這個小販站在他們旁邊，正好聽到了他們的談話。

書就這樣被賣掉了。想想那位可憐的傑佩托，為了給兒子買這本識字課本，如今他在家中還只穿了件襯衫，冷得渾身發抖呢！

第 10 章

木偶們開心地認出了他們的兄弟皮諾丘,並歡迎他的到來。此時,因為偶戲大劇院的團主吃火人的出現,皮諾丘要遭殃了。

當皮諾丘一進入那個小劇院時就發生了一件事,他差點兒引發一場大亂。

那時候布幕已經升起,戲劇也開演了。

舞臺上的兩個小丑,哈利奎因和潘趣乃樂如同以前演出方式:吵吵鬧鬧,還說要互揍對方一頓。

台下的觀眾全神貫注聽著他們吵架對話,爆出陣陣哄堂大笑。台上兩個木偶一邊做著手勢,一邊相互辱罵,演得栩栩如生,就像是現實生活中兩個活生生的人類一樣。

突然間哈利奎因停下了表演,轉過身面對觀眾席,然後用手指著後排的某個人,以誇張的聲調喊道:「我的天啊!這是在做夢還是清醒啊?台下那位不正是皮諾丘嗎?」

「是皮諾丘!」潘趣乃樂也大叫起來。

「真的是他!」羅斯小姐從幕後探頭來看並尖聲叫道。

「是皮諾丘!是皮諾丘!」所有的木偶齊聲喊著,並從四面八方跳上舞臺,「皮諾丘!我們的兄弟皮諾丘!皮諾丘萬歲!」

「皮諾丘,快上到我這兒來。」哈利奎因喊道,「來到木偶兄弟們的懷抱中吧!」

在夥伴們熱情洋溢的邀請下,皮諾丘縱身一跳,就從觀眾席後排跳到前排,再從前排躍上樂隊指揮的頭頂,然後再從樂隊指揮的頭頂跳上舞台。

皮諾丘受到木偶劇院全體演員的熱烈歡迎,就像兄弟姐妹一般,他們緊緊地擁抱著他,環繞著他的脖子、友善地撫摸他,激動之情無法用語言來形容。

毋庸置疑,這個場景令人動容,但因為觀眾們發現偶戲遲遲未再續演,便開始不耐鼓譟起來了,他們大聲喊著:「我們要看戲,繼續演戲!」

觀眾的反應只是白費力氣,木偶們非但沒有繼續演戲,相反他們還激動地提高了尖叫喧嘩的聲音。他們把皮諾丘扛在肩上以勝利的姿態抬到舞台腳燈前面。

正在那時木偶劇院的團主走出來了，他長得高大兇狠，是那種用一個眼神就能讓人感到恐懼的人。他黑如墨汁的鬍鬚，長度幾乎快從下巴延伸到了地面；順便一提，他走起路來腳都要踩到這長鬍子了。還有他的嘴，大得像一口爐灶；雙眼則似兩盞光亮地玻璃紅燈。他手裡不斷地甩著一根用蛇和狼的尾巴交錯綁起來的大鞭子。

　　團主的突然現身讓全場瞬時鴉雀無聲，大家一口氣都不敢喘息，就連蒼蠅飛過的聲音都可以清楚聽得見，這些可憐的木偶們就像狂風吹過樹葉般的瑟瑟發抖。

　　「你為什麼要到我的劇院裡來搗蛋？」劇院團主責問皮諾丘，粗啞的聲音就像是罹患重感冒的大妖怪。

　　「請您相信，敬愛的先生，這不是我的錯！」

　　「夠啦！等到今天晚上演出結束後我們再來算帳。」

　　當結束表演後，團主就走進廚房準備烹煮他的晚餐，一隻用大叉子叉著的肥羊，正在火上慢慢地旋轉烘烤著。他發現火候不夠大，以致於無法烤熟肥羊時，於是喚來了哈利奎因和潘趣乃樂，說：「把那個木偶帶過來，然後把他掛在那釘子上面。我看到他的木質很乾燥，扔進火裡一定能烤熟這隻羊了。」

　　起初，哈利奎因和潘趣乃樂還猶豫著，但是被團主狠狠地瞪了一眼後，便乖乖聽話照辦。不久後他們就把可憐的皮諾丘帶進了廚房。這時的皮諾丘就像一條剛出水的魚，絕望地大叫大喊：「爸爸！爸爸！救救我！我不想死，我不想死！」

第 11 章

木偶劇院團主吃火人再打了個噴嚏後,就饒了皮諾丘一命。隨後,皮諾丘又救了小丑哈利奎因。

我不得不說,那位木偶劇院的團主名叫吃火人的傢伙,看上去雖然是有點恐怖,特別是那把烏漆抹黑的大鬍子,就像圍裙一樣將他的胸口和雙腿完全給遮住了。不過,嚴格來說,他並不是一個壞人。而且事實證明,他一看到可憐的皮諾丘被帶到他面前,使勁掙扎著尖叫道:「我不想死,我不想死!」他馬上就動搖了,還起了憐憫之心。這時候他的鼻子忽然發癢,他雖然拚命忍著,但沒多久還是憋不住地打了一個大大的噴嚏。本來一直因為傷心自責,而向垂柳般彎腰駝背的哈利奎因,一聽見這聲噴嚏,立即喜逐顏開,他靠近了皮諾丘在耳邊輕輕地說著:「好消息,兄弟,團主打噴嚏了,代表他憐憫你,所以最後,你一定會得救的。

　　如您所知大多數人,當他們對某人感到同情時,總是會掉眼淚或至少會假裝擦乾眼淚;吃火人則不一樣,當他真的心軟了,就會打噴嚏,這是他的慣性。

　　打過噴嚏以後,木偶劇院的團主還是一貫的嚴厲表情,但他對皮諾丘大喊:「不要哭了!你哭得我胃疼……就像抽筋一樣疼,就像……就像……哈啾!哈啾!」他又打了兩次噴嚏。

　　「祝您好運!」皮諾丘說。

　　「謝謝!你的爸爸媽媽呢?他們還活著嗎?」吃火人問他。

　　「爸爸還活著,但是,媽媽……我從來沒見過。」

　　「如果把你扔進這炭火堆裡,天知道,你那可憐的老父親該要多悲傷啊!可憐的人家!我真同情他!哈啾!哈啾!哈……啾!」話還沒說完,他又打了三次噴嚏。

　　「祝您好運!」皮諾丘說。

　　「謝謝!但同樣的,也同情同情我吧!你都看到了,因為這兒木頭不夠用,以致無法將這頭羊烤熟。說實話,在這種情形下你本來是對我非常有用處的!可是我已經對你心軟了,所以不忍心燒掉你,既然不燒你,我就必須在劇院裡另外找個木偶,好代替你被扔在鍋子底下燒……嘿,這兒,守門員!」

聽到命令，兩個木偶守衛立刻就過來了。他們又高又瘦，頭上戴著三角帽，手中還握著未出鞘的利劍。

木偶劇院的團主以嘶啞的聲音地對他們說：「抓住哈利奎因，綁緊了，然後扔進火裡去燒。我下定決心了，一定要把這頭羊給烤熟！」

想像哈利奎因該有多可憐吧！他嚇得兩腿一軟，撲倒在地，嘴裡還吃了個滿滿的泥巴。

皮諾丘看見這種悲慘的場景，一下就跪在團主的腳下，悲慟大哭；眼淚嘩啦嘩啦地流個不止，把團主的大鬍子都給噴濕了。他苦苦哀求他說：「吃火人先生，您就發發善心吧！」

「這兒沒有先生！」木偶劇院的團主嚴肅的說。

「發發善心吧，騎士先生！」

「這兒沒有騎士先生！」

「發發善心吧，長官大人！」

「這兒沒有長官大人！」

「發發善心吧，大老爺！」

木偶劇院的團主一聽見他被叫大老爺，就忍不住地笑了，立刻變得非常和藹溫柔起來。他問皮諾丘：「好吧，你想求我什麼事呢？」

「我懇求您，饒恕可憐的哈利奎因吧！」

「沒辦法饒恕他的。我放了你就必須燒他，因為這頭羊我是決心一定要烤好的。」

「既然如此……」皮諾丘站了起來，丟掉頭上用麵包碎屑做成的帽子，大聲說道，「那麼，我明白要怎麼做了。來吧，守衛先生們！把我捆好扔進火焰裡吧！可憐的哈利奎因，我真正的朋友，讓他代替我去死，是不公平的！」

這一番犧牲救人的話語，讓在場的每一個木偶都動容了。就連兩個守衛，儘管是用木頭做成的，也哭得像嬰兒一般停不住。

吃火人最初還不為所動，像冰塊一樣冷酷，可是後來也漸漸地被融化了，他又開始打噴嚏，在一連串打了四五次噴嚏後，他張開懷抱、慈愛地對皮諾丘說：「你是一個勇敢的好小子！過來，親我一下。」

皮諾丘飛跑過去，像松鼠一般抓著木偶劇院團主的大鬍子往上爬，然後對著他的鼻子，真情實意地吻了一下。

「那麼，您原諒我嗎？」可憐的哈利奎因用小得不能再小的聲音問道。

「就饒了你吧！」吃火人回答說；接著又搖搖頭，長歎一聲說：「只能將就湊合一下了！今天晚上，我就只能吃這半生不熟的羊肉了。不過，下一次要是再發生這樣的事，就只能怪那個人倒楣！」

當好消息一傳開，木偶們全都跳到舞臺上進行了一場盛大的演出,舞臺上所有的燈光都亮起了,他們興高采烈地蹦蹦跳跳,一直狂歡到黎明。

第 12 章

木偶劇院的團主吃火人送給了皮諾丘五個金幣,讓他帶回家送給父親傑佩托。但是,皮諾丘卻不自覺地跟著狐狸和貓,一起同行。

　　第二天早上,吃火人把皮諾丘叫到一旁,問他說:「你父親叫什麼名字?」

「傑佩托。」

「他做什麼工作?」

「他是一個乞丐。」

「他賺的錢多嗎?」

「賺很多錢?嗯,在他衣服裡從未見過有一塊錢。你想想就知道，為了我上學要買一本識字課本，他必須賣掉身上唯一的一件外套。那件外套還全是補丁，一塊完整的布料都沒有。」

「可憐的傢伙！我太同情他了。這五個金幣，你馬上帶回家給他，並替我向他問好。」

無須多言，皮諾丘對木偶劇院的團主自是感激萬分。他還一一地擁抱了劇場裡所有的木偶，甚至是那兩個守衛，然後他便歡歡喜喜地回家去了。

當他還沒離開沒多久，便在路上遇到了一隻單腿瘸了的狐狸和一隻雙眼失明的貓。如同患難之交的好友，他們一路互相扶持照顧。瘸腿狐狸依靠著貓朋友前行，而盲貓則靠著狐狸引導前行。

「你好，皮諾丘。」狐狸禮貌地向他問好。

「你怎麼知道我叫什麼？」木偶問他。

「我和你爸爸很熟。」

「你在哪裡見過他？」

「昨天我還在他家門口見到過面呢！」

「他正在做什麼？」

「他穿著一件襯衫，冷得渾身發抖。」

「可憐的爸爸！一切都過去了！從此以後，他再也不用冷到渾身發抖了！」

「為什麼？」

「因為我已經是個紳士啦！」

「紳士……就憑你？」狐狸一說完，他開始粗魯而輕蔑地笑了出聲音；貓也跟著笑了出來，但是他假裝用了前掌整理鬍鬚，好掩飾住他的恥笑。

「一點也不好笑！」皮諾丘生氣地說道，「很抱歉讓你們垂涎欲滴喔！你們若真想知道的話，不妨我就告訴你們吧！我可是有五個黃澄澄的金幣。」

說著，他掏出了吃火人送的金幣。

一聽到金幣叮噹作響的聲音，殘障狐狸那隻看似殘廢的爪子竟不知不覺地往前抓伸，盲貓也睜大了發出綠光的雙眼，當然意識到什麼的又隨即閉上了眼睛，動作之迅速，以至於皮諾丘完全沒有注意到。

「那麼現在……」狐狸問他，「你打算用這些錢做什麼？」

「首先……」皮諾丘回答說，「我準備給爸爸買一件新外套，衣服必須是金絲銀線織成的，最好還嵌著寶石鈕扣；其次，我要買一本識字課本給自己。」

「你自己用？」

「那當然。我要去學校，認認真真學習。」

「你看看我吧！」狐狸說，「我像傻瓜一樣，興沖沖地去讀書，結果是瘸了一條腿。」

61

「你再看看我吧！」貓說話了，「我當初因愚昧的激情而讀書，結果呢，卻讓雙眼失明。」

就在此時，一隻白色的畫眉突然棲息在街道旁的樹籬上，開始了他例行性的歌唱，他說：「皮諾丘，切勿聽損友的話，否則後悔都來不及！」

可憐的畫眉，話都還沒說完，便被貓兒縱身一跳給一把抓住，就這樣連皮帶毛全塞進貓的血盆大口中，那隻鳥連「哎喲」一聲都未能哀叫。

那貓兒一吃掉畫眉，馬上就把嘴巴擦的乾乾淨淨，然後再次閉上雙眼，繼續偽裝盲貓。

「可憐的畫眉！」皮諾丘對貓說，「你怎麼這麼狠心吃掉他呢？」

「我是為了給他一個教訓，這樣下回他便不會在別人說話的時候插嘴了。」

當他們走到將近一半路程後，狐狸突然停了下來，對木偶說：「想不想讓你的金幣變多？」

「有什麼辦法？」

「想不想讓你手頭上那少的可憐的五個金幣，變成一百個，一千個，甚至一萬個？」

「當然想啊！不過，怎麼變呢？」

「辦法非常簡單。但是，你還不能回家，必須跟我們走。」

「你們要帶我去哪裡呢？」

「到貓頭鷹之地去。」

皮諾丘想了一會兒，接著堅定地說：「不，我不去，我離家很近了，要先回家去，爸爸還在家等候呢！昨天我沒有回去，可憐的老人家，誰知道他是怎樣唉聲嘆氣呢！我真是一個壞孩子，會說話的蟋蟀先生說得好：『在這個世界上，壞孩子絕對不會遇到好事。』我的經歷讓我明白了這個道理，我已經遭受過很多罪了。就在昨天，在吃火人的廚房裡，差一點連命都沒了⋯⋯喔！我現在想到都還怕得發抖呢！」

「哦，那麼⋯⋯」狐狸說道，「你真的決定要回家？那你就回家吧，反正吃虧的是你自己喔！」

「吃虧的是你自己喔！」貓跟著複述了一遍。

「你仔細考慮考慮，皮諾丘，不要錯失良機。」

「錯失良機！」貓又跟著複述。

「今明兩天之間，你的五個金幣就要變成兩千個了。」

「兩千個了！」狐狸每說一遍，貓又跟著複述。

「但是，怎麼可能變成那麼多呢？」皮諾丘問道，他驚訝得張大了嘴。

「我這就解釋給你聽。」狐狸說，「我告訴你，在貓頭鷹之地有塊神奇的地方，人們稱它為『奇蹟之地』。只要在這片土地上挖一個小坑，然後，放進去某樣東西，舉例說，像一個金幣吧。然後蓋上一點土壤，接著，澆上兩桶泉水，再撒上兩撮鹽，到了晚上，只要安安靜靜去睡個好覺就等著願望實現。因為，當夜晚沉睡時，這個金幣便會生長並開花。等早上起床後，你來到那掩埋地一看，猜會看到什麼？你將看到一棵美麗的樹，枝頭綴滿了金幣，多得就像六月份沉甸甸的麥穗上掛著滿滿的麥粒。」

「這麼說來……」皮諾丘聽得暈頭轉向的說，「假如我在那塊地裡種上五個金幣，那麼，第二天早上，我可以收穫多少個金幣呢？」

「那很容易算出來嘛！」狐狸回答說，「你掰掰手指頭就算出來了。假定一個金幣可以長出五百個，五百的五倍，也就是說，第二天早上，你的衣服裡就會裝著兩千五百個閃閃發亮的金幣。」

「天哪，真是太美好了！」皮諾丘大叫道，他興奮得手舞足蹈起來：「等我收穫到這些金幣，我自己會留兩千個，另外的五百個，我都送給你們兩位。」

「送給我們？」狐狸感到被侮辱了，他憤怒地說：「你都在想些什麼啊？」

「你都在想什麼啊？」貓又跟著複述了一遍。

「我們，可不是為了這個才這麼做的。」狐狸回答說，「我們這麼做，唯一的目的就是，讓他人發財致富。」

「讓他人發財致富。」貓又跟著複述。

「好善良啊!」皮諾丘心想。此時他幾乎忘記了爸爸的事、忘記了新外套、忘記了識字課本、忘記了他的決心,然後他對狐狸和貓說:「那,我們馬上走吧!我跟你們一起同行。」

第 13 章

紅龍蝦旅館

他們走啊,走啊,走啊,一直走到天都黑了,人也累得精疲力竭了,才看到一家「紅龍蝦旅館」。

「我們在這裡稍微休息會兒吧!」狐狸說,「我們先吃點東西,再睡上一兩個鐘頭,半夜再出發,這樣明日天剛亮,我們就可以走到『奇蹟之地』了。」

他們走進旅館並在桌旁坐下,但是大家都沒有什麼食欲。

貓說她消化不良,覺得噁心,所以只要吃三十五條番茄醬烏魚,四份乳酪醬。後來覺得醬汁不夠入味,又加了三次奶油和乳酪粉!

狐狸說本來是有點食慾,但醫生曾叮囑他要嚴格控制飲食,所以只好勉強自己吃得簡單點,於是點了一隻酸甜醬燒野兔,配上少少的幾隻肥嫩的雛雞。吃完野兔,他又點了鷓鴣、家兔、田雞、蜥蜴等其他點心;接下來,就再也不碰其他食物了,他說已經對那些食物感到反胃,一口也吞不下去了。

　　吃得最少的是皮諾丘。他點了一些核桃,一塊麵包,但是全都留在餐盤裡沒有食用,這可憐的孩子一直想著「奇蹟之地」,似乎光想著那些金幣就已經把他撐飽了。

　　吃完晚飯,狐狸對老闆說:「我們要兩間房間,一間給皮諾丘先生,一間給我和我的夥伴。走之前我們要小睡一會兒。你要記得半夜時把我們叫醒,我們還要接著趕路呢!」

　　「好的,先生們。」老闆回答著,還對著狐狸和貓使了個眼色,似乎是說:「我明白你們要做什麼,大家心裡都有數。」

　　皮諾丘一上床馬上就睡著了,他還做了一個夢。夢裡自己正站在田野中央。這個田野長滿了矮樹,樹上掛著一串串金幣,隨著風兒飄飄蕩蕩,還發出叮、叮、叮的聲音,好像是在說:「誰願意就摘下我們吧。」然而,正當皮諾丘滿心歡喜,打算大把大把地摘下這些閃亮的金幣,全都裝進自己衣服口袋的時候,忽然被房門上響亮的三下敲門聲給驚醒了。

　　原來是旅館老闆過來提醒他,午夜的鐘聲已經響過了。

　　「我的夥伴們都準備好了嗎?」木偶問他。

　　「何止是準備好了,他們兩個小時前就離開了。」

　　「他們為何如此匆忙?」

「因為貓收到消息，說她最大的孩子腳上長了凍瘡，有生命的危險。」

「他們晚餐費用付了嗎？」

「您為何會這樣想呢？他們都是有教養的人，不會對先生您做這種無禮的事。」

「太遺憾了！我倒樂意他們無禮些！」皮諾丘不好意思地抓抓頭說，接著他又問了一句，「我的兩位好朋友有說他們會在何處等我嗎？」

「明天天一亮的時候，在『奇蹟之地』見面。」皮諾丘為自己和他那兩位朋友的那頓晚餐付出了一個金幣，然後就出發了。

旅館外面漆黑一片，伸手不見五指，皮諾丘差不多是摸索著往前走的。四周的田野一片靜寂，連風吹葉子的聲音都聽不到，僅有一些夜行的鳥兒飛越過馬路，從一叢灌木飛到另一叢灌木時，偶爾他們的翅膀還會碰觸到皮諾丘的鼻子，不時地嚇得他直向後跳，還大叫喊著：「什麼人在那裡？」但回應他的只有遠處山崗傳來的陣陣回聲：「什麼人在那裡？什麼人在那裡？什麼人在那裡？」

他還是往前趕路，忽然發現一棵樹幹上有個小昆蟲，一閃一閃地發出昏暗朦朧的亮光，就像是從透明瓷燈罩裡透出來的燈光。

「你是誰？」皮諾丘問。

「我是會說話的蟋蟀先生的幽靈。」那小昆蟲輕聲細語地回答，聲音十分微弱，就像是從另一個世界傳來的。

「你想要我幹嘛嗎？」木偶說。

「我是來給你點忠告的。你帶著剩下的四個金幣往回走吧！把它們帶回家給你可憐的父親，他以為你再也不會回去，正在傷心流眼淚呢！」

「等到明天，我這四個金幣變成了兩千個，爸爸就可以當一位紳士了。」

「我的孩子，不要相信那些人所說的一夜致富的假話。一般來說他們不是發瘋；就是詐騙，聽我的話回家去吧。」

「偏不！我打定主意要往前走。」

「現在已經很晚了。」

「我一定要往前走。」

「夜又那麼黑。」

「我一定要往前走！」

「路上還不安全……」

「我一定要往前走。」

「你要牢記，那些任性的孩子遲早要後悔的。」

「老是說這些話。晚安了，會說話的蟋蟀先生。」

「晚安，皮諾丘，願老天保佑你一路平安！」

當說完這句話後，會說話的蟋蟀先生突然消失了，就像被一陣風吹滅的燈那樣，路變得更漆黑了。

第 14 章

皮諾丘因不聽信會說話的蟋蟀先生的勸告，而陷入了危險之中。

「說實話……」木偶邊往前走邊自言自語說，「我們這些可憐的孩子真是不幸！每個人都要責備我們，每個人都要告誡我們，每個人都說給我們忠告。只要他們一開口，就把自己當成是我們的父親或導師，所有人都這樣，就連那會說話的蟋蟀先生也不例外。看看現在，就因為我不聽那隻煩人的蟋蟀的勸告，他就預告我不知道會遇上多少衰事，但誰知道呢！甚至說我會遇到強盜呢！無論如何，我是不相信存在什麼強盜，我從來就沒有信過。對我而言，所謂強盜都是那些爸爸們捏造出來，用來嚇唬晚上想出門的孩子的。而且，假設我在路上真的碰上強盜了，你認為他們能嚇到我嗎？我一點也不怕。而且我還要迎上去，走到他們面前對他們說：『強盜先生，你們想拿我怎麼樣呢？你們可要記住，不要和我開玩笑！快滾蛋，最好別說話！』聽了我這番義正詞嚴的話，那些可憐的強盜啊！我想他們就會像一陣風一樣逃得無影無蹤，如果他們真的那麼不受教，偏不逃跑，那麼，我先拔腿跑就好了，事情不就解決了嘛！」

皮諾丘還沒來得及把他那長篇大論說完，因為這個時候，他好像聽到身後傳來一陣樹葉沙沙作響的聲音，那聲音非常輕。

他轉身一看，只見黑暗中有兩個看似兇惡的黑影在晃動。他們全身罩著裝炭的麻布袋。他們躡手躡腳地踮著腳尖緊跟在他身後。

「還真有強盜啊！」皮諾丘對自己說。他不知道剩下的四個金幣要藏哪兒好，情急之下他把它們全塞到了嘴裡，然後壓在舌頭下面。

接著他嘗試逃跑，但是都還沒有邁開步伐，就感覺手臂被抓住了，然後聽見兩個毛骨悚然、陰森森的聲音對他說：「要錢還是要命？」

皮諾丘因為嘴裡塞著金幣，所以一句話也無法說。於是，他只能不斷低頭鞠躬，不斷比手勢表達意思。他只想讓那兩個包著麻袋的人明白(他們從口袋上方的兩個小洞裡窺探)自己只是個很窮困的木偶，真的身無分文。「好啦！拿出來！少廢話，把錢拿出來！」兩個劫匪威脅他說。

木偶又做了一個手勢表示：「我沒錢。」

「趕快把錢交出來，否則就要你的命。」高的那個劫匪說。

「殺了你！」另一個重覆道。

「我殺了你之後，還要殺了你父親！」

「殺了你父親！」

「不，不，不，不要殺我可憐的爸爸！」皮諾丘著急地大叫道，可是他一開口，嘴裡的金幣就叮噹作響。

「啊哈，無賴！你還把錢藏在舌頭下面？立刻吐出來！」

但是，皮諾丘還是咬牙堅持著。

「啊哈！你還給我裝瞎？你等著，我們這就找個方法讓你把錢給吐出來！」

果然，他們一個捉住他的鼻尖，一個揪住他的下顎，動作粗魯地甩著，一個往上掰，一個朝下拉，想強迫他把嘴張開。可是毫無作用，木偶的嘴就像用釘子固定了一般，牢牢地合在一起。

於是較矮小的強盜抽出了一把大刀，把它當桿槓或鑿子用力的插進小木偶的唇齒之間。此時皮諾丘動作迅速快如閃電，一把抓住他的手臂，一口就把它給咬斷了，立即吐了出來。想像一下這該有多麼驚嚇，因為，木偶覺察到自己吐出的竟是一隻貓爪，並非是人手。

皮諾丘受到首戰告捷的鼓舞；他再次從強盜的爪子下掙脫

開來,越過路旁的灌木叢,飛快地在田野上奔跑起來。那兩名強盜就像是追趕野兔的兩隻狗,緊隨其後,其中那個失去一隻爪子的強盜,就改用單腳追逐,沒人知道他是怎麼做到的。

跑了幾十英里之後,皮諾丘再也跑不動了。沒有辦法,他只好爬上一棵高聳的松樹,在最高的樹枝上坐了下來。兩個強盜也準備學他爬樹,不過爬到一半就從樹上摔到地上,因而磨傷了手腳的皮。

但強盜可沒輕易就放棄。只見他們撿來一捆乾柴堆在松樹底下,然後點燃柴火。一瞬之間,松樹就燃起熊熊大火,火勢像風吹著蠟燭般迅速蔓延。不一會兒,皮諾丘眼見那火焰越升越高,他不想自己變成一隻烤鴿,於是從最高的樹枝上縱身一躍,然後繼續逃跑。他穿過了田野和葡萄園。兩個強盜一步也不落後地緊跟在後。

天漸漸開始亮了,他們還是緊追不捨。猝不及防,皮諾丘的去路被一條水溝給擋住了。那條水溝既寬且深,還滿是顏色渾濁如是牛奶咖啡的汙水。這下他該怎麼辦?「1!2!3!」木偶喊著節拍,助跑了幾步,隨後猛地一跳,跳躍到溝的對面。兩個強盜也學著跳,但是沒有掌握好距離,撲通!撲通!雙雙掉到溝裡去了。皮諾丘聽到水花飛濺的聲音、放聲大笑,一邊跑一邊叫:「強盜先生,好好洗個澡吧!」

他以為他們會被淹死了,沒想到回頭一看,那兩個強盜鍥而不捨地緊跟在後追趕,身上依然套著還淌著水滴的麻布袋,就像兩個漏了底的水桶。

第 15 章

強盜抓到了皮諾丘,將他吊掛在一棵大橡樹的樹枝上。

皮諾丘一看,頓時就失望了。他已經打定主意,準備直接倒在地上,向那兩個劫匪求饒了。可是他一轉身,眼睛四處轉了轉,發現在遠處樹林深處的中央,閃耀著一幢宛如白雪的小房子。

「只要我有力氣跑到房子那兒……」他對著自己說,「也許我就有救了。」

為了活命,他片刻不延誤的振作起來,他跑著穿過了樹林,而那兩個強盜依舊緊跟其後。

全力衝刺跑了約兩個小時,皮諾丘跑得上氣不接下氣,終於來到那幢小房子的門前,連忙咚、咚、咚的敲門。

沒人應門。

聽到身後追趕的腳步聲越來越近,自己的呼吸聲也越來越粗,他不得不加重力道再次敲門。可是,屋內還是靜悄悄的。

眼見敲門已經沒用了,他開始絕望地用腳使勁踹門,再用拳頭用力的打。終於開窗了,一個美麗的小女孩探出頭來。她有一頭天藍色的頭髮,一張白如蠟像的臉,雙眼緊閉,雙手交叉放胸前,說話時嘴唇絲毫未動,聲音好像從另一個世界傳來的:「房子裡面沒有人。他們都死了。」

「那,至少給我開門吧!」皮諾丘很大聲的哭叫著哀求她說。

「我也死了。」

「死了,那你站在窗口是幹嘛?」

「我在等棺材,等它過來裝走。」

這句話一說完,小女孩就消失不見了。窗戶也悄無聲息地重新關上了。

「嘿,漂亮的藍髮女孩。」皮諾丘大叫,「您行行好,給我開開門吧!同情同情這個可憐的孩子吧!我身後有強盜追著……」

他這句話還沒來得及說完,脖子就被人給掐住了,還是那兩個可怕的聲音,他們在咆哮著威嚇他說:「你休想再從我們手中逃掉！」

木偶覺得死到臨頭了，不由得渾身一顫，雙腿的關節開始嘎吱嘎吱地發出聲音，藏於舌下的金幣也叮噹作響了。

「好了！」兩個強盜盤問他說，「你張嘴還是不張？喲！不說話……那我們動手囉！這次拚命也會把你的嘴撬開！」

他們拿了兩把像剃刀一樣鋒利的長刀比劃著：嚓！嚓！他們試圖刺傷他兩次。

但是木偶是用十分堅硬的木頭做成的，所以很幸運的皮諾丘並未受傷，倒是刀斷成了碎片。拿著手中剩下的刀柄，兩個強盜面面相覷。

「我知道該怎麼做了」其中一個說，「他該被吊起來！把他吊起來吧！」

「把他吊起來吧！」另一個同樣複述。

他們也不浪費時間，馬上就把木偶的雙手反綁，在他脖子上套一個活結，然後將他吊在一棵大橡樹的樹枝上。

完成後他們就坐在草地上，等著木偶作最後的掙扎了。但三個小時過去了，木偶依然睜開雙眼，緊閉嘴巴，雙腿踢得越來越起勁。

最後他們的耐心消失殆盡，於是以嘲諷的語氣對皮諾丘說：「明天再見。希望等我們明天過來時，你能給個方便已經死亡了，最好嘴巴還要張得大大的。」

話一說完，他們就轉身離開。

　　此時，刮起了一陣凜冽的北風。風嗚嗚地咆哮著、怒吼著，將吊在樹上的可憐木偶吹得翻來覆去，皮諾丘在風中劇烈地搖晃著，就像是節日慶典上擺動的大鐘。搖啊～搖啊～經過一陣痛苦的痙攣之後，木偶頸部的活結縮得更緊了，眼見就要喘不過氣來。

　　他的眼前漸漸一片漆黑。儘管，感到死亡一步步逼近，但他依然抱有希望，斷氣前會有善心人士能來解救他，然而一等再等，還是看不到有人過來，真是一個人也沒有。他又想起了可憐的父親，想到他就要死了⋯⋯於是垂危之際斷斷續續地說：「啊，爸爸！爸爸！假如你在這兒就好了！」

　　皮諾丘呼吸困難到無法多說話了，沒多久，他閉上了雙眼，張大了嘴巴，伸長了雙腿，在經過一陣的劇烈顫抖後，最終，他吊在那裡一動也不動了。

第 16 章

美麗的藍髮小姑娘將木偶從樹上解下來,並讓他躺在床上,她請來三位醫生確認他的生死。

　　正當可憐的皮諾丘被吊掛在大橡樹樹枝上,看來似乎凶多吉少時,美麗的藍髮小姑娘又出現在窗邊了。她看到木偶的脖子被綁吊在樹上,當北風吹過時身體便來回飄蕩,非常悽慘;不由得對他產生憐憫之情,於是她輕輕地拍了三下手掌。

　　掌聲一起就傳來了翅膀快速振動的聲音,接著,一隻巨大獵鷹停在窗櫺上。

　　「請問有何吩咐,慈愛的仙女?」獵鷹垂下鳥嘴恭敬地問。必須要說的是,那個藍髮小姑娘確確實實長得十分美麗,她已經在這座森林生活超過千年以上。

「你看到吊在大橡樹樹枝上的那個木偶嗎？」

「看到了。」

「很好。你立刻飛過去，用你那堅硬的利嘴啄開吊著他的繩結，將他輕輕放在橡樹下的草地平躺。」

獵鷹飛走了。兩分鐘後他又飛回來了，說：「我已經按照您的指示都完成了。」

「你感覺他現在怎麼樣？」

「看上去好像是死了，不過可能沒有真的死去，因為我一解開他脖子上的活結，他就吐了一口氣，還小聲嘟囔一句：『現在覺得好多了！』」

於是仙女再次輕輕拍了兩下手，這次出現的是一隻穿著華麗的貴賓犬，他像人一樣是用後腿直立行走。

這隻貴賓犬穿著車夫的制服，頭上戴一頂鑲著金邊的三角帽，白色的假卷髮垂到了肩膀上。身上的巧克力色背心還鑲有寶石鈕扣，衣服上的兩個大口袋裡裝著晚餐時主人賞賜給他的骨頭；下身則穿了一條褐紅色的天鵝絨短馬褲、一雙絲襪及開口柔軟的鞋。在他身後則掛著一個用藍綢緞做成的特殊傘盒，方便他在下雨時能讓尾巴防濕。

「快點，梅多羅，好狗！」仙女對貴賓犬說，「立刻到我的馬廄裡找出最好的馬車趕到森林裡去，一直到大橡樹下面，你將會看到一個可憐的木偶，全身僵硬、半死不活地躺在草地上。請溫柔地抱起他，然後輕放在馬車的坐墊上平躺著，快把他帶到我這兒來,明白了嗎?」

貴賓犬為了表達接受到指令,他搖晃了三四次身後藍綢尾巴傘套,然後像賽馬一樣地飛奔而去。

不久之後,馬廄裡出現了一輛美麗的小馬車。馬車坐墊裡塞滿金絲雀的羽毛,車廂裡還備有奶油、卡士達以及甘藍餅乾。拉車的是一百對白老鼠;貴賓犬坐在駕車臺上,左邊一下右邊一下地揮著鞭子,就像一個怕趕不上時間的車夫一樣。

不到十五分鐘,這輛小馬車就返回了。在門口等待的仙女把可憐的木偶抱在懷裡,隨後將他送進一間壁板上裝飾著珍珠母貝的小房間,隨即派人請來附近最著名的醫生。

三位醫生一個接一個立刻趕來了。他們分別是烏鴉、貓頭鷹以及會說話的蟋蟀先生。

「我期望醫生們能告知我⋯⋯」仙女對圍在皮諾丘床邊的三位醫生說,「我期望醫生們能告知我,這不幸的木偶是生是死呢?」

根據仙女的請求,烏鴉第一個上前來,他先是摸摸皮諾丘的脈搏,接著摸他的鼻子,然後摸他的小腳趾,都仔仔細細地摸過了之後,十分嚴肅地下了個診斷:

「依我的判斷,木偶已經死了。如果他沒死,那應該要有跡象顯示他還活著。」

「我很遺憾」貓頭鷹說,「我不能認同這位鼎鼎有名的同行朋友烏鴉醫生的意見。正好相反的是,依我看木偶還活著。

如果他沒有活著,那也該有跡象證明他確實死了!」

「那麼您呢,您沒有要說的話嗎?」仙女問會說話的蟋蟀先生。

「我的觀點是,一位慎重的醫生,當他尚不清楚真相時,最明智的做法是保持沉默。另外,這個木偶對我來說並非初見面,我認識他有段時間了!」

到目前為止,皮諾丘本來是一動不動的躺著,就像一塊真正的木頭,可是他突然劇烈地抽搐起來,使得整張床都晃動起來。

「那個木偶」會說話的蟋蟀先生繼續說,「是個十足的流氓小子!」皮諾丘的眼睛略略睜開後,一下子又閉上了。

「他是個無賴,無所事事,是個懶鬼……」

皮諾丘把臉埋在被子底下。

「這個木偶是個叛逆的壞兒子,他那可憐的爸爸都快為了他傷心而死!」

這個時候,屋子裡有了哽咽的啜泣聲。所有人都大吃一驚:他們掀開被子原來是皮諾丘在哭。

「死人會哭,這說明他正在慢慢好轉。」烏鴉神情嚴肅地說。

「實在不好意思,我的觀點跟我這位赫赫有名的朋友和同行正好相反」貓頭鷹插進來說,「我說啊,死人會哭,這說明他為自己的死感到遺憾。」

第 17 章

皮諾丘吃了糖,但還是不肯吃藥。但當看到掘墓人要帶走他時,馬上就乖乖吃藥了,之後因撒謊導致鼻子變得越來越長了。

將三位醫生送出門後,仙女就回到皮諾丘身邊,摸摸他的前額發現他正在發高燒,那可不是開玩笑的事。

因此,她拿了一些白色粉末放在半杯水裡溶化,然後端過來給木偶並親切地對他說:「喝下它, 過幾天你的病就會痊癒。」

皮諾丘愁眉苦臉看著水杯,欲哭無淚的問道:「這是甜的還是苦的?」

「苦的,但它能讓你好起來。」

「苦的我就不喝。」

「聽話,喝了它。」

「我不喜歡苦的東西。」

「喝吧,喝完給你吃一塊糖,讓你調整苦味。」

「糖在哪裡呢?」

「在這裡。」仙女說著,從金色的糖盒裡面拿出一塊來。

「先給我吃糖,然後我再喝這種討厭的苦水。」

「你保證?」

「我保證。」

仙女把糖給他,皮諾丘卡嗤卡嗤幾口就咬碎,瞬間就吞下肚,然後舔舔嘴唇說:「如果糖是藥就好了!那我每天都要吃藥。」

「現在該你兌現諾言了,喝下這些藥水將會讓你痊癒。」

皮諾丘不情不願地拿起杯子,把鼻子探進去,然後放到嘴邊,隨後又把鼻子探進去,最後說:「它太苦了!太苦了!我喝不下去。」

「你喝都沒喝,怎麼就知道它太苦呢?」

「我能想像的!聞聞氣味就知道了。你再給我一顆糖,然後我就把藥水喝掉!」

仙女就像一個有耐心的好媽媽,又放了一顆糖在他嘴裡,然後再次把杯子遞給他。

「這個樣子我沒法喝藥水！」木偶做著鬼臉說道。

「怎麼啦？」

「因為那個枕頭放在我的腳上，讓我很困擾。」仙女替他拿開了枕頭。

「沒有用的，我還是沒辦法喝。」

「現在又是什麼問題？」

「那房門半開著，很礙眼啊！」仙女又前去把房門關上。

「總而言之……」皮諾丘流著眼淚大哭道，「我不會喝那討厭的藥水的，不喝，不喝，不喝」

「我的孩子，你會後悔的……」

「我不管……」

「你病得很嚴重。」

「我不管」

「你一直發著高燒，再過幾個小時，你就會死掉的。」

「你不怕死嗎？」

「我不管！」

「我一點都不怕！要我喝這種苦藥水，我寧願死了算了。」

此時房門打開了，四隻黑得像墨汁一樣的兔子走了進來，他們肩膀上共扛著一口小棺材。

「你們要對我做什麼？」皮諾丘大叫一聲，嚇得從床上坐了起來。

「我們要過來抬你進棺材。」最大的一隻兔子回答說。

「抬我？……可是我還沒死呢！」

「是的，現在是還沒死，不過只要你不肯喝這個退燒藥水，那就活不了幾分鐘了！」

聽完這個話，木偶大喊：「哎呀，仙女！仙女！趕快把杯子給我，趕快啊，你行行好，我還不想死，不不不……我還不想死……。」

他雙手接過杯子，一口氣就把它喝光了。

「這下好啦！」兔子們說，「我們白費力氣了。」他們重新把棺材扛上肩就離開了房間，離開時還滿腹牢騷地碎念著。

事實上幾分鐘之後，皮諾丘已經能跳下床了，看來他病都好了。如大家所見，這木偶很幸運的，不但很少生病且恢復起來也特別快。

看見他精神抖擻的滿屋子活蹦亂跳，活像一隻小公雞快樂的不得了，仙女就對他說：「你看，我的藥水真讓你好起來了吧？」

「沒錯！吃藥讓我重新活過來了！」

「那你為什麼要讓我一再懇求才肯喝藥水呢？」

「因為你看我們男孩都是這樣的,和生病相比,我們更害怕喝苦藥水。」

「不害燥嗎,孩子們應該瞭解,及時接受有效的治療,能夠讓他們避免生重病,甚至是死亡。」

「哦!下次我就不會要別人那麼苦求了!我會記得那些抬著棺材的黑兔子……這樣,我就會立刻拿個杯子喝下去!」

「現在到我這兒來,跟我講講你是怎麼被那些強盜給逮住的。」

「事情是這樣的:木偶劇院的團主吃火人給了我幾個金幣,對我說:『走吧,把這些錢帶回家給爸爸!』接著,我在路上遇見了一隻狐狸和一隻貓,兩位非常值得尊敬的朋友。他們對我說:「你想不想讓這些金幣變一千個,甚至是兩千個?跟我們同行,我們將帶你去『奇蹟之地』。我回答說:『好,我們出發吧。』後來,他們說:『我們在紅龍蝦旅館稍作休息。』不過,他們半夜就離開了。等我醒來的時候,他們已經不在旅館了。於是,我在凌晨將至前一個人上路了。你可以想像一下當時天有多黑,就在那個時候,我遇見兩個強盜,他們身上罩著裝炭的麻布袋,對我說:『把錢交出來。』我說:『我沒錢。』因為四個金幣全被我藏在嘴裡了。有個強盜試圖把他的手伸進我的嘴裡,被我一口咬了下來,吐在地上了。不過奇怪的是,吐出來是一隻貓爪子,不是手。後來,兩個強盜對我窮追猛打,跑啊跑啊,最終還是被他們給抓住了。他們套住我的脖子,還把我給吊在森林裡,對我嘲諷的說:『明天我們回來時,希望到那時你就死掉了，還把嘴巴張得大大的，這樣，我們就可以把你藏在舌下的金幣拿出來啦。』」

「你那四個金幣，現在放哪兒了？」仙女問他。

「被我弄丟了！」皮諾丘回答說。不過他這是撒謊，因為錢在他衣服口袋裡。

謊言一出，他那本來就已經夠長的鼻子又長了兩個指頭長。

「你把它們丟到哪裡？」

「這附近的森林裡。」

撒了第二個謊後，他的鼻子更長了。

「如果你是在附近森林裡弄丟的」仙女說，「那我們去找找看，一定可以找到的。因為所有丟在附近那森林裡的東西，通常都可以尋得回來。」

「啊！現在我都記起來了。」木偶心慌意亂地說，「我沒有弄丟那四個金幣，而是我剛剛喝藥水的時候，一不小心給吞肚子裡去了。」

撒了第三個謊後，鼻子已經長到令人驚奇的長度了，可憐的皮諾丘連動都沒法動了。假若他往這邊轉，鼻子就會撞上床或者玻璃窗；假若他往那邊轉，鼻子就會撞到牆或者房門；假如他稍稍抬頭，鼻子就可能插到仙女的一隻眼睛裡去。

仙女盯著他看，噗哧地就笑了起來。

「您笑什麼？」木偶問她。眼看鼻子長到不可思議的地步，他又困惑又著急。

「我笑你說謊話。」

「您怎麼知道我撒謊呢？」

「我的孩子，謊話立即就可以分辨出來。因為一般說來，它們有兩種表現形式：有些讓腿變短，有些讓鼻子變長。照情形看，你是屬於鼻子變長的情況。」

皮諾丘羞得無地自容，只想立刻從房間逃走。不過沒辦法了，他的鼻子已經長到連門也出不去了。

第 18 章

皮諾丘再次遇上狐狸和貓,並和他們一起前往「奇蹟之地」種植金幣。

　　如你所想的那樣,由於鼻子長得出不了房門,仙女任由木偶又哭又鬧的整整半個小時,都不予理會他。她這樣做無非是為了給他一個深刻的教訓,好改正他說謊的壞習慣。這是孩子最糟糕的缺點。可是當他看到木偶哭到臉色都變樣了,眼球都快凸出來,又對他感到了憐惜。於是又拍拍手掌,聽到掌聲後,成千隻啄木鳥從窗戶外飛進房間,全都停在皮諾丘的鼻子上,隨後開始猛力的啄他的鼻子。幾分鐘之後,那荒謬可笑的長鼻子就變回了原來的長度。

　　「您真是一位善良的仙女。」木偶擦乾眼淚說道,「我真是太愛您啦!」

「我也愛你。」仙女回答說,「如果你想繼續留在這裡,就做我的弟弟,我一定會成為你的好小姐姐……」

「我很願意留在這兒……但是我可憐的爸爸怎麼辦呢?」

「我全都想過了,而且已經派人告訴你爸爸了,今天晚上他就能到這兒來。」

「真的?」皮諾丘激動得跳了起來,叫著說:「喔,小仙女,如果您同意的話,我想要去接他!我迫不急待想要親吻那位可憐的老人家,他為我遭受了那麼多罪。我真是等不及了!」

「那你就去吧!不過小心點,不要迷路了。從那條路穿過森林,這樣你就能遇上他了。」

皮諾丘出發了。他一到樹林裡,馬上就像個孩子般的開心奔跑。不過,剛走到大橡樹那兒,他便停下腳步了。因為,他似乎聽到灌木叢裡有人聲。他確實看到兩個影子從灌木叢中鑽出來,出現在路上。你們猜,他們是誰?正是他旅途中的兩個夥伴,狐狸和貓。在紅龍蝦旅館,皮諾丘還和他們一起吃過一頓晚餐呢!

「哎呀,是我們親愛的皮諾丘!」狐狸叫著,對他又親又摟。

「你怎麼在這兒呢?」

「你怎麼在這兒呢?」貓跟著重覆了一遍。

「一言難盡啊!」木偶說,「趁現在有時間跟你們講講。

記得那個晚上，你們先我一步離開旅館，隨後我走在路上就遇到強盜⋯⋯。」

「強盜！⋯⋯天哪，可憐的皮諾丘！他們想要幹嘛？」

「他們想搶我的金幣。」

「惡棍！⋯⋯」狐狸說。

「臭名昭彰的惡棍！⋯⋯」貓跟著複述了一遍。

「我看見他們拔腿就跑」木偶繼續說，「他們跟在我後面猛追。終於他們趕上了我，然後還把我吊在大橡樹的樹枝上。」

皮諾丘用手指比了比兩步以外的大橡樹。

「還會有比這更糟糕的事嗎？」狐狸說，「這是一個多麼悲哀的世界啊！像我們這樣的正派人士，哪裡才是我們的避難所呢？」

就在他們說話的同時，皮諾丘突然發現貓的右前腿瘸了，連指甲帶爪子一起都沒有了，就問說：「你的爪子出什麼事了？」

貓試著想回答卻傻住了。狐狸馬上接話說：「我的朋友實在是太謙虛了，所以不願說，還是我來替他回答吧！我告訴你，一個小時前，我們在路上遇到一隻老狼，因為沒吃東西餓得奄奄一息，他哀求我們給點什麼吃的。但我們手頭連一根魚骨頭也沒有。我這位心地善良的朋友，猜他做了什麼？他竟咬下自己的右前腿，送給可憐的老狼吃，緩解他的饑餓。」

說到這裡，狐狸還擦了擦眼淚。

皮諾丘也深受感動，他走到貓的身邊，在他耳邊說了句悄悄話：「要是所有的貓都像你一樣，老鼠該有多幸運啊！」

「不過，這個時候你來這裡做什麼呢？」狐狸問木偶說。

「我正在等我爸爸，他隨時都有可能到這裡來。」

「那你的金幣呢？」

「除了在紅龍蝦旅館花掉的錢，剩下的都在我口袋裡了。」

「你還是考慮考慮，四個金幣到明天就會變成一兩千個，你怎麼就不聽聽我的意見呢？你為什麼不去『奇蹟之地』，種下它們呢？」

「今天不行，我改天再去吧。」

「改天就太遲啦！」狐狸說。

「為什麼？」

「因為這塊地被一位紳士買下來了，從明天開始任何人再也不能在那兒種金幣了。」

「『奇蹟之地』離這裡有多遠？」

「不到兩英里。你想跟我們一起去嗎？半個小時就能到了然後，你立刻把金幣種下去，用不了幾分鐘就可以收穫兩千個金幣，等晚上回來，你口袋裡就滿滿的都是金幣了。要跟我們一起去嗎？」

皮諾丘猶豫了一會兒，因為他想起了好心的仙女，想起了年老的傑佩托，還想起了會說話的蟋蟀先生的忠告。可是最後，他就像所有沒頭沒腦、沒心沒肺的孩子所做的那樣，最後他點點頭，對狐狸和貓說：「那走吧，我和你們一起去。」

於是他們出發了。

他們走了大半天，最終來到一個叫做「傻瓜陷阱」的城鎮。一進城，皮諾丘就看見大街上滿是奇形怪狀的動物。餓得直打哈欠的癩癩狗；冷得瑟瑟發抖的無毛綿羊；正在乞食的沒有雞冠和垂肉印第安玉米的公雞；失去了璀璨的翅膀再也不能飛的大蝴蝶；沒了尾巴而羞愧的孔雀；哀悼永遠消失了耀眼的金銀色羽毛的野雞，正在不吭一聲抓地洩憤。

在這群羞於見人的乞丐和窮人中間，不時會有一些貴族氣派的馬車穿過。馬車裡面不是坐著一隻狐狸，就是偷竊慣犯喜鵲，要不然就是一些其他捕食小生物的禽類。

「『奇蹟之地』在哪兒？」皮諾丘問道。

「就在這兒，再走兩步就到了。」

他們穿過城鎮，走出城牆來到一塊荒涼的田地前面。這塊田地看上去和其他田地完全一樣。

「我們到了。」狐狸對木偶說，「現在你蹲下來，用手在地上挖一個小坑洞，然後把金幣放進去。」皮諾丘按照狐狸說的做了。他先挖了一個坑，把剩餘四個金幣放進去，接著用點土把坑洞重新掩蓋起來。

「好了,接下來」狐狸說,「你到附近的水溝裡舀一桶水來,澆在你剛才播種的地方。」

皮諾丘走到水溝那裡,因為手上沒桶子就脫下腳上的一隻鞋子裝滿水,澆在挖了坑洞的土地上。

然後他問:「還需要做其他什麼事嗎?」

「不用了。」狐狸回答說,「現在我們可以離開了,二十分鐘之後你再回到這兒,就會看到一棵矮矮的樹破土而出,所有的樹枝上都沉甸甸地結滿了金幣。」

可憐的木偶興奮得不知所以,對狐狸和貓千恩萬謝,還許諾要送給他們一份厚禮。

「我們不需要禮物。」兩個惡棍回答說,「我們非常榮幸教會你,不用辛苦勞動就讓你發財致富,這已經讓我們像過節一樣地開心了!」

他們說完這些話,並預祝皮諾丘有個好收成,然後向他告別就去忙他們自己的事了。

第 19 章

皮諾丘的金幣被偷了,卻被判刑關了四個月的監牢。

木偶回到城裡後,開始一分一秒地數著時間,等他覺得二十分鐘一到,就立刻原路返回「奇蹟之地」。

他一路走得飛快,加速的心跳聲就像客廳裡的掛鐘滴答滴答作響。同時他還幻想連連:「假如樹上不是一千個金幣,而是兩千個呢?假如樹上不是兩千個金幣,而是五千個呢?假如樹上不是五千個,而是一萬個呢?天哪!到那時,我將成為一個多麼富有的紳士啊!⋯⋯我將擁有一座華麗的宮殿;我將擁有一千匹小木馬和一千個馬廄供我自己玩樂;我將擁有一個酒窖,裡面裝滿葡萄酒和甜醬;我將擁有一個書房,裡面擺滿了糖果、餡餅、葡萄乾、蛋糕、杏仁餅乾以及奶酪、點心等等。」

他一邊做著白日夢，一邊走到那塊地附近。他停下腳步四處張望，試圖尋找那麼一棵樹，一棵枝頭結滿金幣的樹。不過，他什麼也沒看到。他朝前再走了一百步，還是什麼也沒有。他走進那塊田地上……筆直走到他埋下金幣的那個小坑那裡，依然什麼也沒有。因此，他在那兒冥思苦想，也管不了什麼社交規範和禮儀了，把手從口袋裡拿出來，在頭上撓了半天。

這個時候，一陣爆發出的笑聲正在接近他，皮諾丘於是抬頭一看，只見有隻大鸚鵡停歇在樹上，正在梳理他身上為數不多的幾根羽毛。

「你笑什麼？」皮諾丘氣憤地問他。

「我笑是因為整理羽毛時，剛好搔到了翅膀底下的癢處。」

木偶沒有理會他。他走到水溝那裡，仍舊用那只鞋子裝滿水，重新澆在掩埋金幣的那塊地上。

這時候荒涼的田地裡再次響起了笑聲，打破了剛才的寂靜。這笑聲聽起來比上次更放肆。

「最後一次……」皮諾丘發瘋似的大叫，「你能不能告訴我，你這沒教養的鸚鵡到底在笑些什麼？」

「我笑有些笨蛋，他們竟然什麼蠢話都相信，讓自己被那些狡猾的人給騙了。」

「你這是在說我嗎？」

「對，我就是說你，可憐的皮諾丘，我說你真是頭腦簡單，居然相信錢和豆子、南瓜一樣，可以在田地裡播種收穫。我曾經也相信過一次，直到如今還深受其害。現在……可惜太晚了！我終於明白了，想要錢就必須學會如何賺錢，或者依靠自己勤勞的雙手，或者依靠自己的聰明才智。」

「我不明白你說些什麼。」木偶說，這時他已經緊張得直發抖了。

「耐心點！我會說得更清楚點。」鸚鵡接著說，「我告訴你，你在城裡的時候，狐狸和貓又回到田裡，他們拿走了你埋下的錢，然後像風一樣的跑掉了。如今要是能抓到他們就能了解的更多！」

皮諾丘驚訝得張大了嘴。他不願意相信鸚鵡的話，開始用手和指甲去挖剛澆過水的土。挖啊，挖啊，挖出了一個很深很深的大坑洞，深得都可以裝進去一個稻草堆了，但是錢已經不在那兒了。

木偶徹底絕望了，立刻跑回城裡向法院告狀去了，舉發兩個騙子偷走了他的錢。

法官是猩猩部落裡的長老；一位德高望重且上了年紀的猩猩，他有著花白鬍子，更特別是還戴著一副沒有鏡片的金絲邊眼鏡。由於眼睛出血困擾了他很多年，因此不得不一直戴著眼睛。

皮諾丘當著法官的面，詳細地敘述了自己深受其害的被欺詐經過。他還說出了兩個惡棍的姓名和其他特徵，最後懇求法官伸張正義。

法官十分和氣地聽著，對他的講述特別用心並被深深地觸動了，表示懇切的同情。

等到木偶表示沒什麼要補充了，他伸出一隻手，搖了一下鈴。

聽到召喚，兩位穿得像法警的獒犬馬上就出現了。接著，法官指著皮諾丘對他們說：「那個可憐的孩子，被人偷走了四個金幣，把他抓起來立刻送到牢房裡去。」木偶聽到這個不可思議的宣判，嚇得目瞪口呆並打算提出抗告。

不過兩個獒犬警察為了不白費時間，摀住他的嘴後，就把他帶走關進監獄了。

木偶在監獄了關了四個月，長夜漫漫的四個月。他本來還要被關得更久，剛好出現轉機救了他一命。原來，統治這個「傻瓜陷阱」城的年輕皇帝打敗敵人，贏了大勝仗，遂下令全城同慶、張燈結綵、燃放煙花、賽車賽馬競賽。為了加深勝利的喜悅，還命令監獄特赦，釋放了所有的盜賊。

「別人都放出去了，我也要出獄。」皮諾丘對獄卒說。

「不，您不行。」獄卒回答說，「因為您不在釋放對象之內。」

「我求求您啦！」皮諾丘回答說，「我也是個受刑人啊！」

「如果是那樣，您就完全符合條件了。」獄卒說著，恭恭敬敬地朝他行了個脫帽禮，然後打開牢門放他離開了。

第 20 章

出獄後,皮諾丘準備回仙女家時,在路上遇到可怕的巨蛇,隨後又被捕獸夾給困住了。

讀者可以想像,重獲自由的皮諾丘多麼樂不可支啊!都還沒有來得及喘口氣就飛也似的離開城鎮,往仙女家的路上奔去。

由於下雨天、路上十分泥濘,走起路來汙泥都快淹沒及膝了。但是木偶一點也不在意。他急切地想要再次看到他的父親,看到他藍髮的仙女小姐姐。像條小獵犬般興奮的跑啊跳啊,全身上下都濺滿了泥漿,他一邊跑一邊對自己說:「我遭遇了多少倒楣事啊!這全是自作自受,誰讓我是個又頑固又衝動的木偶呢!我總是一意孤行,不聽那些關心我和比我聰明千倍的人說的話!不過,從今往後,我決定洗心革面,做一個孝順懂事的孩子。現在，我總算明白了，不聽話的孩子都要自食惡果，什麼也得不到。不過，我的爸爸還在等我嗎？我會在仙女家見到他的！可憐的爸爸，好久都沒見他了，我現在就想緊緊地抱抱他，親吻他！仙女能原諒我做的壞事嗎？想一想，她對我的關心以及無微不至的照顧。多虧了她，我今天才能還活著！還有比我更忘恩負義的孩子嗎？又或者，還有比我更沒心沒肺的孩子嗎？」

他一路這麼自言自語，突然間，停了下來，他快被嚇得魂飛魄散，連著往後退了四步。

他見到什麼？

他見到一條橫躺在路上的巨蛇。他全身都是綠色的，卻有著一雙紅色的眼睛；還有那尖尖的尾巴，活像煙囪似的正往外冒煙。

木偶的恐懼之深是難以描述的。他不停歇地往前跑，一路跑到安全的地方，然後坐在一堆石頭上，眼睛眨也不眨地等待巨蛇自己爬開，好把道路淨空出來。

他等了一個小時，兩個小時，三個小時，可是蛇仍然原處不動。雖然離得很遠，但他還是能看見那雙熾熱的眼睛正放著紅光，他那尾巴尖上升起一股一股的煙霧。

最後皮諾丘鼓足了勇氣，走到離那蛇幾步之遙的地方，用輕聲細語的聲音，刻意討好他說：「不好意思，蛇先生，你可不可以行個方便，往一邊移動，讓出點地方好讓我過去？」

他就像是對牛彈琴，一點回應都沒有。

木偶再次用那溫柔的聲音說道：「我跟您說，蛇先生，我正要回家去，家裡有爸爸正在等我，我已經有好久沒見過他，您能讓我繼續趕路嗎？」

他等著一個回覆，不過蛇並沒有回答他。事實上，那條蛇本來顯得生猛異常的，當下卻一動不動，好像僵硬了一般。他閉上雙眼，尾巴也不再冒煙。

「他真的死了嗎？」皮諾丘搓著手高興地說著。他準備從巨蛇身上跳過去到路另一邊。不過，就在他準備跳的時候，蛇忽然豎起了身體，彷彿被壓下的彈簧的彈了起來。木偶著實嚇了一大跳，因此絆了一下摔倒在地上。

他摔得實在是太滑稽了。整顆頭朝下插在路上的稀泥裡，兩條腿則倒立在半空中。

看著木偶的頭埋在泥漿裡，兩腳在空中用力踢來踢去，巨蛇忍不住狂笑起來。他笑啊，笑啊，笑啊，笑得實在是太厲害了，居然笑斷了腹部的血管，一命嗚呼！這一回，他是真的死啦！

於是皮諾丘再次往前逃跑，他想在天黑前回到仙女的家。但是不久之後，他就餓得饑腸轆轆，無法再忍耐了。他跳進了一片葡萄園，打算摘兩串麝香葡萄吃。唉，他真不該跳進去的！

這才剛到葡萄架底下，只聽到卡嚓一聲，他的兩腳就被兩塊很鋒利的鐵片夾住了，痛得他暈頭轉向，兩眼直冒金星。

可憐的木偶被一個捕獸夾給困住。這種夾子原本是農民用來抓取臭鼬的，他們是附近所有雞窩的瘟神。

第 21 章

農民抓住了皮諾丘，強迫他當雞窩裡的看門狗。

大家可以想像一下，當下皮諾丘必然是放聲大哭尖叫。但是，附近看不見房屋，路上也沒有行人經過，所以，他的眼淚也罷，求饒也罷，全無用處。

黑夜終於降臨了。

可能是因為捕獸夾夾得太緊以致腿骨太痛，還有部分原因可能是田野漆黑一片，獨自一人的恐懼，所以眼看著木偶就要昏過去了。正在此時，一隻螢火蟲從他頭上掠過。他立刻喚住螢火蟲，對他說：「嘿，小螢火蟲，好心點，幫幫忙，把我從這夾子弄出來好嗎？」

「可憐的孩子！」螢火蟲停下來，憐憫地看著他問，「但是，你的腳是怎麼被這些鋒利的鐵片給夾住的呢？」

「我走進這片地裡，打算採兩串麝香葡萄充饑，結果⋯⋯」

「請問葡萄是你的嗎？」

「不是⋯⋯。」

「那麼，是誰教你擅自動別人的財產的？」

「我太餓了⋯⋯。」

「孩子，饑餓並不是你盜用別人東西的充分理由⋯⋯」

「你說得對，你說得對！」皮諾丘大哭著說，「下次我不會這麼做了。」

這個時候，他們的談話被漸行漸近的腳步聲給打斷了。

原來是這塊田地的主人。他躡手躡腳地靠近捕獸夾，想看看有沒有夾住夜裡來吃雞的雞貂。

他從外套底下拿出燈來一照，大大出乎他的意料。他發現抓到的是一個孩子，而不是雞貂。

「啊哈！一個小偷！」

農民憤怒地說，「也就是說，我的雞全是你偷的？」

「不，不是我，真的不是我！」皮諾丘急地啜泣著說，「我來這裡只想摘兩串葡萄！⋯⋯」

「會偷葡萄就有可能會偷雞。看我的，我要好好教訓教訓你，省得你轉眼就忘了。」

他打開捕獸夾，揪住木偶的衣領，像拎著一隻新生的羔羊似的把他拎回了家。

　　當他來到門前的院子裡時，他粗暴地把木偶扔在空地上，一隻腳踩著他的脖子，對著他說：「現在太晚了，我要先去睡覺。明天再好好算帳。剛好我那隻守夜的狗今天死了，你今晚就代替他守夜。你給我好好當一隻看門狗。」

　　說完，他將一個黃銅鈕扣的狗項圈套在木偶的脖子上，然後把項圈收緊，好讓木偶的頭掙脫不出來。項圈上繫著一根沉甸甸的鎖鏈，鎖鏈的一頭拴緊在牆上。

　　「要是晚上下雨了。」農民說，「你可以去那邊的狗屋休息，裡面用乾草鋪了一個床，過去四年，我那可憐的狗一直睡在那裡。萬一小偷來了，你的耳朵要警醒點，記得汪汪地叫。」

　　農民叮囑完就轉身進屋，關了門鎖。

　　於是，空地上就剩可憐的皮諾丘一個人躺著，他饑寒交迫，膽戰心驚，都快半死不活啦！他憤恨地不斷用手抓那個勒住脖子的項圈，哭著說：「我真是活該！毫無疑問，真活該！我是個流氓，我一無是處。我只相信壞朋友的話，所以總是災禍連連。如果我和其他孩子一樣，做個好孩子；如果我願意讀書，喜歡做事；如果我還在家，和我可憐的爸爸一起，那我這時候就不會在這茫茫田野之中，被逼著給一個農民當看門狗了。唉，要是我能重新活過就好了！現在一切都晚了，沒有辦法，我只好忍忍了！」

　　他發洩完內心深處的怨氣之後，就走進狗屋去睡覺了。

第 22 章

皮諾丘發現了小偷,他用忠誠換來了自由之身。

皮諾丘昏沉沉地睡了兩個多鐘頭,到了半夜,突然被一陣嘀嘀咕咕的奇怪聲音給驚醒了,聽著像是從院子裡傳來的。他把鼻尖探出狗屋往外看,只見四隻小動物正站在那裡討論著什麼。他們毛髮烏黑,看上去和貓一樣。不過他們不是貓,而是雞貂,一種肉食性動物,尤其是喜歡吃雞蛋和小雞。其中一隻離開了同伴,他走到開著門的狗屋旁邊來,低聲說:「晚上好,梅拉拉波。」

「我不是梅拉拉波。」木偶回答說。

「哦,那你是誰?」

「我叫皮諾丘。」

「你在這兒做什麼？」

「我在這兒當看門狗。」

「那麼，梅拉拉波去哪裡？住在這狗窩裡的老狗去哪裡？」

「他今天早上死了。」

「死了？可憐的傢伙！他是那麼好的一條狗！不過，從你面相上看，我敢說你也是一條優秀的狗。」

「不好意思，我不是狗！」

「不是狗？那你是什麼？」

「我是一個木偶。」

「然後，你被當成看門狗？」

「你說得太對了，這是對我的懲罰。」

「那好，我和你也訂個協議，和已故的梅拉拉波約定的條件完全一樣，我敢保證你一定會滿意的。」

「什麼協議？」

「老樣子，我們一禮拜光顧這個雞窩一次，夜裡來會抓走八隻雞。這八隻雞，我們吃七隻，留給你一隻。不過要聽清楚了，你要假裝睡熟了，千萬別叫出聲來，把農夫給叫醒了。」

「梅拉拉波就是這麼做的嗎？」皮諾丘問。

「當然！我們和他一向合作得很愉快。你儘管安安靜靜地睡覺，我們走之前一定給你在狗屋裡，留下一隻處理好的肥雞，當你明天的早餐。我們已經講清楚了吧？」

「簡直太清楚了！……」皮諾丘答。他搖搖頭，擺出威嚇的架勢，似乎在說：「哼，咱們走著瞧吧！」

四隻雞貂自以為事情已經談妥了，便迅速靠近狗屋旁邊的雞窩那裡，用他們的牙齒和爪子努力地弄開了木門，一隻接一隻地鑽了進去。等他們一進去，只見身後的木門啪噠一聲，就猛地給關上了。

關門的正是皮諾丘。為了確保萬無一失，他還搬了塊大石頭頂住木門。

隨後他就大叫起來，叫得確實就像一隻看門狗：「汪，汪，汪，汪。」

聽到叫聲，農夫從床上一躍而起，拿起槍走到窗戶邊問道：

「發生什麼事了？」

「來小偷了！」皮諾丘回答。

「他們在哪兒？」

「在雞窩裡。」

「我馬上來。」

事實上，連說一聲「阿門」的時間都不到，農民就已經出來了。他衝進雞窩裡抓住雞貂，把他們全部塞進麻布袋裡，得意洋洋地對他們說：「這下，你們終於落到我手裡了！我本該懲罰你們的，不過我不想做這麼殘忍的事。所以，明天早上我把你們送去附近村莊的一家酒店，剝掉你們的皮，把你們當成野兔，配上糖醋醬，燒成美味佳餚。你們本來不配享有這份無上的榮耀，不過像我這麼心胸寬廣的人，就不在意這點小事啦！」

然後，他走到皮諾丘身邊，親切地擁抱著他，並且問：「你是怎麼發現這四個小偷的？再想想梅拉拉波，我忠誠的梅拉拉波，一直以來什麼也沒發現過！」

木偶本來可以把事實真相都講出來，本來可以向農夫告發狗和雞貂之間的無恥協議。可是一想到狗已經死了，就暗自心想：「告發一個死者有什麼意義呢？死者已矣，還是給他留個好名聲吧！」

「小偷進院子的時候，你是醒著還是睡著了？」農民繼續問他。

「我睡著了。」皮諾丘回答說，「是被他們喋喋不休的說話聲給吵醒了。其中一隻雞貂來到狗屋旁邊對我說：『如果你保證不叫醒主人，我們就送給你一隻處理好的肥雞！……』想到他們竟然敢對我提出這種厚顏無恥的建議！雖然，我只是一個木偶，也許還有這個世界上幾乎所有的缺點，但是我絕對不會和不誠實的人串謀勾結，狼狽為奸！」

「孩子，說得好！」農民拍拍他的肩膀，高聲稱讚道，「你這種想法令人尊敬。為了表明我對你的滿意，我這就放了你，你馬上就可以回家了。」

　　說完，農夫給他解開了狗項圈。

第 23 章

皮諾丘為藍髮小仙女的死感到哀傷。接著遇到了鴿子，載著他去海邊尋找爸爸；為了救傑佩托，他勇敢地跳進海裡。

皮諾丘一脫掉那個沉重的、傷自尊的狗項圈，撒腿就跑。他穿過田野，一刻也不停留，一直跑到通向仙女家的那條馬路。上了馬路，他低下頭看了看底下的平原。肉眼就能清清楚楚地看到那片樹林。就在樹林裡，他很倒楣地遇上了狐狸和貓。此外，還能看見高聳在諸多林木之間的大橡樹，當初他就是被吊在那裡。然而他左看右看，那棟屬於美麗的藍髮仙女的房子，怎麼也看不到。

一種不祥的預感油然而生，他用盡最後一份力，拚命地跑起來，不到幾分鐘工夫就來到那座白屋曾經矗立過的土地上。

現在白屋已經消失不見了，取而代之的只有一塊大理石碑，石碑上篆刻著幾行悲傷的文字：

這裡安眠著藍髮的小仙女，

她的弟弟皮諾丘將她遺棄，

她因悲傷而與世長辭。

當木偶困難地拼出這個墓誌銘後，他的哀傷之情大家可以想像得到。他趴在地上把那塊墓碑親吻了上千遍，失聲大哭起來。他哭了一整夜，當第二天黎明到來之際，他依然在哭泣，儘管眼淚早已哭乾了。

他哭得這般激烈、這般傷心，以至於整個山崗都回盪著傷心欲絕的哭泣聲。

他一邊哭一邊說：「噢，我的仙女，你為什麼死了？為什麼死的是你而不是我，我這麼壞，而你那麼善良？⋯⋯我的爸爸呢？他又在哪兒啊！喔，我的仙女，請你告訴我，我該去哪兒找他，我要永遠和他在一起，再也不離開他，再也不離開！⋯⋯喔，我的仙女，請你告訴我，這不是真的，你還沒有死！⋯⋯要是你真的愛你的弟弟，那你就活過來⋯⋯跟從前一樣活過來吧！⋯⋯你看著我孤身一人，被所有的人拋棄了，你不覺得傷心嗎？⋯⋯如果那兩個強盜再把我吊在樹枝上⋯⋯那我真的就要死了。我一個人活在這世上，讓我怎麼過呢？你不在了，我爸爸也不在了，那誰給我吃的呢？晚上我睡哪兒呢？誰替我做新衣裳呢？噢，我還不如也死了好，要好上一百倍！真的，我要死⋯⋯嗚！嗚！嗚！」

他絕望得想要扯掉自己的頭髮,可是他的頭髮是用木頭做的,不要說是扯了,就連手指也插不進去。

這時候一隻大鴿子從他頭頂飛過。鴿子張開雙翅停在半空,低下頭對木偶叫道:「跟我說,孩子,你在那兒做什麼呀?」

「你難道沒看見嗎?我在哭!」皮諾丘抬起頭來,朝聲音傳來的方向看去,並用衣服擦了擦眼睛。

「告訴我。」鴿子接著問,「在你認識的人中間,有沒有一個叫皮諾丘的木偶?」

「皮諾丘?⋯⋯你說皮諾丘?」木偶重覆了一遍,迅速跳了起來,「我就是皮諾丘!」

聽到這個回答,鴿子快速地飛下來落到地面上。這鴿子比一隻火雞還大。

「那你也認識傑佩托嘍?」他問木偶。

「豈止是認識!他是我可憐的爸爸!他有向你提起過我嗎?你可以帶我去找他嗎?他是不是還活著?請你大發慈悲告訴我,他還活著嗎?」

「三天以前,我和他在海邊分開了。」

「他在那裡做什麼?」

「他正在造一隻小船,打算橫渡海洋。在過去的三個多月的時間裡,那位可憐的老人在全世界不停地找你,都沒有找到。如今,他只想著去新大陸那些遙遠的國家裡找尋。」

「從這兒到海邊有多遠?」皮諾丘屏息問道。

「六百多英里。」

「六百多英里?噢,漂亮的鴿子,你有一對翅膀真是太美妙了!」

「要是你想去,我就帶你去。」

「怎麼去呢?」

「你坐在我背上。你重不重?」

「我沒有什麼重量,輕如鴻毛。」皮諾丘二話不說,縱身跳上了鴿子的背,兩條腿叉開坐著就像騎馬一般,他開心地大叫:「快,快,我的小馬,我一心想快點到……」鴿子扇著翅膀往上飛,幾分鐘之內就貼近了天邊的雲彩。木偶發現自己來到這麼高的地方,忍不住內心的好奇心,他低頭往下看去。但是他頭一轉,嚇得心都要跳出來了。為了不讓自己摔下去,只好緊緊環住他那匹長著羽毛的飛馬的脖子。

他們一整天都在飛,等到天黑了,鴿子說:「我好渴!」

「我好餓喔!」皮諾丘跟著說。

「我們停到鴿舍那裡休息幾分鐘,然後接著趕路,這樣明天天一亮就能到海邊。」

說著說著,他們降落到一個廢棄的鴿舍上。那裡除了一盆滿滿的水和一籃野豌豆外,再沒有別的東西。

木偶自出生以來還沒有吃過野豌豆，據了解，他看到野豌豆就會噁心反胃。不過，那個晚上他大吃特吃，一籃子都快吃見底了，才轉身對鴿子說：「我從來沒想過野豌豆居然如此美味！」

　　「記住，孩子。」鴿子對他說，「人啊，到非常餓的時候，當下又沒別的食物，即使野豌豆也變成美食啦！饑餓，可不會讓你挑三揀四的！」

　　就這樣，很快地吃了點東西後，他們又開始旅程，重新起飛了。次日早上，他們來到海邊。鴿子把皮諾丘放在地上，他做了好事又很謙虛地不要人致謝，於是馬上飛上天空，消失了。

　　海邊擠滿了人。民眾面向大海大喊大叫，還做著各種手勢。

　　「發生什麼事了？」皮諾丘問一位老婦人。

　　「是這樣的，一位可憐的父親坐的小船不見了，他丟失了自己的孩子，想坐小船到海的另一邊去尋找。不過，今天海上有暴風雨，所以，那小船隨時有沉沒的危險。」

　　「小船呢？」

　　「在那邊，正對著我手指的地方。」老婦人指著遙遠的一隻小船說。

　　那只船離得太遠，看著就像一個核桃殼裡面坐著一個小小的人。

皮諾丘轉過頭去，定睛一看，立時大聲尖叫起來：「那是我爸爸！那是我爸爸！」

這個時候，一陣巨浪打過來，小船不久後就消失在洶湧的浪潮中，一會兒又被拋上浪峰，載浮載沉。皮諾丘站到一塊高高的岩石上面，不停地叫喊著父親的名字，還一直揮舞著雙手、手帕，乃至他的帽子，以引起父親的注意。

儘管，傑佩托離岸邊有點遠，但他顯然也認出了自己的兒子，他也脫掉帽子揮舞示意，打著手勢，竭力要讓孩子看見；如果可以，他想立刻掉頭了。可是，海上風浪太大，連船槳都不能用，更別說想要靠岸了。

突然，一個可怕的巨浪打過來，船消失了。大家等啊等的，希望它重新浮上海面，可惜再也沒有浮上來。

「可憐的人！」聚集在海岸邊的漁民們喃喃地說。隨後，他們低聲禱告一番，只能抱憾各自回家了。

就在這個時候，他們聽到一聲絕望的哀號；轉身一看，只見一個孩子從岩石上面跳進了大海，嘴裡還呼喊著：「我要救我的爸爸！」

皮諾丘因為是木頭做的，所以輕易就能浮在水面上，好像魚一樣地游了起來。岸上的人看著他一會兒被海浪壓翻到水裡，沒了蹤影；一會兒又掙扎著，重新露出一條腿或者一條手臂。直到最後，終於消失在大家的視野之中，再也看不見那個孩子了。

「可憐的孩子！」聚集在岸邊的漁民們感慨說。他們又是低聲禱告一番，感到非常遺憾的解散了。

第 24 章

皮諾丘抵達了「勤勞蜜蜂之鄉」的小島,在島上再次遇到了仙女。

皮諾丘只想著能夠及時救起他可憐的爸爸,在海裡游了一整晚。

這真是一個讓人戰慄的夜晚!大雨傾盆而下,還夾著大冰雹,雷聲驚天動地,閃電連連,把夜晚照得如同白晝。

破曉時分,他終於看見不遠處,出現了一片狹長的陸地。這是茫茫大海中的一個孤島。

他用盡全力努力想游上岸,不過都徒勞無功。巨浪不停的翻滾著,浪花互相追逐著,拋來拋去,就像他是一根樹枝或是一捆稻草。幸運的是,最後一個洶湧澎湃的巨浪拍打過來,把他拋在了遠遠的沙灘上。

他重重地落在地上，這一下摔得可不輕啊！他全身的骨頭和關節都在嘎吱作響。不過自我安慰地說：「這一回是大難不死啦！」

這時天空漸漸明亮，太陽躍出海平面放出萬道光芒。海浪平靜下來，陽光猶如一面明鏡。

木偶將濕衣服脫下來，讓太陽烘乾。接著他四下打探，想在浩瀚的水面上尋找那條小船，尋找在船上那個小小的人兒。可是，他看啊看啊，見到的只有藍天、大海以及幾面船帆，因為離得很遠，船帆看上去像蒼蠅似的。

「要是，我知道這個島叫什麼名字就好了！」他一面說一面走，「至少能瞭解這島上的居民是不是作風正派。我的意思是說，這些人會不會有把孩子吊在樹枝上的習慣？不過，我能向誰打聽消息呢？找誰呢？這兒可是一個人也沒有。」

一想到自己孤零零一個人，身處這杳無人煙的國度，他就憂愁得想哭了。就在他快哭的時候，突然看見不遠的岸邊游過來一條大魚。這條魚把整個頭露在水面上，只管安靜自在地游著。

不知道這是條什麼魚，木偶只是大聲喊著期望他能聽見：「喂，大魚先生，能和您說一句話嗎？」

「要是你喜歡，講兩句也行啊。」那條魚回答說。原來是條海豚，他很有禮貌，這在海洋世界中相當少見。

「請問,這島上有沒有一些村莊,可以讓我找點吃的東西,又不會被人吃掉?」

「當然有。」海豚回答說,「在離這兒不遠的地方就有。」

「我應該走哪條路過去呢?」

「沿著左邊那條小路,順著你的長鼻子直走。不會走錯的。」

「再向您打聽一件事?您日日夜夜都在海上游,有沒有見過一條小船,船上載著我的爸爸?」

「你爸爸是誰?」

「他是世界上最好的爸爸,同時,卻有著我這個世界上最壞的兒子。」

「昨晚狂風暴雨……」海豚回答說,「那小船肯定葬身海底了。」

「那我爸爸呢?」

「他一定是被那條可怕的鯊魚吞到肚子裡去了。這些日子以來,他一直在我們這些水域大肆破壞,橫掃一切。」

「這條鯊魚十分的大嗎?」皮諾丘問道。他顯然害怕得瑟瑟發抖了。

「大極啦!」海豚回答說,「為了讓你大概知道他的尺寸,我這麼跟你說吧!他比一棟五層高的樓房還大,嘴巴又寬又深,都可以一口吞下一列帶著火車頭的火車。」

「老天爺保佑啊！」木偶驚嚇得大叫起來。他以最快的速度穿好衣服後，轉身對海豚說：「再見，海豚先生。給您添麻煩了，非常感謝您的好意。」

一刻也不停留的立即走上那條小路，走得非常快。因為走太快了，以至於看上去就像在奔跑一樣，一有點風吹草動，他就忙不迭回頭，生怕那條可怕的鯊魚，嘴裡跑出一列火車緊追其後。

走了半小時，他來到一個名字叫做「勤勞蜜蜂之鄉」的小村莊。大街上的人來來往往，都在勤快工作。所有人全都在做事，所有人都有事做。即使打著燈籠，也找不到一個遊手好閒的人或者是流浪漢。

「啊哈！」懶惰的皮諾丘馬上說道，「這個地方永遠不適合我的！我生來可不是做事的！」

可是，這時候他餓到不行了，都連續廿四小時沒吃過任何東西了，即使一顆野豌豆也沒有吃。他該怎麼辦呢？

他要得到吃的，只有兩條路好選；或者是找份工作，或者是乞討，以求得點小錢或一口麵包。

行乞，對他來說是一件丟人的事。因為他父親一再提醒，只有老人和生病殘障的人才能夠乞討。在這個世界上，真正值得我們憐憫和援助的窮人，只有那些因為年老或者病人，因為他們沒有辦法依靠自己的雙手勞動去獲取食物。其他普通人都有義務去勞動，如果有人不勞動而挨餓，那就是自作自受。

正在這時候，大路上過來一個人，看似累得氣喘吁吁。他居然獨自一人艱難地拉著滿滿的兩大車煤礦。

從外表看，皮諾丘覺得他是一個好心的人，於是就走上前去，羞愧地垂著眼睛，輕輕地對他說：「你能不能發發好心，賞給我一枚錢，我都快要餓死啦！」

「我打算不止給你一枚錢。」拉煤人回答說，「而是四枚，只要你能幫我把這兩車煤給拉回家。」

「你讓人很意外！」木偶用不友善的口氣回答，「實話告訴您，我不習慣做拉驢車的工作，我從來沒有拉過車！」

「那你就這樣好了。」拉煤人說，「孩子，要是你真的餓極了，就吃那兩大片自尊活吧！不過，要小心啊！可不要吃撐了。」

又過了幾分鐘，一個泥水匠走過來了，肩上扛著一桶石灰。

「慷慨的人，請給個方便，給我這可憐的孩子一枚錢，我都餓得直打哈欠了！」

「樂意之至。」泥水匠回答說，「過來幫我抬這桶石灰，我給你五枚錢而不是一枚那麼少。」

「但這石灰太重了。」皮諾丘回說，「我不想累著我自己。」

「假若不想累著你自己，那麼，孩子，你就打著哈欠自娛自樂吧！希望它會給你帶來很多好處。」

不到半個鐘頭，又走過其他二十個人。皮諾丘向他們每個人討錢，不過他們都回答說：「你這樣乞討，不覺得丟臉嗎？不要在這路上閒逛了，還是去找點兒工作做，學著靠勞力賺口飯吃吧！」

後來，一位善良的小婦人提著兩瓦罐水，走了過來。

「能讓我從您的瓦罐裡喝點水嗎？」皮諾丘說，他的嗓子乾得都冒煙了。

「孩子，要是渴了就喝吧！」小婦人說著，隨即放下那兩個瓦罐。

皮諾丘像久逢甘霖的魚兒一樣喝飽了水，然後擦擦嘴、低聲咕噥著：「不口渴了，但若是肚子也不餓就好啦！」

善良的小婦人聽到這些話，馬上接著說：「如果你幫我把這兩瓦罐水送回家，我就給你一大片麵包。」

皮諾丘看著瓦罐，既沒答應也沒拒絕。

「除了麵包，還給你一大盤油醋花椰菜。」好心的小婦人又補充說。

皮諾丘又看著瓦罐一眼，還是既不說是也不說不。

「吃過花椰菜，我再給你一塊美味的酒心糖。」

最後一樣美食的誘惑力，實在是太大了。皮諾丘再也不能抵抗了，下定決心說：「那好吧！我幫您把這兩瓦罐水送到家去吧!」

瓦罐很重,木偶只用手是搬不動的,只好頂在頭上。

到了婦人家裡之後,她讓皮諾丘坐在一張已經佈置好的小桌子旁邊,然後給他擺上了麵包、花椰菜和酒心糖。

皮諾丘不是用吃的,而是用吞的。他的胃就像一個五個月沒有住人的空房間。

轆轆饑腸多少得到緩解後,他抬起頭來打算感謝這位大恩人。可是一看到她,他就驚奇說:「啊……」了一聲,然後目不轉睛地盯著她,眼睛張的大大的,楞到叉子都舉在半空中,嘴巴裡塞滿了麵包和花椰菜,就像被施了魔法一樣。

「你怎麼會這樣驚訝啊?」善良的小婦人微笑著問道。

「您是……」皮諾丘回答,「您是……您是…您看上去……您讓我想起……是的,是的,是的,一樣的聲音……一樣的眼睛……一樣的頭髮……是的,是的,是的……您也是藍色的頭髮和她一樣!哦,我的仙女!哦,我的仙女!……告訴我就是您吧!確確實實就是您吧!……不要讓我再哭了!如果您知道……我已經哭太多了,我已經遭受太多懲罰了!」

皮諾丘撲倒在這位神秘小婦人的腳下,抱住她的膝蓋,痛哭流涕。

第 25 章

皮諾丘向仙女保證要做個好孩子,努力學習。他已經厭倦再做木偶了,他希望能成為一個真正的好男孩。

善良的小婦人起初堅持不肯說自己是那位藍髮的仙女。但後來意識到被識破了,也就不想再演戲了,終於承認就是仙女。她對皮諾丘說:「你這小機靈鬼!你怎麼發現是我的?」

「我太愛您了,一看到就認出是您了。」

「你還記得嗎?你離開我的時候,我還是個女孩。現在,我們再次重逢,我已經是個婦人了,一位年紀大得足夠當你媽媽的婦人。」

「這樣我很開心,因為現在我就不用叫您姐姐,可以叫您媽媽了。一直以來,我多希望能和其他孩子一樣有個媽媽!……不過,您是用什麼方法長得這麼快的?」

「這是一個秘密。」

「教教我吧,我也盼望長大一點。難道您沒看出來嗎?我還是只有一個木樁那麼高。」

「但你是不會長大的。」仙女回答說。

「為什麼?」

「因為木偶永遠都不會長大。他們生出來是木偶,出生時是木偶,死了還是木偶。」

「喔!我討厭做個木偶!」皮諾丘拍了自己一下,哭著說,「現在我想做個人。」

「如果你知道,怎麼樣才能做為一個人類的話,你就會是人了。」

「真的嗎?我要怎麼做才能是人呢?」

「非常簡單,只要你學著做個好孩子,就行了。」

「難道,我不是個好孩子嗎?」

「完全不是!好孩子會聽話,但是你呢?」

「我從來不聽話。」

「好孩子喜歡學習,喜歡工作,但是你呢?」

「剛好相反,我整年都懶懶散散,遊手好閒。」

「好孩子永遠講真話……」

「但我通常都說假話。」

「好孩子都願意去學校……」

「學校讓我渾身不舒服。但是從今天開始，我要改變自己的生活。」

「你可以向我保證嗎？」

「我向你保證。我會成為一個好孩子，我還會變成我爸爸的慰藉……不過，這個時候，我可憐的爸爸在哪裡呢？」

「我不知道。」

「我還能再見到他、親吻他嗎？我能有這份幸運嗎？」

「我認為你有，真的，我保證。」

聽到這個回答，皮諾丘又興奮起來，抓著仙女的手不顧一切地親吻。然後，他仰著臉熱切地注視著仙女問道：「告訴我，好媽媽，你的死不是真的吧？」

「似乎不是。」仙女微笑著回答。

「你不知道，那個時候我多麼傷心，當我讀著：『這裡躺著……』那些文字，我的喉嚨都緊縮了。」

「我知道，那也是我原諒你的理由。你的傷心是真真切切的，這讓我明白，你保有一顆善良的心。一個心地善良的孩子，儘管有些調皮，儘管有點不良的習慣，但總是有希望的。也就是說，總是有希望能重新回歸正途的。所以，我才來這兒找你，成為你的媽媽。」

「啊，真是太好了！」皮諾丘大叫道，興奮得跳了起來。

「你必須聽我的話，我說什麼你就做什麼。」

「我願意，我願意，我願意！」

「那，從明天開始……」仙女接著說，「你就去上學。」皮諾丘立刻就沒那麼激動了。

「然後根據你的意願，選一門手藝或者一種行業……」

這下，皮諾丘的臉嚴肅起來了。

「你在牙齒縫裡嘀咕些什麼呢？」仙女生氣地問他。

「我是說……」木偶輕聲抱怨著，「我現在才去上學，似乎遲了點……」

「不會遲的，孩子。你記著，讀書、學習是永遠不嫌遲的。」

「可是我不想學手藝或選擇一種行業什麼的。」

「怎麼呢？」

「因為工作實在是太累人了。」

「我的孩子！」仙女說，「這樣說的人，最後幾乎不是進監獄，或者就進醫院了。我告訴你，在這個世界上，一個人生下來不管貧困還是富足，都得做點事，都必須勞動。懶惰的人，是不會善終的。懶惰是一種可怕的毛病，從孩提時代就要馬上糾正。否則，等年紀大了，就再也矯正不過來了！」

這一番話觸動了皮諾丘的心。他迅速把頭抬起來，對仙女說：「我要學習，我要工作，你說的話我全都照辦。說實在的，木偶的生活我已經厭倦了，不管要付出什麼，我都要變成一個孩子。你說過我可以的，不是嗎？」

「我已經承諾過了。現在一切取決於你。」

第 26 章

皮諾丘跟同學一起去海邊看那條可怕的大鯊魚。

第二天,皮諾丘就去了一所公立學校。

大家想一下就知道,那些調皮搗蛋鬼看見一個木偶走進他們的學校,該有多麼興奮!他們沒完沒了地大聲笑著。對著木偶人坐著各種各樣的惡作劇。一個孩子摘掉他的帽子,另一個孩子就從身後拉他的小夾克。有人還試圖用墨水在他鼻子底下畫兩撇鬍鬚,有人則嘗試著把線綁在他的腳上和手上,好扯著線讓他舞蹈。

最初,皮諾丘還假裝不在意,專心做自己的事情。不過後來他爆怒了,轉過身去朝著那些一直糾纏、捉弄他最厲害的人,扳著臉說:「當心點,孩子們。我來學校可不是讓你們戲弄的。我尊重你們，也希望你們同樣尊重我。」

「真會說！小鬼！說的像書上寫的，好個出口成章！」那些淘氣鬼喊叫著，瘋狂笑到都要扭曲變形了。他們中間最膽大妄為的孩子，突然伸出手就要抓木偶的鼻尖。

不過，他還沒來得及抓住，皮諾丘就從課桌下伸出腳來，狠狠地踢了他的小腿一下。

「哎喲！你的腳也太硬了！」那孩子大叫一聲，用力地揉著被木偶踢傷的地方。

「哎喲！還有手肘！……比腳還硬！」另外一個孩子也尖叫著。他因為開了粗魯的玩笑，肚子被木偶打了一拳。

不過，這一踢一拳卻讓皮諾丘得到全校學生的認同和尊重。大家都願意和他交朋友，真心喜歡他。

甚至連老師也誇獎他，因為他上課聚精會神，學習刻苦用功，並且聰明過人。他總是第一個進學校，最後一個放學回家的學生。

他唯一的缺點就是，結交了太多朋友。其中還有一些小搗蛋鬼，他們以不愛學習、喜歡作弄別人而全校聞名。

老師每天都提醒他，連善良的仙女也時常反反覆覆叮囑他說：「要小心啊，皮諾丘！早晚有一天，這些問題同學會帶壞你不愛學習的，說不定，哪一天還可能讓你倒大楣。」

「不要擔心！」木偶聳聳肩膀，還用了食指比著前額，好像是說,「我這兒清醒得很呢!」

　　終於在某一天,當他正走在上學的路上,那幫問題學生迎面而來,問他說,「有一個重大的消息,你聽說了嗎?」

「沒有。」

「這附近海邊出現了一條鯊魚,聽說有一座山那麼大。」

「真的?吃掉我可憐的爸爸的鯊魚,有可能是同一條嗎?」

「我們打算到海邊去看看。你和我們一起去嗎?」

「不去,我還要去上學。」

「不去學校有什麼關係?隔天再去上學就好了。反正多上一節課,少上一節課,也沒什麼差別。我們一樣還是笨蛋。」

「但是老師會怎麼說呢?」

「他愛說不說。他就靠整天嘮嘮叨叨地賺錢呢!」

「不過我媽媽呢?」

「媽媽們什麼也不會知道的。」這些壞小孩說。

「你們猜,我怎麼做呢?」皮諾丘說,「因為某種理由,我也想去看看這條大鯊魚,不過我要等放學後再去。」

「可憐的蠢驢!」某個孩子大聲說,「你以為這麼大一條魚,會等在那裡,隨便你什麼時候去看嗎?他要是在那裡待煩了,馬上就會去其他地方了,等你再去的時候,就太遲啦!」

「從這裡到海邊要多長時間？」木偶問道。

「來回大約一個鐘頭。」

「那，出發囉！」皮諾丘叫道，「看誰跑得最快、最厲害！」起跑的信號一響，這些孩子就把他們的課本、練習本都夾在腋下裡，穿越田野飛奔過去。皮諾丘一路領先，雙腳感覺像長了翅膀一樣地快速。

他不時回過頭去，向著那些落後在他後面好遠的同學，嘲笑一番。看著他們跑得氣喘吁吁、全身沾了泥巴、舌頭都吐出來的模樣，他開心地大笑起來。這個倒楣的孩子，還不知道自己正面臨著什麼樣的恐怖和災難呢！

第 27 章

皮諾丘和同伴們打了激烈的一架了;其中一個還受了傷。皮諾丘被警察逮捕了。

一到海邊,皮諾丘立刻向海平面望去。然而,他並沒有看見什麼鯊魚。大海寧靜得就像一面大的水晶鏡子。

「鯊魚在哪兒呢?」他回頭問他的夥伴。

「他啊!肯定去吃早餐了。」一個同學大笑著回答說。

「要不然啊!就是上床打瞌睡去了。」另一個同學樂不可支地補充了一句。

聽到這些亂七八糟的回答和他們的傻笑,皮諾丘意識到,那些同學在愚弄他,誘騙他相信了一個謠言。他很生氣,聲色俱厲地向他們說:「好了,現在你們告訴我,拿鯊魚的謊話來騙我，這很值得開心嗎？」

「哈，有趣極了！」那些壞同學異口同聲地回答。

「有什麼樂趣？」

「就是要你和我們一起翹課。你每天都準時上學，一課不落後的，難道不覺得羞恥嗎？你那麼勤奮刻苦地學習，難道不覺得羞恥嗎？」

「就算我學習用功，這又跟你們有什麼關係呢？」

「跟我們關係可大著呢！因為你這樣，會讓老師對我們留下不好的印象。」

「為什麼？」

「在有人認真學習的比較下，像我們這樣不想學習的人，就顯得更惡劣了。那太丟臉了！我們也有自尊啊！」

「那我怎麼做，你們才高興呢？」

「你也應該和我們一樣，討厭學校，討厭功課，討厭老師，討厭我們認為的這三大敵人。」

「要是我想繼續學習呢？」

「如果那樣的話，我們就沒什麼好說的了。只要一逮到機會，我們就要你好看。」

「真的是……」木偶邊搖頭邊說，「你們才叫我覺得好笑。」

「喂！皮諾丘！」其中最大的孩子走到他跟前叫道，「別擺出一副高高在上的樣子，別到這兒來說廢話！如果你不怕我們，那我們也不怕你！你記住了，你一個要對我們七個。」

「七個！剛好湊成七宗罪。」皮諾丘大笑著說。

「你們聽聽！他辱罵我們大家！他管我們叫七宗罪！」

「皮諾丘！快點道歉……否則我們要對你不利喔！」

「咕咕！」木偶學布穀鳥的叫聲，還用食指摸摸鼻尖的諷刺他們。

「皮諾丘！你會很悲慘的！」

「咕咕！」

「我們要揍死你！」

「咕咕！」

「我們要打爛你的鼻子！」

「咕咕！」

「哈，我們這就來給你一個『咕咕』！」膽子最大的孩子說道，「你好好享用，留給你今晚當飯吃。」

他說著，然後一拳頭揍在了木偶的腦袋上。

有道是：一報還一報。因此不出所料，木偶立刻就回敬他一拳。一時之間，這場架就越打越厲害，越打越混亂了。

儘管，皮諾丘只有一個人，但他就像個自衛的英雄。他不停地踢著那兩條用世界上最硬的木頭做成的腿,好讓那些對手們躲得遠遠的,不敢走近。因為,他們不管哪裡都會被他的腿踢到,然後留下一塊淤青,作為永久的印記。

　　孩子們眼看空手無法靠近木偶的身體,心裡開始急躁起來,只好尋找其他武器了。他們打開書包,朝著他扔學校的書本;語法書、詞典、識字課本、地理書以及一些其他的學校用書。可是木偶眼明手快,都一一及時閃開了,因此,書全從他頭上擦邊而過,通通都掉到海裡去了。

　　可想而知,海裡的魚兒們有多麼驚奇!他們還以為那些書,是什麼美味的東西,趕緊在淺灘附近聚集起來。他們試吃了一兩頁後,快把前言頁面都啃光時,突然又一口吐出來,然後露出怪異的神色,好像說:「這不是給我們吃的,我們海裡吃得比這東西好太多了!」

　　就在孩子們打架打得越來越激烈的時候,一隻大螃蟹浮出水面,動作緩慢地朝岸邊爬去,一面爬還一面像拿著擴音器似的高喊著:「不要打啦,你們這些壞小孩!像你們這樣打架的孩子們,是不會有好事發生的,以後肯定要闖大禍!」

　　可憐的螃蟹,根本是在白費唇舌。皮諾丘反而轉過頭盯著他,無禮地嘲笑他說:「煩人的螃蟹,閉上你的嘴!你最好還是去吃點甘草, 先把你那破嗓子治一治。或者趁早上床睡覺吧!」

　　這時候,那群孩子將自己的書已經給扔完了,看見不遠處有皮諾丘的書包,說時遲那時快,他們快速地跑過去一把搶了過來。

在書包裡,有一本用厚紙板裝幀的書,書脊和書角還包著羊皮紙。這是一本數學書。大家想想看,這本書該有多重!

其中一個孩子抓起這本書,用力地朝皮諾丘的腦袋扔過去。不過,他沒砸中木偶,卻砸在另一個同學的太陽穴上了。這個同學的臉,馬上白得就像一張紙,然後尖叫了兩聲:「天哪,媽媽,救救我⋯⋯我要死了!」然後,就全身僵硬地倒在沙灘上了。想到他可能死了,那些孩子嚇得拔腿就逃,一眨眼的工夫全失去蹤影。

但是,皮諾丘卻留了下來。儘管,他已經被傷心和恐懼折磨得半死不活了,可還是跑過去查看。他在海水裡把手帕浸濕,然後跑回來敷在那位可憐的同學的太陽穴上。皮諾丘一邊絕望地痛哭流涕,一邊叫他的名字:「尤金!⋯⋯我可憐的尤金!⋯⋯你睜開眼睛,看著我!你為什麼不出聲啊?不是我砸你的,真的不是我把你傷成這樣的!你要相信我,不是我做的!你睜開眼吧,尤金⋯⋯如果你一直閉著眼睛,我也活不下了⋯⋯啊!我該怎麼辦啊?我要怎麼回家呢?我怎麼有臉見善良的媽媽啊?我將面對什麼事呢?有什麼地方可以讓我逃避呢?唉!要是我當初堅持去學校那該多好啊,要比現在好上一千倍!⋯⋯我為什麼要相信那些壞同學的話呢?他們就是我的災難啊!老師曾經告誡過我!我媽媽也再三強調說:『當心壞同學!』可我總是不聽⋯⋯我真是一個頑固的傻瓜⋯⋯他們的話被我當做耳邊風!現在好了,有苦頭吃啦!從我來到這個世上起,就因為這種個性,我片刻的歡樂都沒有享受過。我的

「天哪！我要怎麼辦啊？我要怎麼辦啊？我要怎麼辦啊？」

皮諾丘哭個不停，一直嗚咽著，他不停地用拳頭，敲打著腦袋，自責地叫著可憐尤金的名字，一直到……一陣腳步聲傳過來。

他回過頭去，看到了兩個警察。

「你趴在地上做什麼？」他們問皮諾丘。

「我正在救護我的同學。」

「他受傷了嗎？」

「看上去是的！」

「真的受傷了！」一個騎兵蹲下來，湊近仔細看了看尤金，「這孩子的太陽穴受傷了。誰傷害他？」

「不是我。」木偶結結巴巴地說，他一口氣也不敢喘息。

「不是你，那會是誰？」

「不是我。」皮諾丘重覆一遍。

「他為什麼受傷的？」

「這本書。」皮諾丘從地上撿起那本用厚紙板和羊皮紙裝幀的數學書，遞給警察看。

「這本書是誰的？」

「是我的。」

「這就夠了,什麼也不用再說了。立刻站起來,跟我們走。」

「但是,我……」

「跟我們走!」

「但是,我是清白的。」

「跟我們走!」

就在他們離開之際,剛好有漁民駕船從附近岸邊經過。兩個騎兵叫住幾個漁民,對他們說:「躺在這裡的孩子,就交給你們了。他頭部受傷了。你們把他帶回家好好好照顧,等明天我們再來看他。」

隨後,他們回轉到皮諾丘身邊,把他夾在兩人中間,用指揮官的語氣命令說:「預備,走!走快點!否則,要你好看!」

沒等他們說第二遍,木偶就朝通往村莊的這條路走了起來。不過這時,那個可憐的小子幾乎不知道自己身處何方。他覺得自己一定是在做夢,一個非常恐怖的噩夢!他嚇得魂飛魄散。兩眼發昏,雙腿發抖,舌頭緊貼著牙根,連一個音也發不出來。不過,儘管處於這種渾渾噩噩、迷迷糊糊的狀態,他還是感到心裡一陣刺痛。因為他想到,他就要被夾在兩個警察中間,從那位善良的仙女的窗前經過。這下他倒真是情願死了,一了百了。

他們已經走到了村口,突然一陣狂風吹過,把皮諾丘頭上的小圓帽吹走了十步遠的距離。

141

木偶對兩個員警說：「可以允許我去把帽子撿回來嗎？」

「那好，你去吧！不過得快點。」

木偶走過去，撿起帽子……可是他沒有把帽子戴到頭上，而是把它咬在嘴裡，然後拔腿就向海邊，狂奔而去。

兩個警察眼看追上他似乎是不可能了，於是就放出一條大型警犬去追他。這條狗在比賽中還拿過冠軍呢。皮諾丘拚命跑，但是狗跑得比他更快。所有的人不是從窗戶探出頭來，就是擠在大街上，急迫地想要看到這場激烈賽跑的結果。不過，他們的願望很快就落空了，因為那條警犬和皮諾丘一跑過，就揚起了漫天灰塵。不用幾分鐘的時間，他們就沒了蹤影。

第 28 章

皮諾丘陷入危機了,他差點就像一條魚被放進煎鍋裡給煎熟了。

這場猶如亡命之徒的追逐賽,已經到了決定生死的時刻。此刻皮諾丘驚恐不已,想著自己可能就要輸了。如眾所皆知阿利多羅,就是那條警犬的名字,他的動作迅猛如閃電,幾乎快要趕上木偶了。

木偶聽到這條猛犬的喘氣聲,正在漸漸逼近他。他們之間的距離,連一個手掌都不到;他甚至感覺到警犬呼出的熱氣。

不過幸運的是,海岸近了。離海邊只有幾步之遙了。

一到海邊木偶便縱身一躍,跳到海裡去了,連青蛙都沒有他的動作俐落。

但相反的是，阿利多羅突然停住腳步。可是由於衝跑力度太大，沒能來得及停下來，直接撲通一聲落進水裡了。可憐的狗他不會游泳啊！於是兩隻前掌在水裡拚命地比劃著，想讓自己能浮在水面上。但是越划沉得越快，最後整個頭都埋進海裡去了。

等他再次把頭探出水面時，雙眼裡全是恐慌的眼神，嚇得汪汪大叫著：「我快淹死了！我快淹死了！」

「淹吧，你！」眼見自己的危機已解除，皮諾丘忿忿地回了一句。

「救救我吧，親愛的皮諾丘！……救救我吧！……」

可是，聽到狗淒慘的哀求聲，本性善良的木偶禁不住心軟下來。他轉身對狗說：「要是我救你，你能承諾再也不找我麻煩，再也不追我了嗎？」

「我答應，我答應！快點吧，你行行好，如果你再遲個半分鐘，我就淹死啦！」

皮諾丘還在遲疑不定，不過後來想起父親常跟他說過的話，做好事絕不會吃虧。於是，就游到阿利多羅身邊，兩手抓著他的尾巴，安然無恙地把他拉上沙灘上。

這條可憐的狗，連站都站不穩了。他迫不得已喝了好多海水進肚，肚子脹得像個大氣球。不過，木偶還是不敢太相信他，心裡想著還是謹慎點好，於是重新跳進水裡。他游出岸邊很大一段距離後，才對救起來的朋友喊道：「再見，阿利多羅，一路順風，代我問候你的家人。」

「再見，皮諾丘。」警犬回答說，「衷心感謝您救了我一命。您幫了我的大忙，這是一個善惡有報的世界；如果有機會，我一定會報答您的。」

皮諾丘緊靠著岸邊繼續往前游去，終於來到一個他認為安全的地方。沿著海岸看過去，只見岩石之間有個山洞，從山洞裡升起了嫋嫋的煙霧。

「那山洞裡肯定有火。」他自言自語道，「真是太好啦！我先上去把身體烘乾，暖和暖和，接下來呢？接下來，再說吧。」

他打定了主意，就朝那片岩石游過去。但是，就在他準備爬上岸時，突然覺察到水底下有樣東西越升越高，一直把他升到了半空。他打算馬上逃跑，可是已經太遲了。因為，他萬分驚訝地發現，自己竟然在一個大漁網裡，夾在一大群游魚中間。這些魚形狀、大小各異，正拚了老命地在漁網裡掙扎。

與此同時，一個漁夫從山洞裡走了出來，長相十分醜陋，醜得實在是慘不忍睹，像個海怪似的。他的頭上長的不是頭髮，而是茂密的草叢。他的皮膚是綠色，雙眼是綠色，連長到地面的鬍子，也是綠色的。簡而言之，他的外表活像是一隻會站立的大蜥蜴。

漁夫從海裡面收起漁網，滿心歡喜地叫道：「謝天謝地！今天我又能享受一頓豐盛的海鮮大餐囉！」

「老天保佑，我不是魚！」皮諾丘似乎重新獲得了勇氣，心裡暗想道。

滿滿的一網子魚，都被漁夫帶進了山洞。山洞裡面很黑，且濃煙滾滾。山洞中央架著一隻大油鍋，盛滿油的煎鍋裡，發出一股令人窒息的菌類的氣味。

「好啦！讓我來看看，網住了一些什麼魚！綠色漁夫說著，接著，把他那隻巨大的、活像鍋鏟的手，伸進漁網裡，掏出了一把烏魚。

「這些烏魚還不錯！」他這樣說。然後，沾沾自喜地看了又看，聞了又聞。聞完之後，隨手就把魚扔到了一個盤子裡。

他把前面那一套動作，重複了很多遍。綠色漁夫邊挑魚、邊流起口水，而且，還傻笑的自言自語：「多麼好的鱈魚啊！」

「多麼肥美的鱈魚啊！」

「這些沙丁魚很可口！」

「螃蟹也不錯哦！」

「鯤魚長得多美妙啊！」

接下來，不用多說也能知道，這些鱈魚、沙丁魚、比目魚、螃蟹、鯤魚，全都被地丟到盤子裡，跟最初扔進的烏魚做伴去了。

最後，網裡剩下的就只有皮諾丘了。

漁夫把他一掏出來，嚇得瞪圓了他那雙綠色的大眼睛，半是驚訝、半是害怕地尖叫出聲來：「這是一種什麼魚？我怎麼不記得曾吃過這種魚！」

他把木偶認認真真地再看一遍，檢視完之後，歸結一句話：「我知道了。他是小龍蝦。」

被誤會成一隻龍蝦，皮諾丘很生氣地說：「龍蝦？你以為我是一隻龍蝦？看看你，把我當什麼啦！實話告訴你，我是一個木偶。」

「木偶？」漁夫反問道，「說實在的，對我來說，木偶可是全新的一種食物，那真是太好了！我更想吃你了。」

「吃我？你還不明白嗎？我不是魚。難道，你沒有聽出來，我和您一樣，會說話、會思考嗎？」

「那倒是真的。」漁夫接著說，「不過，我認為你還是魚，一條和我一樣，有說話和思考能力的魚而已，所以，我很願意給你應得的照顧。」

「那種照顧？」

「為了表示我的友好，和對你的特別關注。我給你機會，讓你自由選擇自己喜歡的煮法。你是想在煎鍋裡煎呢？還是想要淋上番茄醬呢？」

「實話實說吧。」皮諾丘回答說，「假如，真要我選擇的話，我寧願你給我自由，放我回家去。」

「你在開玩笑吧！難得有一個吃罕見魚類的機會，你覺得我會放棄嗎？我告訴你，在這附近的海域，可不是每天都能捕到木偶魚的！還是我做主吧！把你和所有其他的魚一塊兒放在煎鍋裡，保證你百分百滿意，和那麼多魚一起被油炸，多少也是一種安慰。」聽到這番話，皮諾丘不管了，開始大哭大鬧，苦苦求饒。最後他哭哭啼啼地說道：「要是當初我去上學了，該有多好啊！都是我聽信了同學的話，現在有苦頭吃了！……哎！……哎！……哎！」

木偶像條鰻魚一樣蠕動，千方百計想從綠色漁夫的手裡掙脫出去。不過，這是白費氣力。漁夫拿起一束扎實的燈芯草，像捆香腸一樣，把皮諾丘的雙手雙腳綁得更緊了，然後扔到盤子裡和其他的魚在一起。

接著，他端出一大木碗麵粉，依次在魚身上裹好麵粉；裹好之後，就把他們扔到煎鍋裡炸。

最先在煮沸的油裡蹦跳的是可憐的鱈魚；接下來，就是螃蟹，然後是沙丁魚、鰓魚，最後就輪到了皮諾丘。眼看著自己死期將至，而且是這種悲慘的死法，皮諾丘嚇得渾身劇烈顫抖，害怕得既出不了聲，也透不過氣來，現在就算求饒肯定也沒用了。

於是，那可憐的孩子只好用眼神來求饒！然而，那綠色漁夫根本就不在意。他把木偶扔進麵粉裡滾了五六遍，直到皮諾丘全身上下，都裹滿了麵粉，看上去就像個石膏像。接著，他一把抓住他的頭，然後……。

第 29 章

皮諾丘回到了仙女的家。仙女承諾次日就讓他擺脫木偶,做個真正的男孩。為了慶祝這件大事,他們邀請所有同學參加有著咖啡牛奶等的豐盛早宴。

就在綠色漁夫正準備把皮諾丘扔進煎鍋裡炸的時候,山洞裡跑進來一條大狗。這條狗是被炸魚濃郁的香味給吸引過來的。

「滾出去!」漁夫威嚇的對大狗吼道,手裡依然拎著那個渾身裹滿麵粉的木偶。

但是,那條可憐的狗餓得實在是不行,哀怨地搖搖尾巴,好像在說:「只要你給我口魚吃,我馬上就離開。」

「滾出去，沒聽到嗎？」漁夫又吼了一聲，還伸出腿來，踢了他一腳。

不過，當一隻狗餓到極限的時候，才不理會這樣的威脅。那條狗對著漁夫咆哮起來，還露出了恐怖的獠牙。

這時，山洞裡響起一個微弱的聲音，苦苦哀求他說：「救救我，阿利多羅！要是你不救我，我就要被油炸了！」

狗瞬間認出了皮諾丘的聲音。不過，讓他覺得最驚奇的是，那些聲音是從漁夫抓著的那團麵粉裡面傳出來的。

猜猜看，他做了什麼？只見他縱身一躍，把那團麵粉叼在嘴，風馳電掣般地溜走了。

眼看著自己一心想吃的那條魚被搶走了，漁夫一陣狂怒，追著那條狗就跑了出去。可是還沒追多久，他就突然咳起來，只好放棄了。

這時，阿利多羅已經跑到通往村莊的小徑。他停下腳步，把他的朋友皮諾丘輕輕地放在了地上。

「我真不知道要怎麼感謝你！」木偶說。

「不用謝。」狗回答說，「你救過我的命，現在我回過頭救你一命，你知道生活在這世上，我們本來就要互相幫忙。」

「不過，你是怎麼到那山洞裡去的？」

「我本來是半死不活地躺在海邊的，突然一陣風吹過，帶來了陣陣炸魚的香味。這股味道勾起了我的食欲，循著香味就到了那裏。如果，我要遲來那麼一秒鐘的話……」

「你不要說了！」皮諾丘呻吟著，還停不住全身顫抖，「你不要說了！如果你遲來一秒鐘，我現在已經被油炸，然後被吃掉、消化了。呃！……一想到這裡，我就忍不住打冷顫！」

阿利多羅微微一笑，朝木偶伸出了他的右爪，木偶緊緊地握住狗爪，表達了自己友善感恩的心意。接著，他們就此告別了。

就這樣，狗兒上路回家了。留下皮諾丘一個人，朝不遠處的一間茅舍走去，茅舍門前正坐著一位曬太陽的老人家。木偶問他說：「向您打聽件事，善良的老人家，您有沒有聽說一個名叫尤金的可憐的孩子，他的腦部受傷了？」

「幾名漁夫把一個孩子送來過這間茅舍。但是如今……」

「如今他死了！」皮諾丘非常悲傷地打斷了他的話。

「不，他還活著，現在已經回家了。」

「真的嗎？真的嗎？」木偶激動得跳了起來，大聲說道，「這樣說來，他的傷不嚴重囉！」

「可是它的後果有可能十分嚴重，甚至是致命的。」小老頭兒回答他說，「因為打中他腦袋的是一本厚紙板裝幀的書。」

「是誰打中了他呢？」

「他的一個同學，叫皮諾丘的……」

「這皮諾丘是誰？」木偶假裝不知道地追問。

「他們說他是個壞孩子，是個流氓，是個真正的廢物。」

「造謠！全都是毀謗！」

「你認識這個皮諾丘？」

「見過！」木偶回答說。

「那你覺得他是一個什麼樣的人？」小老頭兒問他。

「據我所知，他是個極好的孩子，一心向學，為人乖巧，愛他的父親和家人……」

木偶像放機關槍一樣，撒著一串的謊言；說完後他摸摸鼻子，感覺它已經長了不止一隻手掌長度。他慌張得叫了起來：「好心的老人家，您可不要相信剛剛我跟您說的話。那個皮諾丘，我很熟悉。我可以肯定地告訴您，他真的是個十足的壞孩子，不聽話，懶惰，不去上學，卻跟著一群同學四處遊蕩！」

話剛說完，他的鼻子就變短了，回到了原來的模樣。

「你怎麼全身都是白色的？」老年人突然問他。

「是這樣的……我一個沒留神，身體碰上了一堵新刷白的牆上。」木偶回答說。他不好意思坦白，自己被當成魚，還裹上麵粉，差點就扔進煎鍋裡給油炸了。

「哦，那你的外套、褲子還有帽子，又是怎麼回事呢？」

「我遇上了強盜，他們把我剝光了。善良的老人家，您能不能給我一些衣服，讓我好穿回家去？」

「我的孩子,說到衣服,我這兒就只有一個裝豆子的小口袋子。如果你要就拿走吧,它在那邊。」

皮諾丘不等他說第二遍,立刻拿起那個小口袋子,用一把剪刀在底部剪了一個洞,在左右兩邊又各剪了一個洞,把它當做襯衫。穿上這件小衣服,他便動身往村裡走去。

可是,他一路走著,心裡總覺得有些不自在。事實上,他是走一步又退一步,還不停地自說自話:「我要怎麼去面對善良的仙女呢?她見到我會說些什麼呢?……我又犯錯了,她能寬恕我嗎?……我敢打賭她不會寬恕我……哎!她肯定不會寬恕我……這是我自作自受,誰叫我是個小渾蛋。我經常保證說要改過自新,但是我從來就不兌現諾言。」

他回到村裡的時候,已經是晚上了,天色十分黑暗。還颳起了暴風,外面下著傾盆大雨。他直接回到仙女家,下定決心前去敲門,希望能進得了門。

可是一到那裡,他的勇氣就消失殆盡了,不僅沒去敲門,反而來回跑了二十來步。然後,他再次走到門前,卻依然下不了決心。後來,他第三次前去,還是不敢敲門。直到第四次他才戰戰兢兢地拿起門環,輕輕地敲了一下。

他等啊等啊,半個小時過去之後,終於最高一層(這棟樓有四層)的窗戶打開了,皮諾丘看見一隻大蝸牛頭上舉著一支蠟燭,探身出來。這蝸牛對皮諾丘說:「這個時候,是誰呀?」

「仙女在家嗎?」木偶問蝸牛。

「仙女睡著了,要人不要吵醒她。不過,你是誰啊?」

「是我!」

「這個『我』是誰啊?」

「皮諾丘。」

「皮諾丘又是誰啊?」

「是原來住在仙女家的木偶。」

「啊,我知道了。」蝸牛說,「你在那兒等著,我立刻下來給你開門。」

「麻煩你快一點,我都要凍死了。」

「孩子,我是一隻蝸牛,蝸牛是永遠也快不起來的。」

一個小時過去了,兩個小時過去了,可是門還沒有開。皮諾丘全身濕透,一個人又冷又怕,在那兒發抖。他只好再鼓起勇氣,又敲了一次門,這回敲得比上回聲大。

第二次敲門聲響起之後,四層下面的窗戶打開了,還是那隻蝸牛出現在窗戶。

「美麗善良的蝸牛。」皮諾丘從大街上叫道,「我都等了兩個小時啦!這麼糟糕的夜晚,兩個小時可比兩年還要長啊!您發發善心,快一點吧。」

「孩子⋯⋯」蝸牛不急不徐地冷靜回答說,「孩子,我是一隻蝸牛,蝸牛永遠都快不了。」

接著，窗戶又關起來了。

不久，午夜的鐘聲敲響了，隨後是半夜一點，之後是兩點，而門依然是關著的。

皮諾丘終於忍無可忍。他怒氣衝天地抓住門環，打算狠狠地敲，讓整棟樓都聽得到聲音。但是，那個鐵門環突然變成了活生生的鰻魚，從他手裡滑脫出來，掉進大街中央的水坑裡，就消失不見了。

「啊！怎麼會這樣？」皮諾丘都氣暈了，叫道，「既然門環不見了，那我就自己來踢。」

他後退幾步，然後猛衝上前去，對著門狠踢一腳。這一腳踢得太大力，結果半條腿都插進木頭裡，卡住了。木偶拚命想把腿拔出來，可是他怎麼用力也拔不出來，牢固得就像是一顆被錘子釘進去的釘子。

讀者們，想一想這個可憐的皮諾丘，整個後半夜，他就被迫這麼站著，一條腿立在地上，一條腿蹺在空中。

第二天拂曉時分，那扇門終於開了。那隻機靈的蝸牛花了整整九個小時，才從四樓下來走到大門口。很顯然，他已經盡了最大的努力了！

「你把一條腿插進門裡做什麼啊？」他笑著問木偶。

「這是個意外。您試試，好蝸牛，看有沒有辦法能讓我不受這份罪。」

「孩子，這是木匠的工作，我可不是一個木匠。」

「那你幫我求求仙女。」

「仙女睡了，不讓人吵醒。」

「那你說說看，我整天釘在這門上能做什麼呢？」

「您就……數數從街上經過的螞蟻，自娛自樂吧！」

「您至少給我送點吃的過來吧，我都餓得精疲力盡了。」

「馬上！」蝸牛說。

實際上，過了整整三個半小時之後，那隻蝸牛才頭上頂著個托盤，回到皮諾丘身邊。托盤上放著一個麵包、一隻烤雞，和四個成熟的杏子。

「這是仙女讓我送給你的早餐。」蝸牛說。

木偶看到這些好吃的，精神為之一振。等到他開始吃的時候，才倒胃口地發現，麵包是石灰做的，烤雞是用厚紙板做的，四個杏子是上色的石膏！

他想哭。傷心絕望之際，打算連著托盤和上面的東西，一起丟開。但是，也許是由於悲痛，也許是太餓了，他一下子就暈了過去。

一覺醒來，他發現自己正躺在一張沙發上，而仙女就守在他旁邊。

「我再原諒你這一次。」仙女對他說。「但是，如果你要再做錯一次,就有得你受了!」

皮諾丘賭咒發誓,說他會好好學習,在將來的日子裡,嚴格要求自己。

在這一年剩下的時間裡,他都遵守了自己的承諾。確實如此,期末考試中,他獲得了全校第一名的好成績。品行也令人滿意,值得稱道。仙女因此十分歡喜,對他說:「明天你的願望就能得到滿足了!」

「什麼願望?」

「從明天開始,你就不再是一個木偶,而要成為一個真正的孩子啦。」

大家是沒看到,聽到這個期盼已久的消息,皮諾丘的興奮之情難以言喻。所有同學都被邀請到仙女家,參加第二天的盛大早宴。他們要一起慶祝這件大喜事。仙女準備了兩百杯牛奶和咖啡以及四百片雙面都塗滿奶油的麵包。那一天必定是最開心、最美妙的一天;但是……就是那麼不幸,在木偶的人生中老是有一個「但是」,它把一切都給毀了。

第 30 章

皮諾丘並沒有變成一個真正的男孩!因為,他和朋友燈芯偷偷地去了「享樂園」。

　　自然地,皮諾丘馬上就請求仙女同意,讓他進城去邀請宴會的客人。仙女同意並叮囑說:「如果你要的話就去吧!把你的同學們,請來參加明天的早宴吧。不過,你記得在天黑前要趕回家,知道嗎?」

　　「我保證一個小時之內就回來。」木偶回答說。

　　「小心點,皮諾丘!孩子們總是承諾得很快,但是,經常不能兌現他們的諾言。」

　　「我跟別的孩子不同。我既然說了,就會做到。」

　　「那我們來驗證吧!你要是不聽話,會有大苦頭吃的。」

「為什麼？」

「因為，孩子若不聽見識比他們多的人勸告，總是會遭遇一些不幸，或者其他什麼事的。」

「我已經經歷過了。」皮諾丘說，「同樣的錯誤我不會再犯了！」

「是真是假，我們等著看了！」

木偶不再多說話，就跟像媽媽般待他的善良仙女告別了，然後唱唱跳跳地出門去了。

不到一個小時，他就邀請到了所有的朋友。有些人一聽就痛快地接受了邀請。有些人還要先拜託他們，不過他們一聽可以喝到牛奶和咖啡，還能吃上兩面抹奶油的麵包，最後就都說：「為了讓你開心開心，我們會去的。」

現在，要向大家說明的是，在皮諾丘所有的朋友和同學間，有一個他最願意親近、關係最好的，他的名字叫做羅密歐。不過，大家通常都是叫他的綽號「燈芯」，因為他又瘦又直，就像晚上點在小油燈裡的一根燈芯。

燈芯是全校最懶散最調皮的學生，但皮諾丘跟他很投緣。

事實上，他是第一個就去燈芯家，邀請他參加早宴，不過卻沒有遇見到他。於是，他又去了第二次，結果燈芯還是不在家。後來，他第三次過去還是白跑一趟。到底，去哪兒能找到他呢？他東找西找，終於發現燈芯正躲在一間農舍的走廊裡。

「你在這兒做什麼？」皮諾丘走過去問他。

「我在等半夜到來，然後動身……」

「怎麼，你要去哪裡？」

「去很遠很遠很遠的地方！」

「我去你家找過你三次了。」

「你找我做什麼呢？」

「你沒有聽說這個重大的消息嗎？你還不知道我好運來了嗎？」

「什麼好運？」

「從明天開始，我就不再是木偶了，而是一個真正的孩子了，和你和其他人一樣了。」

「祝你心想事成。」

「因此，我期待你明天能去我家赴早宴。」

「但是，我跟你說了，我今天晚上就要離開這裡了！」

「幾點離開？」

「短時間內。」

「你打算去哪兒？」

「去一個國家……全世界最幸福的國家，一塊真正的人間樂土！」

「那個國家叫什麼名字?」

「叫『享樂園』。你為什麼不和我一起去呢?」

「我?不,我絕對不去!」

「這就大錯特錯了,皮諾丘!相信我,要是你不去,將來一定會後悔的。對我們孩子而言,你上哪裡去找一個比它更好的國家呢?那兒沒有學校,沒有教師,沒有課本。在那個幸福的國度裡,沒有人需要學習。在那兒禮拜四不用上學,一個禮拜有六個禮拜四,和一個禮拜日。你就想像一下吧!秋假從一月一號開始,一直到十二月最後一天結束。這個國家簡直太對我的胃口了!所有的文明國家都應該和它一樣……」

「在『享樂園』裡,是怎麼生活的?」

「從早到晚就變各種花招玩啊!然後等晚上了,就上床睡覺。第二天早上開始,又重新玩耍。你覺得怎麼樣?」

「嗯!……」皮諾丘嗯了一聲,不由得微微地點了點頭,好像是在說,「那種生活,我也想要。」

「那麼,你要和我一起去嗎?去、還是不去?快點做個決定吧!」

「不去,不去,不去,絕對不去。我已經跟好心的仙女保證過,要做一個聽話的孩子,我要說話算話。現在,我看太陽快下山了,我得走了,要趕緊跑啦!再見,祝你旅途愉快。」

「你這麼急呼呼的要上哪兒去啊?」

「回家。我的好仙女希望我天黑之前到家。」

「再等兩分鐘吧。」

「那我就要晚了。」

「兩分鐘而已啦。」

「要是仙女責罵我呢?」

「那就讓她罵好了。她要罵完了就不會再罵了。」燈芯不懷好意地說。

「你打算怎麼去?獨自一人還是跟夥伴們一起去?」

「獨自一人?我們一百多個人一起呢!」

「你們要走著去嗎?」

「不久會有一輛馬車經過,把我們送去那個快樂的國家。」

「要是那輛馬車現在能來,那我願意付出任何代價!」

「為什麼?」

「那樣我就能看著你們大家一起出發了。」

「你稍微再等一會兒,就能看見了。」

「不行,不行,我必須回家了。」

「再等兩分鐘吧。」

「我已經耽誤很長時間了。仙女肯定要為我著急了。」

「可憐的仙女!她是擔心蝙蝠會吃了你嗎?」

「不過……」皮諾丘繼續說,「你真的肯定那裡沒有學校嗎?」

「連學校的影子都沒有一個。」

「也沒有老師?」

「一個老師也沒有。」

「也用不著學習嗎?」

「不用,不用,不用!」

「多美好的國家呀!」皮諾丘說,感覺連口水都要流下來了,

「多美妙的國家呀!雖然我沒去過那裡,但我完全可以想像得出……」

「那你為什麼不一起來呢?」

「你慫恿我也沒用的。我已經向我的好仙女保證過,要做個有判斷力的孩子,我不會違背諾言的。」

「那我們就說再見吧!替我向同學們問好,要是你在大街上遇到同學,也替我向他們問好。」

「再見,燈芯,祝你一路順風,玩得開心,時常想想你的朋友們。」

木偶說完就轉身回家,剛走兩步,又停了下來,扭過頭去問他的朋友:「你真的敢肯定,那國家每個禮拜都是六個禮拜

四,和一個禮拜日嗎?」

「百分百肯定。」

「你確實知道,它的假期都是從一月一號開始,一直到十二月最後一天嗎?」

「的的確確!」

「多麼美妙的國家呀!」皮諾丘再次感慨說,簡直是心醉神迷。然後他定了定神,下定決心急急忙忙地說:「這次真的再見了,旅途愉快。」

「你們什麼時候出發?」

「不久就走了!」

「真可惜!如果你們一個小時之內就動身的話,我還能夠再等。」

「那仙女呢?」

「反正現在也已經遲了⋯⋯早一個小時晚一小時回家也沒什麼差別。」

「可憐的皮諾丘!要是仙女罵你怎麼辦呢?」

「就讓她罵吧!讓她罵吧,罵夠了,就不會再罵了」

這個時候,夜幕已經降臨,外面一片漆黑。突然,他們看見遠處有一點燈光在移動⋯⋯隨後他們還聽到說話聲和喇叭聲,那聲音又輕又細,就像是蚊子嗡嗡的叫聲!

「來了！」燈芯大喊一聲，跳了起來。

「誰來了？」皮諾丘低聲問道。

「接我的馬車來了。你要來嗎？來、還是不來？」

「不過，那都是真的嗎？」木偶問道，「在那個國家裡，孩子們都不用被逼著學習？」

「不用，不用，不用！」

「多麼美妙的國家啊！……多麼美妙的國家啊！……多麼美妙的國家啊！」

第 31 章

在「享樂園」生活五個月後,皮諾丘驚訝地發現,自己長了一對美麗的驢耳朵。他變成了一隻真正的小驢子,還有驢尾巴和所有驢子該具備的樣子。

車子終於到了跟前,由於輪子上包著乾草和破布,一路過來沒有發出一點聲音。

拉車的是十二對驢子,所有的驢子體形都一樣,不過毛色各異。有灰色的、白色的;有些是斑點的,像撒了胡椒和鹽一樣;而有些則長著黃色和綠色的大條紋。

不過最特別的事情是:這十二對也就是說廿四頭驢子,和其他拉車馱貨的驢子不一樣,他們的腳沒有打上鐵掌,而是像人那樣穿著白色羊皮靴。

那駕車的車夫呢？

不妨給自己想像的畫面。那個矮小的男人身材粗短，有著鬆弛油膩的感覺，就像一坨軟爛的奶油塊；圓滾滾的臉像顆橘子；略小的嘴巴總是帶著笑意的嘴角；聲音溫柔就像，貓要討好優雅的女主人時發出的聲音。

所有的孩子一見到他，就不由自主地喜歡上了他，都爭搶著要上他的車，帶他們去那個真正的快樂國度。這國家在地圖上被命名為「享樂園」。

事實上，車上已經擠滿了八歲到十二歲的孩子，他們一個疊一個就像是疊著的一桶鮮魚。坐在裡面特別不舒服，人擠著人幾乎連氣都透不過來。可是沒有一個人唉聲嘆氣，也沒有一個人抱怨。大家都感到欣慰，因為他們知道再過幾個小時，他們就能到達一個國家；那兒沒有課本，沒有學校，也沒有老師。他們興奮得什麼都能忍受，他們不感覺苦，也沒感覺累；沒感覺餓，也不感覺渴，甚至沒感覺想打瞌睡。

車子一停，車夫便轉頭看著燈芯，他臉上滿是假笑，裝模作樣地問說：「告訴我，我的好孩子，你也想去那個幸運的國家嗎？」

「當然，我想去。」

「不過，我可要提醒你，我親愛的孩子，車上已經沒有空位啦！你自己也看到了，裡面真的很滿啦！」

「不要緊。」小燈芯回答說，「如果馬車裡坐不下了，我可以將就地著坐在車轅上。」

他一說完隨即就跳上車轅,並劈腿坐下。

「那你,我的寶貝?」車夫轉身過來,刻意討好的問皮諾丘,「你有什麼計畫呢?是跟我們一起去呢,還是一個人留下?」

「我留下。」皮諾丘回答說,「我要回家。我要和所有聽話的孩子一樣,在學校裡好好學習,好好做人。」

「祝你一切順利!」

「皮諾丘!」燈芯大喊著,「你聽我說,和我們一道去吧!我們會過得很開心的。」

「不去,不去,不去!」

「和我們一起去,我們會過得很開心的。」車廂內傳來另外四個孩子的聲音。

「和我們一起去,我們會過得很開心的。」車廂內一百多個孩子齊聲說話。

「要是我和你們一起去了,那好心的仙女會說什麼呢?」木偶雖然這樣說,但他的心已經開始動搖了。

「不要去想這種傷腦筋的事。你就想著,我們要到一個國家去,在那裡我們能夠自由自在地,從早玩到晚。」

皮諾丘沒有說話,只是長歎一聲,接著,又歎了第二聲,再歎了第三聲,終於他說:「給我讓出點位子,我也要去。」

「都擠滿了。」車夫回答說,「不過,為了表示對你的歡迎,我把我的座位讓給你⋯⋯。」

「那您呢?」

「哦,我走路就好了。」

「當然,我是不會讓那種事發生的。這樣我還不如去騎一頭驢子!」皮諾丘叫道。

說完,他就朝第一隊右手邊的那頭驢子走過去,準備騎上去。但是那頭驢子突然轉過身來,朝著他的肚子狠狠地踢了一腳,把他踢得兩腳朝天。

大家可以想像,在場的孩子們一看到這個場景,全都放肆的狂笑起來!

車夫卻一點也笑不出來。他走近那頭反抗的驢子身邊,做出一副要親他的樣子,卻一口咬下了他半隻耳朵。

與此同時,皮諾丘暴怒地從地上爬起來,一下子就跳上了這頭可憐的傢伙的後背。他跳得乾脆俐落,孩子們馬上止住了哄笑,為他喝彩叫道:「皮諾丘萬歲!」還為他不停的鼓掌。

可是驢子又忽然跳了起來,兩隻後腿用力一蹬,把可憐的木偶不偏不倚的甩到馬路中央的石頭堆上面。

孩子們又哄堂大笑。車夫依然沒有笑,再次佯裝十分喜愛那隻難以馴育的驢子,假裝要去親吻他,卻一口又咬掉了他另外半隻耳朵。隨後車夫對木偶說:「現在不用怕了,騎上去吧!」

這頭小驢子有點倔強，我已經跟他咬過兩次耳朵了，我想他應該變乖，變得能說理了。」

皮諾丘騎上驢子後，車子就出發了。正當驢子飛速行進，拉著車子碾過圓石子大路上時，木偶感覺自己聽到一個很輕的聲音，輕得幾乎只有他才能聽得明白。那聲音說：「可憐的笨蛋！如果你一定要我行我素的話，你會後悔的！」

皮諾丘有點害怕，他向四周看了看，想找出這聲音到底是從哪兒來的。可是他一個人也沒看到。驢子在拉車，車子在前進，車裡的孩子在睡覺，燈芯像小老鼠縮著打呼熟睡，車夫坐在駕車位上，在齒間輕輕哼著歌：

「夜裡大家都熟睡了，只有我從未睡覺……」

車子行進約莫一英里後，皮諾丘再次聽見那又輕又細的聲音對他說：「傻瓜，你要記住！不肯讀書，一見到課本、學校和老師就轉身離去，一心只想玩樂，這樣的孩子遲早要遭殃的！這是我的親身經歷……我明確的跟你說，終有一天，你也會像我今天一樣哭泣……只是等到那個時候，一切就都晚啦！」

木偶聽到這番像竊竊私語一般的話，感到了前所未有的恐懼。他害怕得從驢背上跳了下來，跑過去一把摀住了驢子的嘴。

大家可以想見，當木偶看到這頭驢子在哭的時候，心裡該有多麼驚訝……那頭驢哭得就像個孩子一樣啊！

「喂，車夫先生。」皮諾丘對車夫叫道，「這真是一件神奇的事！您看，這隻驢子在哭呢！」

「讓他哭去吧！到他當新郎的時候就會笑了。」

「那您有沒有教會他講話呢？」

「沒有。他和一群受過訓的狗一起生活過三年，也許，他自己學會了嘀咕兩句話。」

「可憐的畜牲！」

「快，快！」車夫說，「不要浪費時間去看一頭驢子哭了。騎上去吧，我們要上路了。晚上很冷，路還長著呢。」

皮諾丘照車夫說的做了。第二天一清早，他們就平安地到達了「享樂園」。

這是一個和世界上其他國家都不相同的地方。整個國家全都是孩子，其中最大的十四歲，最小的還不到八歲。大街上到處充斥著嬉戲聲、吵鬧聲、叫嚷聲，讓人感覺暈頭轉向。四處都是成群結隊的孩子。有些人玩堅果核，有些人踢毽子，有些人打球，有騎腳踏車的，也有騎木馬的。一群孩子在捉迷藏，另一幫孩子在玩追人的遊戲。有些孩子扮成小丑在吞火。有朗誦的，有唱歌的，有翻跟斗的。有些人玩著倒立行走，還有些身穿將軍裝，頭戴紙頭盔，向著一隊厚紙板做的假騎兵發號施令。有人在笑，有人在高呼，有人在叫，有人在鼓掌，有人在吹口哨，有人在學母雞生蛋時咯咯叫。總之一句話，整個街上一片熙熙攘攘，嘰嘰喳喳，亂七八糟，讓人不得不用棉花塞住耳朵,以防耳朵給震聾了。每一個廣場都有帆布搭建的劇院,裡面從早到晚擠滿了孩子。每一所房子的牆上,都可以看到木炭塗鴉,寫著他們的美好願望,如「玩具萬歲,我們不要學校,打倒數學」以及其他一些拼寫錯誤的標語。

剛踏進城裡,皮諾丘、燈芯,以及車夫帶來的一群孩子,瞬間就陷入了巨大的混亂之中。就在短短的幾分鐘內,每一個人就熟悉起來。在哪裡還能找到比他們更幸福、更滿足的孩子們呢?

在這種無窮無盡、花樣繁多的玩樂當中,一個小時接一個小時,一天接一天,一個禮拜接一個禮拜,就那麼閃電般一閃而過了。

「噢!多麼無憂無慮的生活啊!」皮諾丘每次遇見燈芯都要這樣說。

「瞧,我說的沒錯吧?」燈芯回答說,「想想你當初還不願意來呢!就一個心思地想著回仙女的家去,想著把光陰浪費在學習上呢!如今,你不用再為課本和學校的事情煩惱了,是不是不得不承認這都得感謝我;感謝我的忠告和勸說。只有真正的朋友,才會提供給你這麼大的幫助。」

「你說得對,燈芯!現在我變成一個真正幸福的孩子,全都是你的功勞。但你知道嗎?老師以前都是怎麼跟我說你的嗎?他經常對我說:『不要和燈芯那個淘氣鬼打混,他是個壞同學,只會帶著你做傻事!』」

「可憐的老師!」燈芯搖著頭回答說,「我都知道得一清二楚,他不喜歡我,老是以中傷我為樂,但是我心胸寬闊,我原諒他!」

「你真是太寬容啦!」皮諾丘說著,他親熱地擁抱著他的朋友,在他額頭上一再親吻。

這種樂不思蜀的生活,一連過了五個月。那些日子裡,他們不必想著書本、想著學校,整天就是一直玩樂。直到某日早上,皮諾丘醒過來遭遇了一個意外的打擊。一時之間,什麼心情都沒有了。

第 32 章

皮諾丘發現,自己不但長了驢耳朵,還變成了一頭真正的驢子。接著,開始發出了驢子的嘶叫聲。

發生了一個意外,是什麼呢?

親愛的讀者,這個意外就是,當皮諾丘一早醒來習慣性地抓抓頭時,可是他一抓頭⋯⋯猜猜看,他究竟發現了什麼?

他大驚失色,哇!兩隻耳朵居然變得比手掌還大。

讀者也知道,木偶自出生起,耳朵就一直非常的小,小得連肉眼也看不到。大家再想想看,在一夜之間,發現自己的兩隻耳朵,竟然長得像兩把板刷那麼長的時候,該有多麼令人驚嚇啊!

他立刻去找鏡子,想看看自己變成什麼模樣了。但鏡子沒找著,於是他只好把洗臉檯上的洗臉盆裝滿水,然後往水裡一看,看見了他這輩子都不會想看見的事情,他看見自己的頭上⋯⋯多了一對活生生的驢耳朵。

可憐的皮諾丘!一時間悲傷、羞恥和絕望一起湧上了他的心頭。

他哇哇的大哭起來,還邊哭邊用頭撞牆。可是,他越哭、耳朵就長得越長。它們長啊長啊,直到耳朵尖上都長出毛來。

聽到號啕大哭的聲音,一隻住在樓上的小土撥鼠走進了木偶的房間,看見他悲慟欲絕的樣子,關切地問道:「發生什麼事啦,親愛的房客?」

「親愛的小土撥鼠,我病了,而且病得很嚴重⋯⋯得這種病可真叫人恐懼!你懂得把脈嗎?」

「懂一點。」

「那就給我把把脈,看看我是不是發燒了。」

小土撥鼠伸出右前爪,把過皮諾丘的脈象以後,歎了一口氣說:「我的朋友,我很遺憾,但也只能把這個不幸的消息告訴你!」

「是什麼?」

「你在發高燒!」

「是什麼樣的高燒?」

「是發驢子的高燒。」

「那是一種什麼高燒,我不清楚!」木偶嘴裡這麼說著,但其實心裡再清楚不過了。

「那我解釋給你聽吧。」土撥鼠說,「我告訴你,在接下來的兩三個小時之內,你就不再是一個木偶,也不再是一個孩子了⋯⋯」

「那我會變成什麼呢?」

「在兩三個小時之內,你就會變成一頭貨真價實的小驢子了,跟那些拉車和馱著高麗菜、生菜到市場去的驢子,都一樣。」

「喔!我太倒楣啦!我太倒楣啦!」皮諾丘哭叫著,用手抓著那兩隻耳朵,狂暴地又拉又扯的,似乎那是別人的耳朵一樣。

「我親愛的孩子。」土撥鼠勸慰他說,「你怎麼能阻止它呢?一切都是天意。智慧書上早就寫著,那些懶惰的孩子,那些討厭課本、討厭學校、討厭老師的孩子,那些整天嬉戲玩樂的孩子,遲早都要變成這種小驢子的。」

「真的是這樣嗎?」木偶嗚咽著問。

「千真萬確!事到如今,哭也沒用。你應該早點想到的!」

「可是這又不是我的錯。相信我,小土撥鼠,這全是燈芯的錯!」

「這個燈芯是誰啊?」

「是我的一個同學。我本來要回家的,想做個聽話的孩子,想好好學習,好好做人……但燈芯對我說:『你為什麼要學習,要自討苦吃呢?你為什麼要上學呢?還是跟我一起去『享樂園』吧!到那裡以後,我們就再也不用學習了,可以成天玩耍,永遠開開心心的。』」

「那你為什麼要聽信那個壞朋友、壞同學的話呢?」

「為什麼……我親愛的小土撥鼠,因為我是一個木偶,沒有大腦……沒心沒肺。唉,我要是有一點兒良心就好了,我就不會離開好心的仙女了,她一直像媽媽那樣愛護我,替我做了很多很多的事情!……而且,這時候我本來應該不再是個木偶……應該已經是個真正的孩子了,和其他許許多多的孩子一樣!我要是再遇上燈芯,我一定給他好看!我要罵他個狗血淋頭!」

他說完就打算出門。可他剛走到門口,就記起了那對驢耳朵,實在是羞於讓大家看到。猜,他想到了一個什麼主意?他拿起一頂大棉帽,將它戴在頭上,一直拉低到鼻尖那兒。

他出門四處尋找燈芯。找遍了所有的大街,全部的廣場,每一個小劇院,以及其他可能的地方。但是都沒有見到燈芯,他還問遍了每個他遇到的人,可是誰也沒見過他。

於是,他只好找上了燈芯的家,到門口敲了敲門。

「誰呀?」燈芯在房間裡問道。

「是我！」木偶回答說。

「等一會兒，我馬上過來開門。」

半小時後，門終於打開了。皮諾丘看見朋友燈芯，竟然也戴著一頂大棉帽，帽子一直拉到了鼻樑那裏。

皮諾丘一見那頂帽子，心裡覺得憂些欣慰，暗自想到：「我這位朋友是不是跟我罹患同樣的病呢？他是不是也有了驢子發燒的症狀呢？」

不過，他裝出一副毫不知情的樣子，微笑問燈芯說：「你過得怎麼樣，我親愛的小燈芯？」

「好極了，好得就像一隻掉到帕瑪森起士裡的老鼠。」

「你這是說真的？」

「我為什麼要跟你說謊呢？」

「實在不好意思。不過，你為什麼要戴那頂棉帽，還遮住耳朵呢？」

「因為，我膝蓋受傷了，醫生囑咐一定要戴帽子的。親愛的木偶，那你為什麼要把那頂棉帽壓到鼻樑呢？」

「我的一隻腳擦傷了，醫生囑咐我這麼做。」

「喔，可憐的皮諾丘！」

「喔，可憐的燈芯！」

說完這些話以後，兩人陷入了長久的沉默，誰都不開口，只是用嘲諷的眼光打量著對方。

最後，木偶用又溫柔又甜膩的聲音對他的同伴說：「親愛的小燈芯，我真的很好奇。你能不能告訴我，你耳朵得過病嗎？」

「從來沒有！⋯⋯你呢？」

「從來沒有！不過從今早開始，我有一隻耳朵感覺有些疼。」

「我的耳朵也這樣。」

「你也這樣？你是哪邊耳朵痛呢？」

「兩邊都痛。你呢？」

「和你一樣。難道我們得了同樣的病嗎？」

「我恐怕是的。」

「你可以幫我一個忙嗎，燈芯？」

「很樂意！樂意之至。」

「能讓我看看你的耳朵嗎？」

「這有什麼不行的？不過，親愛的皮諾丘，我想先瞧瞧你的。」

「不行，你要先給我看。」

「不，親愛的！你先給我看，然後我再給你看！」

「那好！」木偶說，「我們定個君子協議。」

「說來聽聽。」

「我們兩個一齊把帽子摘了。你同意嗎？」

「同意。」

「好，預備！」

皮諾丘開始大聲數「1！2！3」一說完，兩個孩子同時脫掉帽子，把它們扔到空中。

接下來發生的事情，要不是親眼所見，實在讓人難以置信。原來皮諾丘和燈芯，看見兩個人都遇到了同一件倒楣事，非但不覺得丟人和傷心，倒是相互盯著對方長得醜陋不堪的耳朵，做出各種古怪滑稽的動作。最後，兩人還忍不住哄然大笑起來。

他們笑啊，笑啊，笑啊，笑得都直不起腰來了，只能彼此相扶著。然而，就在他們嘻嘻哈哈的時候，燈芯突然止住了笑，開始左搖右晃，神色大變，然後對他的朋友說：「救命啊，救命啊，皮諾丘！」

「發生什麼事啦？」

「哎喲！我再也站不穩啦！」

「我也站不穩了。」皮諾丘也開始腳步蹣跚，大哭起來。

他們倆說話的當下，身體也不由自主地往下彎下去，然後手腳並用，在房間裡繞圈圈轉地跑了起來。他們跑著跑著，手變成了腳，臉還拉長成了一張驢子臉，背上長滿了淺灰色的毛，上面還散布著黑色的斑點。

對這兩個不幸的孩子而言，你知道他們最悲慘的是哪一刻嗎？他們最悲慘、最丟人的時刻，就是發現自己長了尾巴。他們又羞恥又悲傷，忍不住號啕大哭起來，哀悼他們的悲慘命運。

哦，如果只是這樣也已經夠倒楣了。沒料到，後來他們連歎息和哭泣都再也不能了，只能像驢一樣地叫著，齊聲嘶吼著：「咿——呀，咿——呀，咿——呀。」

正在這個時候，一陣敲門聲響了起來，一個聲音在外面說著：「開門！是我，那個把你們帶來這個國家的車夫。立刻給我開門，否則你們就遭殃了！」

第 33 章

皮諾丘變成了真正的小驢子。他被賣給了小丑馬戲團的團長,被迫學習跳舞、跳鐵環等等技術。但是某晚他的腳受傷了,後來就又被轉賣給了準備用驢皮來做大鼓的人。

那個男人發現門遲遲不開後,於是一腳就把門踹開了。然後就走進去,帶著他一貫的假笑,對皮諾丘和燈芯說:「幹得好,孩子們!你們叫得真好,我一聽到你們的聲音就識別出來了。所以,我就馬上趕到這兒來了。」

聽到這些話,兩頭驢子瞬間心如死灰,低著頭,垂下耳朵,夾住尾巴,站在那裡動也不動。

那人先是這兒拍拍、那兒摸摸,然後拿出一把刷子,把他們身上的毛刷整齊。他反覆地刷啊刷啊,一直把他們刷得油光發亮,都可以當鏡子用了,這才在他們的脖子上套上韁繩,牽到市場上去,希望賣掉他們,好發筆橫財。

事實上,買主馬上就出現了。燈芯被一個農民給買走了,他的驢子前一天剛好死了。而買走皮諾丘的,則是一個小丑馬戲團的團長。他買皮諾丘是為了訓練他,以便讓他跟馬戲團的其他動物,一起蹦蹦跳跳地表演。

讀者們,現在大家應該都明白,那個車夫是做什麼惡行的吧!那個壞心的惡魔,長著一張抹過牛奶和蜂蜜的臉,趕著他的馬車行騙天下,沿途許下各種諾言,說著巴結討好的話,把那些厭惡課本和學校的懶孩子一一找出來。等裝滿一車之後,就把他們帶到這個「享樂園」來,先讓他們無憂無慮地玩上一陣子。等到那些可憐的孩子沉迷其中,只知道一味地玩耍,不再學習,最後都變成小驢子以後,他就歡歡喜喜地做他們的主人,然後把他們帶到市集或市場上賣掉。就這樣沒有幾年的工夫,他就撈到了一大筆錢,成了一個百萬富翁。

燈芯後來下落怎麼樣,並不清楚;只知道,皮諾丘從第一天開始,就必須忍受艱苦難熬、疲憊不堪的日子。

他的主人把他關進畜欄,然後在食槽裡撒了些麥稈。皮諾丘嚐了一口,立即就把它給吐出來了。

主人嘟嘟囔囔碎念兩句,又在食槽裡撒了些乾草,皮諾丘還是不喜歡吃。

「啊!乾草你也不喜歡吃?」主人生氣大叫起來,「好吧,親愛的驢子,我們走著瞧。要是你真那麼任性的話,我就找個方法治治你！」

為了教訓教訓皮諾丘，他拿起鞭子在驢腿上抽了一鞭。

皮諾丘痛得哇哇大哭，還不停地哀叫著：「哎呀，哎呀，我的胃消化不了麥稭！」

「那就試試乾草吧！」主人說得好像很懂驢子似的。

「哎呀，哎呀，吃了乾草，我肚子會疼！」

「你是說，像你這樣的驢子，我還要用雞胸肉和全雞孝敬你嗎？」主人說著越生氣，抬手又給了他一鞭。

皮諾丘被打這第二鞭，於是學聰明了閉上嘴，再也不多說話了。

隨後，畜欄的門關上了，留皮諾丘一人待在裡面。他都已經好幾個小時沒吃東西了，餓得直打哈欠。但他一打哈欠，就讓人看到了那張大得像爐口似的嘴巴。

食槽裡再也找不到別的東西，他也就只好認命了，嚼了幾口乾草，嚼爛之後、閉著眼睛硬是給嚥下去了。

「這乾草還不算太糟糕。」他暗想，「假如我繼續學習，我吃的比這可要好多了！……這會兒，我就不用吃乾草，而是吃著一塊新鮮的麵包，加美味的香腸了！但是現在我只好將就著吃了！」

第二天早上睡醒了，他想在食槽裡再找點乾草，但卻也找不著一點了，因為昨天晚上都被自己吃光光了。

於是，他只好吃一口剁碎的麥稈。嚼著嚼著，發現剁碎的麥稈嚐起來，既完全不像美味可口的通心粉，也不像炒飯。

「但是，我只能將就了！」他重覆說著，嘴裡不停地咀嚼，「希望所有不聽話的孩子，所有不想學習的孩子，都能知道我的教訓。現在，我只有忍耐！……忍耐！……」

「你確實要忍忍！」這個時候主人剛好走進畜欄，朝他說道，「我的小驢子，你認為我把你買回來，是為了好吃好喝地供著你 嗎？我買下你，是為了讓你替我做事，替我賺錢的。好了，過來吧！跟我到馬戲場去。在那兒，我要教你鑽鐵環，鑽紙框，跳華爾滋和波爾卡，教你倒立行走。」

可憐的皮諾丘不論是情願或脅迫，只能學這些技術了。不過，他學了三個月才終於學會，全身的皮膚都被抽打得傷痕累累。

終於到了這一天，他的主人對外宣稱，有一場特別的節目即將上演，大街小巷都張貼著色彩斑斕的海報進行宣傳。

正如所料，那天晚上節目開場前的一個小時，戲院就高朋滿座了。

不管是前座還是後座，哪怕是包廂，你就算掏一個金幣，也別想換到一個位子。

環繞著馬戲場的長椅上，坐滿了各個年齡層的孩子們，他們都迫不及待地想看聞名遐邇的驢子演員皮諾丘跳舞。

演出的第一場結束後，馬戲團的經理穿著黑上衣、白馬褲和及膝的長筒皮靴出現在舞臺上。他深深地一鞠躬，然後，表情嚴肅地發表了一一場荒謬可笑的演說：「尊敬的觀眾朋友，女士們和先生們！鄙人路過貴市，很高興、也很榮幸，能向智慧、尊貴的各位來賓，介紹一隻大名鼎鼎的驢子。他曾有幸為歐洲各大王室的皇帝陛下登臺獻藝。」

「衷心感謝各位前來捧場，感謝大家的鼓勵和支持，不足之處，敬請海涵。」

他這番話招來了大家的笑聲和掌聲。等到小驢子皮諾丘登上戲場的中央時，掌聲越發響亮，最後變成如雷鳴一般。臺上的皮諾丘，經過一番盛裝打扮：他套著一根閃亮的漆皮韁繩，皮韁繩上裝飾著黃銅扣環和特製螺絲釘，雙耳各戴著一朵白色茶花，鬃毛打成很多鼓瓣子，上面紮著彩色的綢緞，全身纏繞了金銀交錯的帶子，整條尾巴用紫紅色和藍色的天鵝絨帶子，交叉編織起來。

總而言之，就是一隻人見人愛的小驢子！

經理向觀眾介紹時，又插入了這麼一段話：「各位尊貴的觀眾！我毫不誇張地告訴諸位，為了馴服這頭驢子，我可是歷盡了千辛萬苦。想當初，他可是一隻生在熱帶原野的山林中，自由自在地生活著的野獸。在這兒，敬請諸位仔細看看，他雙眼散發出野性的光芒。為了馴服他，使他適應馴養的生活方式，我費勁了各種手段，均以失敗而告終，甚至嘗試著用鞭子來和他交流。但是，我的一片苦心並沒有換來他的感激之情，相反，還助長了他的惡習。不過，根據高爾系統理論，我在他的顱骨上發現了一塊凸出的軟骨;巴黎醫學院認為,這是頭髮與舞蹈的再生之源。出於這個緣故,我不僅訓練他跳舞,而且還教他跳鐵環和紙框。還請各位多多鼓勵,多多指點!最後,在我離場之前,女士們先生們,請允許我邀請大家來觀看明晚的演出。不過,如果下雨的話,那時間就改為明天上午、午前十一點。」

說完,經理再一次深深鞠躬,然後轉身對皮諾丘說:「打起精神來!皮諾丘!在表演之前,先給在座各位尊敬的觀眾、女士們、先生們、小朋友們,行個禮吧!」

皮諾丘聽從團長的指示,雙膝著地跪在地上,直到經理甩了一下鞭子,對他大聲喊道:「預備,走!」

接著,驢子站了起來,開始繞著馬戲場悠閒地走著。

不久之後,團長又命令道:「小步跑!」皮諾丘順從地改變動作。

「大步跑!」皮諾丘加快腳步跑。

「全速跑!」於是皮諾丘揚蹄飛奔。他正像賽馬一樣快跑的時候,團長舉起一支手槍,朝天開了一槍。

聽到槍聲,小驢子立刻佯裝受傷,身體直直地摔倒在地上,似乎真的死了。

在一片轟動的歡呼聲、喝彩聲以及掌聲中間,他從地上爬了起來,然後很自然地就抬頭向上看了看……他一眼就看到了包廂裡的一位漂亮的女士,她脖子上戴著一根很粗的金項鍊,項鍊上吊著一個圓形墜子。墜子表面印著的竟是木偶的畫像。

「那是我的畫像啊！……這位女士是仙女！」皮諾丘當即就認出她來。隨後，他實在是太興奮了，就試圖喊出來：「哦，我的仙女！哦！我的仙女！」

不過，他嘴裡喊出來的，可不是人話而是驢叫聲，叫聲洪亮又悠長，惹得戲院裡的所有觀眾，尤其是小朋友們，爆發出哄堂大笑。

團長為了給他一個教訓，讓他明白在公眾面前發出驢的叫聲，是很不禮貌的行為，就用鞭子柄對著他的鼻子使勁敲了一下。

可憐的驢子痛的舌頭伸出一寸長，在鼻子上舔了至少五分鐘之久，想著這樣也許能夠減輕一些痛楚。

但是，讓他失望的是，等他再次回頭的時候，包廂已經沒人了，仙女不知道什麼時候走了！

他感覺自己馬上就要死了，眼睛裡面飽含淚水，忍不住掉了下來。然而，大家都沒有注意到這一點，至少團長沒有注意到。他揚起鞭子叫道「加油，皮諾丘！現在讓觀眾們看看，你是如何靈巧地鑽過這個鐵環的。」

皮諾丘試了兩三次，不過，每次他都只是走到了鐵環前面，因為他發現從鐵環下溜過去，可比鑽過鐵環容易多了。最終，他還是從環裡鑽了過去。然而不幸的是，後腿被鐵環絆了一下，使他啪嗒一聲摔在鐵環的另一邊，疼得縮成一團。

等到他從地上起來之後,腳已經受傷了,後來費了九牛二虎之力,才回到了畜欄。

「皮諾丘出來!我們要看小驢子!小驢子出來!」戲場裡,所有的孩子們大叫,對這件糟糕的事情,表現出了深切的遺憾。

可是,那天晚上後,驢子再也沒有出現過了。

第二天早上,一位獸醫,亦即專門給動物看病的醫生,過來診斷之後下結論說,他這一輩子都要瘸腿了。

聽完醫生的話,團長對畜欄管理員說:「你說說看,我養著一頭瘸腿驢子,有什麼用呢?除了白吃白喝,他一點錢也賺不回來。把他拉到市場上去賣了吧!」

剛到市場上,買主就找上門來。他問畜欄管理員說:「這頭跛腳的驢子,你開價多少?」

「二十法郎。」

「我給你二十便士。不過,你可別誤會我買下他,是為了讓他幹活。我買他僅僅是看中了他的驢皮,看上去挺厚的,我打算用它給我們村的樂隊做一面大鼓。」

讀者們,當可憐的皮諾丘聽到,他就要變成一個大鼓時,他的感覺將會如何呢?相信大家可以感受得到。

事實就是,買主付了二十便士之後,就把驢子牽到了海邊。然後,他拿一塊大石頭吊在驢脖子上,用一根繩子綁住他的腿,繩子另一端抓在手裡,接著猛地一推,把他推到海裡去了。

　　皮諾丘就這樣綁著那麼大塊石頭,咚一聲就沉到海底去了。買主仍然緊緊地抓著繩子,他坐在岩石上,安靜地等著驢子淹死了,然後再來剝離他的外皮。

第 34 章

皮諾丘被扔進海裡時,被一條魚給吃掉了;但隨後,卻變回了之前的木偶了。正當他游往安全的地方時,卻又被一條可怕的大鯊魚給吞下了肚。

皮諾丘沉下海裡五十分鐘以後,買主自言自語說:「到這個時候,那隻可憐的瘸腿驢應該已經淹死吧!等把他從水裡面拉起來,就能剝皮做出最好的大鼓了。」

於是,他動手拉一拉綁在驢子腿上的繩子,拉啊、拉啊、拉啊,拉到最後⋯⋯讀者們,您猜猜,出現在水面上的是什麼東西?竟然不是一隻死驢,而是一個活生生的木偶!那木偶還像鰻魚一樣蠕動著。

看到這個木偶,那個可憐的人還以為自己是在做夢,驚嚇得啞口無言,驚得嘴巴都合不攏,連眼珠子都要掉出來了。

等他從最初的驚慌失措中,漸漸冷靜下來之後,他用戰戰兢兢的聲音問道:「被我扔進海裡去的小驢子呢?他怎麼啦?」

「我就是那隻小驢子!」木偶笑著回答他說。

「是你?」

「是我。」

「啊!你這個小淘氣!你竟然敢拿我開玩笑!」

「拿您尋開心?不是這樣的,親愛的主人,我說的都是實話。」

「不久之前,你還是一頭驢子呢!怎會在海裡的短短的時間,就變成一個木偶呢?」

「這一定是海水的作用,是大海製造了這個非凡的奇蹟。」

「小心點,木偶,給我小心點!……別想背地裡嘲笑我。如果惹我生氣,那你就不好過喔!」

「那好,我的主人,想知道事實真相嗎?您給我解開綁在腳上的繩子,我就把一切都告訴您。」

那個好心的人,實在是太好奇了。於是,馬上就解開拴在皮諾丘身上的繩結。皮諾丘馬上便自由得像天空中的鳥兒,開始講了自己的故事了:「告訴你,我原本就是個木偶,模樣跟現在絲毫沒差,我曾經差點兒……就要變成一個真實的孩子,和世界上其他的孩子一樣。但是，由於我討厭學習，還聽信壞同學的建議，離家出走了……後來有一天，我醒過來發現自己變成了一頭驢子，長了一對長長的耳朵……還有一條長尾巴！……這真是一件讓人覺得羞辱的事情！……親愛的主人，但願聖安東尼奧庇佑您，從未遭受這種恥辱！之後，我被帶到市場上，被一個馬戲團的團長買下來了。他竟然希望我成為一個著名的舞者，成為一個優秀的跳圈演員。有一天晚上在演出中，我重重地摔倒在場地中央，兩條腿都摔傷了。團長不需要一隻瘸腿的驢子，於是把我給賣掉了。而您就是那個買主！」

「實在難以置信！我花了二十便士才把你買回來。現在，我該找誰去討回那倒楣的 20 便士呢？」

「您為什麼要買下我呢？是想用我的皮去做一面大鼓！一面大鼓！」

「實在難以置信！如今我去哪兒再找另一張皮呢？」

「不要傷心，主人。這個世界上，還有許許多多其他的驢子！」

「告訴我，你這個沒禮貌的淘氣鬼，你的故事說完了沒有？」

「沒有……」木偶回答說，「我再補充幾句，這個故事才算結束了。您買下我後，把我牽到這個地方，打算殺死我。後來您於心不忍，只好在我的脖子上吊一塊大石頭，然後把我推進海裡。您的仁慈讓人敬仰，我一輩子都會感激您的。說實在的，親愛的主人，如果沒有仙女，您這一次就能得償所願了⋯⋯。」

「這個仙女是誰？」

「她是我的媽媽，跟其他的好媽媽沒有兩樣，都對自己的孩子總是關懷備至。自始至終全心關注他們，總是向他們伸出援助之手。哪怕他們做了一些愚蠢邪惡的事情，活該被捨棄，任其自生自滅。所以說，好心的仙女一見到我就要淹死，忙不迭就派了一大群魚。他們把我當成是一頭真正的死驢子，大吃特吃！他們的嘴可真是貪婪啊！我從來沒見過比孩子們更貪吃的魚！⋯⋯他們有的吃耳朵，有的吃嘴唇，有的吃脖子，有的吃鬃毛，有的吃腿上的皮，有的吃背上的皮⋯⋯其中夾著一尾小魚，他居然連我的尾巴也不放過，吃得津津有味。」

「自此以後⋯⋯」買主一臉反感地說，「我發誓，我再也不碰魚了。要是我剖開一條烏魚，或者一條炸鱈魚，居然在腹腔裡發現了一條驢子的尾巴，那該有多麼恐怖！」

「我也這樣認為。」木偶笑著回答，「無論如何，我還是要告訴您，當魚把我全身的驢肉吃光了之後，理所當然，就碰到了我的骨頭⋯⋯抑或說是，碰到了我的木頭。正如您所見，我是用最堅硬的木頭做成的。那些魚咬了幾口之後，就發覺連自己的牙齒也咬不動，對這種不消化的東西感到十分厭煩，所以，連一句感謝的話也沒有說，就各自游開了。現在，我把所有的事情都講給您聽了，那麼，您應該也明白，為什麼您抓住繩子拉上來的不是一隻死驢，而是一個木偶。」

「你的故事還真叫人發笑！」買主怒火直冒地喊道，「我只知道我花了二十便士才把你給買下來,而今我得想辦法把錢賺回來。你知道我要怎麼做嗎?我要將你重新拉到市場上,把你當成是能生火的乾木頭給稱重賣掉。」

「只要您喜歡,您就賣吧。我樂意之至。」皮諾丘說。

可是他話音剛落就猛然一跳,撲通一聲跳到水裡去了。他得意洋洋地游離岸邊,對可憐的買主叫道:「再見了,主人!萬一您還是要張驢皮做大鼓,就想想我吧!」

他說完就一邊笑著一邊游走了,沒游多久,他又轉過頭來,比剛才叫得更響:「再見了,主人!萬一您需要一些乾木頭生火,就想想我吧。」

眨眼之間,他已經游了好遠好遠,遠得都要看不見身影了。放眼望去,整個人就只剩下海平面上一個黑點,只見得這個黑點時不時把腳伸出水面,翻跟斗,活蹦亂跳的,就像一隻正在嬉戲的海豚。

皮諾丘漫無目的地在海裡游啊遊啊,忽然在大海中央,看見了一塊礁石,就像一塊潔白如雪的大理石。在礁石的最高處,站著一隻漂亮的小山羊,正咩咩咩地叫著,熱情地招呼著他過去。

而且最特別的是,這隻小山羊的毛,跟一般的山羊很不相同,它不是白色的,也不是黑色的,更不是黑白混雜的,而是藍色的。並且,還是很鮮豔的藍色,像極了漂亮仙女頭髮的顏色。

可憐的皮諾丘，他的心在那兒怦怦直跳，激動之情可想而知。他加倍努力地朝那塊雪白的礁石游去。就在他游到一半時，忽然從水裡冒出一個可怕的大海怪腦袋，直直地對著他游過來。他的嘴張得像洞穴一般大，露出兩排陰森森的牙齒，讓人一看就膽戰心驚。

讀者們，您知道這個大海怪是什麼嗎？

這海怪不是別的什麼東西，正是一條大鯊魚。在這個故事中，我們已經多次提到過他了。由於他喜好殺戮，且貪得無厭，所以被人稱作「魚和漁夫的魔王。」

可憐的皮諾丘，見到這個怪物該有多麼驚慌！於是，他換個方向游去，想儘量避開，他絞盡腦汁想逃跑。但是，那個龐然大物，就這樣張開血盆大口，像離了弦的箭一般朝他衝了過來。

「皮諾丘，拜託你快點！」那頭美麗的小山羊急得咩咩咩的叫喚。

皮諾丘用雙手、用胸口、用雙腿、用雙腳，拚了命地加速往前游。

「趕快，皮諾丘，那隻怪物馬上就要抓到你了！」

皮諾丘越游越快，像出膛的子彈一樣，眼看他就要到礁石了。那隻小山羊向海面傾著身子，朝他伸出了前蹄，想助他一臂之力。

但是，一切都太晚了！大海怪已經趕上他了，對著他深深地吸了一口氣，就像吸顆雞蛋一般，就這樣把那可憐的木偶給吸到嘴裡去了。然後，囫圇一吞。一眨眼的工夫，皮諾丘就被吞進了大鯊魚的肚子裡，他在鯊魚的體內被重重地撞了一下，昏昏沉沉大概有一刻鐘之久。

等他清醒過來時，連自己在哪裡都搞不明白了。他身邊一片漆黑，深沉沉的黑暗，就像是整個人埋進了墨水瓶裡。他張著耳朵聽了聽，沒有一點聲響，只是臉上偶爾能感覺有一陣風吹過。一開始，他還不清楚那風是從哪裡來的，不過後來總算明白了，是從怪物的肺裡出來的。原來，鯊魚患了很嚴重的哮喘病，每當他呼吸的時候，就像刮北風一樣。最初皮諾丘還強裝振作，不過，後來確認自己是被禁錮在大海怪的肚子裡時，他就開始又哭又鬧，嗚咽地流著淚說：「救命啊！救命啊！喔，我真是太倒楣了！有沒有人能救救我啊？」

「可憐的傢伙，你認為誰可以救你呢？」黑暗中一個類似走調的吉他聲出現。

「是誰在說話？」皮諾丘問，他嚇得汗毛都豎了起來。

「是我！一條可憐的鮪魚，跟你同時被鯊魚吸進了肚裡。你是什麼品種的魚？」

「我和魚一點也不像，我不過是一個木偶而已。」

「如果你不是魚，怎麼會讓自己被這個怪物給吞了？」

「不是故意讓自己被吞的，是他主動把我給吞了！當下，這黑漆漆的，我們該怎麼辦呢？」

「聽天由命吧,我們就等著被鯊魚消化掉!」

「可是,我不願意讓他給消化掉!」皮諾丘咆哮著說,他又哭了起來。

「我也不願意被他給消化掉。」鮪魚接著說,「但我是一個實實在在的哲學家,既然生下來就是一條魚,那麼能在水裡死去,總好過在油鍋裡死去。這麼一想,我心裡就舒服多了⋯⋯」

「胡說八道!」皮諾丘叫道。

「這只是我個人看法。」鮪魚回答說,「不過,正如鮪魚政治家所說的,只要是看法都應當得到尊重!」

「無論如何⋯⋯我想從這兒離開⋯⋯我想逃走。」

「要是可以,那就逃啊!」

「吞下我們的這條鯊魚大不大?」木偶問道。

「非常大。你想想看,除去尾巴,光是他的身子就有兩英里長。」

就在他們摸黑說話的當下,皮諾丘覺得遠處好像發出了微弱的光亮。

「那些光,又是怎麼回事?」皮諾丘又問。

「那應該是和我們一樣的倒楣傢伙,都在等著被消化呢!」

「我要去會會他。你不覺得他有可能是一條經驗老到的魚,能給我們指出一條生路嗎?」

「我衷心希望能夠如你所願,親愛的木偶。」

「再見,鮪魚。」

「再見,木偶,祝你好運。」

「我們回頭在哪裡見面?」

「誰知道呢?……最好,還是想都別想吧!」

第 35 章

皮諾丘在鯊魚的身體裡尋覓光源,他發現了誰呢?看完這一章就知道答案了。

　　皮諾丘離開了他的好朋友鮪魚,開始在鯊魚的肚子裡摸黑找路,一步一步地,朝著遙遠的那點閃爍朦朧的亮光走去。

　　他越是往前,那光點就越是明亮放大。

　　他一直走啊走啊,終於到了目的地。等他走到那裡⋯⋯猜他看見什麼啦?怎麼猜也猜不到吧!他看見了一張鋪設好的小桌子,桌上擺著一個綠色的玻璃瓶,瓶裡插著一支點燃的蠟燭。桌旁坐著一個老人,他正吃著活生生的魚。那些魚實在是太新鮮了,甚至有時候吃著吃著,魚就從他嘴裡面蹦了出來。

　　可憐的皮諾丘一見到這個人,瞬間感到喜出望外,興奮得幾乎都要暈過去了。他一會兒想笑，一會兒想哭，心裡有千言萬語想要說出口，可最終只能結結巴巴地亂說一通。最後，他好不容易發出聲來，歡呼著張開雙臂，撲過去一把抱住老頭兒的脖子，大聲嚷嚷起來：「喔！我親愛的爸爸！我終於找到您了！我再也不離開您了，再也不離開了，再也不離開了！」

「我看到的都是真的嗎？」老人揉揉眼睛問道，「真是我親愛的皮諾丘嗎？」

「是的，是的，是的，我是皮諾丘！您已經原諒我了，是不是？喔！我親愛的爸爸，您真是太好了！……再想想我，我卻那麼壞……喔！您不知道，有多少災難降臨在我頭上，我遭遇了多少不幸的事情啊！回想那一天，我可憐的爸爸，您賣掉了自己的上衣，替我買了一本上學用的識字課本，可是我卻跑去看木偶戲。木偶劇院的團主，想把我扔進火堆去烤他那隻羊羔。不過，後來他給了我五個金幣，讓我帶回去給您。但是，我遇到一隻狐狸和一隻貓，他們把我帶去『紅龍蝦旅館』，他們在那裡飽餐一頓，然後留我孤身一人，半夜離開旅館。在路上碰到兩個強盜一直追我。我在前面跑，他們便在後面追。我繼續跑，他們也不停地追。最終，我還是被他們給抓住了，吊在一棵大橡樹的樹枝上。後來，一位藍髮的漂亮仙女派車把我救走。醫生診斷之後，立即說：「假如他還沒有死，那就說明還活著。」隨後，因為我撒謊，我的鼻子就開始長長，一直長到連房門也出不去。接下來，我跟著狐狸和貓去種四個金幣。因為有一個金幣已經在旅館裡用掉了。一隻鸚鵡嘲笑我，我不但沒有收穫兩千個金幣，相反，連最後一個金幣也沒有了。法官聽說我被偷了，反而為了讓小偷們滿意，就立刻把我關進了監獄。出了監獄，我路過一片碩果纍纍的葡萄園，結果被捕獸夾給困住了。農夫當然有足夠的理由在我的脖子上戴了一個狗項圈，讓我看守雞窩。等他意識到我是無辜的之後，就把我放走了。之後，我遇到一條尾巴冒煙的蛇，他笑啊笑啊，把肚子上的血管笑到爆了。就這樣，我又回到了美麗仙女的家，可是她已經死了。鴿子見到我在哭，就告訴我說：『我見過你爸爸了，他造了一隻小船要出海去找你。』我對他說『喔！要是我有翅膀就好了！』他隨即對我說：『你想到你爸爸那兒去嗎？』我回答說：『不用說，我肯定想去！可是誰帶我過去呢？』他對我說：『我帶你去。』我就問他：『要怎麼去呢？』他說：『你坐在我背上來。』就這樣，我們飛了整整一夜。等到第二天，天一亮，所有的漁民都盯著大海，對我說：『有一個可憐人坐在一條小船上，馬上就要被淹死了。雖然隔著很遠，但我一眼就認出是您，因為我的心就是這麼告訴我的。於是，我打著手勢讓您回到岸上來……』

「我也認出你來了。」傑佩托說，「我也很想回到岸上，但是我做不到！大海上波濤洶湧，一個巨浪過來，就把小船掀翻了。當時那條可怕的大鯊魚就在附近，他一看見我落水了，立刻向我游過來，伸出舌頭一捲，就把我捲進嘴裡，然後像吞一隻波倫亞餃子似的，把我吞了下去。」

「您困在這裡面多長時間啦？」皮諾丘問。

「從那一天直到現在，差不多都有兩個年頭了。我親愛的皮諾丘，這兩年對我來說就像兩個世紀一樣漫長啊！」

「您都是怎麼生活的？這蠟燭是從哪裡弄來的？點蠟燭的火柴呢？這些都是誰給您的？」

「好了，我把所有的事情都講給你聽。跟你說，那一場風暴不僅掀翻我的船，還同時打翻一艘商船。船員全都得救了，不過船沉到了海底。那一天，這條鯊魚的胃口大開，他吞下我之後，又把那條船也吞進來了。」

「怎麼吞的？」

「他一口就把整條船給吞了進來，只把一根主桅桿吐了出去。關鍵還是因為，那主桅杆像根魚刺一樣卡在他的牙縫裡。我運氣很好，這條船裝滿了保存完好的罐頭肉、餅乾、瓶裝酒、葡萄乾、乳酪、咖啡、砂糖、蠟燭，以及成箱的火柴。真是上天保佑，我才能活著過了兩年。但是，如今所有的物品都已經消耗殆盡了，一點儲備都沒有了，你現在見到的這支燃燒著的蠟燭，它已經是最後一支了……」

「那之後要怎麼過呢？」

「以後啊，我親愛的孩子，我們就得一直生活在黑暗中了。」

「那麼，我親愛的爸爸。」皮諾丘說，「我們已經沒有可以浪費的時間了，我們要立刻想辦法逃走。」

「想辦法逃走？……怎麼逃？」

「我們從鯊魚嘴裡溜出去，跳進海裡，然後游走。」

「你說得倒是有理。不過親愛的皮諾丘，我不會游泳啊！」

「那有什麼關係？……我可是個游泳高手，您只要坐在我的肩膀上，我就能夠把您平安地帶上岸。」

「不要有錯覺啊！孩子！」傑佩托回答說，同時苦笑著搖搖頭，「像你這樣一個……約莫僅有一米高的木偶想背著我游泳，你覺得你的力氣足夠嗎？」

「您試試就知道了！」

皮諾丘不再多言，把蠟燭拿在手上，走在前面作為照明，還回過頭對他爸爸說：「跟在我後面，不要擔心。」

他們就這樣走了很長一段時間，穿過了鯊魚的身體和肚子，一直走到了海怪的喉嚨口。到這裡後想著最好還是先停下來，好好打探一番，然後，再找一個最恰當的時機溜出去。

之前已經告訴過大家，這條鯊魚已經上年紀了，再加上患了哮喘病和心臟病，只能張著嘴巴睡覺。因此，皮諾丘靠近他的喉嚨口往上看，可以從張開的嘴巴縫裡，看到一大片繁星點點的天空，以及美麗的月光。

「這是逃跑的最好時機了。」他轉身對父親竊竊私語，「鯊魚已經睡熟了，大海一片寧靜，亮如白晝。親愛的爸爸，您跟著我，很快我們就安全啦！」

二話不說，他們順著這海怪的喉嚨往上爬，一直爬到他碩大無比的嘴巴那裡，然後，他們踮起腳尖走在他的舌頭上。

在最後跳進海裡之前，木偶對他的爸爸說：「坐到我肩膀上，兩隻手抱著我的脖子，其他的就都交給我好了。」

　　傑佩托在兒子的肩膀坐穩了。皮諾丘自信滿滿地跳進水裡，游了起來。大海光滑如絲，沒有一點漣漪。月華如洗，皎潔明亮。而那隻鯊魚依舊酣睡著，看來連大炮也轟不醒他。

第 36 章

終於,皮諾丘不再是木偶了。他變成了一個真正的男孩。

皮諾丘迅速地朝岸邊遊著,突然發現坐在肩上的爸爸不停地發抖,因為他的雙腿都泡在水裡,就像是一個罹患瘧疾的可憐老人。

但發抖究竟是因為寒冷呢?還是驚嚇呢?也可能兩者都有。不過,皮諾丘認為他應該是感到恐懼居多,於是安慰說:「不要擔心,爸爸!再過幾分鐘,我們就能安全上岸了。」

「可是,海岸到底在哪裡啊?」老人問道。他心裡越來越忐忑不安,半眯著眼睛像縫線穿針那樣地,望著前方。「四周看過去,除了一望無際的大海和天空,其他什麼也沒有啊!」

「但我看見海岸了。」木偶說。

「你要知道，我像貓一樣，夜間的視力可是比白天更清楚。」

可憐的皮諾丘只是假裝一副活力充沛的樣子，實際上呢？他其實已經感到沮喪了。他漸漸失去氣力，大口大口地喘氣，其實再也游不動了。但是，海岸邊還離得很遠呢！

他用盡最後一點力量，然後轉頭對著傑佩托，斷斷續續地說：「我的爸爸，救救我……我要死了！」

眼看著父子倆就要被淹沒之際，突然他們聽到一個像是走調的吉他聲說：「誰快死啦？」

「是我和我可憐的父親！」

「這聲音我很熟！你是皮諾丘吧！」

「正是。你是誰啊？」

「我是鮪魚，和你一起被困在鯊魚肚子裡的患難之交。」

「那，你是怎麼逃出來的呢？」

「我就有樣學樣。你既然開了路，我就跟在你後面逃出來了。」

「鮪魚，你來得正是時候！求求你幫幫忙，否則我們就要死在這裡了。」

「我很樂意之至。你們倆趕快抓住我的尾巴，我給你們帶路,四分鐘就能把你們送到岸邊。」

不用多說,大家也可以想像得到,傑佩托和皮諾丘立即接受幫助。不過,不是抓著鮪魚的尾巴,而是直接騎在他背上,他們覺得這樣更輕鬆一些。

到了岸邊,皮諾丘先跳上去,然後再把爸爸拉上岸。之後他轉過身來,充滿感激地對鮪魚說:「我的朋友,你救了我的爸爸一命!我實在不知道該說些什麼話來感謝你才好!但是,至少讓我親親你,表達我沒齒難忘的感激之情!」

鮪魚把頭伸出水面,皮諾丘跪在地上,對著他的嘴溫柔地吻了一下。可憐的鮪魚面對皮諾丘真心實意的感謝,感到非常不自在,激動得無以復加,又不好意思讓人看見,他哭得像個小孩子似的,只好把頭鑽到水裡,然後消失不見了。

這時候,曙光初露。傑佩托都站不穩了。皮諾丘將手伸給他, 對他說:「您靠在我的手臂上,親愛的爸爸,我們走吧!一步一步慢慢地,就像螞蟻一樣走,等走累了就在路邊休息一會兒。」

「可是,我們去哪兒呢?」

「我們去找個有房子或茅屋的地方。到了那裡,好心的人們會願意給我們一口麵包吃,再給我們一點稻草睡覺的。」

走了還不到一百步,他們就看到路邊有兩個奇醜無比的人正在行乞。

他們正是那兩隻貓和狐狸,不過,他們的外表變得幾乎都快令人認不出來了。大家回想一下，那隻貓一直以來都在裝瞎，但這回是真瞎了。狐狸年紀大了，身上長滿疥瘡，身體還一邊癱瘓了，甚至連尾巴都不見了。那個惡賊也終於到了山窮水盡的地步，被迫把他好看的尾巴，賣給一個小販作為拂塵去了。

「喔！皮諾丘。」狐狸大哭起來，「行行好，賞點什麼，給我們兩個可憐的體弱多病的人吃吧！」

「體弱多病的人！」貓重覆了一遍。

「滾開，騙子！」木偶回答說，「我已經上過一次當，你們不要想再騙我第二次。」

「你一定要相信我，皮諾丘，我們現在真的是又貧困又倒楣啦！」

「你們要是真窮了，那也是自作自受。俗話說得好：『偷錢永遠不會致富。』滾開，騙子！」

說完，皮諾丘扶著傑佩托默默地接著趕路。走了約一百步遠，他們看見田野中間那條小路的盡頭，矗立著一座精緻的茅草屋，用磚和瓦層疊的屋頂。

「那座小屋裡一定有人住。」皮諾丘說，「我們走過去看看。」

於是，他們走到門前敲了敲門。

「誰在那兒？」裡面有個細微的聲音問道。

「我們是一對可憐的父子，沒有飯吃，沒有地方住。」木偶回答說。

「你轉動一下鑰匙，門就開了。」還是那聲音。

皮諾丘扭了扭鑰匙，把門打開了。然後，他們走了進去，繞著滿屋瞧了又瞧，但是一個人也沒有看到。

「喔！請問房子的主人在嗎？」皮諾丘驚奇地說。

「我在你們頭頂上！」

父子倆一齊抬頭望向天花板，只見會說話的蟋蟀先生正棲息在一根橫樑上。

「喔！親愛的會說話的蟋蟀先生！」皮諾丘說道，並十分禮貌地向他鞠躬。

「啊哈！如今你知道叫我『親愛的蟋蟀』了，你還記得嗎？那時，為了把我從你家趕出去，朝我用力扔了一個錘子把手嗎？」

「你是對的，會說話的蟋蟀先生！你也把我趕出去吧！也用錘子的把手扔我吧！但是，請你能憐憫我可憐的爸爸……」

「我會同情你們父子倆的。不過是想提醒你，我從你這兒受過的粗暴對待。目的也是想教訓你。在這個世界上，如果我們想獲得別人應有的尊重，那麼，我們也應該盡可能的，對每一個人都謙恭有禮。」

「你是對的，會說話的蟋蟀先生，你說得對。我會牢牢記住，你給我的教訓，不過，請你先告訴我，你是如何買下這棟精緻的茅草屋。」

「這棟茅草屋，是昨天一隻山羊送給我的，那隻山羊有一身藍色的羊毛，好看極了。」

「那隻山羊現在去哪裡了？」皮諾丘迫不及待地問道。

「我也不清楚。」

「那他什麼時候回來？」

「他不會回來了，昨天他離開時非常傷心，一直咩咩咩地哀叫，似乎在說：『可憐的皮諾丘……我永遠都見不到他了……都這個時候了，鯊魚肯定已經把他吃掉！』」

「他真是這麼說的？……那就是她！……就是她！……就是我親愛的仙女！」皮諾丘大聲喊完，便哇哇地哭了起來。

哭了好長一段時間之後，他擦乾眼淚，用乾草鋪了一張舒適的床，讓老傑佩托躺在上面。之後，他繼續問會說話的蟋蟀先生：「告訴我，會說話的蟋蟀先生，我可以到哪裡，給我可憐的爸爸弄來一杯牛奶呢？」

「離這兒大概三塊田遠的地方，住著一位名叫詹吉奧的花匠，他養了好幾隻奶牛。你去他那裡一定能得到想要的牛奶。」

皮諾丘飛快地跑去了詹吉奧家裡，那位花匠問他：

「你需要多少牛奶？」

「我想要一滿杯。」

211

「一杯牛奶半便士。先給我半便士。」

「但是,我一枚錢也沒有。」皮諾丘既傷心又苦惱地回答說。

「那可不行啊!我的木偶。」花匠回答說,「你要是一枚錢也沒有,那我可就一滴牛奶也沒有。」

「那我也無能為力!皮諾丘說完,轉身便要離開。

「你先等一會兒。」詹吉奧說,「我們還可以商量一下。你願意搖水車嗎?」

「水車是什麼?」

「它是一個木頭的工具,可以用來將水從蓄水池裡拉上來好澆在菜上。」

「我能試一試……」

「那好,你試試看,要是你能拉一百桶水上來,我就給你一杯牛奶作為報酬。」

「就這麼說定了。」

詹吉把木偶帶到菜園,教他怎麼使用水車。說完,皮諾丘立即就工作了。可是一百桶水還沒有全部拉上來,他已經從頭到腳全都濕透了。他這一輩子都還沒這麼疲累過。

「到目前為止。」花匠說,「搖水車這個活兒,都是由我的驢子來完成的。不過,現在這頭可憐的畜牲,馬上就要死了。」

「您能帶我去看看他嗎?」皮諾丘當即問道。

「當然好啊。」

皮諾丘走進畜欄,一眼就看見有頭漂亮的小驢子,直挺挺地躺在乾草上,他又餓又累,已經奄奄一息了。皮諾丘認認真真地打量之後,心緒不寧地自言自語道:「我敢肯定,我認識這頭小驢子!他的臉⋯⋯對我來說並不陌生。」

他彎下身,用驢子的語言問他說:「你是誰?」

聽到這句話,小驢子睜開垂死的雙眼,也用相同的話斷斷續續地回答:「我是燈⋯⋯燈⋯⋯芯⋯⋯。」

說完,他再次闔上眼睛,斷氣了。

「噢,可憐的燈芯!」皮諾丘低聲驚呼道。隨後他抓了一把乾草,擦掉了從臉上滾落下來的淚水。

「這頭驢子沒有花你一分錢,你卻為他那麼惋惜?」花匠說,「我可是花了一筆錢才把他給買回來的,我該要多可惜啊?」

「我跟您說⋯⋯他是我的朋友!」

「你的朋友?」

「是我的一個同學!」

「怎麼可能?」詹吉奧大笑著說,「怎麼可能?你竟然會有驢子同學?你的學習怎麼樣那就可想而知了!」

聽到這些話,木偶感覺十分羞恥,沒好意思回話。他接過一杯微熱的牛奶,便回茅屋去了。

從那天開始,待在這裡五個多月的時間裡,他每天都堅持黎明就起床,然後去搖水車,換回一杯牛奶。就靠著這杯奶,他父親衰弱的身體才一天天地好起來了。不過,他仍然不滿足。因此,白天他學著用燈芯草來編筐子,編籃子,賣了這些東西賺回的錢,夠他省吃儉用地滿足日常開銷了。此外,他還做了一輛精巧的輪椅,天氣好的時候就推著輪椅,帶爸爸出去散散步,呼吸一些新鮮空氣。

憑著他的勤勉與智慧,以及對工作的渴望,他克服了種種困難;不僅使他體弱多病的父親過舒服的日子,他還想方設法賺了四十便士,想替自己買件新上衣。

一天早上,他對父親說:「我打算去附近的市場上,為自己買一件夾克,一頂帽子和一雙鞋。等我回家的時候……」他笑著往下說,「我一定打扮得體體面面,讓您以為我是一位有修養的紳士。」

出了家門,他就滿心喜悅地奔跑起來。突然,他聽到有人叫他的名字。他回頭一看,看見一隻大蝸牛從樹籬裡緩緩地爬出來。

「難道你不認識我了嗎?」蝸牛問道。

「我好像認識……但是又不確定……」

「藍髮仙女的那隻僕人蝸牛,記不起來嗎?那一次,我從樓上下來給你開門,你還把一隻腳插進房門裡,被困在那兒了,記不起來了嗎?」

「我全都想起來啦!!皮諾丘叫道,「你趕快告訴我,美麗的蝸牛,我那好心的仙女,現在在哪裡呢?她正在幹些什麼?她饒恕我了嗎?她還惦念我嗎?她還希望我好嗎?她離這裡遠不遠?我能不能去看看她?」

皮諾丘說話飛快,一口氣提出一連串問題。蝸牛還是像往常一樣,慢慢悠悠地回答道:「親愛的皮諾丘!可憐的仙女現在正躺在醫院的床上!」

「在醫院裡?……」

「真是太糟糕了!在無窮的打擊之下,她得了重病,而且窮得連替自己買一口麵包的錢,也沒有了。」

「這是真的嗎?……噢!多麼令人難過的消息啊!喔!可憐的仙女!可憐的仙女!……要是我手頭有一百萬,我就馬上跑過去送給她了,但是,我只有四十便士……全都在這兒了。我準備去買件新外套。你都拿著吧,蝸牛,立刻把它們帶給我好心的仙女。」

「那你的新衣服呢?……」

「我的新衣服又有什麼關係?只要能夠幫得上她,我這身破衣服都可以賣掉。去吧,蝸牛,你動作快一點。兩天後你再回來,希望到時候我可以再給你湊一些錢。到現在為止,我工作是為了賺錢養活我爸爸。從今往後,我每天要多工作五個小時，爭取也能養活我的好媽媽。再見了，蝸牛，兩天後我還在這兒等你。」

蝸牛一反常態的拔腿快跑，就像是一隻在八月炎炎烈日下奔走的蜥蜴。

和往常不一樣，這天晚上皮諾丘到十點了，還沒有上床睡覺，而是一直坐到午夜的鐘聲都敲響才休息。他編了不止八個籃子，而是十六個。

因此，他一躺到床上就進入夢鄉。在夢中似乎見到美麗的仙女，她微笑著吻了吻他後，對他說：「做得好，皮諾丘！為了回報你的好心，我將原諒你過往的種種行為。那些體貼地照顧自己父母的孩子，一一幫助父母渡過苦難，戰勝病魔，儘管，他們不能被當做聽話和品行優良的楷模，也理應受到讚美，獲得喜愛。在未來的日子裡，再接再厲，好好做人，你會快樂的。」

夢到這裡就結束了，皮諾丘睜開眼睛，醒了過來。

可以想像一下，他這時候該有多麼的訝異，因為他一覺醒來，發現自己不再是一個木偶，而變成了一個百分之百的真實男孩，和其他孩子沒有絲毫差別！他環顧四周，只見原來那棟茅屋的乾草牆壁不見了，取而代之的是一個漂亮的小房間，室內的裝飾擺設優雅大方。他連忙跳下床，看見一套為他準備的新衣服，一頂新帽子和一雙皮靴子，搭配再完美不過了。

他一穿上衣服，就很自然地把手伸進了口袋，從裡面掏出了象牙的小錢包。錢包上寫著如下文字：「藍髮的仙女還給她親愛的皮諾丘四十便士，並感謝他的善心。」他打開錢包一看，裡面裝的可不止四十便士，而是四十個金幣，四十個新鮮出爐的金幣，還閃爍著金色的光芒呢！

隨後，皮諾丘跑去照照鏡子，感覺就像是另外一個人。映入眼簾的不再是原來的木偶，而是一個聰明伶俐的漂亮的孩子：一頭栗色的頭髮，一雙藍色的眼眸，整個人看上去喜氣洋洋的，就像在過復活節一樣。

神奇的事一樁接一樁地發生，皮諾丘感覺困惑不已。他已經沒法分辨，他是真的清醒呢？還是睜著眼睛做夢？

「我的爸爸在哪裡？」他突然驚叫一聲，趕忙跑去隔壁房間。只見老傑佩托跟原來一樣，身體健康，神清氣爽，心情歡愉。他又做起了老本行——木雕，當下他正在設計一個畫框，畫框上面刻著各種葉子，各色鮮花以及各類動物的頭，看上去真是美極了。

「親愛的爸爸，你就滿足一下我的好奇心吧！」

皮諾丘撲過去摟住他的脖子，親著他問，「這一切變得太快了，究竟是怎麼回事呢？」

「我們家的種種改變，全都是你的功勞。」傑佩特回答說。

「怎麼都是我的功勞？」

「因為當一個孩子全然醒悟，由壞變好的時候，他就具備了一種力量，一種可以帶給家人滿足和快樂的力量。」

「原來的木偶皮諾丘藏到哪兒去了呢？」

「就在那裡。」傑佩托回答說，並用手指著一個大木偶。那個木偶坐靠在一張椅子上，頭偏到一側，兩條手臂下垂，雙腿交叉著蜷曲起來，那種模樣讓人看了，覺得它要是能站起來，還真是個奇蹟。

皮諾丘轉過身去，目不轉睛地盯著，看了好半天之後，心滿意足地暗想道：「回想我還是個木偶的時候，生活得如此幼稚不懂事；現在，我很高興自己變成了一個品行良好的小男孩！」

The Adventure of Pinocchio

Pinocchio

Chapter 1

How it came to pass that Master Cherry the carpenter found a Piece of wood that laughed and cried like a child.

THERE was once upon a time...

"A king!" my little readers will instantly exclaim.

No, children, you are wrong. There was once upon a time a piece of wood.

This wood was not valuable: it was only a common log like those that are burnt in winter in the stoves and fireplaces to make a cheerful blaze and warm the rooms.

I cannot say how it came about, but the fact is, that one fine day this piece of wood was lying in the shop of an old carpenter of the name of Master Antonio. He was, however, called by everybody Master Cherry, on account of the end of his nose, which was always as red and polished as a ripe cherry.

No sooner had Master Cherry set eyes on the piece of wood than his face beamed with delight; and, rubbing his hands together with satisfaction, he said softly to himself: "This wood has come at the right moment; it will just do to make the leg of a little table, "

Having said this he immediately took a sharp axe with which to remove the bark and the rough surface. Just, however, as he was going to give the first stroke he remained with his arm suspended in the air, for he heard a very small voice saying imploringly, "Do not strike me so hard!"

Picture to yourselves the astonishment of good old Master Cherry!

He turned his terrified eyes all round the room to try and discover where the little voice could possibly have come from, but he saw nobody! He looked under the bench - nobody; he looked into a cupboard that was always shut - nobody; he looked into a basket of shavings and sawdust- nobody; he even opened the door of the shop and gave a glance into the street and still nobody. Who, then, could it be?

"I see how it is, " he said, laughing and scratching his wig; "evidently that little voice was all my imagination. Let us set to work again."

And taking up the axe he struck a tremendous blow on the piece of wood.

"Oh! oh! you have hurt me!" cried the same little voice dolefully.

This time Master Cherry was petrified. His eyes started out of his head with fright, his mouth remained open, and his tongue hung out almost to the end of his chin, like a mask on a fountain. As soon as he had recovered the use of his speech, he began to say, stuttering and trembling with fear: "But where on earth can that little voice have come from that said Oh! oh!?...Here there is certainly not a living soul. Is it possible that this piece of wood can have learnt to cry and to lament like a child? I cannot believe it. This piece of wood, here it is; a log for fuel like all the others, and thrown on the fire it would about suffice to boil a saucepan of beans...How then? Can anyone be hidden inside it? If anyone is hidden inside, so much the worse for him. I will settle him at once."

So saying, he seized the poor piece of wood and commenced beating it without mercy against the walls of the room.

Then he stopped to listen if he could hear any little voice lamenting. He waited two minutes - nothing; five minutes - nothing; ten minutes still- nothing!

"I see how it is, " he then said, forcing himself to laugh and pushing up his wig; "evidently the little voice that said Oh! oh! was all my imagination! Let us set to work again."

But as all the same he was in a great fright, he tried to sing to give himself a little courage.

Putting the axe aside he took his plane, to plane and polish the bit of wood; but whilst he was running it up and down he heard the same little voice say, laughing: "Have done! you are tickling me all over!"

This time poor Master Cherry fell down as if he had been struck by lightning. When he at last opened his eyes he found himself seated on the floor.

His face was quite changed, even the end of his nose, instead of being crimson, as it was nearly always, had become blue from fright.

Chapter 2

Master Cherry makes a present of the piece of wood to his friend Geppetto, who takes it to make for himself a wonderful puppet, that shall know how to dance, and to fence, and to leap like an acrobat.

AT that moment some one knocked at the door.

"Come in," said the carpenter, without having the strength to rise to his feet.

A lively little old man immediately walked into the shop. His name was Geppetto, but when the boys of the neighbourhood wished to put him in a passion they called him by the nickname of Polendina, because his yellow wig greatly resembled a pudding made of Indian corn.

Geppetto was very fiery. Woe to him who called him Polendina! He became furious, and there was no holding him.

"Good day, Master Antonio," said Geppetto; "what are you doing there on the floor?"

"I am teaching the alphabet to the ants."

"Much good may that do you."

"What has brought you to me, neighbour Geppetto?"

"My legs. But to say the truth, Master Antonio, I am come to ask a favour of you."

"Here I am, ready to serve you," replied the carpenter, getting on to his knees.

"This morning an idea came into my head."

"Let us hear it."

"I thought I would make a beautiful wooden puppet; but a wonderful puppet that should know how to dance, to fence, and to leap like an acrobat. With this puppet I would travel about the world to earn a piece of bread and a glass of wine. What do you think of it?"

"Bravo, Polendina!" exclaimed the same little voice, and it was impossible to say where it came from.

Hearing himself called Polendina Geppetto became as red as a turkey-cock from rage, and turning to the carpenter he said in a fury: "Why do you insult me?"

"Who insults you?"

"You called me Polendina! ..."

"It was not I!"

"Would you have it, then, that it was I? It was you, I say!"

"No!"

"Yes!"

"No!"

"Yes!"

And becoming more and more angry, from words they came to blows, and flying at each other they bit, and fought, and scratched manfully.

When the fight was over Master Antonio was in possession of Geppetto's yellow wig, and Geppetto discovered that the grey wig belonging to the carpenter had remained between his teeth.

"Give me back my wig," screamed Master Antonio.

"And you, return me mine, and let us make friends."

The two old men having each recovered his own wig shook hands, and swore that they would remain friends to the end of their lives.

"Well then, neighbour Geppetto," said the carpenter, to prove that peace was made, "what is the favour that you wish of me?"

"I want a little wood to make my puppet; will you give me some?"

Master Antonio was delighted, and he immediately went to the bench and fetched the piece of wood that had caused him so much fear. But just as he was going to give it to his friend the piece of wood gave a shake, and wriggling violently out of his hands struck with all its force against the dried up shins of poor Geppetto.

"Ah! is that the courteous way in which you make your presents, Master Antonio? You have almost lamed me! ..."

"I swear to you that it was not I! ..."

"Then you would have it that it was I? ..."

"The wood is entirely to blame! ..."

"I know that it was the wood; but it was you that hit my legs with it! ..."

"I did not hit you with it!.."

"Liar!"

"Geppetto, don't insult me or I will call you Polendina! ..."

"Ass!"

"Polendina!"

"Donkey!"

"Polendina!"

"Baboon!"

"Polendina!"

On hearing himself called Polendina for the third time Geppetto, blind with rage, fell upon the carpenter and they fought desperately.

When the battle was over, Master Antonio had two more scratches on his nose, and his adversary had two buttons too little on his waistcoat. Their accounts being thus squared they shook hands, and swore to remain good friends for the rest of their lives.

Geppetto carried off his fine piece of wood and, thanking Master Antonio, returned limping to his house.

Chapter 3

Geppetto having returned home begins at once to make a puppet, to which he gives the name of Pinocchio. The first tricks played by the puppet.

GEPPETTO lived in a small ground-floor room that was only lighted from the staircase. The furniture could not have been simpler, -a bad chair, a poor and a broken-down table. At the end of the room there was a fireplace with a lighted fire; but the fire was painted, and by the fire was a painted saucepan that was boiling cheerfully, and sending out a cloud of smoke that looked exactly like real smoke.

As soon as he reached home Geppetto took his tools and set to work to cut out and model his puppet.

"What name shall I give him?" he said to himself; "I think I will call him Pinocchio. It is a name that will bring him luck. I once knew a whole family so called. There was Pinocchio the father, Pinocchia the mother, and Pinocchi the children, and all of them did well. The richest of them was a beggar."

Having found a name for his puppet he began to work in good earnest, and he first made his hair, then his forehead, and then his eyes.

The eyes being finished, imagine his astonishment when he peceived that they moved and looked fixedly at him.

Geppetto seeing himself stared at by those two wooden eyes took it almost in bad part, and said in an angry voice: "Wicked wooden eyes, why do you look at me?"

No one answered.

He then proceeded to carve the nose; but no sooner had he made it than it began to grow. And it grew, and grew, and grew, until in a few minutes it had become an immense nose that seemed as if it would never end.

Poor Geppetto tired himself out with cutting it off; but the more he cut and shortened it, the longer did that impertinent nose become!

The mouth was not even completed when it began to laugh and deride him.

"Stop laughing!" said Geppetto, provoked; but he might as well have spoken to the wall.

"Stop laughing, I say!" he roared in a threatening tone.

The mouth then ceased laughing, but put out its tongue as far as it would go.

Geppetto, not to spoil his handiwork, pretended not to see, and continued his labours. After the mouth he fashioned the chin, then the throat, then the shoulders, the stomach, the arms and the hands.

The hands were scarcely finished when Geppetto felt his wig snatched from his head. He turned round, and what did he see? He saw his yellow wig in the puppet's hand.

"Pinocchio!...Give me back my wig instantly!"

But Pinocchio, instead of returning it, put it on his own head, and was in consequence nearly smothered.

Geppetto at this insolent and derisive behaviour felt sadder and more melancholy than he had ever been in his life before; and turning to Pinocchio he said to him: "You young rascal! You are not yet completed, and you are already beginning to show want of respect to your father! That is bad, my boy, very bad!"

And he dried a tear.

The legs and the feet remained to be done.

When Geppetto had finished the feet he received a kick on the point of his nose.

"I deserve it!" he said to himself; "I should have thought of it sooner! Now it is too late!"

He then took the puppet under the arms and placed him on the floor to teach him to walk.

Pinocchio's legs were stiff and he could not move, but Geppetto led him by the hand and showed him how to put one foot before the other.

When his legs became flexible Pinocchio began to walk by himself and to run about the room; until, having gone out of the house door, he jumped into the street and escaped.

Poor Geppetto rushed after him but was not able to overtake him, for that rascal Pinocchio leapt in front of him like a hare, and knocking his wooden feet together against the pavement made as much clatter as twenty pairs of peasants' clogs.

"Stop him! stop him!" shouted Geppetto; but the people in the street, seeing a wooden puppet running like a racehorse, stood still in astonishment to look at it, and laughed, and laughed, and laughed, until it beats description.

At last, as good luck would have it, a carabineer arrived who, hearing the uproar, imagined that a colt had escaped from his master. Planting himself courageously with his legs apart in the middle of the road, he waited with the determined purpose of stopping him, and thus preventing the chance of worse disasters.

When Pinocchio, still at some distance, saw the carabineer barricading the whole street, he endeavoured to take him by surprise and to pass between his legs. But he failed signally.

The carabineer without disturbing himself in the least caught him cleverly by the nose it was an immense nose of ridiculous proportions that seemed made on purpose to be laid hold of by carabineers and consigned him to Geppetto. Wishing to punish him, Geppetto intended to pull his ears at once. But imagine his feelings when he could not succeed in finding them. And do you know the reason? It was that, in his hurry to model him, he had forgotten to make them.

He then took him by the collar, and as he was leading him away he said to him, shaking his head threateningly: "We will go home at once, and as soon as we arrive we will regulate our accounts, never doubt it."

At this announcement Pinocchio threw himself on the ground and would not take another step. In the mean while a crowd of idlers and inquisitive people began to assemble and to make a ring round them.

Some of them said one thing, some another.

"Poor puppet!" said several, "he is right not to wish to return home! Who knows how Geppetto, that bad old man, will beat him! ..."

The Adventure of Pinocchio

And the others added maliciously: "Geppetto seems a good man! but with boys he is a regular tyrant! If that poor puppet is left in his hands he is quite capable of tearing him in pieces! ..."

It ended in so much being said and done that the carabineer at last set Pinocchio at liberty and conducted Geppetto to prison. The poor man, not being ready with words to defend himself, cried like a calf, and as he was being led away to prison sobbed out:"Wretched boy! And to think how I have laboured to make him a well-conducted puppet! But it serves me right! I should have thought of it sooner! ..."

What happened afterwards is a story that really is past all belief, but I will relate it to you in the following chapters.

Chapter 4

The story of Pinocchio and the Talking-cricket, from which we see that naughty boys cannot endure to be corrected by those who know more than they do.

WELL then, children, I must tell you that whilst poor Geppetto was being taken to prison for no fault of his, that imp Pinocchio, finding himself free from the clutches of the carabineer, ran off as fast as his legs could carry him. That he might reach home the quicker he rushed across the fields, and in his mad hurry he jumped high banks, thorn hedges, and ditches full of water, exactly as a kid or a leveret would have done if pursued by hunters.

Having arrived at the house he found the street door ajar. He pushed it open, went in, and having secured the latch threw himself seated on the ground and gave a great sigh of satisfaction.

But his satisfaction did not last long, for he heard some one in the room who was saying: "Cri-cri-cri!"

"Who calls me?" said Pinocchio in a fright.

"It is I!"

Pinocchio turned round and saw a big cricket crawling slowly up the wall. "Tell me, Cricket, who may you be?"

"I am the Talking-cricket, and I have lived in this room a hundred years and more."

"Now, however, this room is mine, " said the puppet, " and if you would do me a pleasure go away at once, without even turning round."

"I will not go, " answered the Cricket, " until I have told you a great truth."

"Tell it me, then, and be quick about it."

"Woe to those boys who rebel against their parents, and run away capriciously from home. They will never come to any good in the world, and sooner or later they will repent bitterly."

"Sing away, Cricket, as you please, and as long as you please. For me, I have made up my mind to run away tomorrow at daybreak, because if I remain I shall not escape the fate of all other boys; I shall be sent to school and shall be made to study either by love or by force. To tell you in confidence, I have no wish to learn; it is much more amusing to run after butterflies, or to climb trees and to take the young birds out of their nests."

"Poor little goose! But do you not know that in that way you will grow up a perfect donkey, and that every one will make game of you?"

"Hold your tongue, you wicked ill-omened croaker!" shouted Pinocchio.

But the Cricket, who was patient and philosophical, instead of becoming angry at this impertinence, continued in the same tone: "But if you do not wish to go to school why not at least learn a trade, if only to enable you to earn honestly a piece of bread!"

"Do you want me to tell you?" replied Pinocchio, who was beginning to lose patience. "Amongst all the trades in the world there is only one that really takes my fancy."

"And that trade – what is it?"

"It is to eat, drink, sleep, and amuse myself, and to lead a vagabond life from morning to night."

"As a rule, " said the Talking-cricket with the same composure, "all those who follow that trade end almost always either in a hospital or in prison."

"Take care, you wicked ill-omened croaker! Woe to you if I fly into a passion!..."

The Adventure of Pinocchio

"Poor Pinocchio! I really pity you!..."

"Why do you pity me?"

"Because you are a puppet and, what is worse, because you have a wooden head."

At these last words Pinocchio jumped up in a rage, and snatching a wooden hammer from the bench he threw it at the Talking-cricket.

Perhaps he never meant to hit him; but unfortunately it struck him exactly on the head, so that the poor Cricket had scarcely breath to cry cri-cri-cri, and then he remained dried up and flattened against the wall.

Chapter 5

Pinocchio is hungry and searches for an egg to make himself an omelet; but just at the most interesting moment the omelette flies out of the window.

NIGHT was coming on, and Pinocchio, remembering that he had eaten nothing all day, began to feel a gnawing in his stomach that very much resembled appetite.

But appetite with boys travels quickly, and in fact after a few minutes his appetite had become hunger, and in no time his hunger became ravenous - a hunger that was really quite insupportable.

Poor Pinocchio ran quickly to the fire-place where a saucepan was boiling, and was going to take off the lid to see what was in it, but the saucepan was only painted on the wall. You can imagine his feelings. His nose, which was already long, became longer by at least three fingers.

He then began to run about the room, searching in the drawers and in every imaginable place, in hopes of finding a bit of bread. If it was only a bit of dry bread, a crust, a bone left by a dog, a little mouldy pudding of Indian corn, a fish bone, a cherry stone-in fact anything that he could gnaw. But he could find nothing, nothing at all, absolutely nothing.

And in the meanwhile his hunger grew and grew; and poor Pinocchio had no other relief than yawning, and his yawns were so tremendous that sometimes his mouth almost reached his ears. And after he had yawned he spluttered, and felt as if he was going to faint.

Then he began to cry desperately, and he said: "The Talking-cricket was right. I did wrong to rebel against my papa and to run away from home... If my papa was here I should not now be dying of yawning! Oh! What a dreadful illness hunger is!"

Just then he thought he saw something in the dust-heap something round and white that looked like a hen's egg. To give a spring and seize hold of it was the affair of a moment. It was indeed an egg.

Pinocchio's joy beats description; it can only be imagined. Almost believing it must be a dream he kept turning the egg over in his hands, feeling it and kissing it. And as he kissed it he said: "And now, how shall I cook it? Shall I make an omelet?...No, it would be better to cook it in a saucer!...Or would it not be more savoury to fry it in the frying-pan? Or shall I simply boil it? No, the quickest way of all is to cook it in a saucer: I am in such a hurry to eat it!"

Without loss of time he placed an earthenware saucer on a brazier full of red-hot embers. Into the saucer instead of oil or butter he poured a little water; and when the water began to smoke, tac!...he broke the egg-shell over it that the contents might drop in. But instead of the white and the yolk a little chicken popped out very gay and polite. Making a beautiful courtesy it said to him: "A thousand thanks, Master Pinocchio, for saving me the trouble of breaking the shell. Adieu until we meet again. Keep well, and my best compliments to all at home!"

Thus saying it spread its wings, darted through the open window, and flying away was lost to sight.

The poor puppet stood as if he had been bewitched, with his eyes fixed, his mouth open, and the egg-shell in his hand. Recovering, however, from his first stupefaction, he began to cry and scream, and to stamp his feet on the floor in desperation, and amidst his sobs he said: "Ah! indeed the Talkingcricket was right. If I had not run away from home, and if my papa was here, I should not now be dying of hunger! Oh! what a dreadful illness hunger is!..."

And as his stomach cried out more than ever and he did not know how to quiet it, he thought he would leave the house and make an excursion in the neighbourhood in hopes of finding some charitable person who would give him a piece of bread.

Chapter 6

Pinocchio falls asleep with his feet on the brazier, and wakes in the morning to find them burnt off.

IT was a wild and stormy winter's night. The thunder was tremendous and the lightning so vivid that the sky seemed on fire. A bitter blusterous wind whistled angrily, and raising clouds of dust swept over the country, causing the trees to creak and groan as it passed.

Pinocchio had a great fear of thunder, but hunger was stronger than fear. He therefore closed the house door and made a rush for the village, which he reached in a hundred bounds, with his tongue hanging out and panting for breath, like a dog after game.

But he found it all dark and deserted. The shops were closed, the windows shut, and there was not so much as a dog in the street. It seemed the land of the dead.

Pinocchio, urged by desperation and hunger, laid hold of the bell of a house and began to peal it with all his might, saying to himself: "That will bring somebody."

And so it did. A little old man appeared at a window with a nightcap on his head, and called to him angrily: "What do you want at such an hour?"

"Would you be kind enough to give me a little bread?"

"Wait there, I will be back directly, " said the little old man, thinking he had to do with one of those rascally boys who amuse themselves at night by ringing the house bells to rouse respectable people who are sleeping quietly.

After half a minute the window was again opened, and the voice of the same little old man shouted to Pinocchio: "Come underneath and hold out your cap."

Pinocchio pulled off his cap; but just as he held it out an enormous basin of water was poured down on him, watering him from head to foot as if he had been a pot of dired-up geraniums.

He returned home like a wet chicken quite exhausted with fatigue and hunger; and having no longer strength to stand, he sat down and rested his damp and muddy feet on a brazier full of burning embers.

And then he fell asleep; and whilst he slept his feet, which were wooden, took fire, and little by little they burnt away and became cinders.

Pinocchio continued to sleep and to snore as if his feet belonged to some one else. At last about day break he awoke because some one was knocking at the door.

"Who is there?" he asked, yawning and rubbing his eyes.

"It is I!" answered a voice.

And the voice was Geppetto's voice.

Chapter 7

Geppetto returns home, makes the puppet new feet, and gives him the breakfast that the poor man had brought for himself.

POOR Pinocchio, whose eyes were still half shut from sleep, had not as yet discovered that his feet were burnt off. The moment, therefore, that he heard his father's voice he slipped off his stool to run and open the door; but after stumbling two or three times he fell his whole length on the floor.

And the noise he made in falling was as if a sack of wooden ladles had been thrown from a fifth story.

"Open the door!" shouted Geppetto from the street.

"Dear papa, I cannot," answered the puppet, crying and rolling about on the ground.

"Why cannot you?"

"Because my feet have been eaten."

"And who has eaten your feet?"

"The cat, " said Pinocchio, seeing the cat, who was amusing herself by making some shavings dance with her forepaws.

"Open the door, I tell you!" repeated Geppetto. "If you don't, when I get into the house you shall have the cat from me!"

"I cannot stand up, believe me. Oh, poor me! poor me! I shall have to walk on my knees for the rest of my life!..."

Geppetto, believing that all this lamentation was only another of the puppet's tricks, thought of a means of putting an end to it, and climbing up the wall he got in at the window.

He was very angry, and at first he did nothing but scold; but when he saw his Pinocchio lying on the ground and really without feet he was quite overcome. He took him in his arms and began to kiss and caress him and to say a thousand endearing things to him, and as the big tears ran down his cheeks, he said, sobbing: "My little Pinocchio! how did you manage to burn your feet?"

"I don't know, papa, but believe me it has been an infernal night that I shall remember as long as I live. It thundered and lightened, and I was very hungry, " and then the Talking-cricket said to me: "It serves you right; you have been wicked and you deserve it, " and I said to him: "Take care, Cricket!"...and he said: "You are a puppet and you have a wooden head, " and I threw the handle of a hammer at him, and he died, but the fault was his, for I didn't wish to kill him, and the proof of it is that I put an earthenware saucer on a brazier of burning embers, but a chicken flew out and said "Adieu until we meet again, and many compliments to all at home": and I got still more hungry, for which reason that little old man in a nightcap opening the window said to me: "Come underneath and hold out your hat, and poured a basinful of water on my head, because asking for a little bread isn't a disgrace, is it? and I returned home at once, and because I was always very hungry I put my feet on the brazier to dry them, and then you returned, and I found they were burnt off, and I am always hungry, but I have no longer any feet! Ih! Ih! Ih! Ih!..." And poor Pinocchio began to cry and to roar so loudly that he was heard five miles off.

Geppetto, who from all this jumbled account had only understood one thing, which was that the puppet was dying of hunger, drew from his pocket three pears, and giving them to him said: "These three pears were intended for my breakfast; but I will give them to you willingly. Eat them, and I hope they will do you good."

"If you wish me to eat them, be kind enough to peel them for me."

"Peel them?" said Geppetto, astonished. "I should never have thought, my boy, that you were so dainty and fastidious. That is bad! In this world we should accustom ourselves from childhood to like and to eat everything, for there is no saying to what we may be brought. There are so many chances!..."

"You are no doubt right, " interrupted Pinocchio, "but I will never eat fruit that has not been peeled. I cannot bear rind."

So that good Geppetto fetched a knife, and arming himself with patience peeled the three pears, and put the rind on a corner of the table.

Having eaten the first pear in two mouthfuls, Pinocchio was about to throw away the core; but Geppetto caught hold of his arm and said to him: "Do not throw it away; in this world everything may be of use."

"But core I am determined I will not eat, " shouted the puppet, turning upon him like a viper.

"Who knows! there are so many chances!..." repeated Geppetto without losing his temper.

And so the three cores, instead of being thrown out of the window, were placed on the corner of the table together with the three rinds.

Having eaten, or rather having devoured the three pears, Pinocchio yawned tremendously, and then said in a fretful tone: "I am as hungry as ever!"

"But, my boy, I have nothing more to give you!"

"Nothing, really nothing?"

"I have only the rind and the cores ofthe three pears."

"One must have patience!" said Pinocchio; if there is nothing else I will eat a rind."

And he began to chew it. At first he made a wry face; but then one after another he quickly disposed of the rinds: and after the rinds even the cores, and when he had eaten up everything he clapped his hands on his sides in his satisfaction, and said joyfully: "Ah! now I feel comfortable."

"You see now, " observed Geppetto, "that I was right when I said to you that it did not do to accustom ourselves to be too particular or too dainty in our tastes. We can never know, my dear boy, what may happen to us. There are so many chances!..."

Chapter 8

Geppetto makes Pinocchio new feet, and sells his own coat to buy him a Spelling-book.

NO sooner had the puppet appeased his hunger than he began to cry and to grumble because he wanted a pair of new feet.

But Geppetto, to punish him for his naughtiness, allowed him to cry and to despair for half the day. He then said to him: "Why should I make you new feet? To enable you, perhaps, to escape again from home?"

"I promise you, " said the puppet, sobbing, " that for the future I will be good."

"All boys, " replied Geppetto, "when they are bent upon obtaining something, say the same thing."

"I promise you that I will go to school, and that I will study and earn a good character."

"All boys, when they are bent on obtaining something, repeat the same story."

"But I am not like other boys! I am better than all of them and I always speak the truth. I promise you, papa, that I will learn a trade, and that I will be the consolation and the staff of your old age."

Geppetto, although he put on a severe face, had his eyes full of tears and his heart big with sorrow at seeing his poor Pinocchio in such a pitiable state. He did not say another word, but taking his tools and two small pieces of well-seasoned wood he set to work with great diligence.

In less than an hour the feet were finished: two little feet swift, well-knit, and nervous. They might have been modelled by an artist of genius.

Geppetto then said to the puppet: "Shut your eyes and go to sleep!"

And Pinocchio shuthis eyes and pretended to be asleep.

And whilst he pretended to sleep, Geppetto, with a little glue which he had melted in an egg-shell, fastened his feet in their place, and it was so well done that not even a trace could be seen of where they were joined.

No sooner had the puppet discovered that he had feet than he jumped down from the table on which he was lying, and began to spring and to cut a thousand capers about the room, as if he had gone mad with the greatness of his delight.

"To reward you for what you have done for me, " said Pinocchio to his father, "I will go to school at once."

"Good boy."

"But to go to school I shall want some clothes." Geppetto, who was poor, and who had not so much as a farthing in his pocket, then made him a little dress of flowered paper, a pair of shoes from the bark of a tree, and a cap of the crumb of bread.

Pinocchio ran immediately to look at himself in a crock of water, and he was so pleased with his appearance that he said, strutting about like a peacock: "I look quite like a gentleman!"

"Yes indeed, " answered Geppetto, "for bear in mind that it is not fine clothes that make the gentleman, but rather clean clothes."

"By the bye, " added the puppet, "to go to school I am stillin want- indeed I am without the best thing, and the most important."

"And what is it?"

"I have no spelling-book."

"You are right: but what shall we do to get one?"

"It is quite easy. We have only to go to the bookseller's and buy it."

"And the money?"

"I have got none."

"No more have I, " added the good old man very sadly.

And Pinocchio, although he was a very merry boy, became sad also; because poverty, when it is real poverty, is understood by everybody - even by boys.

"Well, patience!" exclaimed Geppetto, all at once rising to his feet, and putting on his old fustian coat, all patched and darned, he ran out of the house.

He returned shortly, holding in his hand a spelling-book for Pinocchio, but the old coat was gone. The poor man was in his shirt sleeves, and out of doors it was snowing.

"And the coat, papa?"

"I have sold it."

"Why did you sell it?"

"Because I found it too hot."

Pinocchio understood this answer in an instant, and unable to restrain the impulse of his good heart he sprang up, and throwing his arms round Geppetto's neck he began kissing him again and again.

Chapter 9

Pinocchio sells his spelling-book that he may go and see a puppet-show.

AS soon as it had done snowing Pinocchio set out for school with his fine spelling-book under his arm. As he went along he began to imagine a thousand things in his little brain, and to build a thousand castles in the air, one more beautiful than the other.

And talking to himself he said: "Today at school I will learn to read at once; then tomorrow I will begin to write, and the day after tomorrow to cipher. Then with my acquirements I will earn a great deal of money, and with the first money I have in my pocket I will immediately buy for my papa a beautiful new cloth coat. But what am I saying? Cloth, indeed! It shall be all made of gold and silver, and it shall have diamond buttons. That poor man really deserves it; for to buy me books and have me taught he has remained in his shirt sleeves…And in this cold! It is only fathers who are capable of such sacrifices!…"

Whilst he was saying this with great emotion he thought that he heard music in the distance that sounded like fifes and the beating of a big drum: fifi-fi, fi-fi-fi, zum, zum, zum, zum.

He stopped and listened. The sounds came from the end of a cross street that took to a little village on the seashore.

"What can that music be? What a pity that I have to go to school, or else…"

And he remained irresolute. It was, however, necessary to come to a decision. Should he go to school? or should he go after the fifes?

"Today I will go and hear the fifes, and tomorrow I will go to school," finally deiced the young scapegrace, shrugging his shoulders.

The more he ran the nearer came the sounds of the fifes and the beating of the big drum: fi-fi-fi, zum, zum, zum, zum.

At last he found himself in the middle of a square quite full of people, who were all crowding round a building made of wood and canvas, and painted a thousand colours.

"What is that building?" asked Pinocchio, turning to a little boy who belonged to the place.

"Read the placard-it is all written-and then you will know."

"I would read it willingly, but it so happens that today I don't know how to read."

"Bravo, blockhead! Then I will read it to you. The writing on that placard in those letters red as fire is:

"GREAT PUPPET THEATRE."

"Has the play begun long?"

"It is beginning now."

"How much does it cost to go in?"

"Twopence."

Pinocchio, who was in a fever of curiosity, lost all control of himself, and without any shame he said to the little boy to whom he was talking: "Would you lend me twopence until tomorrow?"

"I would lend them to you willingly, " said the other, taking him off, "but it so happens that today I cannot give them to you."

"I will sell you my jacket for twopence!" the puppet then said to him.

"What do you think that I could do with a jacket of flowered paper? If there was rain and it got wet, it would be impossible to get it off my back."

"Will you buy my shoes?"

"They would only be of use to light the fire."

"How much will you give me for my cap?"

"That would be a wonderful acquisition indeed! A cap of bread crumb! There would be a risk of the mice coming to eat it whilst it was on my head."

Pinocchio was on thorns. He was on the point of making another offer, but he had not the courage. He hesitated, felt irresolute and remorseful. At last he said: "Will you give me twopence for this new spelling-book?"

"I am a boy and I don't buy from boys," replied his little interlocutor, who had much more sense than he had.

"I will buy the spelling-book for twopence," called out a hawker of old clothes, who had been listening to the conversation.

And the book was sold there and then. And to think that poor Geppetto had remained at home trembling with cold in his shirt sleeves, that he might buy his son a spelling-book!

Chapter 10

The puppets recognise their brother Pinocchio, and receive him with delight; but at that moment their master Fire-eater, makes his appearance and Pinocchio is in danger of coming to a bad end.

WHEN Pinocchio came into the little puppet theatre, an incident occurred that almost produced a revolution.

I must tell you that the curtain was drawn up, and the play had already begun.

On the stage Harlequin and Punchinello were as usual quarrelling with each other, and threatening every moment to come to blows.

The audience, all attention, laughed till they were ill as they listened to the bickerings of these two puppets, who gesticulated and abused each other so naturally that they might have been two reasonable beings, and two persons of the world.

All at once Harlequin stopped short, and turning to the public he pointed with his hand to some one far down in the pit, and exclaimed in a dramatic tone: "Gods of the firmament! do I dream, or am I awake? But surely that is Pinocchio!..."

"It is indeed Pinocchio!" cried Punchinello.

"It is indeed himself!" screamed Miss Rose, peeping from behind the scenes.

"It is Pinocchio! it is Pinocchio!" shouted all the puppets in chorus, leaping from all sides on to the stage. "It is Pinocchio! It is our brother Pinocchio! Long live Pinocchio!..."

"Pinocchio, come up here to me, " cried Harlequin, "and throw yourself into the arms of your wooden brothers!"

At this affectionate invitation Pinocchio made a leap from the end of the pit into the reserved seats; another leap landed him on the head of the leader of the orchestra, and he then sprang upon the stage.

The embraces, the hugs, the friendly pinches, and the demonstrations of warm brotherly affection that Pinocchio received from the excited crowd of actors and actresses of the puppet dramatic company beat description.

The sight was doubtless a moving one, but the public in the pit, finding that the play was stopped, became impatient, and began to shout: "We will have the play - go on with the play!"

It was all breath thrown away. The puppets, instead of continuing the recital, redoubled their noise and outcries, and putting Pinocchio on their shoulders they carried him in triumph before the footlights.

At that moment out came the showman. He was very big, and so ugly that the sight of him was enough to frighten anyone. His beard was as black as ink, and so long that it reached from his chin to the ground. I need only say that he trod upon it when he walked. His mouth was as big as an oven, and his eyes were like two lanterns of red glass with lights burning inside them.

He carried a large whip made of snakes and foxes' tails twisted together, which he cracked constantly.

At his unexpected appearance there was a profound silence: no one dared to breathe. A fly might have been heard in the stillness. The poor puppets of both sexes trembled like so many leaves.

"Why have you come to raise a disturbance in my theatre?" asked the showman of Pinocchio, in the gruff voice of a hob-goblin suffering from a severe cold in the head.

"Believe me, honoured sir, that it was not my fault!..."

"That is enough! To-night we will settle our accounts."

As soon as the play was over the showman went into the kitchen where a fine sheep, preparing for his supper, was turning slowly on the spit in front of the fire. As there was not enough wood to finish roasting and browning it, he called Harlequin and Punchinello, and said to them: "Bring that puppet here: you will find him hanging on a nail. It seems to me that he is made of very dry wood, and I am sure that if he was thrown on the fire he would make a beautiful blaze for the roast."

At first Harlequin and Punchinello hesitated; but, appalled by a severe glance from their master, they obeyed. In a short time they returned to the kitchen carrying poor Pinocchio who was wriggling like an eel taken out of water, and screaming desperately: "Papa! papa! save me! I will not die, I will not die!..."

Chapter 11

Fire-eater sneezes and pardons Pinocchio, who then saves the life of his friend Harlequin.

THE showman Fire-eater for that was his name-looked, I must say, a terrible man, especially with his black beard that covered his chest and legs like an apron. On the whole, however, he had not a bad heart. In proof of this, when he saw poor Pinocchio brought before him, struggling and screaming "I will not die, I will not die!" he was quite moved and felt very sorry for him. He tried to hold out, but after a little he could stand it no longer and he sneezed violently. When he heard the sneeze, Harlequin, who up to that moment had been in the deepest affliction, and bowed down like a weeping willow, became quite cheerful, and leaning towards Pinocchio he whispered to him softly: "Good news, brother. The showman has sneezed, and that is a sign that he pities you, and consequently you are saved."

For you must know that whilst most men, when they feel compassion for somebody, either weep or at least pretend to dry their eyes, Fire-eater, on the contrary, whenever he was really overcome, had the habit of sneezing.

After he had sneezed, the showman, still acting the ruffian, shouted to Pinocchio: "Have done crying! Your lamentations have given me a pain in my stomach...I feel a spasm, that almost...Etci! etci!" and he sneezed again twice.

"Bless you!" said Pinocchio.

"Thank you! And your papa and your mamma, are they still alive?" asked Fire-eater.

"Papa, yes; my mamma I have never known."

"Who can say what a sorrow it would be for your poor old father if I was to have you thrown amongst those burning coals! Poor old man! I compassionate him!...Etci! etci! etci!" and he sneezed again three times.

"Bless you!" said Pinocchio.

"Thank you! All the same, some compassion is due to me, for as you see I have no more wood with which to finish roasting my mutton, and to tell you the truth, under the circumstances you would have been of great use to me! However, I have had pity on you, so I must have patience. Instead of you will bum under the spit one of the puppets belonging to my company. Ho there, gendarmes!"

At this call two wooden gendarmes immediately appeared. They were very long and very thin, and had on cocked hats, and held unsheathed swords in their hands.

The showman said to them in a hoarse voice: " Take Harlequin, bind him securely, and then throw him on the fire to bum. I am determined that my mutton shall be well roasted."

Only imagine that poor Harlequin! His terror was so great that his legs bent under him, and he fell with his face on the ground.

At this agonising sight Pinocchio, weeping bitterly, threw himself at the showman's feet, and bathing his long beard with his tears he began to say in a supplicating voice: "Have pity, Sir Fire-eater!..."

"Here there are no sirs, " the showman answered severely.

"Have pity, Sir Knight!..."

"Here there are no knights!"

"Have pity, Commander!..."

"Here there are no commanders!"

"Have pity, Excellence!..."

Upon hearing himself called Excellence the showman began to

smile, became at once kinder and more tractable. Turning to Pinocchio he asked: "Well, what do you want from me?"

"I implore you to pardon poor Harlequin."

"For him there can be no pardon. As I have spared you he must be put on the fire, for I am determined that my mutton shall be well roasted."

"In that case, "cried Pinocchio proudly, rising and throwing away his cap of bread crumb-"in that case I know my duty. Come on gendarmes! Bind me and throw me amongst the flames. No, it is not just that poor Harlequin, my true friend, should die for me!..."

These words, pronounced in a loud heroic voice, made all the puppets who were present cry. Even the gendarmes, although they were made of wood, wept like two newly-born lambs.

Fire-eater at first remained as hard and unmoved as ice, but little by little he began to melt and to sneeze. And having sneezed four or five times, he opened his arms affectionately, and said to Pinocchio: "You are a good, brave boy! Come here and give me a kiss."

Pinocchio ran at once, and climbing like a squirrel up the showman's beard he deposited a hearty kiss on the point of his nose.

"Then the pardon is granted?" I asked poor Harlequin in a faint voice that was scarcely audible.

"The pardon is granted!" I answered Fire-eater; he then added, sighing and shaking his head: "I must have patience! To-night I shall have to resign myself to eat the mutton half raw; but another time, woe to him who chances!..."

At the news of the pardon the puppets all ran to the stage, and having lighted the lamps and chandeliers as if for a full-dress performance, they began to leap and to dance merrily. At dawn they were still dancing.

The Adventure of Pinocchio

Chapter 12

The showman, Fire-eater, makes Pinocchio a present of five gold pieces to take home to his father, Geppetto; but Pinocchio instead allows himself to be taken in by the Fox and the Cat, and goes with them.

THE following day Fire-eater called Pinocchio on one side and asked him:

"Wha tis your father's name?"

"Geppetto."

"And what trade does he follow?"

"He is a beggar."

"Does he gain much?"

"Gain much? Why, he has never a penny in his pocket. Only think, to buy a Spelling-book for me to go to school he was obliged to sell the only coat he had to wear - a coat that, between patches and darns, was not fit to be seen."

"Poor devil! I feel almost sorry for him! Here are five gold pieces. Go at once and take them to him with my compliments."

You can easily understand that Pinocchio thanked the showman a thousand times. He embraced all the puppets of the company one by one, even to the gendarmes, and beside himself with delight set out to return home.

But he had not gone far when he met on the road a Fox lame of one foot, and a Cat blind of both eyes, who were going along helping each other like good companions in misfortune. The Fox, who was lame, walked leaning on the Cat, and the Cat, who was blind, was guided by the Fox.

"Good day, Pinocchio, " said the Fox, accosting him politely .

"How do you come to know my name?" asked the puppet.

"I know your father well."

"Where did you see him?"

"I saw him yesterday at the door of his house."

"And what was he doing?"

"He was in his shirt sleeves and shivering with cold."

"Poor papa! But that is over; for the future he shall shiver no more!..."

"Why?"

"Because I am become a gentleman."

"A gentleman - you!" said the Fox, and he began to laugh rudely and scornfully. The Cat also began to laugh, but to conceal it she combed her whiskers with her forepaws.

"There is little to laugh at," cried Pinocchio angrily. "I am really sorry to make your mouths water, but if you know anything about it, you can see that these here are five gold pieces."

And he pulled out the money that Fire-eater had made him a present of.

At the sympathetic ring of the money the Fox, with an involuntary movement, stretched out the paw that had seemed crippled, and the Cat opened wide two eyes that looked like two green lanterns. It is true that she shut them again, and so quickly that Pinocchio observed nothing.

"And now," asked the Fox, "what are you going to do with all that money?"

"First of all," answered the puppet, "I intend to buy a new coat for my papa, made of gold and silver, and with diamond buttons; and then I will buy a spelling-book for myself."

"For yourself?"

"Yes indeed: for I wish to go to school to study in earnest."

"Look at me!" said the Fox. "Through my foolish passion for study I have lost a leg."

"Look at me!" said the Cat." Through my foolish passion for study I have lost the sight of both my eyes."

At that moment a white Blackbird, that was perched on the hedge by the road, began his usual song, and said: "Pinocchio, don't listen to the advice of bad companions: if you do you will repent it!..."

Poor Blackbird! If only he had not spoken! The Cat, with a great leap, sprang upon him, and without even giving him time to say Oh! ate him in a mouthful, feathers and all.

Having eaten him and cleaned her mouth she shut her eyes again and feigned blindness as before.

"Poor Blackbird!" said Pinocchio to the Cat, "why did you treat him so badly?"

"I did it to give him a lesson. He will learn another time not to meddle in other people's conversation."

They had gone almost half-way when the Fox, halting suddenly, said to the puppet: "Would you like to double your money?"

"In what way?"

"Would you like to make out of your five miserable sovereigns, a hundred, a thousand, two thousand?"

"I should think so! But in what way?"

"The way is easy enough. Instead of returning home you must go with us." "And where do you wish to take me?"

"To the land of the Owls."

Pinocchio reflected a moment, and then he said resolutely: "No, I will not go. I am already close to the house, and I will return home to my papa who is waiting for me. Who can tell how often the poor old man must have sighed yesterday when I did not come back! I have indeed been a bad son, and the Talking-cricket was right when he said: 'Disobedient boys never come to any good in the world.' I have found it to my cost, for many misfortunes have happened to me. Even yesterday in Fire eater's house I ran the risk...Oh! it makes me shudder only to think of it!"

"Well, then, " said the Fox, " you are quite decided to go home? Go, then, and so much the worse for you."

"So much the worse for you!" repeated the Cat.

"Think well of it, Pinocchio, for you are giving a kick to fortune."

"To fortune!" repeated the Cat.

"Between today and tomorrow your five sovereigns would have become two thousand."

"Two thousand!" repeated the Cat.

"But how is it possible that they could have become so many?" asked Pinocchio, remaining with his mouth open from astonishment.

"I will explain it to you at once," said the Fox. "You must know that in the land of the Owls there is a sacred field called by everybody the Field of Miracles. In this field you must dig a little hole, and you put into it, we will say, one gold sovereign. You then cover up the hole with a little earth: you must water it with two pails of water from the fountain, then sprinkle it with two pinches of salt, and when night comes you can go quietly to bed. In the meanwhile, during the night, the gold piece will grow and flower, and in the morning when you get up and return to the field, what do you find? You find a beautiful tree laden with as many gold sovereigns as a fine ear of corn has grains in the month of June."

"So that," said Pinocchio, more and more bewildered, "supposing I buried my five sovereigns in that field, how many should I find there the following morning?"

"That is an exceedingly easy calculation," replied the Fox, "a calculation that you can make on the ends of your fingers. Put that every sovereign gives you an increase of five hundred: multiply five hundred by five, and the following morning will find you with two thousand five hundred shining gold pieces in your pocket."

"Oh! how delightful!" cried Pinocchio, dancing for joy. "As

soon as ever I have obtained those sovereigns, I will keep two thousand for myself, and the other five hundred I will make a present of to you two."

"A present to us?" cried the Fox with indignation and appearing much offended.

"What are you dreaming of ?"

"What are you dreaming of ?" repeated the Cat.

"We do not work, " said the Fox, "for dirty interest: we work solely to enrich others."

"Others!" repeated the Cat.

"What good people!" thought Pinocchio to himself: and forgetting there and then his papa, the new coat, the spelling-book, and all his good resolutions, he said to the Fox and the Cat: "Let us be off at once. I will go with you."

Chapter 13

The inn of The Red Craw-fish.

THEY walked, and walked, and walked, until at last, towards evening, they arrived dead tired at the Inn of The Red Craw-fish.

"Let us stop here a little, " said the Fox, " that we may have something to eat and rest ourselves for an hour or two. We will start again at midnight, so as to arrive at the Field of miracles by dawn tomorrow morning."

Having gone into the inn they all three sat down to table: but none of them had any appetite.

The Cat, who was suffering from indigestion and feeling seriously indisposed, could only eat thirty-five mullet with tomato sauce, and four portions of tripe with Parmesan cheese; and because she thought the tripe was not seasoned enough, she asked three times for the butter and grated cheese!

The Fox would also willingly have picked a little, but as his doctor had ordered him a strict diet, he was forced to content himself simply with a hare dressed with a sweet and sour sauce, and garnished lightly with fat chickens and early pullets. After the hare he sent for a made dish of partridges, rabbits, frogs, lizards, and other delicacies; he could not touch anything else. He had such a disgust to food, he said, that he could put nothing to his lips.

The one who ate the least was Pinocchio. He asked for some walnuts and a hunch of bread, and left everything on his plate. The poor boy, whose thoughts were continually fixed on the Field of Miracles, had got in anticipation an indigestion of gold pieces.

When they had supped, the Fox said to the host: "Give us two good rooms, one for Mr Pinocchio, and the other for me and my companion. We will snatch a little sleep before we leave. Remember, however, that at midnight we wish to be called to continue our journey."

"Yes, gentlemen, " answered the host, and he winked at the Fox and the Cat, as much as to say: "I know what you are up to. We understand one another!"

No sooner had Pinocchio got into bed than he fell asleep at once and began to dream. And he dreamt that he was in the middle of a field, and the field was full of shrubs covered with clusters of gold sovereigns, and as they swung in the wind they went zin, zin, zin, almost as if they would say: "Let who will, come and take us. " But when Pinocchio was at the most interesting moment, that is, just as he was stretching out his hand to pick handfuls of those beautiful gold pieces and to put them in his pocket, he was suddenly wakened by three violent blows on the door of his room.

It was the host who had come to tell him that midnight had struck. "Are my companions ready?" asked the puppet.

"Ready! Why, they left two hours ago."

"Why were they in such a hurry?"

"Because the Cat had received a message to say that her eldest kitten was ill with chilblains on his feet, and was in danger of death."

"Did they pay for the supper ?"

"What are you thinking of ? They are much too well educated to dream of offering such an insult to a gentleman like you."

"What a pity! It is an insult that would have given me so much pleasure!" said Pinocchio, scratching his head. He then asked: "And where did my good friends say they would wait for me?"

"At the Field of Miracles, tomorrow morning at daybreak."

Pinocchio paid a sovereign for his supper and that of his companions, and then left.

The Adventure of Pinocchio

Outside the inn it was so pitch dark that he had almost to grope his way, for it was impossible to see a hand's breadth in front of him. In the adjacent country not a leaf moved. Only some night-birds flying across the road from one hedge to the other brushed Pinocchio's nose with their wings as they passed, which caused him so much terror that, springing back, he shouted: "who goes there?" and the echo in the surrounding hills repeated in the distance: "Who goes there? Who goes there? Who goes there?"

As he was walking along he saw a little insect shining dimly on the trunk of a tree, like a night-light in a lamp of transparent china.

"Who are you?" asked Pinocchio.

"I am the ghost of the Talking-cricket," answered the insect in a low voice, so weak and faint that it seemed to come from the other world.

"What do you want with me?" said the puppet.

"I want to give you some advice. Go back, and take the four sovereigns that you have left to your poor father, who is weeping and in despair because you have never returned to him."

"By tomorrow my papa will be a gentleman, for these four sovereigns will have become two thousand."

"Don't trust, my boy, to those who promise to make you rich in a day.

Usually they are either mad or rogues! Give ear to me, and go back." "On the contrary, I am determined to go on."

"The hour is late!..."

"I am determined to go on."

"The night is dark!..."

"I am determined to go on."

"The road is dangerous!..."

"I am determined to go on."

"Remember that boys who are bent on following their caprices, and will have their own way, sooner or later repent it."

"Always the same stories. Good-night, Cricket."

"Good-night, Pinocchio, and may Heaven preserve you from dangers and from assassins.

No sooner had he said these words than the Talking-cricket vanished suddenly like a light that has been blown out, and the road became darker than ever.

Chapter 14

> **Pinocchi, because he would not heed the good counsels of the Talking-cricket, falls amongst assassins.**

"REALLY, " said the puppet to himself as he resumed his journey, "how unfortunate we poor boys are. Everybody scolds us, everybody admonishes us, everybody gives us good advice. To let them talk, they would all take it into their heads to be our fathers and our masters - all: even the Talkingcricket. See now; because I don't choose to listen to that tiresome Cricket, who knows, according to him, how many misfortunes are to happen to me! I am even to meet with assassins! That is, however, of little consequence, for I don't believe in assassins-I have never believed in them. For me, I think that assassins have been invented purposely by papas to frighten boys who want to go out at night.

Besides, supposing I was to come across them here in the road, do you imagine they would frighten me? not the least in the world. I should go to meet them and cry: 'Gentlemen assassins, what do you want with me? Remember that with me there is no joking. Therefore go about your business and be quiet!' At this speech, said in a determined tone, those poor assassins - I think I see them - would run away like the wind. If, however, they were so badly educated as not to run away, why, then, I would run away myself, and there would be an end of it..."

But Pinocchio had not time to finish his reasoning, for at that moment he Thought that he heard a slight rustle of leaves behind him.

He turned to look, and saw in the gloom two evil-looking black figures completely enveloped in charcoal sacks. They were running after him on tiptoe, and making great leaps like two phantoms.

"Here they are in reality!" he said to himself, and not knowing where to hide his gold pieces he put them in his mouth precisely under his tongue.

Then he tried to escape. But he had not gone a step when he felt himself seized by the arm, and heard two horrid sepulchral voices saying to him: "Your money or your life!"

Pinocchio, not being able to answer in words, owing to the money that was in his mouth, made a thousand low bows and a thousand pantomimes. He tried thus to make the two muffled figures, whose eyes were only visible through the holes in their sacks, understand that he was a poor puppet, and that he had not as much as a false farthing in his pocket. "Come now! Less nonsense and outwith the money!" cried the two brigands threateningly.

And the puppet made a gesture with his hands to signify: "I have got none.

"Deliver up your money or you are dead, " said the tallest of the brigands.

"Dead!" repeated the other.

"And after we have killed you, we will also kill your father."

"Also your father!"

"No, no, no, not my poor papa!" cried Pinocchio in a despairing tone; and as he said it, the sovereigns clinked in his mouth.

"Ah! you rascal! Then you have hidden your money under your tongue!

Spit it out at once!"

But Pinocchio was obdurate.

"Ah! you pretend to be deaf, do you? Wait a moment, leave it to us to find a means to make you spit it out."

And one of them seized the puppet by the end of his nose, and the other took him by the chin, and began to pull them brutally, the one up and the other down, to constrain him to open his mouth. But it was all to no purpose. Pinocchio's mouth seemed to be nailed and riveted together.

Then the shorter assassin drew out an ugly knife and tried to force it between his lips like a lever or chisel. But Pinocchio, as quick as lightning, caught his hand with his teeth, and with one bite bit it clean off and spat it out. Imagine his astonishment when instead of a hand he perceived that he had spat a cat's paw on to the ground.

Encouraged by this first victory he used his nails to such purpose that he succeeded in liberating himself from his assailants, and jumping the hedge by the roadside he began to fly across country. The assassins ran after him like two dogs chasing a hare: and the one who had lost a paw ran on one leg, and no one ever knew how he managed it.

After a race of some miles Pinocchio could do no more. Giving himself up for lost he climbed the stem of a very high pinetree and seated himself in the topmost branches. The assassins attempted to climb after him, but when they had reached half-way up the stem they slid down again, and arrived on the ground with the skin grazed from their hands and knees.

But they were not to be beaten by so little: collecting a quantity of dry wood they piled it beneath the pine and set fire to it. In less time than it takes to tell the pine began to bum and to flame like a candle blown by the wind. Pinocchio, seeing that the flames were mounting higher every instant, and not wishing to end his life like a roasted pigeon, made a stupendous leap from the top of the tree and started afresh across the fields and vineyards. The assassins followed him, and kept behind him without once giving in.

The day began to break and they were still pursuing him. Suddenly Pinocchio found his way barred by a wide deep ditch full of dirty water the colour of coffee. What was he to do? "One! two! three!" cried the puppet, and making a rush he sprang to the other side. The assassins also jumped, but not having measured the distance properly - splash, splash!... they fell into the very middle of the ditch. Pinocchio, who heard the plunge and the splashing of the water, shouted out, laughing, and without stopping: "A fine bath to you, gentleman assassins."

And he felt convinced that they were drowned, when, turning to look, he perceived that on the contrary they were both running after him, still enveloped in their sacks, with the water dripping from them as if they had been two hollow baskets.

Chapter 15

The assassins pursue Pinocchio; and having overtaken him hang him to a branch of the Big Oak.

AT this sight the puppet's courage failed him, and he was on the point of throwing himself on the ground and giving himself over for lost. Turning, however, his eyes in every direction, he saw at some distance, standing out amidst the dark green of the trees, a small house as white as snow.

"If I had only breath to reach that house, " he said to himself, "perhaps I should be saved."

And without delaying an instant, he recommenced running for his life through the wood, and the assassins after him.

At last, after a desperate race of nearly two hours, he arrived quite breathless atthe door of the house, and knocked.

No one answered.

He knocked again with great violence, for he heard the sound of steps approaching him, and the heavy panting of his persecutors. The same silence. Seeing that knocking was useless he began in desperation to kick and pommel the door with all his might. The window then opened and a beautiful Child appeared at it. She had blue hair and a face as white as a waxen image; her eyes were closed and her hands were crossed on her breast. Without moving her lips in the least, she said in a voice that seemed to come from the other world: "In this house there is no one. They are all dead."

"Then at least open the door for me yourself, " shouted Pinocchio, crying and imploring.

"I am dead also."

"Dead? then what are you doing there at the window?" "I am waiting for the bier to come to carry me away."

Having said this she immediately disappeared, and the window was closed again without the slightest noise.

"Oh! beautiful Child with blue hair, "cried Pinocchio, "open the door for pity's sake! Have compassion on a poor boy pursued by assas-"

But he could not finish the word, for he felt himself seized by the collar, and the same two horrible voices said to him threateningly: "You shall not escape from us again!"

The puppet, seeing death staring him in the face, was taken with such a violent fit of trembling that the joints of his wooden legs began to creak, and the sovereigns hidden under his tongue to clink.

"Now then, " demanded the assassins, "will you open your mouth, yes or no? Ah! no answer...Leave it to us: this time we will force you to open it!..."

And drawing out two long horrid knives as sharp as razors, clash...they attempted to stab him twice.

But the puppet, luckily for him, was made of very hard wood; the knives therefore broke into a thousand pieces, and the assassins were left with the handles in their hands staring at each other.

"I see what we must do, " said one of them. "He must be hung! let us hang him!"

"Let us hang him!" repeated the other.

Without loss of time they tied his arms behind him, passed a running noose round his throat, and then hung him to the branch of a tree called the Big Oak.

They then sat down on the grass and waited for his last struggle. But at the end of three hours the puppet's eyes were still open, his mouth closed, and he was kicking more than ever.

Losing patience they turned to Pinocchio and said in a bantering tone: "Good-bye till tomorrow. Let us hope that when we return you will be polite enough to allow yourself to be found quite dead, and with your mouth wide open."

And they walked off.

In the meantime a tempestuous northerly wind began to blow and roar angrily, and it beat the poor puppet as he hung from side to side, making him swing violently like the clatter of a bell ringing for a wedding. And the swinging gave him atrocious spasms, and the running noose, becoming still tighter round his throat, took away his breath.

Little by little his eyes began to grow dim, but although he felt that death was near he still continued to hope that some charitable person would come to his assistance before it was too late. But when, after waiting and waiting, he found that no one came, absolutely no one, then he remembered his poor father, and thinking he was dying...he stammered out: "Oh, papa! papa! if only you were here!"

His breath failed him and he could say no more. He shut his eyes, opened his mouth, stretched his legs, gave a long shudder, and hung stiff and insensible.

Chapter 16

The beautiful Child with blue hair has the puppet taken down: has him put to bed and calls in three doctors to know if he is alive or dead.

WHILST poor Pinocchio, suspended to a branch of the Big Oak, was apparently more dead than alive, the beautiful Child with blue hair came again to the window. When she saw the unhappy puppet hanging by his throat, and dancing up and down in the gusts of the north wind, she was moved by compassion. Striking her hands together she made three little claps.

At this signal there came a sound of the sweep of wings flying rapidly, and a large Falcon flew on to the window-sill.

"What are your orders, gracious Fairy?" he asked, inclining his beak in sign of reverence - for I must tell you that the Child with blue hair was no more and no less than a beautiful Fairy, who for more than a thousand years had lived in the wood.

"Do you see that puppet dangling from a branch of the Big Oak?"

"I see him."

"Very well. Fly there at once: with your strong beak break the knot that keeps him suspended in the air, and lay him gently on the grass at the foot of the tree."

The Falcon flew away, and after two minutes he returned, saying: "I have done as you commanded."

"And how did you find him?"

"To see him he appeared dead, but he cannot really be quite dead, for I had no sooner loosened the running noose that tightened his throat than, giving a sigh, he muttered in a faint voice: "Now I feel better!..."

The Fairy then striking her hands together made two little claps, and a magnificent Poodle appeared, walking upright on his hind-legs exactly as if he had been a man.

He was in the full-dress livery of a coachman. On his head he had a threecornered cap braided with gold, his curly white wig came down on to his shoulders, he had a chocolate-coloured waistcoat with diamond buttons, and two large pockets to contain the bones that his mistress gave him at dinner. He had besides a pair of short crimson velvet breeches, silk stockings, cutdown shoes, and hanging behind him a species of umbrella-case made of blue satin, to put his tail into when the weather was rainy.

"Be quick, Medora, like a good dog!" said the Fairy to the Poodle. "Have the most beautiful carriage in my coach-house putto, and take the road to the wood. When you come to the Big Oak you will find a poor puppet stretched on the grass half dead. Pick him up gently, and lay him flat on the cushions of the carriage and bring him here to me. Have you understood?"

The Poodle, to show that he had understood, shook the case of blue satin that he had on three or four times, and ran off like a racehorse.

Shortly afterwards a beautiful little carriage came out of the coach-house. The cushions were stuffed with canary feathers, and it was lined in the inside with whipped cream, custard, and Savoy biscuits. The little carriage was drawn by a hundred pairs of white mice, and the Poodle, seated on the coachbox, cracked his whip from side to side like a driver when he is afraid that he is behind time.

A quarter of an hour had not passed when the carriage returned. The Fairy, who was waiting at the door of the house, took the poor puppet in her arms, and carried him into a little room that was wainscotted with mother-of-pearl, and sent at once to summon the most famous doctors in the neighbourhood.

The doctors came immediately one after the other: namely a Crow, an Owl, and a Talking-cricket.

"I wish to know from you gentlemen, "said the Fairy, turning to the three doctors who were assembled round Pinocchio's bed- "I wish to know from you gentlemen, if this unfortunate puppetis alive or dead!..."

At this request the Crow, advancing first, felt Pinocchio's pulse; he then felt his nose, and then the little toe of his foot: and having done this carefully, he pronounced solemnly the following words:

"To my belief the puppet is already quite dead; but if unfortunately he should not be dead, then it would be a sign that he is still alive!"

"I regret, " said the Owl, "to be obliged to contradict the Crow, my illustrious friend and colleague; but in my opinion the puppet is still alive: but if unfortunately he should not be alive, then it would be a sign that he is dead indeed!"

"And you - have you nothing to say?"asked the Fairy of the Talkingcricket.

"In my opinion the wisest thing a prudent doctor can do, when he does not know what he is talking about, is to be silent. For the rest, that puppet there has a face that is not new to me. I have known him for some time!..."

Pinocchio, who up to that moment had lain immovable, like a real piece of wood, was seized with a fit of convulsive trembling that shook the whole bed.

"That puppet there, " continued the Talking-cricket, " is a confirmed rogue..."

Pinocchio opened his eyes, but shut them again immediately.

"He is a ragamuffin, a do-nothing, a vagabond..."

Pinocchio hid his face beneath the clothes.

"That puppet there is a disobedient son who will make his poor father die of a broken heart!..".

At that instant a suffocated sound of sobs and crying was heard in the room. Imagine everybody's astonishment when, having raised the sheets a little, it was discovered that the sounds came from Pinocchio.

"When the dead person cries, it is a sign that he is on the road to get well, " said the Crow solemnly.

"I grieve to contradict my illustrious friend and colleague, " added the Owl; "but for me, when the dead person cries, it is a sign that he is sorry to die."

Chapter 17

Pinocchio eats the sugar, but will not take his medicine: when, however, he sees the grave-diggers, who have arrived to carry him away, he takes it. He then tells a lie, and as a punishmen t his nose grows longer.

AS soon as the three doctors had left the room the Fairy approached Pinocchio, and having touched his forehead she perceived that he was in a high fever that was not to be trifled with.

She therefore dissolved a certain white powder in half a tumbler of water, and offering it to the puppet she said to him lovingly: "Drink it, and in a few days you will be cured."

Pinocchio looked at the tumbler, made a wry face, and then asked in a plaintive voice: "Is it sweet or bitter?"

"It is bitter, but it will do you good."

"If it is bitter, I will not take it."

"Listen to me: drink it."

"I don't like anything bitter."

"Drink it, and when you have drunk it I will give you a lump of sugar to take away the taste."

"Where is the lump of sugar?"

"Here it is, " said the Fairy, taking a piece from a gold sugar-basin.

"Give me first the lump of sugar, and then I will drink that bad bitter water..."

"Do you promise me?"

"Yes..."

The Fairy gave him the sugar, and Pinocchio, having crunched it up and swallowed it in a second, said, licking his lips: "It would be a fine thing if sugar was medicine!...I would take it every day."

"Now keep your promise and drink these few drops of water, which will restore you to health."

Pinocchio took the tumbler unwillingly in his hand and put the point of his nose to it: he then approached it to his lips: he then again put his nose to it, and at last said: "It is too bitter! too bitter! I cannot drink it. ..."

"How can you tell that, when you have not even tasted it?"

"I can imagine it! I know it from the smell. I want first another lump of sugar...and then I will drink it!..."

The Fairy then, with all the patience of a good mamma, put another lump of sugar in his mouth, and then again presented the tumbler to him.

"I cannot drink it so!" said the puppet, making a thousand grimaces.

"Why?"

"Because that pillow that is down there on my feet bothers me."

The Fairy removed the pillow.

"It is useless. Even so I cannot drink it..."

"What is the matter now?"

"The door of the room, which is half open, bothers me."

The Fairy went and closed the door.

"In short, " cried Pinocchio, bursting into tears, "I will not drink that bitter water - no, no, no!..."

"My boy, you will repent it..."

"I don't care..."

"Your illness is serious..."

"I don't care..."

"The fever in a few hours will carry you into the other world..."

"I don't care..."

"Are you not afraid of death?"

"I am not in the least afraid!...I would rather die than drink that bitter medicine."

At that moment the door of the room flew open, and four rabbits as black as ink entered carrying on their shoulders a little bier.

"What do you want with me?" cried Pinocchio, sitting up in bed in a great fright.

"We are come to take you," said the biggest rabbit.

"To take me?...But I am not yet dead!..."

"No, not yet: but you have only a few minutes to live, as you have refused the medicine that would have cured you of the fever."

"Oh, Fairy, Fairy!" the puppet then began to scream, "give me the tumbler at once...be quick, for pity's sake, for I will not die no...I will not die..."

And taking the tumbler in both hands he emptied it at a draught.

"We must have patience!" said the rabbits; "this time we have made our journey in vain." And taking the little bier again on their shoulders they left the room, grumbling and murmuring between their teeth.

In fact, a few minutes afterwards Pinocchio jumped down from the bed quite well: because you must know that wooden puppets have the privilege of being seldom ill and of being cured very quickly.

The Fairy, seeing him running and rushing about the room as gay and as lively as a young cock, said to him: "Then my medicine has really done you good?"

"Good, I should think so! It has restored me to life!..."

"Then why on earth did you require so much persuasion to take it?"

"Because you see that we boys are all like that! We are more afraid of medicine than of the illness."

"Disgraceful! Boys ought to know that a good remedy taken in time may save them from a serious illness, and perhaps even from death..."

"Oh! but another time I shall not require so much persuasion. I shall remember those black rabbits with the bier on their shoulders...and then I shall immediately take the tumbler in my hand, and down it will go!..."

"Now come here to me, and tell me how it came about that you fell into the hands of those assassins."

It came about that the showman Fire-eater gave me some gold pieces and said to me: "Go, and take them to your father!" and instead I met on the road a Fox and a Cat, two very respectable persons, who said to me: "Would you like those pieces of gold to become a thousand or two? Come with us and we will take you to the Field of Miracles, " and I said: "Let us go." And they said: "Let us stop at the Inn of the Red Craw-fish, " and after midnight they left. And when I awoke I found that they were no longer there, because they had gone away. Then I began to travel by night, for you cannot imagine how dark it was; and on that account I met on the road two assassins in charcoal sacks who said to me: "Out with your money, " and I said to them: "I have got none, " because I had hidden the four gold pieces in my mouth, and one of the assassins tried to put his hand in my mouth, and I bit his hand off and spat it out, but instead of a hand I spat out a cat's paw. And the assassins ran after me, and I ran, and ran, until at last they caught me, and tied me by the neck to a tree in this wood, and said to me:" Tomorrow we shall return here, and then you will be dead with your mouth open, and we shall be able to carry off the pieces of gold that you have hidden under your tongue."

"And the four pieces - where have you put them?"asked the Fairy.

"I have lost them!" said Pinocchio; but he was telling a lie, for he had them in his pocket.

He had scarcely told the lie when his nose, which was already long, grew at once two fingers longer.

"And where did you lose them?"

"In the wood near here."

At this second lie his nose went on growing.

"If you have lost them in the wood near here, " said the Fairy, "we will look for them, and we shall find them: because everything that is lost in that wood is always found."

"Ah! now I remember all about it, " replied the puppet, getting quite confused; "I didn't lose the four gold pieces, I swallowed them inadvertently whilst I was drinking your medicine."

At this third lie his nose grew to such an extraordinary length that poor Pinocchio could not move in any direction. If he turned to one side he struck his nose against the bed or the window-panes, if he turned to the other he struck it against the walls or the door, if he raised his head a little he ran the risk of sticking it into one of the Fairy's eyes.

And the Fairy looked at him and laughed.

"What are you laughing at?" asked the puppet, very confused and anxious at finding his nose growing so prodigiously.

"I am laughing at the lie you have told."

"And how can you possibly know that I have told a lie?"

"Lies, my dear boy, are found out immediately, because they are of two sorts. There are lies that have short legs, and lies that have long noses. Your lie, as it happens, is one of those that have a long nose."

Pinocchio, not knowing where to hide himself for shame, tried to run out of the room; but he did not succeed, for his nose had increased so much that it could no longer pass through the door.

Chapter 18

Pinocchio meets again the Fox and the Cat, and goes with them to bury his money in the Field of miracles.

THE Fairy, as you can imagine, allowed the puppet to cry and to roar for a good half-hour over his nose, which could no longer pass through the door of the room. This she did to give him a severe lesson, and to correct him of the disgraceful fault of telling lies - the most disgraceful fault that a boy can have. But when she saw him quite disfigured, and his eyes swollen out of his head from weeping, she felt full of compassion for him. She therefore beat her hands together, and atthat signal a thousand large birds called Woodpeckers flew in at the window. They immediately perched on Pinocchio's nose, and began to peck at it with such zeal that in a few minutes his enormous and ridiculous nose was reduced to its usual dimensions.

"What a good Fairy you are, " said the puppet, drying his eyes, "and how much I love you!"

"I love you also, " answered the Fairy; "and if you will remain with me, you shall be my little brother and I will be your good little sister…"

"I would remain willingly…but my poor papa?"

"I have thought of everything. I have already let your father know, and he will be here to-night."

"Really?" shouted Pinocchio, jumping for joy." Then, little Fairy, if you consent, I should like to go and meet him. I am so anxious to give a kiss to that poor old man, who has suffered so much on my account, that I am counting the minutes."

"Go, then, but be careful not to lose yourself. Take the road through the wood and I am sure that you will meet him."

Pinocchio set out; and as soon as he was in the wood he began to run like a kid. But when he had reached a certain spot, almost in front of the Big Oak, he stopped, because he thought that he heard people amongst the bushes. In fact, two persons came out on to the road. Can you guess who they were?… His two travelling companions, the Fox and the Cat, with whom he had supped at the Inn of the Red Craw-fish,

"Why, here is our dear Pinocchio!" cried the Fox, kissing and embracing him.

"How come you to be here?"

"How come you to be here?" repeated the Cat.

"It is a long story," answered the puppet, " which I will tell you when I have time. But do you know that the other night, when you left me alone at the inn, I met with assassins on the road..."

"Assassins!...Oh, poor Pinocchio! And what did they want?"

"They wanted to rob me of my gold pieces."

"Villains!..."said the Fox.

"Infamous villains!" repeated the Cat.

"But I ran away from them," continued the puppet, "and they followed me: and at last they overtook me and hung me to a branch of that oak-tree..."

And Pinocchio pointed to the Big Oak, which was two steps from them.

"Is it possible to hear of anything more dreadful?" said the Fox. "In what a world we are condemned to live! Where can respectable people like us find a safe refuge?"

Whilst they were thus talking Pinocchio observed that the Cat was lame of her front right leg, for in fact she had lost her paw with all its claws. He therefore asked her: "What have you done with your paw?"

The Cat tried to answer but became confused. Therefore the Fox said immediately: "My friend is too modest, and that is why she doesn't speak. I will answer for her. I must tell you that an hour ago we met an old wolf on the road, almost fainting from want of food, who asked alms of us. Not having so much as a fishbone to give him, what did my friend, who has really the heart of a Caesar, do? She bit off one of her fore paws, and threw it to that poor beast that he might appease his hunger."

And the Fox, in relating this, dried a tear.

Pinocchio was also touched, and approaching the Cat he whispered into her ear: "If all cats resembled you, how fortunate the mice would be!"

"And now, what are you doing here?" asked the Fox of the puppet.

"I am waiting for my papa, whom I expect to arrive every moment."

"And your gold pieces?"

"I have got them in my pocket, all but one that I spent at the Inn of the Red Craw-fish."

"And to think that, instead of four pieces, by tomorrow they might become one or two thousand! Why do you not listen to my advice? why will you not go and bury them in the Field of Miracles?"

"Today itis impossible: I will go another day."

"Another day it will be too late!..."said the Fox.

"Why?"

"Because the field has been bought by a gentleman, and after tomorrow no one will be allowed to bury money there."

"How far off is the Field of Miracles?"

"Not two miles. Will you come with us? In half an hour you will be there. You can bury your money at once, and in a few minutes you will collect two thousand, and this evening you will return with your pockets full. Will you come with us?"

Pinocchio thought of the good Fairy, old Geppetto, and the warnings of the Talking-cricket, and he hesitated a little before answering. He ended, however, by doing as all boys do who have not a grain of sense and who have no heart he ended by giving his head a little shake, and saying to the Fox and the Cat: "Let us go: I will come with you."

And they went.

After having walked half the day they reached a town that was called "Trap for Blockheads." As soon as Pinocchio entered this town, he saw that the streets were crowded with dogs who had lost their coats and who were yawning from hunger, shorn sheep trembling with cold, cocks without combs or crests who were begging for a grain of Indian com, large butterflies who could no longer fly because they had sold their beautiful coloured wings, peacocks who had no tails and were ashamed to be seen, and pheasants who went scratching about in a subdued fashion, mourning for their brilliant gold and silver feathers gone for ever.

In the midst of this crowd of beggars and shame-faced creatures, some lordly carriage passed from time to time containing a Fox, or a thieving Magpie, or some other ravenous bird of prey.

"And where is the Field of Miracles?" asked Pinocchio.

"It is here, not two steps from us."

They crossed the town, and having gone beyond the walls they came to a solitary field which to look at resembled all other fields.

"We are arrived," said the Fox to the puppet. "Now stoop down and dig with your hands a little hole in the ground and put your gold pieces into it."

Pinocchio obeyed. He dug a hole, put into it the four gold pieces that he had left, and then filled up the hole with a little earth.

"Now, then," said the Fox, "go to that canal close to us, fetch a can of water, and water the ground where you have sowed them."

Pinocchio went to the canal, and as he had no can he took off one of his old shoes, and filling it with water he watered the ground over the hole.

He then asked: "Is there anything else to be done?"

"Nothing else," answered the Fox. "We can now go away. You can return in about twenty minutes, and you will find a shrub already pushing through the ground, with its branches quite loaded with money."

The poor puppet, beside himself with joy, thanked the Fox and the Cat a thousand times, and promised them a beautiful present.

"We wish for no presents," answered the two rascals. "It is enough for us to have taught you the way to enrich yourself without undergoing hard work, and we are as happy as folk out for a holiday."

Thus saying they took leave of Pinocchio, and, wishing him a good harvest, went about their business.

Chapter 19

Pinocchio is robbed of his money, and as a punishment he is sent to prison for four months.

THE puppet returned to the town and began to count the minutes one by one; and when he thought that it must be time he took the road leading to the Field of Miracles.

And as he walked along with hurried steps his heart beat fast tic, tac, tic, tac, like a drawing-room clock when it is really going well Meanwhile he was thinking to himself: "And if instead of a thousand gold pieces, I was to find on the branches of the tree two thousand?...And instead of two thousand supposing I found five thousand? and instead of five thousand that I found a hundred thousand? Oh! what a fine gentleman I should then become!...

I would have a beautiful palace, a thousand little wooden horses and a thousand stables to amuse myself with, a cellar full of currant-wine and sweet syrups, and a library quite full of candies, tarts, plum-cakes, macaroons, and biscuits with cream."

Whilst he was building these castles in the air he had arrived in the neighbourhood of the field, and he stopped to look if by chance he could perceive a tree with its branches laden with money: but he saw nothing. He advanced another hundred steps-nothing: he entered the field... he went right up to the little hole where he had buried his sovereigns-and nothing. He then became very thoughtful, and forgetting the rules of society and good manners he took his hands out of his pocket and gave his head a long scratch.

At that moment he heard an explosion of laughter close to him, and looking up he saw a large Parrot perched on a tree, who was pruning the few feathers he had left.

"Why are you laughing?" asked Pinocchio in an angry voice.

"I am laughing because in pruning my feathers I tickled myself under my wings.

The puppet did not answer, but went to the canal and, filling the same old shoe full of water, he proceeded to water the earth afresh that covered his gold pieces.

Whilst he was thus occupied another laugh, and still more impertinent than the first, rang out in the silence of that solitary place.

"Once for all, " shouted Pinocchio in a rage, "may I know, you ill-educated Parrot, what you are laughing at?"

"I am laughing at those simpletons who believe in all the foolish things that are told them, and who allow themselves to be entrapped by those who are more cunning than they are."

"Are you perhaps speaking of me?"

"Yes, I am speaking of you, poor Pinocchio-of you who are simple enough to believe that money can be sown and gathered in fields in the same way as beans and gourds. I also believed it once, and today I am suffering for it. Today-but it is too late-I have at last learnt that to put a few pennies honestly together it is necessary to know how to earn them, either by the work of our own hands or by the cleverness of our own brains."

"I don't understand you, " said the puppet, who was already trembling with fear.

"Have patience! I will explain myself better, " rejoined the Parrot. "You must know, then, that whilst you were in the town the Fox and the Cat returned to the field: they took the buried money and then fled like the wind. And now he that catches them will be clever."

Pinocchio remained with his mouth open, and not choosing to believe the Parrot's words he began with his hands and nails to dig up the earth that he had watered. And he dug, and dug, and dug, and made such a deep hole that a rick of straw might have stood up right in it: but the money was no longer there.

He rushed back to the town in a state of desperation, and went at once to the Courts of Justice to denounce the two knaves who had robbed him to the judge.

The judge was a big ape of the gorilla tribe-an old ape respectable for his age, his white beard, but especially for his gold spectacles without glasses that he was always obliged to wear, on account of an inflammation of the eyes that had tormented him for many years.

Pinocchio related in the presence of the judge all the particulars of the in famous fraud of which he had been the victim. He gave the names, the surnames, and other details, of the two rascals, and ended by demanding justice.

The judge listened with great benignity; took a lively interest in the story; was much touched and moved; and when the puppet had nothing further to say he stretched out his hand and rang a bell.

At this summons two mastiffs immediately appeared dressed as gendarmes. The judge then, pointing to Pinocchio, said to them: "That poor devil has been robbed of four gold pieces; take him up, and put him immediately into prison.

The puppet was petrified on hearing this unexpected sentence, and tried to protest; but the gendarmes, to avoid losing time, stopped his mouth, and carried him off to the lock-up.

And there he remained for four months-four long months - and he would have remained longer still if a fortunate chance had not released him. For I must tell you that the young Emperor who reigned over the town of "Trap for blockheads, " having won a splendid victory over his enemies, ordered great public rejoicings. There were illuminations, fire-works, horse races, and velocipede races, and as a further sign of triumph he commanded that the prisons should be opened and all the prisoners liberated.

"If the others are to be let out of prison, I will go also, " said Pinocchio to the jailor.

"No, not you, " said the jailor, "because you do not belong to the fortunate class."

"I beg your pardon, " replied Pinocchio, "I am also a criminal."

"In that case you are perfectly right, " said the jailor; and taking off his hat and bowing to him respectfully he opened the prison doors and let him escape.

The Adventure of Pinocchio

Chapter 20

Liberated from prison, he starts to return to the Fairy's house; but on the road he meets with a horrible Serpent, and afterwards he is caught in a trap.

YOU can imagine Pinocchio's joy when he found himself free. Without stopping to take breath he immediately left the town and took the road that led to the Fairy's house.

On account of the rainy weather the road had become a marsh into which he sank knee-deep. But the puppet would not give in. Tormented by the desire of seeing his father and his little sister with blue hair again he ran and leapt like a grey-hound, and as he ran he was splashed with mud from head to foot. And he said to himself as he went along: "How many misfortunes have happened to me... and I deserved them! for I am an obstinate, passionate puppet...I am always bent upon having my own way, without listening to those who wish me well, and who have a thousand times more sense than I have!... But from this time forth I am determined to change and to become orderly and obedient...For at last I have seen that disobedient boys come to no good and gain nothing. And will my papa have waited for me? Shall I find him at the Fairy's house! Poor man, it is so long since I last saw him: I am dying to embrace him, and to cover him with kisses! And will the Fairy forgive me my bad conduct to her?...To think of all the kindness and loving care I received from her...to think that if I am now alive I owe it to her!... Would it be possible to find a more ungrateful boy, or one with less heart than I have!..."

Whilst he was saying this he stopped suddenly, frightened to death, and made four steps backwards.

What had he seen?...

He had seen an immense Serpent stretched across the road. Its skin was green, it had red eyes, and a pointedtail that was smoking like a chimney.

It would be impossible to imagine the puppet's terror. He walked away to a safe distance, and sitting down on a heap of stones waited until the Serpent should have gone about its business and had left the road clear.

He waited an hour; two hours; three hours; but the Serpent

was always there, and even from a distance he could see the red light of his fiery eyes and the column of smoke that ascended from the end of his tail.

At last Pinocchio, trying to feel courageous, approached to within a few steps, and said to the Serpent in a little, soft, insinuating voice: "Excuse me, Sir Serpent, but would you be so good as to move a little to one side, just enough to allow me to pass?"

He might as well have spoken to the wall. Nobody moved.

He began again in the same soft voice: "You must know, Sir Serpent, that I am on my way home, where my father is waiting for me, and it is such a long time since I saw him last!...Will you therefore allow me to continue my road?"

He waited for a sign in answer to this request, but there was none: in fact the Serpent, who up to that moment had been sprightly and full of life, became motionless and almost rigid. He shut his eyes and his tail ceased smoking.

"Can he really be dead?" said Pinocchio, rubbing his hands with delight; and he determined to jump over him and reach the other side of the road. But just as he was going to leap the Serpent raised himself suddenly on end, like a spring set in motion; and the puppet, drawing back, in his terror caught his feet and fell to the ground.

And he fell so awkwardly that his head stuck in the mud and his legs went into the air.

At the sight of the puppet kicking violently with his head in the mud the Serpent went into convulsions of laughter, and he laughed, and laughed, and laughed, until from the violence of his laughter he broke a blood-vessel in his chest and died. And that time he was really dead.

Pinocchio then set off running in hopes that he should reach the Fairy's house before dark. But before long he began to suffer so dreadfully from hunger that he could not bear it, and he jumped into a field by the wayside intending to pick some bunches of muscatel grapes. Oh, that he had never done it!

He had scarcely reached the vines when crac... his legs were caught between two cutting iron bars, and he became so giddy with pain that stars of every colour danced before his eyes.

The poor puppet had been taken in a trap put there to capture some big polecats who were the scourge of the poultry-yards in the neighbourhood.

Chapter 21

Pinocchio is taken by a peasant, who obliges him to fill the place of his watch-dog in the poultry-yard.

PINOCCHIO, as you can imagine, began to cry and scream: but his tears and groans were useless, for there was not a house to be seen, and not a living soul passed down the road.

At last night came on.

Partly from the pain of the trap that cut his legs, and a little from fear at finding himself alone in the dark in the midst of the fields, the puppet was on the point of fainting. Just at that moment he saw a Firefly flitting over his head. He called to it and said: "Oh, little Firefly, will you have pity on me and liberate me from this torture?"

"Poor boy!" said the Firefly, stopping and looking at him with compassion, "but how could your legs have been caught by those sharp irons?"

"I came into the field to pick two bunches of these muscatel grapes, and..."

"But were the grapes yours?"

"No..."

"Then who taught you to carry off other people's property?"

"I was so hungry..."

"Hunger, my boy, is not a good reason for appropriating what does not belongto us..."

"That is true, that is true!" said Pinocchio, crying. "I will never do it again. "

At this moment their conversation was interrupted by a slight sound of approaching footsteps. It was the owner of the field coming on tiptoe to see if one of the polecats that ate his chickens during the night had been caught in his trap.

His astonishment was great when, having brought out his lantern from under his coat, he perceived that instead of a polecat a boy had been taken.

"Ah, little thief" said the angry peasant, "then it is you who carry off my chickens?"

"No, it is not I; indeed it is not!" cried Pinocchio, sobbing." I only came into the field to take two bunches of grapes!..."

"He who steals grapes is quite capable of stealing chickens. Leave itto me, I will give you a lesson that you will not forget in a hurry."

Opening the trap he seized the puppet by the collar, and carried him to his house as if he had been a young lamb.

When he reached the yard in front of the house he threw him roughly on the ground, and putting his foot on his neck he said to him: "It is late, and I want to go to bed; we will settle our accounts tomorrow. In the meanwhile, as the dog who kept guard at night died today, you shall take his place at once. You shall be my watch-dog."

And taking a great collar covered with brass knobs he strapped it tightly round his throat that he might not be able to draw his head out of it. A heavy chain attached to the collar was fastened to the wall.

"If it should rain to-night, " he then said to him, "you can go and lie down in the kennel; the straw that has served as a bed for my poor dog for the last four years is still there. If unfortunately robbers should come, remember to keep your ears pricked and to bark."

After giving him this last injunction the man went into the house, shut the door, and put up the chain.

Poor Pinocchio remained lying on the ground more dead than alive from the effects of cold, hunger, and fear. From time to time he put his hands angrily to the collar that tightened his throat and said, crying: "It serves me right!...Decidedly it serves me right! I was determined to be a vagabond and a good-for-nothing... I would listen to bad companions, and that is why I always meet with misfortunes. If I had been a good little boy as so many are; if I had been willing to learn and to work; if I had remained at home with my poor papa, I should not now be in the midst of the fields and obliged to be the watch-dog to a peasant's house. Oh, if I could be born again! But now it is too late, and I must have patience!"

Relieved by this little outburst, which came straight from his heart, he went into the dog-kennel and fell asleep.

Chapter 22

Pinocchio discovers the robbers, and as a reward for his fidelity is set at liberty.

HE had been sleeping heavily for about two hours when, towards midnight, he was roused by a whispering of strange voices that seemed to come from the courtyard. Putting the point of his nose out of the kennel he saw four little beasts with dark fur, that looked like cats, standing consulting together. But they were not cats; they were polecats-carnivorous little animals, especially greedy for eggs and young chickens. One of the pole-cats, leaving his companions, came to the opening of the kennel and said in a low voice: "Good evening, Melarapo."

"My name is not Melampo," answered the puppet.

"Oh! then who are you??:

"I am Pinocchio."

"And what are you doing here?"

"I am acting as watch-dog."

"Then where is Melampo? Where is the old dog who lived in this kennel?" "He died this morning."

"Is he dead? Poor beast! He was so good. But judging you by your face I should say that you were also a good dog."

"I beg your pardon, I am not a dog."

"Not a dog? Then what are you?"

"I am a puppet."

"And you are acting as watch-dog?"

"That is only too true-as a punishment."

"Well, then, I will offer you the same conditions that we made with the deceased Melampo, and I am sure you will be satisfied with them."

"What are these conditions?"

"One night in every week you are to permit us to visit this poultry-yard as we have hither to done, and to carry off eight chickens. Of these chickens seven are to be eaten by us, and one we will give to you, on the express understanding, however, that you pretend to be asleep, and that it never enters your head to bark and to wake the peasant."

"Did Melampo actin this manner?" asked Pinocchio.

"Certainly, and we were always on the best terms with him. Sleep quietly, and rest assured that before we go we will leave by the kennel a beautiful chicken ready plucked for your breakfast tomorrow. Have we understood each other clearly?"

"Only too clearly!..." answered Pinocchio, and he shook his head threateningly as much as to say: "You shall hear of this shortly!"

The four polecats thinking themselves safe repaired to the poultry-yard, which was close to the kennel, and having opened the wooden gate with their teeth and claws, they slipped in one by one. But they had only just passed through when they heard the gate shut behind them with great violence.

It was Pinocchio who had shut it; and for greater security he put a large stone against it to keep it closed.

He then began to bark, and he barked exactly like a watch-dog: bow-wow, bow-wow.

Hearing the barking the peasant jumped out of bed, and taking his gun he came to the window and asked: "What is the matter?"

"There are robbers!" answered Pinocchio.

"Where are they?"

"In the poultry-yard."

"I will come down directly."

In fact, in less time than it takes to say Amen, the peasant came down. He rushed into the poultry-yard, caught the polecats, and having put them into a sack, he said to them in a tone of great satisfaction: "At last you have fallen into my hands! I might punish you, but I am not so cruel. I will content myself instead by carrying you in the morning to the innkeeper of the neighbouring village, who will skin and cook you as hares with a sweet and sour sauce. It is an honour that you don't deserve, but generous people like me don't consider such trifles!..."

He then approached Pinocchio and began to caress him, and amongst other things he asked him: "How did you manage to discover the four thieves? To think that Melampo, my faithful Melampo, never found out anything!..."

The puppet might then have told him the whole story; he might have informed him of the disgraceful conditions that had been made between the dog and the polecats; but he remembered that the dog was dead, and he thought to himself: "What is the good of accusing the dead?...The dead are dead, and the best thing to be done is to leave them in peace!..."

"When the thieves got into the yard were you asleep or awake?" the peasant went on to ask him.

"I was asleep," answered Pinocchio, "but the polecats woke me with their chatter, and one of them came to the kennel and said to me: 'If you promise not to bark, and not to wake the master, we will make you a present of a fine chicken ready plucked!...' To think that they should have had the audacity to make such a proposal to me! For although I am a puppet, possessing perhaps nearly all the faults in the world, there is one that I certainly will never be guilty of, that of making terms with, and sharing in the gains of, dishonest people!"

"Well said, my boy!" cried the peasant, slapping him on the shoulder. "Such sentiments do you honour: and as a proof of my gratitude I will at once set you at liberty, and you may return home."

And he removed the dog's collar.

Chapter 23

Pinocchio mourns the death of the beautiful Child with the blue hair. He then meets with a Pigeon who flies with him to the seashore, and there he throws himself into the water to go to the assistance of his father Geppetto.

AS soon as Pinocchio was released from the heavy and humiliating weight of the dog-collar he started off across the fields, and never stopped until he had reached the high road that led to the Fairy's house. There he turned and looked down into the plain beneath. He could see distinctly with his naked eye the wood where he had been so unfortunate as to meet with the Fox and the Cat; he could see amongst the trees the top of the Big Oak to which he had been hung; but although he looked in every direction the little house belonging to the beautiful Child with the blue hair was nowhere visible.

Seized with a sad presentiment he began to run with all the strength he had left, and in a few minutes he reached the field where the little white house had once stood. But the little white house was no longer there. He saw instead a marble stone, on which were engraved these sad words:

HERE LIES
THE CHILD WITH THE BLUE HAIR
WHO DIED FROM SORROW
BECAUSE SHE WAS ABANDONED BY HER
LITTLE BROTHER PINOCCHIO

I leave you to imagine the puppet's feelings when he had with difficulty spelt out this epitaph. He fell with his face on the ground and, covering the tombstone with a thousand kisses, burst into an agony of tears. He cried all night, and when morning came he was still crying although he had no tears left, and his sobs and lamentations were so acute and heart-breaking that they roused the echoes in the surrounding hills.

And as he wept he said: "Oh, little Fairy, why did you die? Why did not I die instead of you, I who am so wicked, whilst you were so good?... And my papa? Where can he be? Oh, little Fairy, tell me where I can find him, for I want to remain with him always and never to leave him again, never again!... Oh, little Fairy, tell me that it is not true that you are dead!... If you really love me...if you really love your little brother, come to life again...come to life as you were before!...Does it not grieve you to see me alone and abandoned by everybody?...If assassins come they will hang me again to the branch of a tree...and then I should die indeed. What do you imagine that I can do here alone in the world? Now that I have lost you and my papa, who will give me food? Where shall I go to sleep at night? Who will make me a new jacket?

Oh, it would be better, a hundred times better, that I should die also! Yes, I want to die...ih! ih! ih!"

And in his despair he tried to tear his hair; but his hair, being made of wood, he could not even have the satisfaction of sticking his fingers into it.

Just then a large pigeon flew over his head, and stopping with distended wings called down to him from a great height: "Tell me, child, what are you doing there?"

"Don't you see? I am crying!" said Pinocchio, raising his head towards the voice and rubbing his eyes with his jacket.

"Tell me, " continued the Pigeon, "amongst your companions, do you happen to know a puppet who is called Pinocchio?"

"Pinocchio?...Did you say Pinocchio?" repeated the puppet, jumping quickly to his feet. "I am Pinocchio!"

The Pigeon at this answer descended rapidly to the ground. He was larger than a turkey.

"Do you also know Geppetto?" he asked.

"If I know him! He is my poor papa! Has he perhaps spoken to you of me? Will you take me to him? Is he still alive? Answer me for pity's sake: is he still alive?"

"I left him three days ago on the sea-shore."

"What was he doing?"

"He was building a little boat for himself, to cross the ocean. For more than three months that poor man has been going all round the world looking for you. Not having succeeded in finding you he has now taken it into his head to go to the distant countries of the new world in search of you."

"How far is it from here to the shore?" asked Pinocchio breathlessly. "More than six hundred miles."

"Six hundred miles? Oh, beautiful Pigeon, what a fine thing it would be to have your wings!..."

"If you wish to go, I will carry you there."

"How?"

"Astride on my back. Do you weigh much?"

"I weigh next to nothing. I am as light as a feather."

And without waiting for more Pinocchio jumped at once on the Pigeon's back, and putting a leg on each side of him as men do on horseback, he exclaimed joyfully: "Gallop, gallop, my little horse, for I am anxious to arrive quickly!..."

The Pigeon took flight, and in a few minutes had soared so high that they almost touched the clouds. Finding himself at such an immense height the puppet had the curiosity to turn and look down; but his head spun round, and he became so frightened, that to save himself from the danger of falling he wound his arms tightly round the neck of his feathered steed.

They flew all day. Towards evening the Pigeon said: "I am very thirsty!" And I am very hungry!" rejoined Pinocchio.

"Let us stop at that dovecot for a few minutes; and then we will continue our journey that we may reach the seashore by dawn to-morrow."

They went into a deserted dovecot, where they found nothing but a basin full of water and a basket full of vetch.

The puppet had never in his life been able to eat vetch: according to him it made him sick and revolted him. That evening, however, he ate to repletion, and when he had nearly emptied the basket he turned to the Pigeon and said to him: "I never could have believed that vetch was so good!"

"Be assured, my boy, " replied the Pigeon, "that when hunger is real, and there is nothing else to eat, even vetch becomes delicious. Hunger knows neither caprice nor greediness."

Having quickly finished their little meal they recommenced

their journey and flew away. The following morning they reached the seashore.

The pigeon placed Pinocchio on the ground, and not wishing to be troubled with thanks for having done a good action, flew quickly away and disappeared.

The shore was crowded with people who were looking out to sea, shouting and gesticulating.

"What has happened?" asked Pinocchio of an old woman.

"A poor father who has lost his son has gone away in a boatto search for him on the other side of the water, and today the sea is tempestuous and the little boat is in danger of sinking."

"Where is the little boat?"

"It is out there in a line with my finger, " said the old woman, pointing to a little boat which, seen at that distance, looked like a nutshell with a very little man in it.

Pinocchio fixed his eyes on it, and after looking attentively he gave a piercing scream, crying: "It is my papa! It is my papa!"

The boat meanwhile, beaten by the fury of the waves, at one moment disappeared in the trough of the sea, and the next came again to the surface. Pinocchio, standing on the top of a high rock, kept calling to his father by name, and making every kind of signal to him with his hands, his handkerchief, and his cap.

And although he was so far off, Geppetto appeared to recognise his son, for he also took off his cap and waved it, and tried by gestures to make him understand that he would have returned if it had been possible, but that the sea was so tempestuous that he could not use his oars or approach the shore.

Suddenly a tremendous wave rose and the boat disappeared. They waited, hoping it would come again to the surface, but it was seen no more.

"Poor man!" said the fishermen who were assembled on the shore, and murmuring a prayer they turned to go home.

Just then they heard a desperate cry, and looking back they saw a little boy who exclaimed, as he jumped from a rock into the sea: "I will save my papa!"

Pinocchio, being made of wood, floated easily and he swam like a fish. At one moment they saw him disappear under the water, carried down by the fury of the waves; and next he reappeared struggling with a leg or an arm. At last they lost sight of him, and he was seen no more.

"Poor boy!" said the fishermen who were collected on the shore, and murmuring a prayer they returned home.

Chapter 24

Pinocchio arrives at the island of the "Industrious Bees" and finds the Fairy again.

PINOCCHIO, hoping to be in time to help his father, swam the whole night.

And what a horrible night it was! The rain came down in torrents, it hailed, the thunder was frightful, and the flashes of lightning made it as light as day Towards morning he saw a long strip of land not far off. It was an island in the midst of the sea.

He tried his utmost to reach the shore: but it was all in vain. The waves, racing and tumbling over each other, knocked him about as if he had been a stick or a wisp of straw. At last, fortunately for him, a billow rolled up with such fury and impetuosity that he was lifted up and thrown violently far on to the sands.

He fell with such force that, as he struck the ground, his ribs and all his joints cracked, but he comforted himself, saying: "This time also I have made a wonderful escape!"

Little by little the sky cleared, the sun shone out in all his splendour, and the sea became as quiet and smooth as oil.

The puppet put his clothes in the sun to dry, and began to look in every direction in hopes of seeing on the vast expanse of water a little boat with a little man in it. But although he looked and looked, he could see nothing but the sky, and the sea, and the sail of some ship, but so far away that it seemed no bigger than a fly.

"If I only knew what this island was called!" he said to himself. "If I only knew whether it was inhabited by civilised people -I mean by people who have not got the bad habit of hanging boys to the branches of the trees. But who can I ask? who, if there is nobody?..."

This idea of finding himself alone, alone, all alone, in the midst of this great uninhabited country, made him so melancholy that he was just beginning to cry. But at that moment, at a short distance from the shore, he saw a big fish swimming by; it was going quietly on its own business with its head out of the water.

Not knowing its name the puppet called to it in a loud voice to make himself heard: "Eh, Sir fish, will you permit me a word with you?"

"Two if you like, " answered the fish, who was a Dolphin, and so polite that few similar are to be found in any sea in the world.

"Will you be kind enough to tell me if there are villages in this island where it would be possible to obtain something to eat, without running the danger of being eaten?"

"Certainly there are," replied the Dolphin. "Indeed you will find one at a short distance from here."

"And what road must I take to go there?"

"You must take that path to your left and follow your nose. You cannot make a mistake."

"Will you tell me another thing? You who swim about the sea all day and all night, have you by chance met a little boat with my papa in it?"

"And who is your papa?"

"He is the best papa in the world, whilst it would be difficult to find a worse son than I am."

"During the terrible storm last night," answered the Dolphin, "the little boat must have gone to the bottom."

"And my papa?"

"He must have been swallowed by the terrible Dog-fish who for some days Past has been spreading devastation and ruin in our waters."

"Is this Dog-fish very big?" asked Pinocchio, who was already beginning to quake with fear.

"Big!..." replied the Dolphin. "That you may form some idea of his size, I need only tell you that he is bigger than a five-storied house, and that his mouth is so enormous and so deep that a railway train with its smoking engine could pass easily down his throat."

"Mercy upon us!" exclaimed the terrified puppet; and putting on his clothes with the greatest haste he said to the Dolphin: "Good-bye, Sir fish: excuse the trouble I have given you, and many thanks for your politeness."

He then took the path that had been pointed out to him and began to walk fast-so fast, indeed, that he was almost running. And at the slightest noise he turned to look behind him, fearing that he might see the terrible Dog-fish with a railway train in its mouth following him.

After a walk of half an hour he reached a little village called "The village of the Industrious Bees." The road was alive with people running here and there to attend to their business: all were at work, all had something to do. You could not have found an idler or a vagabond, not even if you had searched for him with a lighted lamp.

"Ah!" said that lazy Pinocchio at once, "I see that this village will never suit me! I wasn't born to work!"

In the meanwhile he was tormented by hunger, for he had eaten nothing for twenty-four hours-not even vetch. What was he to do?

There were only two ways by which he could obtain food-either by asking for a little work, or by begging for a halfpenny or for a mouthful of bread.

He was ashamed to beg, for his father had always preached to him that no one had a right to beg except the aged and the infirm. The really poor in this world, deserving of compassion and assistance, are only those who from age or sickness are no longer able to earn their own bread with the labour of their hands. It is the duty of every one else to work; and if they will not work, so much the worse for them if they suffer from hunger.

At that moment a man came down the road, tired and panting for breath. He was dragging alone, with fatigue and difficulty, two carts full of charcoal. Pinocchio, judging by his face that he was a kind man, approached him, and casting down his eyes with shame he said to him in a low voice: "Would you have the charity to give me a halfpenny, for I am dying of hunger?"

"You shall have not only a halfpenny, " said the man, "but I will give you twopence, provided that you help me to drag home these two carts of charcoal."

"I am surprised at you!" answered the puppet in a tone of offence. "Let me tell you that I am not accustomed to do the work of a donkey: I have never drawn a cart!..".

"So much the better for you, " answered the man. "Then, my boy, if you are really dying of hunger, eat two fine slices of your pride, and be careful not to get an indigestion."

A few minutes afterwards a mason passed down the road carrying on his shoulders a basket of lime.

"Would you have the charity, good man, to give a half penny to a poor boy who is yawning for want of food?"

"Willingly, " answered the man. "Come with me and carry the lime, and instead of a halfpenny I will give you five."

"But the lime is heavy, " objected Pinocchio, "and I don't want to tire myself."

"If you don't want to tire yourself, then, my boy, amuse yourself with yawning, and much good may it do you."

In less than half an hour twenty other people went by; and Pinocchio asked charity of them all, but they all answered: "Are you not ashamed to beg? Instead of idling about the roads, go and look for a little work and learn to earn your bread, "

At last a nice little woman carrying two cans of water came by.

"Will you let me drink a little water out of your can?" asked Pinocchio, who was burning with thirst.

"Drink, my boy, if you wish it!" said the little woman, setting down the two cans.

Pinocchio drank like a fish, and as he dried his mouth he mumbled: "I have quenched my thirst. If I could only appease my hunger!.."

The good woman hearing these words said at once: "If you will help me to carry home these two cans of water, I will give you a fine piece of bread."

Pinocchio looked at the can and answered neither yes nor no.

"And besides the bread you shall have a nice dish of cauliflower dressed with oil and vinegar, " added the good woman.

Pinocchio gave another look at the can, and answered neither yes nor no. "And after the cauliflower I will give you a beautiful bonbon full of syrup."

The temptation of this last dainty was so great that Pinocchio could resist no longer, and with an air of decision he said: "I must have patience! I will carry the can to your house."

The can was heavy, and the puppet not being strong enough to carry it in his hand, had to resign himself to carry it on his head.

When they reached the house the good little woman made Pinocchio sit down at a small table already laid, and she placed before him the bread, the cauliflower, and the bonbon.

Pinocchio did not eat, he devoured. His stomach was like an apartment that had been left empty and uninhabited for five months.

When his ravenous hunger was somewhat appeased he raised his head to thank his benefactress; but he had no sooner looked at her than he gave a prolonged Oh-h-h! of astonishment, and continued staring at her, with wide open eyes, his fork in the air, and his mouth full of bread and cauliflower, as if he had been bewitched.

"What has surprised you so much?" I asked the good woman, laughing.

"It is..." answered the puppet, "it is... it is... that you are like... that you remind me...yes, yes, yes, the same voice...the same eyes... the same hair... yes, yes, yes...you also have blue hair...as she had... Oh, little Fairy!...tell me that it is you, really you!...Do not make me cry any more! If you knew... I have cried so much, I have suffered so much..."

And throwing himself at her feet on the floor, Pinocchio embraced the knees of the mysterious little woman and began to cry bitterly.

Chapter 25

Pinocchio promises the Fairy to be good and studious, for he is quite sick of being a puppet and wishes to become an exemplary boy.

AT first the good little woman maintained that she was not the little Fairy with blue hair; but seeing that she was found out, and not wishing to continue the comedy any longer, she ended by making herself known, and she said to Pinocchio: "You little rogue! how did you ever discover who I was?"

"It was my great affection for you that told me."

"Do you remember? You left me a child, and now that you have found me again I am a woman-a woman almost old enough to be your mamma."

"I am delighted at that, for now, instead of calling you little sister, I will call you mamma. I have wished for such a long time to have a mamma like other boys!...But how did you manage to grow so fast?"

"That is a secret."

"Teach it to me, for I should also like to grow. Don't you see? I always remain no bigger than a ninepin."

"But you cannot grow," replied the Fairy.

"Why?"

"Because puppets never grow. They are born puppets, live puppets, and die puppets."

"Oh, I am sick of being a puppet!" cried Pinocchio, giving himself a slap. "It is time that I became a man..."

"And you will become one, if you know how to deserve it "

"Not really? And what can I do to deserve it?"

"A very easy thing: by learning to be a good boy."

"And you think I am not?"

"You are quite the contrary. Good boys are obedient, and you..."

"And I never obey."

"Good boys like to learn and to work, and you..."

"And I instead lead an idle vagabond life the year through."

"Good boys always speak the truth..."

"And I always tell lies."

"Good boys go willingly to school..."

"And school gives me pain all over my body. But from today I will change my life."

"Do you promise me?"

"I promise you. I will become a good little boy, and I will be the consolation of my papa... Where is my poor papa at this moment?"

"I do not know."

"Shall I ever have the happiness of seeing him again and kissing him?"

"I think so; indeed I am sure of it."

At this answer Pinocchio was so delighted that he took the Fairy's hands and began to kiss them with such fervour that he seemed beside himself. Then raising his face and looking at her lovingly, he asked: "Tell me, little mamma: then it was not true that you were dead?"

"It seems not, " said the Fairy, smiling.

"If you only knew the sorrow I felt and the tightening of my throat when I read, 'here lies...'"

"I know it, and it is on that account that I have forgiven you. I saw from the sincerity of your grief that you had a good heart; and when boys have good hearts, even if they are scamps and have got bad habits, there is always something to hope for: that is, there is always hope that they will turn to better ways. That is why I came to look for you here. I will be your mamma..."

"Oh, how delightful!" shouted Pinocchio, jumping for joy.

"You must obey me and do everything that I bid you."

"Willingly, willingly, willingly!"

"Tomorrow, " rejoined the Fairy, "you will begin to go to school."

Pinocchio became at once a little less joyful.

"Then you must choose an art, or a trade, according to your own wishes."

Pinocchio became very grave.

"What are you muttering between your teeth?" asked the Fairy in an angry voice.

"I was saying, " moaned the puppet in a low voice, "that it seemed to me too late for me to go to school now..."

"No, sir. Keep it in mind that it is never too late to learn and to instruct ourselves."

"But I do not wish to follow either an art or a trade."

"Why?"

"Because it tires me to work."

"My boy," said the Fairy, "those who talk in that way end almost always either in prison or in the hospital. Let me tell you that every man, whether he is born rich or poor, is obliged to do something in this world-to occupy himself, to work. Woe to those who lead slothful lives. Sloth is a dreadful illness and must be cured at once, in childhood. If not, when we are old it can never be cured."

Pinocchio was touched by these words, and lifting his head quickly he said to the Fairy: "I will study, I will work, I will do all that you tell me, for indeed I have become weary of being a puppet, and I wish at any price to become a boy. You promised me that I should, did you not?"

"I did promise you, and it now depends upon yourself."

Chapter 26

Pinocchio accompanies his schoolfellows to the seashore to see the terrible Dog-fish.

THE following day Pinocchio went to the government school.

Imagine the delight of all the little rogues when they saw a puppet walk into their school! They setup a roar of laughter that never ended. They played him all sorts of tricks. One boy carried off his cap, another pulled his jacket behind; one tried to give him a pair of inky mustachios just under his nose, and another attempted to tie strings to his feet and hands to make him dance.

For a short time Pinocchio pretended not to care and got on as well as he could; but at last, losing all patience, he turned to those who were teasing him most and making game of him, and said to them, looking very angry: "Beware, boys: I am not come here to be your buffoon. I respect others, and I intend to be respected."

"Well said, boaster! You have spoken like a book!" howled the young rascals, convulsed with mad laughter; and one of them, more impertinent than the others, stretched out his hand intending to seize the puppet by the end of his nose.

But he was not in time, for Pinocchio stuck his leg out from under the table and gave him a great kick on his shins.

"Oh, what hard feet!" roared the boy, rubbing the bruise that the puppet had given him.

"And what elbows!... even harder than his feet!..."said another, who for his rude tricks had received a blow in the stomach.

But nevertheless the kick and the blow acquired at once for Pinocchio the sympathy and the esteem of all the boys in the school. They all made friends with him and liked him heartily.

And even the master praised him, for he found him attentive, studious, and intelligent—always the first to come to school, and the last to leave when school was over.

But he had one fault: he made too many friends; and amongst them were several young rascals well known for their dislike to study and love of mischief.

The master warned him every day, and even the good Fairy never failed to tell him, and to repeat constantly: "Take care, Pinocchio! Those bad schoolfellows of yours will end sooner or later by making you lose all love of study, and perhaps even they may bring upon you some great misfortune."

"There is no fear of that!" answered the puppet, shrugging his shoulders and touching his forehead as much as to say: "There is so much sense here!"

Now it happened that one fine day, as he was on his way to school, he met several of his usual companions who, coming up to him, asked: "Have you heard the great news?"

"No."

"In the sea near here a Dog-fish has appeared as big as a mountain."

"Not really? Can it be the same Dog-fish that was there when my poor papa was drowned?"

"We are going to the shore to see him. Will you come with us?"

"No; I am going to school."

"What matters school? We can go to school tomorrow. Whether we have a lesson more or a lesson less, we shall always remain the same donkeys."

"But what will the master say?"

"The master may say what he likes. He is paid on purpose to grumble all day."

"And my mamma?..."

"Mammas know nothing, " answered those bad little boys.

"Do you know what I will do?" said Pinocchio. "I have reasons for wishing to see the Dog-fish, but I will go and see him when school is over."

"Poor donkey!" exclaimed one of the number. "Do you suppose that a fish of that size will wait your convenience? As soon as he is tired of being here he will stail for another place, and then it will be too late."

"How long does it take from here to the shore?" asked the puppet.

"We can be there and back in an hour."

"Then away!" shouted Pinocchio, "and he who runs fastest is the best!" Having thus given the signal to start, the boys, with their books and copybooks under their arms, rushed off across the fields, and Pinocchio was always the first-he seemed to have wings to his feet.

From time to time he turned to jeer at his companions, who were some distance behind, and seeing them panting for breath, covered with dust and their tongues hanging out of their mouths, he laughed heartily. The unfortunate boy little knew what terrors and horrible disasters he was going to meet with!

Chapter 27

Great fight between Pinocchio and his companions. One of them is wounded, and Pinocchio is arrested by the gendarmes.

WHEN he arrived on the shore Pinocchio looked out to sea; but he saw no Dog-fish. The sea was as smooth as a great crystal mirror.

"Where is the Dog-fish?" he asked, turning to his companions.

"He must have gone to have his breakfast," said one of them, laughing.

"Or he has thrown himself on to his bed to have a little nap," added another, laughing still louder.

From their absurd answers and silly laughter Pinocchio perceived that his companions had been making a fool of him, in inducing him to believe a tale with no truth in it. Taking it very badly he said to them angrily: "And now may I ask what fun you could find in deceiving me with the story of the Dogfish?"

"Oh, it was great fun!" answered the little rascals in chorus.

"And in what did it consist?"

"In making you miss school, and persuading you to come with us. Are you not ashamed of being always so punctual and so diligent with your lessons? Are you not ashamed of studying so hard?"

"And if I study hard what concern is it of yours?"

"It concerns us excessively, because it makes us appear in a bad light to the master."

"Why?"

"Because boys who study make those who, like us, have no wish to learn seem worse by comparison. And that is too bad. We too have our pride!..."

"Then what must I do to please you?"

"You must follow our example and hate school, lessons, and the master - our three greatest enemies."

"And if I wish to continue my studies?"

"In that case we will have nothing more to do with you, and at the first opportunity we will make you pay for it."

"Really, " said the puppet, shaking his head, "you make me inclined to laugh."

"Eh, Pinocchio!" shouted the biggest of the boys, confronting him. "None of your superior airs: don't come here to crow over us!...for if you are not afraid of us, we are not afraid of you. Remember that you are one against seven of us."

"Seven, like the seven deadly sins, " said Pinocchio with a shout of laughter.

"Listen to him! He has insulted us all! He called us the seven deadly sins! ..."

"Pinocchio! beg pardon...or it will be the worse for you!..."

"Cuckoo!" sang the puppet? putting his fore-finger to the end of his nose scoifingly.

"Pinocchio! it will end badly!..."

"Cuckoo!"

"You will get as many blows as a donkey!..."

"Cuckoo!"

"You will return home with a broken nose!..."

"Cuckoo!"

"Ah, you shall have the cuckoo from me!" said the most courageous of the boys. "Take that to begin with, and keep it for your supper to-night."

And so saying he gave him a blow on the head with his fist.

But it was give and take; for the puppet, as was to be expected, immediately returned the blow, and the fight in a moment became general and desperate.

Pinocchio, although he was one alone, defended himself like a hero. He used his feet, which were of the hardest wood, to such purpose that he kept his enemies at a respectful distance. Wherever they touched they left a bruise by way of reminder.

The boys, becoming furious at not being able to measure themselves hand to hand with the puppet, had recourse to other weapons. Loosening their satchels they commenced throwing their school-books at him-grammars, dictionaries, spelling-books, geography books, and other scholastic works. But Pinocchio was quick and had sharp eyes, and always managed to duck in time, so that the books passed over his head and all fell into the sea.

Imagine the astonishment of the fish! Thinking that the books were something to eat they all arrived in shoals, but having tasted a page or two, or a frontispiece, they spat it quickly out and made a wry face that seemed to say: "It isn't food for us; we are accustomed to something much better!"

The battle meantime had become fiercer than ever, when a big crab, who had come out of the water and had climbed slowly up on to the shore, called out in a hoarse voice that sounded like a trumpet with a bad cold: "Have done with that, you young ruffians, for you are nothing else! These hand-to-hand fights between boys seldom finish well. Some disaster is sure to happen!..."

Poor crab! He might as well have preached to the wind. Even that young rascal Pinocchio, turning round, looked at him mockingly and said rudely: "Hold your tongue, you tiresome crab! You had better suck some liquorice lozenges to cure that cold in your throat. Or better still, go to bed and try to get a reaction!"

Just then the boys, who had no more books of their own to throw, spied at a little distance the satchel that belonged to Pinocchio, and took possession of it in less time than it takes to tell.

Amongst the books there was one bound in strong cardboard with the back and points of parchment. It was a Treatise on Arithmetic. I leave you to imagine if it was big or not!

One of the boys seized this volume, and aiming at Pinocchio's head threw it at him with all the force he could muster. But instead of hitting the puppet it struck one of his companions on the temple, who, turning as white as a sheet, said only: "Oh, mother, help...I am dying!..." and fell his whole length on the sand. Thinking he was dead the terrified boys ran off as hard as their legs could carry them, and in a few minutes they were out of sight.

But Pinocchio remained. Although from grief and fright he was more dead than alive, nevertheless he ran and soaked his handkerchief in the sea and began to bathe the temples of his poor schoolfellow. Crying bitterly in his despair he kept calling him by name and saying to him: "Eugene!... my poor Eugene!.. open your eyes and look at me!... why do you not answer? I did not do it, indeed it was not I that hurt you so! believe me, it was not! Open your eyes, Eugene...If you keep your eyes shut I shall die too...Oh! what shall I do? how shall I ever return home? How can I ever have the courage to go back to my good mamma? What will become of me?... Where can I fly to?...Oh! how much better it would have been, a thousand times better, if I had only gone to school!... Why did I listen to my companions? they have been my ruin. The master said to me, and my mamma repeated it often: 'Beware of bad companions!' But I am obstinate... a wilful fool... I let them talk and then I always take my own way! and I have to suffer for it...And so, ever since I have been in the world, I have never had a happy quarter of an hour. Oh dear! what will become of me, what will become of me, what will become of me?..."

And Pinocchio began to cry and sob, and to strike his head with his fists, and to call poor Eugene by his name. Suddenly he heard the sound of approaching footsteps.

He turned and saw two carabineers.

"What are you doing there lying on the ground?" they asked Pinocchio.

"I am helping my schoolfellow."

"Has he been hurt?"

"So it seems."

"Hurt indeed!" said one of the carabineers, stooping down and examining Eugene closely. "This boy has been wounded in the temple. Who wounded him?"

"Not I," stammered the puppet breathlessly.

"If it was not you, who then did it?"

"Not I," repeated Pinocchio.

"And with what was he wounded?"

"With this book." And the puppet picked up from the ground the Treatise on Arithmetic, bound in cardboard and parchment, and showed it to the carabineer.

"And to whom does this book belong?"

"To me."

"That is enough: nothing more is wanted. Get up and come with us at once.

"But I..."

"Come along with us!..."

"But I am innocent..."

"Come along with us!"

Before they left, the carabineers called some fishermen, who were passing at that moment near the shore in their boat, and said to them: "We give this boy who has been wounded in the head into your charge. Carry him to your house and nurse him. Tomorrow we will come and see him."

They then turned to Pinocchio, and having placed him between them they said to him in a commanding voice: "Forward! and walk quickly! or it will be the worse for you."

Without requiring it to be repeated, the puppet set out along the road leading to the village. But the poor little devil hardly knew where he was. He thought he must be dreaming, and what a dreadful dream! He was beside himself. He saw double: his legs shook: his tongue clung to the roof of his mouth, and he could not utter a word. And yet in the midst of his stupefaction and apathy his heart was pierced by a cruel thorn - the thought that he would have to pass under the windows of the good Fairy's house between the carabineers. He would rather have died.

They had already reached the village when a gust of wind blew Pinocchio's cap off his head and carried it ten yards off.

"Will you permit me, " said the puppet to the carabineers, "to go and get my cap?"

"Go, then; but be quick about it."

The puppet went and picked up his cap...but instead of putting it on his head he took it between his teeth and began to run as hard as he could towards the seashore.

The carabineers, thinking it would be difficult to overtake him, sent after him a large mastiff who had won the first prizes at all the dog-races. Pinocchio ran, but the dog ran faster. The people came to their windows and crowded into the streetin their anxiety to see the end of the desperate race. But they could not satisfy their curiosity, for Pinocchio and the dog raised such clouds of dust that in a few minutes nothing could be seen of either of them.

Chapter 28

Pinocchio is in danger of being fried in a frying-pan like a fish.

THERE came a moment in this desperate race-a terrible moment when Pinocchio thought himself lost: for you must know that Alidoro - for so the mastiff was called-had run so swiftly that he had nearly come up with him.

The puppet could hear the panting of the dreadful beast close behind him; there was not a hand's breadth between them, he could even feel the dog's hot breath.

Fortunately the shore was close and the sea but a few steps off.

As soon as he reached the sands the puppet made a wonderful leap-a frog could have done no better-and plunged into the water.

Alidoro, on the contrary, wished to stop himself; but carried away by the impetus of the race he also went into the sea. The unfortunate dog could not swim, but he made great efforts to keep himself afloat with his paws; but the more he struggled the farther he sank head downwards under the water.

When he rose to the surface again his eyes were rolling with terror, and he barked out: "I am drowning! I am drowning!"

"Drown!" shouted Pinocchio from a distance, seeing himself safe from all danger.

"Help me, dear Pinocchio!... save me from death!..."

At that agonising cry the puppet, who had in reality an excellent heart, was moved with compassion, and turning to the dog he said: "But if I save your life, will you promise to give me no further annoyance, and not to run after me?"

"I promise! I promise! Be quick, for pity's sake, for if you delay another half-minute I shall be dead."

Pinocchio hesitated: but remembering that his father had often told him that a good action is never lost, he swam to Alidoro, and taking hold of his tail with both hands brought him safe and sound on to the dry sand of the beach.

The poor dog could not stand. He had drunk, against his will, so much salt water that he was like a balloon. The puppet, however, not wishing to trust him too far, thought it more prudent to jump again into the water. When he had swum some distance from the shore he called out to the friend he had rescued: "Good-bye, Alidoro; a good journey to you, and take my compliments to all at home."

"Good-bye, Pinocchio," answered the dog; "a thousand thanks for having saved my life. You have done me a great service, and in this world what is given is returned. If an occasion offers I shall not forget it."

Pinocchio swam on, keeping always near the land. At last he thought that he had reached a safe place. Giving a look along the shore he saw amongst the rocks a kind of cave from which a cloud of smoke was ascending.

"In that cave," he said to himself, "there must be a fire. So much the better.

I will go and dry and warm myself, and then?...and then we shall see."

Having taken this resolution he approached the rocks; but as he was going to climb up, he felt something under the water that rose higher and higher and carried him into the air. He tried to escape, but it was too late, for to his extreme surprise he found himself enclosed in a great net, together with a swarm of fish of every size and shape, who were flapping and struggling like so many despairing souls.

At the same moment a fisherman came out of the cave; he was so ugly, so horribly ugly, that he looked like a sea monster. Instead of hair his head was covered with a thick bush of green grass, his skin was green, his eyes were green, his long beard that came down to the ground was also green. He had the appearance of an immense lizard standing on its hind-paws.

When the fisherman had drawn his net out of the sea, he exclaimed with great satisfaction: "Thank Heaven! Again today I shall have a splendid feast of fish!"

"What a mercy that I am not a fish!" said Pinocchio to himself, regaining a little courage.

The net full of fish was carried into the cave, which was dark and smoky. In the middle of the cave a large frying-pan full of oil was frying, and sending out a smell of mushrooms that was suffocating.

"Now we will see what fish we have taken!" said the green fisherman; and putting into the net an enormous hand, so out of all proportion that it looked like a baker's shovel, he pulled out a handful of mullet.

"These mullets are good!" he said, looking at them and smelling them complacently. And after he had smelt them he threw them into a pan without water.

He repeated the same operation many times; and as he drew out the fish, his mouth watered and he said, chuckling to himself: "What good whiting!…"

"What exquisite sardines!…"

"These soles are delicious!.. "

"And these crabs excellent!..."

"What dear little anchovies!..."

I need not tell you that the whiting, the sardines, the soles, the crabs, and the anchovies were all thrown promiscuously into the pan to keep company with the mullet.

The last to remain in the net was Pinocchio.

No sooner had the fisherman taken him out than he opened his big green eyes with astonishment, and cried, half-frightened: "What species of fish is this? Fish of this kind I never remember to have eaten!"

And he looked at him again attentively, and having examined him well all over, he ended by saying: "I know: he must be a craw-fish."

Pinocchio, mortified at being mistaken for a craw-fish, said in an angry voice: "A craw-fish indeed! do you take me for a craw-fish? What treatment! Let me tell you that I am a puppet."

"A puppet?" replied the fisherman. "To tell the truth, a puppet is quite a new fish for me. All the better! I shall eat you with greater pleasure."

"Eat me! but will you understand that I am not a fish? Do you hear that I talk and reason as you do?"

"That is quite true," said the fisherman; "and as I see that you are a fish possessed of the talent of talking and reasoning as I do, I will treat you with all the attention that is your due."

"And this attention?..."

"In token of my friendship and particular regard, I will leave you the choice of how you would like to be cooked. Would you like to be fried in the frying-pan, or would you prefer to be stewed with tomato sauce?"

"To tell the truth," answered Pinocchio, "if I am to choose, I should prefer to be set at liberty and to return home."

"You are joking! Do you imagine that I would lose the opportunity of tasting such a rare fish? It is not every day, I assure you, that a puppet fish is caught in these waters. Leave it to me, I will fry you in the frying-pan with the other fish, and you will be quite satisfied. It is always consolation to be fried in company."

At this speech the unhappy Pinocchio began to cry and scream and to implore for mercy; and he said, sobbing: "How much better it would have been if I had gone to school!... I would listen to my companions and now I am paying for it! Ih!...Ih!...Ih!..."

And he wriggled like an eel, and made indescribable efforts to slip out of the clutches of the green fisherman. But it was useless: the fisherman took a long strip of rush, and having bound his hands and feet as if he had been a sausage, he threw him into the pan with the other fish.

He then fetched a wooden bowl full of flour and began to flour them each in turn, and as soon as they were ready he threw them into the frying-pan.

The first to dance in the boiling oil were the poor whiting; the crabs followed, then the sardines, then the soles, then the anchovies, and at last it was Pinocchio's turn. Seeing him selfso near death, and such a horrible death, he was so frightened, and trembled so violently, that he had neither voice nor breath left for further entreaties.

But the poor boy implored with his eyes! The green fisherman, however, without caring in the least, plunged him five or six times in the flour, until he was white from head to foot, and looked like a puppet made of plaster.

He then took him by the head, and...

Chapter 29

He returns to the Fairy's house. She promises him that the following day he shall cease to be a puppet and shall become a boy. Grand breakfast of coffee and milk to celebrate this great event.

JUST as the fisherman was on the point of throwing Pinocchio into the frying-pan a large dog entered the cave, enticed there by the strong and savoury odour of fried fish.

"Get out!" shouted the fisherman threateningly, holding the floured puppet in his hand.

But the poor dog, who was as hungry as a wolf, whined and wagged his tail as much as to say: "Give me a mouthful of fish and I will leave you in peace."

"Get out, I tell you?" repeated the fisherman, and he stretched out his leg to give him a kick.

But the dog, who, when he was really hungry, would not stand trifling, turned upon him, growling and showing his terrible tusks.

At that moment a little feeble voice was heard in the cave saying entreatingly: "Save me, Alidoro! If you do not save me I shall be fried!..."

The dog recognised Pinocchio's voice, and to his extreme surprise perceived that it proceeded from the floured bundle that the fisherman held in his hand.

So what do you think he did? He made a spring, seized the bundle in his mouth, and holding it gently between his teeth he rushed out of the cave and was gone like a flash of lightning.

The fisherman, furious at seeing a fish he was so anxious to eat snatched from him, ran after the dog; but he had not gone many steps when he was taken with a fit of coughing and had to give it up.

Alidoro, when he had reached the path that led to the village, stopped, and put his friend Pinocchio gently on the ground.

"How much I have to thank you for!" said the puppet.

"There is no necessity, " replied the dog, " You saved me and I have now returned it. You know that we must all help each other in this world."

"But how came you to come to the cave?"

"I was lying on the shore more dead than alive when the wind brought to me the smell of fried fish. The smell excited my appetite, and I followed it up. If I had arrived a second later..."

"Do not mention it!" groaned Pinocchio, who was still trembling with fright. "Do not mention it! If you had arrived a second later I should by this time have been fried, eaten, and digested. Brrr!... it makes me shudder only to think of it!..."

Alidoro, laughing, extended his right paw to the puppet, who shook it heatily in token of great friendship, and they then separated.

The dog took the road home; and Pinocchio, left alone, went to a cottage not far off, and said to a little old man who was warming himself in the sun: "Tell me, good man, do you know anything of a poor boy called Eugene who was wounded in the head!..."

"The boy was brought by some fishermen to this cottage, and now..."

"And now he is dead!..."interrupted Pinocchio with great sorrow.

"No, he is alive, and has returned to his home."

"Not really? not really?" cried the puppet, dancing with delight. "Then the wound was not serious?..."

"It might have been very serious and even fatal, " answered the little old man, "for they threw a thick book bound in cardboard at his head."

"And who threw it at him?"

"One of his schoolfellows, a certain Pinocchio..."

"And who is this Pinocchio?" asked the puppet, pretending ignorance.

"They say that he is a bad boy, a vagabond, a regular good-for-nothing..". "Calumnies! all calumnies!"

"Do you know this Pinocchio?"

"By sight!" answered the puppet.

"And what is your opinion of him?" asked the little man.

"He seems to me to be a very good boy, anxious to learn, and obedient and affectionate to his father and family..."

Whilst the puppet was firing off all these lies, he touched his nose and perceived that it had lengthened more than a hand. Very much alarmed he began to cry out: "Don't believe, good man, what I have been telling you. I know Pinocchio very well, and I can assure you that he is really a very bad boy, disobedient and idle, who instead of going to school runs off with his companions to amuse himself."

He had hardly finished speaking when his nose became shorter and returned to the same size that it was before.

"And why are you all covered with white?" asked the old man suddenly.

"I will tell you... Without observing it I rubbed myself against a wall which had been freshly whitewashed, " answered the puppet, ashamed to confess that he had been floured like a fish prepared for the frying-pan.

"And what have you done with you jacket, your trousers, and your cap?"

"I met with robbers who took them from me. Tell me, good old man, could you perhaps give me some clothes to return home in?"

"My boy, as to clothes, I have nothing but a little sack in which I keep beans. If you wish for it, take it; there itis."

Pinocchio did not wait to be told twice. He took the sack at once, and with a pair of scissors he cut a hole at the end and at each side, and put it on like a shirt. And with this slight clothing he set off for the village.

But as he went he did not feel at all comfortable-so little so, indeed, that for a step forward he took another backwards, and he said, talking to himself:"How shall I ever present myself to my good little Fairy? What will she say when she sees me?...Will she forgive me this second escapade?...I bet that she will not forgive me! Oh, I am sure that she will not forgive me!...And it serves me right, for I am a rascal. I am always promising to correct myself, and I never keep my word!..."

When he reached the village it was night and very dark. A storm had come on, and as the rain was coming down in torrents he went straight to the Fairy's house, resolved to knock at the door, and hoping to be let in.

But when he was there his courage failed him, and instead of knocking he ran away some twenty paces. He returned to the door a second time, but could not make up his mind; he came back a third time, still he dared not; the fourth time he laid hold of the knocker and, trembling, gave a little knock.

He waited and waited. At last, after half an hour had passed, a window on the top floor was opened-the house was four stories high-and Pinocchio saw a big Snail with a lighted candle on her head looking out. She called to him: "Who is there at this hour?"

"Is the Fairy at home? "asked the puppet.

"The Fairy is asleep and must not be awakened; but who are you?"

"It is I!"

"Who is I? "

"Pinocchio."

"And who is Pinocchio?"

"The puppet who lives in the Fairy's house."

"Ah, I understand!" said the Snail."Wait for me there. I will come down and open the door directly."

"Be quick, for pity's sake, for I am dying of cold."

"My boy, I am a snail, and snails are never in a hurry."

An hour passed, and then two, and the door was not opened. Pinocchio, who was wet through, and trembling from cold and fear, at last took courage and knocked again, and this time he knocked louder.

At this second knock a window on the lower story opened, and the same Snail appeared at it.

"Beautiful little Snail, " cried Pinocchio from the street, "I have been waiting for two hours! And two hours on such a bad night seem longer than two years. Be quick, for pity's sake."

"My boy, "answered the calm, phlegmatic little animal-"my boy, I am a snail, and snails are never in a hurry."

And the window was shut again.

Shortly afterwards midnight struck; then one o'clock, then two o'clock, and the door remained still closed.

Pinocchio at last, losing all patience, seized the knocker in a rage, intending to give a blow that would resound through the house. But the knocker, which was iron, turned suddenly into an eel, and slipping out of his hands disappeared in the stream of water that ran down the middle of the street.

"Ah! is that it?" shouted Pinocchio, blind with rage. "Since the knocker has disappeared, I will kick instead with all my might."

And drawing a little back he gave a tremendous kick against the house door. The blow was indeed so violent that his foot went through the wood and stuck; and when he tried to draw it back again it was trouble thrown away, for it remained fixed like a nail that has been hammered down.

Think of poor Pinocchio! He was obliged to spend the remainder of the night with one foot on the ground and the other in the air.

The following morning at daybreak the door was at last opened. That clever little Snail had taken only nine hours to come down from the fourth storey to the house door. It is evident that her exertions must have been great.

"What are you doing with your foot stuck in the door?" she asked the puppet, laughing.

"It was an accident. Do try, beautiful little Snail, if you cannot release me from this torture."

"My boy, that is the work of a carpenter, and I have never been a carpenter."

"Beg the Fairy from me!..."

"The Fairy is asleep and must not be wakened."

"But what do you suppose that I can do all day nailed to this door?"

"Amuse yourself by counting the ants that pass down the street."

"Bring me at least something to eat, for I am quite exhausted."

"Atonce, " said the Snail.

In fact, after three hours and a half she returned to Pinocchio carrying a silver tray on her head. The tray contained a loaf of bread, a roast chicken, and four ripe apricots.

"Here is the breakfast that the Fairy has sent you, " said the Snail.

The puppet felt very much comforted at the sight of these good things. But when lie began to eat them, what was his disgust at making the discovery that the bread was plaster, the chicken cardboard and the four apricots painted alabaster.

He wanted to cry. In his desperation he tried to throw away the tray and all that was on it; but instead, either from grief or exhaustion, he fainted away. When he came to himself he found that he was lying on a sofa, and the Fairy was beside him.

"I will pardon you once more, " the Fairy said, "but woe to you if you behave badly a third time!..."

Pinocchio promised, and swore that he would study, and that for the future he would always conduct himself well.

And he kept his word for the remainder of the year. Indeed, at the examinations before the holidays, he had the honour of being the first in the school, and his behaviour in general was so satisfactory and praiseworthy that the Fairy was very much pleased, and said to him: "Tomorrow your wish shall be gratified."

"And that is?"

"Tomorrow you shall cease to be a wooden puppet, and you shall become a boy."

No one who had not witnessed it could ever imagine Pinocchio's joy at this long-sighed-for good fortune. All his schoolfellows were to be invited for the following day to a grand breakfast at the Fairy's house, that they might celebrate together the great event. The Fairy had prepared two hundred cups of coffee and milk, and four hundred rolls cut and buttered on each side. The day promised to be most happy and delightful, but...

Unfortunately in the lives of puppets there is always a "but" that spoils everything.

Chapter 30

Pinocchio, instead of becoming a boy, starts secretly with his friend Candlewick for the "Land of Boobies"

PINOCCHIO, as was natural, asked the Fairy's permission to go round the town to make the invitations; and the Fairy said to him: "Go if you like and invite your companions for the breakfast tomorrow, but remember to return home before dark. Have you understood?"

"I promise to be back in an hour," answered the puppet.

"Take care, Pinocchio! Boys are always very ready to promise; but generally they are little given to keep their word."

"But I am not like other boys. When I say a thing, I do it."

"We shall see. If you are disobedient, so much the worse for you."

"Why?"

"Because boys who do not listen to the advice of those who know more than they do always meet with some misfortune or other."

"I have experienced that, " said Pinocchio. "But I shall never make that mistake again."

"We shall see if that is true."

Without saying more the puppet took leave of his good Fairy, who was like a mamma to him, and went out of the house singing and dancing.

In less than an hour all his friends were invited. Some accepted at once heartily; others at first required pressing; but when they heard that the rolls to be eaten with the coffee were to be buttered on both sides, they ended by saying: "We will come also, to do you a pleasure."

Now I must tell you that amongst Pinocchio's friends and schoolfellows there was one that he greatly preferred and was very fond of. This boy's name was Romeo; but he always went by the nickname of Candlewick, because he was so thin, straight, and bright like the new wick of a little nightlight Candlewick was the laziest and the naughtiest boy in the school; but Pinocchio was devoted to him. He had indeed gone at once to his house to invite him to the breakfast, but he had not found him. He returned a second time, but Candlewick was not there. He went a third time, but it was in vain. Where could he search for him? He looked here, there, and everywhere, and at last he saw him hiding in the porch of a peasant's cottage.

"What are you doing there?" asked Pinocchio, coming up to him.

"I am waiting for midnight, to start..."

"Why, where are you going?"

"Very far, very far, very far away."

"And I have been three times to your house to look for you."

"What did you want with me?"

"Do you not know the great event? Have you not heard of my good fortune?"

"What is it?"

"Tomorrow I cease to be a puppet, and become a boy like you, and like all the other boys."

"Much good may it do you."

"Tomorrow, therefore, I expect you to breakfast at my house."

"But when I tell you that I am going away to-night."

"At what o'clock?"

"In a short time."

"And where are you going"

"I am going to live in a country...the most delightful country in the world: a real land of Cocagne!..."

"And how is it called?"

"It is called the" Land of Boobies. "Why do you not come too?"

"I? No, never!"

"You are wrong, Pinocchio. Believe me, if you do not come you will repent it. Where could you find a better country for us boys? There are no schools there: there are no masters: there are no books. In that delightful land nobody ever studies. On Thursday there is never school; and every week consists of six Thursdays and one Sunday. Only think, the autumn holidays begin on the 1stof January and finish on the last day of December. That is the country for me! That is what all civilised countries should be like!..."

"But how are the days spent in the 'Land of Boobies'?"

"They are spent in play and amusement from morning till night. When night comes you go to bed, and recommence the same life in the morning. What do you think of it?"

"Hum!..." said Pinocchio; and he shook his head slightly as much as to say, "That is a life that I also would willingly lead."

"Well, will you go with me? Yes or no? Resolve quickly."

"No, no, no, and again no. I promised my good Fairy to become a well-conducted boy, and I will keep my word. And as I see that the sun is setting I must leave you at once and run away. Good-bye, and a pleasant journey to you."

"Where are you rushing off to in such a hurry?"

"Home. My good Fairy wishes me to be back before dark."

"Wait another two minutes."

"It will make me too late."

"Only two minutes."

"And if the Fairy scolds me?"

"Let her scold. When she has scolded well she will hold her tongue," said That rascal Candlewick.

"And what are you going to do? Are you going alone or with companions?"

"Alone? We shall be more than a hundred boys."

"And do you make the journey on foot?"

"A coach will pass by shortly which is to take me to that happy country."

"What would I not give for the coach to pass by now!..."

"Why?"

"That I might see you all start together."

"Stay here a little longer and you will see us."

"No, no, I must go home."

"Wait another two minutes."

"I have already delayed too long. The Fairy will be anxious about me."

"Poor Fairy-Is she afraid that the bats will eat you?"

"But now, " continued Pinocchio, "are you really certain that there are no schools in that country?..."

"Not even the shadow of one."

"And no masters either?..."

"Not one."

"And no one is ever made to study?"

"Never, never, never!"

"What a delightful country!" said Pinocchio, his mouth watering. "What a delightful country! I have never been there, but I can quite imagine it..."

"Why will you not come also?"

"It is useless to tempt me. I promised my good Fairy to become a sensible boy, and I will not break my word."

"Good-bye, then, and give my compliments to all the boys at

the gymnasiums, and also to those of the lyceums, if you meet them in the street."

"Good-bye, Candlewick: a pleasant journey to you, amuse yourself, and think sometimes of your friends."

Thus saying the puppet made two steps to go, but then stopped, and turning to his friend he inquired: "But are you quite certain that in that country all the weeks consist of six Thursdays and one Sunday?"

"Most certain."

"But do you know for certain that the holidays begin on the 1st of January and finish on the last day of December?"

"Assuredly."

"What a delightful country!" repeated Pinocchio, looking enchanted. Then, with a resolute air, he added in a great hurry: "This time really good-bye, and a pleasant journey to you."

"Good-bye."

"When do you start?"

"Shortly."

"What a pity! If really it wanted only an hour to the time of your start, I should be almost tempted to wait.

And the Fairy?"

"It is already late...If I return home an hour sooner or an hour later it will be all the same."

"Poor Pinocchio! And if the Fairy scolds you?"

"I must have patience! I will let her scold. When she has scolded well she will hold her tongue."

In the meantime night had come on and it was quite dark. Suddenly they saw in the distance a small light moving...and they heard a noise of talking, and the sound of a trumpet, but so small and feeble that it resembled the hum of a mosquito.

"Here it is!" shouted Candlewick, jumping to his feet.

"What is it?" asked Pinocchio in a whisper.

"It is the coach coming to take me. Now will you come, yes or no?"

"But is it really true, " asked the puppet, "that in that country boys are never obliged to study?"

"Never, never, never!"

"What a delightful country!... What a delightful country!... What a delightful country!

Chapter 31

After five months' residence in the land of Boobies, Pinocchio, to his great astonishment, grows a beautiful pair of donkey's ears, and he becomes a little donkey, tail and all.

AT last the coach arrived; and it arrived without making the slightest noise, for its wheels were bound round with tow and rags.

It was drawn by twelve pairs of donkeys, all the same size but of different colours.

Some were gray, some white, some brindled like pepper and salt, and others had large stripes of yellow and blue.

But the most extraordinary thing was this: the twelve pairs, that is, the twenty-four donkeys, instead of being shod like other beasts of burden, had on their feet men's boots made of white kid.

And the coachman?...

Picture to yourself a little man broader than he was long, flabby and greasy like a lump of butter, with a small round face like an orange, a little mouth that was always laughing, and a soft caressing voice like a cat when she is trying to insinuate herself into the good graces of the mistress of the house.

All the boys as soon as they saw him fell in love with him, and vied with each other in taking places in his coach to be conducted to the true land of Cocagne, known on the geographical map by the seducing name of the "Land of Boobies."

The coach was in fact quite full of boys between eight and twelve years old, heaped one upon another like herrings in a barrel. They were uncomfortable, packed close together and could hardly breathe: but nobody said Oh!-nobody grumbled. The consolation of knowing that in a few hours they would reach a country where there were no books, no schools, and no masters, made them so happy and resigned that they felt neither fatigue nor inconvenience, neither hunger, nor thirst, nor want of sleep.

As soon as the coach had drawn up the little man turned to Candlewick, and with a thousand smirks and grimaces said to him, smiling: "Tell me, my fine boy, would you also like to go to that fortunate country",

"I certainly wish to go."

"But I must warn you, my dear child, that there is not a place left in the coach. You can see for yourself that it is quite full..."

"No matter," replied Candlewick; "if there is no place inside, I will manage to sit on the springs."

And giving a leap he seated himself astride on the springs.

"And you, my love!..."said the little man, turning in a flattering manner to Pinocchio, "what do you intend to do? Are you coming with us, or are you going to remain behind?"

"I remain behind," answered Pinocchio. "I am going home. I intend to study and to earn a good character at school, as all well-conducted boys do."

"Much good may it do you!"

"Pinocchio!" called out Candlewick, "listen to me: come with us and we shall have such fun."

"No, no, no!"

"Come with us, and we shall have such fun," cried four other voices from the inside of the coach.

"Come with us, and we shall have such fun," shouted in chorus a hundred voices from the inside of the coach.

"But if I come with you, what will my good Fairy say?" said the puppet, who was beginning to yield.

"Do not trouble your head with melancholy thoughts. Consider only that we are going to a country where we shall be at liberty to run riot from morning till night."

Pinocchio did not answer; but he sighed: he sighed again: he sighed for the third time, and he said finally:" Make a little room for me, for I am coming too."

"The places are all full, " replied the little man; "but to show you how welcome you are, you shall have my seat on the box..."

"And you?..."

"Oh, I will go on foot."

"No, indeed, I could not allow that. I would rather mount one of these donkeys, " cried Pinocchio.

Approaching the right-hand donkey of the first pair he attempted to mount him, but the animal turned on him, and giving him a great blow in the stomach rolled him over with his legs in the air.

You can imagine the impertinent and immoderate laughter of all the boys who witnessed this scene.

But the little man did not laugh. He approached the rebellious donkey and, pretending to give him a kiss, bit off half of his ear.

Pinocchio in the meantime had got up from the ground in a fury, and with a spring he seated him-self on the poor animal's back. And he sprang so well that the boys stopped laughing and began to shout: " Hurrah, Pinocchio!" and they clapped their hands and applauded him as if they would never finish.

But the donkey suddenly kicked up its hind-legs, and backing violently threw the poor puppet into the middle of the road on to a heap of stones.

The roars of laughter recommenced: but the little man, instead of laughing, felt such affection for the restive ass that he kissed him again, and as he did so he bit half of his other ear clean off. He then said to the puppet: "Mount him now without fear. That little donkey had got some whim into his head; but I whispered two little words into his ears which have, I hope, made him gentle and reasonable."

Pinocchio mounted, and the coach started. Whilst the donkeys were galloping and the coach was rattling over the stones of the high road, the puppet thought that he heard a low voice that was scarcely intelligible saying to him: "Poor fool! you would follow your own way, but you will repent it!"

Pinocchio, feeling almost frightened, looked from side to side to try and discover where these words could come from: but he saw nobody. The donkeys galloped, the coach rattled, the boys inside slept, Candlewick snored liked a dormouse, and the little man seated on the box sang between his teeth: During the night all sleep, But I sleep never...

After they had gone another mile, Pinocchio heard the same

little low voice saying to him: "Bear it in mind, simpleton! Boys who refuse to study, and turn their backs upon books, schools, and masters, to pass their time in play and amusement, sooner or later come to a bad end...I know it by experience... and I can tell you. A day will come when you will weep as I am weeping now... but then it will be too late!..."

On hearing these words whispered very softly the puppet, more frightened than ever, sprang down from the back of his donkey and went and took hold of his mouth.

Imagine his surprise when he found that the donkey was crying...and he was crying like a boy!

"Eh! Sir coachman, " cried Pinocchio to the little man, "here is an extraordinary thing! This donkey is crying."

"Let him cry; he will laugh when he is a bridegroom."

"But have you by chance taught him to talk?"

"No; but he spent three years in a company of learned dogs, and he learnt to mutter a few words."

"Poor beast!"

"Come, come, " said the little man, "don't let us waste time in seeing a donkey cry. Mount him, and let us go on: the night is cold and the road is long."

Pinocchio obeyed without another word. In the morning about daybreak they arrived safely in the "Land of Boobies."

It was a country unlike any other country in the world. The population was composed entirely of boys. The oldest were fourteen, and the youngest scarcely eight years old. In the streets there was such merriment, noise, and shouting, that it was enough to turn anybody's head. There were troops of boys everywhere. Some were playing with nuts, some with battledores, some with balls. Some rode velocipedes, others wooden horses. A party were playing at hide and seek, a few were chasing each other. Boys dressed in straw were eating lighted tow; some were reciting, some singing, some leaping. Some were amusing themselves with walking on their hands with their feet in the air; others were trundling hoops, or strutting about dressed as generals, wearing leaf helmets and commanding a squadron of cardboard soldiers. Some were laughing, some shouting, some were calling out; others clapped their hands, or whistled, or clucked like a hen who has just laid an egg. To sum it all up, it was such a pandemonium, such a bedlam, such an uproar, that not to be deafened it would have been necessary to stuff one's ears with cotton wool. In every square, canvas theatres had been erected, and they were crowded with boys from morning till evening. On the walls of the houses there were inscriptions written in charcoal: "Long live playthings, we will have no more schools: down with arithmetic:" and similar other fine sentiments all in bad spelling.

Pinocchio, Candlewick, and the other boys who had made the journey with the little man, had scarcely set foot in the town before they were in the thick of the tumult, and I need not tell you that in a few minutes they had made acquaintance with everybody. Where could happier or more contented boys be found?

In the midst of continual games and every variety of amusement, the hours, the days, and the weeks passed like lightning.

"Oh, what a delightful life!" said Pinocchio, whenever by chance he met Candlewick.

"See, then, if I was not right?" replied the other. "And to think that you did not want to come! To think that you had taken it into your head to return home to your Fairy, and to lose your time in studying!...If you are at this moment free from the bother of books and school, you must acknowledge that you owe it to me, to my advice and to my persuasions. It is only friends who know how to render such great services."

"It is true, Candlewick! If I am now a really happy boy, itis all your doing. But do you know what the master used to say when he talked to me of you? He always said to me: "Do not associate with that rascal Candlewick, for he is a bad companion, and will only lead you into mischief!..."

"Poor master!" replied the other, shaking his head. "I know only too well that he disliked me, and amused himself by calumniating me; but I am generous and I forgive him!"

"Noble soul!" said Pinocchio, embracing his friend affectionately, and kissing him between the eyes.

This delightful life had gone on for five months. The days had been entirely spent in play and amusement, without a thought of books or school, when one morning Pinocchio awoke to a most disagreeable surprise that put him into a very bad humour.

Chapter 32

Pinocchio gets donkey's ears; and then he becomes a real little donkey and begins to bray.

WHAT was this surprise?

I will tell you, my dear little readers. The surprise was that Pinocchio when he awoke scratched his head; and in scratching his head he discovered. Can you guess in the least what he discovered?

He discovered to his great astonishment that his ears had grown more than a hand.

You know that the puppet from his birth had always had very small ears-so small that they were not visible to the naked eye.

You can imagine then what he felt when he found that during the night his ears had become so long that they seemed like two brooms.

He went at once in search of a glass that he might look at himself, but not being able to find one he filled the basin of his washing-stand with water, and he saw reflected what he certainly would never have wished to see. He saw his head embellished with a magnificent pair of donkey's ears!

Only think of poor Pinocchio's sorrow, shame, and despair!

He began to cry and roar, and he beat his head against the wall; but the more he cried the longer his ears grew: they grew, and grew, and became hairy towards the points.

At the sound of his loud outcries a beautiful little Marmot that lived on the first floor came into the room. Seeing the puppet in such grief she asked earnestly: "What has happened to you, my dear fellow-lodger?"

"I am ill, my dear little Marmot, very ill…and of an illness that frightens me. Do you understand counting a pulse?"

"A little."

"Then feel and see if by chance I have got fever."

The little Marmot raised her right fore-paw; and after having felt Pinocchio's pulse she said to him, sighing: "My friend, I am grieved to be obliged to give you bad news!…"

"What is it?"

"You have got a very bad fever!..."

"What fever is it?"

"It is donkey fever."

"That is a fever that I do not understand, " said the puppet, but he understood it only too well.

"Then I will explain it to you, " said the Marmot. " You must know that in two or three hours you will be no longer a puppet, or a boy..."

"Then what shall I be?"

"In two or three hours you will become really and truly a little donkey, like those that draw carts and carry cabbages and salad to market."

"Oh! unfortunate that I am! Unfortunate that I am!" cried Pinocchio, seizing his two ears with his hands, and pulling them and tearing them furiously as if they had been some one else's ears.

"My dear boy, " said the Marmot, by way of consoling him, "what can you do to prevent it? It is destiny. It is written in the decrees of wisdom that all boys who are lazy, and who take a dislike to books, to schools, and to masters, and who pass their time in amusement, games, and diversions, must end sooner or later by becoming transformed into so many little donkeys."

"But is it really so?" asked the puppet, sobbing.

"It is indeed only too true! And tears are now useless. You should have thought of it sooner!"

"But it was not my fault: believe me, little Marmot, the fault was all Candlewick's!..."

"And who is this Candlewick?"

"One of my schoolfellows. I wanted to return home: I wanted to be obedient. I wished to study and to earn a good character... but Candlewick said to me:'Why should you bother yourself by studying? Why should you go to school? Come with us instead to the 'Land of Boobies': there we shall none of us have to learn: there we shall amuse ourselves from morning to night, and we shall always be merry.'"

"And why did you follow the advice of that false friend? of that bad companion?"

"Why?...Because, my dear little Marmot, I am a puppet with no sense... and with no heart. Ah! If I had had the least heart I should never have left that good Fairy who loved me like a mamma, and who had done so much for me!... and I should be no longer a puppet...for I should by this time have become a little boy like so many others! But if I meet Candlewick, woe to him! He shall hear what I think of him!..."

And he turned to go out. But when he reached the door he remembered his donkey's ears, and feeling ashamed to show them in public, what do you think he did? He took a big cotton cap, and putting it on his head he pulled it well down over the point of his nose.

He then set out, and went everywhere in search of Candlewick. He looked for him in the streets, in the squares, in the little theatres, in every possible place; but he could not find him. He inquired for him of everybody he met, but no one had seen him.

He then went to seek him at his house; and having reached the door he knocked.

"Who is there?" asked Candlewick from within.

"It is I!" answered the puppet.

"Wait a moment and I will let you in."

After half an hour the door was opened, and imagine Pinocchio's feelings when upon going into the room he saw his friend Candlewick with a big cotton cap on his head which came down over his nose.

At the sight of the cap Pinocchio felt almost consoled, and thought to himself: "Has my friend got the same illness that I have? Is he also suffering from donkey fever?..."

And pretending to have observed nothing he asked him, smiling: "How are you, my dear Candlewick?"

"Very well; as well as a mouse in a Parmesan cheese."

"Are you saying that seriously?"

"Why should I tell you a lie?"

"Excuse me; but why, then, do you keep that cotton cap on your head which covers up your ears?"

"The doctor ordered me to wear it because I have hurt this knee. And you, dear puppet, why have you got on that cotton cap pulled down over your nose?"

"The doctor prescribed it because I have grazed my foot."

"Oh, poor Pinocchio!..."

"Oh, poor Candlewick!..."

After these words a long silence followed, during which the two friends did nothing but look mockingly at each other.

At last the puppet said in a soft mellifluous voice to his companion: "Satisfy my curiosity, my dear Candlewick: have you ever suffered from disease of the ears?"

"Never!...And you?"

"Never! Only since this morning one of my ears aches."

"Mine is also paining me."

"You also?...And which of your ears hurts you?"

"Both of them. And you?"

"Both of them. Can we have got the same illness?"

"I fear so."

"Will you do me a kindness, Candlewick?"

"Willingly! With all my heart."

"Will you let me see your ears?"

"Why not? But first, my dear Pinocchio, I should like to see yours."

"No, you must be the first."

"No, dear! First you and then I!"

"Well, " said the puppet, "let us come to an agreement like good friends."

"Let us hear it."

"We will both take off our caps at the same moment. Do you agree?"

"I agree."

"Then attention!"

And Pinocchio began to count in a loud voice: "One! Two! Three!"

At the word three! the two boys took off their caps and threw them into the air.

And then a scene followed that would seem incredible if it was not true. That is, that when Pinocchio and Candlewick discovered that they were both struck with the same misfortune, instead of feeling full of mortification and grief, they began to prick their ungainly ears and to make a thousand antics, and they ended by going into bursts of laughter.

And they laughed, and laughed, and laughed, until they had to hold themselves together. But in the midst of their merriment, Candlewick suddenly stopped, staggered, and changing colour said to his friend: "Help, help, Pinocchio!"

"What is the matter with you?"

"Alas, I cannot any longer stand upright."

"No more can I, " exclaimed Pinocchio, tottering and beginning to cry.

And whilst they were talking they both doubled up and began to run round the room on their hands and feet. And as they ran, their hands became hoofs, their faces lengthened into muzzles, and their backs became covered with a light grey hairy coat sprinkled with black.

But do you know what was the worst moment for these two wretched boys? The worst and the most humiliating moment was when their tails grew Vanquished by shame and sorrow they wept and lamented their fate.

Oh, if they had but been wiser! But instead of sighs and lamentations they could only bray like asses; and they brayed loudly and said in chorus: "j-a, j-a, j-a.

Whilst this was going on some one knocked at the door, and a voice on the outside said: "Open the door! I am the little man, I am the coachman, who brought you to this country. Open at once, or it will be the worse for you!"

Chapter 33

Pinocchio having become a genuine little donkey, is taken to be sold, and is bought by the director of a company of buffoons to be taught to dance, and to jump through hoops: but one evening he lames himself, and then he is bought by a man who purposes to make a drum of his skin.

FINDING that the door remained shut the little man burst it open with a violent kick, and coming into the room he said to Pinocchio and Candlewick with his usual little laugh: "Well done, boys! You brayed well, and I recognised you by your voices. That is why I am here."

At these words the two little donkeys were quite stupefied, and stood with their heads down, their ears lowered, and their tails between their legs.

At first the little man stroked and caressed them; then taking out a currycomb he currycombed them well. And when by this process he had polished them till they shone like two mirrors, he put a halter round their necks and led them to the market-place, in hopes of selling them and making a good profit.

And indeed buyers were not wanting. Candlewick was bought by a peasant whose donkey had died the previous day. Pinocchio was sold to the director of a company of buffoons and tight-rope dancers, who bought him that he might teach him to leap and to dance with the other animals belonging to the company.

And now, my little readers, you will have understood the fine trade that little man pursued. The wicked little monster, who had a face all milk and honey, made frequent journeys round the world with his coach. As he went along he collected, with promises and flattery, all the idle boys who had taken an aversion to books and school. As soon as his coach was full he conducted them to the "Land of Boobies, " that they might pass their time in games, in uproar, and in amusement. When these poor deluded boys, from continual play and no study, had become so many little donkeys, he took possession of them with great delight and satisfaction, and carried them off to the fairs and markets to be sold. And in this way he had in a few years made heaps of money and had become a millionaire.

What became of Candlewick I do not know; but I do know that Pinocchio from the very first day had to endure a very hard, laborious life.

When he was put into his stall his master filled the manger with straw; but Pinocchio, having tried a mouthful, spat it out again.

Then his master, grumbling, filled the manger with hay; but neither did the hay please him.

"Ah!" exclaimed his master in a passion. "Does not hay please you either? Leave it to me, my fine donkey; if you are so full of caprices I will find a way to cure you!..."

And by way of correcting him he struck his legs with his whip.

Pinocchio began to cry and to bray with pain, and he said, braying:"J-a, j-a, I cannot digest straw!..."

"Then eat hay!" said his master, who understood perfectly the asinine dialect.

"J-a, j-a, hay gives me a pain in my stomach."

"Do you mean to pretend that a little donkey like you must be kept on breasts of chickens, and capons in jelly?" asked his master, getting more and more angry, and whipping him again.

At this second whipping Pinocchio prudently held his tongue and said nothing more.

The stable was then shut and Pinocchio was left alone. He had not eaten for many hours, and he began to yawn from hunger. And when he yawned he opened a mouth that seemed as wide as an oven.

At last, finding nothing else in the manger, he resigned himself, and chewed a little hay; and after he had chewed it well, he shut his eyes and swallowed it.

"This hay is not bad, " he said to himself; "but how much better it would have been if I had gone on with my studies!... Instead of hay I might now be eating a hunch of new bread and a fine slice of sausage! But I must have patience!..."

The next morning when he woke he looked in the manger for a little more hay; but he found none, for he had eaten it all during the night.

Then he took a mouthful of chopped straw; but whilst he was chewing it he had to acknowledge that the taste of chopped straw did not in the least resemble a savoury dish of macaroni or rice.

"But I must have patience!" he repeated as he went on chewing. "May my example serve at least as a warning to all disobedient boys who do not want to study. Patience!...patience!..."

"Patience indeed!" shouted his master, coming at that moment into the stable. "Do you think, my little donkey, that I bought you only to give you food and drink? I bought you to make you work, and that you might earn money for me. Up, then, at once!

you must come with me into the circus, and there I will teach you to jump through hoops, to go through frames of paper head foremost, to dance waltzes and polkas, and to stand upright on your hind legs."

Poor Pinocchio, either by love or by force, had to learn all these fine things Butit took him three months before he had learnt them, and he got many a whipping that nearly took off his skin.

At last a day came when his master was able to announce that he would give a really extraordinary representation and many-coloured placards were stuck on the street comers.

On that evening, as you may imagine, an hour before the play was to begin the theatre was crammed.

There was not a place to be had either in the pit or the stalls, or in the boxes even, by paying its weight in gold.

The benches round the circus were crowded with children and with boys of all ages, who were in a fever of impatience to see the famous little donkey Pinocchio dance.

When the first part of the performance was over, the director of the company, dressed in a black coat, white shorts, and big leather boots that came above his knees, presented himself to the public, and after making a profound bow he began with much solemnity the following ridiculous speech: "Respectable public, ladies and gentlemen! The humble undersigned being a passer-by in this illustrious city, I have wished to procure for myself the honour, not to say the pleasure, of presenting to this intelligent and distinguished audience a celebrated little donkey, who has already had the honour of dancing in the presence of His Majesty the Emperor of all the principal Courts of Europe. "

"And thanking you, I beg of you to help us with your inspiring presence and to be indulgent to us."

This speech was received with much laughter and applause; but the applause redoubled and became tumultuous when the little donkey Pinocchio made his appearance in the middle of the circus. He was decked out for the occasion. He had a new bridle of polished leather with brass buckles and studs, and two white camelias in his ears. His mane was divided and curled, and each curl was tied with bows of coloured ribbon. He had a girth of gold and silver round his body, and his tail was plaited with amaranth and blue velvet ribbons. He was, in fact, a little donkey to fall in love with!

The director, in presenting him to the public, added these few words: "My respectable auditors! I am not here to tell you falsehoods of the great difficulties that I have overcome in understanding and subjugating this mammifer, whilst he was grazing at liberty amongst the mountains in the plains of the torrid zone. I beg you will observe the wild rolling of his eyes. Every means having been tried in vain to tame him, and to accustom him to the life of domestic quadrupeds, I was often forced to have recourse to the convincing argument of the whip. But all my goodness to him, instead of gaining his affections, has, on the contrary, increased his viciousness. However, following the system of Gall, I discovered in his cranium a bony cartilage, that the Faculty of Medicine in Paris has itself recognised as the regenerating bulb of the hair, and of dance. For this reason I have not only taught him to dance, but also to jump through hoops and through frames covered with paper. Admire him, and then pass your opinion on him! But before taking my leave of you, permit me, ladies and gentlemen, to invite you to the daily performance that will take place tomorrow evening; but in the apotheosis that the weather should threaten rain, the performance will be postponed till tomorrow morning at eleven antemeridian of postmeridian."

Here the director made another profound bow; and then turning to Pinocchio, he said: "Courage, Pinocchio! before you begin your feats make your bow to this distinguished audience-ladies, gentlemen, and children."

Pinocchio obeyed, and bent both his knees till they touched the ground, and remained kneeling until the director, cracking his whip, shouted to him: "At a foot's pace!"

Then the little donkey raised himself on his four legs and began to walk round the theatre, keeping at a foot's pace.

After a little the director cried: "Trot!" and Pinocchio, obeying the order, changed to a trot.

"Gallop!" and Pinocchio broke into a gallop.

"Full gallop!" and Pinocchio went full gallop. But whilst he was going full speed like a racehorse the director, raising his arm in the air, fired off a pistol.

At the shot the little donkey, pretending to be wounded, fell his whole length in the circus, as if he was really dying.

As he got up from the ground amidst an outburst of applause, shouts, and clapping of hands, he naturally raised his head and looked up...and he saw in one of the boxes a beautiful lady who wore round her neck a thick gold chain from which hung a medallion. On the medallion was painted the portrait of a puppet.

"That is my portrait!...that lady is the Fairy!" said Pinocchio to himself, recognising her immediately; and overcome with delight he tried to cry: "Oh, my little Fairy! Oh, my little Fairy!"

But instead of these words a bray came from his throat, so sonorous and so prolonged that all the spectators laughed, and more especially all the children who were in the theatre.

Then the director, to give him a lesson, and to make him understand that it is not good manners to bray before the public, gave him a blow on his nose with the handle of his whip.

The poor little donkey put his tongue out an inch, and licked his nose for at least five minutes, thinking perhaps that it would ease the pain he felt.

But what was his despair when, looking up a second time, he saw that the box was empty and that the Fairy had disappeared!..

He thought he was going to die: his eyes filled with tears and he began to weep. Nobody, however, noticed it, and least of all the director who, cracking his whip, shouted: "Courage, Pinocchio! Now let the audience see how gracefully you can jump through the hoops."

Pinocchio tried two or three times, but each time that he came in front of the hoop' instead of going through it, he found it easier to go under it. At last he made a leap and went through it; but his right leg unfortunately caught in the hoop, and that caused him to fall to the ground doubled up in a heap on the other side.

When he got up he was lame, and it was only with great difficulty that he managed to return to the stable.

"Bring out Pinocchio! We want the little donkey! Bring out the little donkey!" shouted all the boys in the theatre, touched and sorry for the sad accident.

But the little donkey was seen no more that evening.

The following morning the veterinary, that is, the doctor of animals, paid him a visit, and declared that he would remain lame for life.

The director then said to the stable-boy: "What do you suppose I can do with a lame donkey? He would eat food without earning it. Take him to the market and sell him."

When they reached the market a purchaser was found at once. He asked the stable-boy: "How much do you want for that lame donkey?"

"Twenty francs."

"I will give you twenty pence. Don't suppose that I am buying him to make use of; I am buying him solely for his skin. I see that his skin is very hard, and I intend to make a drum with it for the band of my village."

I leave it to my readers to imagine poor Pinocchio's feelings when he heard that he was destined to become a drum!

As soon as the purchaser had paid his twenty pence he conducted the little donkey to the seashore. He then put a stone round his neck, and tying a rope, the end of which he held in his hand, round his leg, he gave him a sudden push and threw him into the water.

Pinocchio, weighed down by the stone, went at once to the bottom; and his owner, keeping tight hold of the cord, sat down quietly on a piece of rock to wait until the little donkey was drowned, intending then to skin him.

Chapter 34

Pinocchio, having been thrown into the sea, is eaten by the fish and becomes a puppet as he was before. Whilst he is swimming away to save his life he is swallowed by the terrible Dog-fish.

AFTER Pinocchio had been fifty minutes under the water, his purchaser said aloud to himself: "My poor little lame donkey must by this time be quite drowned. I will therefore pull him out of the water, and I will make a fine drum of his skin."

And he began to haul in the rope that he had tied to the donkey's leg; and he hauled, and hauled, and hauled, until at last.. what do you think appeared above the water? Instead of a little dead donkey he saw a live puppet, who was wriggling like an eel.

Seeing this wooden puppet the poor man thought he was dreaming, and, struck dumb with astonishment, he remained with his mouth open and his eyes starting out of his head.

Having somewhat recovered from his first stupefaction, he asked in a quavering voice: "And the little donkey that I threw into the sea? What has become of him?"

"I am the little donkey!" said Pinocchio, laughing.

"You?"

"I."

"Ah, you young scamp! Do you dare to make game of me?"

"To make game of you? Quite the contrary, my dear master; I am speaking seriously."

"But how can you, who, but a short time ago, were a little donkey, have become a wooden puppet, only from having been left in the water?"

"It must have been the effect of sea-water. The sea makes extraordinary changes."

"Beware, puppet, beware!... Don't imagine that you can amuse yourself at my expense. Woe to you, if I lose patience!..."

"Well, master, do you wish to know the true story? If you will set my leg free I will tell it you."

The good man, who was curious to hear the true story, immediately untied the knot that kept him bound; and Pinocchio, finding himself as free as a bird in the air, commenced as follows: "You must know that I was once a puppet as I am now, and I was on the point of becoming a boy like the many that there are in the world. But instead, induced by my dislike to study and the advice of bad companions, I ran away from home…and one fine day when I awoke I found myself changed into a donkey with long ears… and a long tail!…What a disgrace it was to me!-a disgrace, dear master, that the blessed St Anthony would not inflict even upon you! Taken to the market to be sold I was bought by the director of an equestrian company, who took it into his head to make a famous dancer of me, and a famous leaper through hoops. But one night during a performance I had a bad fall in the circus and lamed both my legs. Then the director, not knowing what to do with a lame donkey, sent me to be sold, and you were the purchaser!…"

"Only too true! And I paid twenty pence for you. And now who will give me back my poor pennies?"

"And why did you buy me? You bought me to make a drum of my skin!… a drum!…"

"Only too true! And now where shall I find another skin?…"

"Don't despair, master. There are such a number of little donkeys in the world!"

"Tell me, you impertinent rascal, does your story end here?"

"No, " answered the puppet; "I have another two words to

say and then I shall have finished. After you had bought me you brought me to this place to kill me; but then, yielding to a feeling of compassion, you preferred to tie a stone round my neck and to throw me into the sea. This humane feeling does you great honour, and I shall always be grateful to you for it. But nevertheless, dear master, this time you made your calculations without considering the Fairy!..."

"And who is this Fairy?"

"She is my mamma, and she resembles all other good mammas who care for their children, and who never lose sight of them, but help them lovingly, even when, on account of their foolishness and evil conduct, they deserve to be abandoned and left to themselves. Well, then, the good Fairy, as soon as she saw that I was in danger of drowning, sent immediately an immense shoal of fish, who, believing me really to be a little dead donkey, began to eat me. And what mouthfuls they took! I should never have thought that fish were greedier than boys!...Some ate my ears, some my muzzle, others my neck and mane, some the skin of my legs, some my coat.. and amongst them there was a little fish so polite that he even condescended to eat my tail."

"From this time forth, " said his purchaser, horrified, "I swear that I will never touch fish. It would be too dreadful to open a mullet, or a fried whiting, and to find inside a donkey's tail!"

"I agree with you, " said the puppet, laughing. "However, I must tell you that when the fish had finished eating the donkey's hide that covered me from head to foot, they naturally reached the bone...or rather the wood, for as you see I am made of the hardest wood. But after giving a few bites they soon discovered that I was not a morsel for their teeth, and, disgusted with such indigestible food, they went off, some in one direction and some in another, without so much as saying thank you to me. And now, at last, I have told you how it was that when you pulled up the rope you found a live puppet instead of a dead donkey."

"I laugh at your story, " cried the man in a rage. "I know only that I spent twenty pence to buy you, and I will have my money back. Shall I tell you what I will do? I will take you back to the market and I will sell you by weight as seasoned wood for lighting fires."

"Sell me if you like; I am content, " said Pinocchio.

But as he said it he made a spring and plunged into the water. Swimming gaily away from the shore he called to his poor owner: "Good-bye, master; if you should be in want of a skin to make a drum, remember me."

And he laughed and went on swimming; and after a while he turned again and shouted louder: "Good-bye, master; if you should be in want of a little well-seasoned wood for lighting the fire, remember me."

In the twinkling of an eye he had swum so far off that he was scarcely visible. All that could be seen of him was a little black speck on the surface of the sea that from time to time lifted its legs out of the water and leapt and capered like a dolphin enjoying himself.

Whilst Pinocchio was swimming he knew not whither he saw in the midst of the sea a rock that seemed to be made of white marble, and on the summit there stood a beautiful little goat who bleated lovingly and made signs to him to approach.

But the most singular thing was this. The little goat's hair, instead of being white or black, or a mixture of two colours as is usual with other goats, was blue, and of a very vivid blue, greatly resembling the hair of the beautiful Child.

I leave you to imagine how rapidly poor Pinocchio's heart began to beat. He swam with redoubled strength and energy towards the white rock; and he was already half-way when he saw, rising up out of the water and coming to meet him, the horrible head of a sea-monster. His wide-open cavernous mouth and his three rows of enormous teeth would have been terrifying to look at even in a picture.

And do you know what this sea-monster was?

This sea-monster was neither more nor less than that gigantic Dog-fish who has been mentioned many times in this story, and who, for his slaughter and for his insatiable voracity, had been named the "Attila of fish and fishermen."

Only think of poor Pinocchio's terror at the sight of the monster. He tried to avoid it, to change his direction; he tried to escape; but that immense wideopen mouth came towards him with the velocity of an arrow.

"Be quick, Pinocchio, for pity's sake, " cried the beautiful little goat, bleating.

And Pinocchio swam desperately with his arms, his chest, his legs, and his feet.

"Quick, Pinocchio, the monster is close upon you!... "

And Pinocchio swam quicker than ever, and flew on with the rapidity of a ball from a gun. He had nearly reached the rock, and the little goat, leaning over towards the sea, had stretched out her fore-legs to help him out of the water!...

But it was too late! The monster had overtaken him, and, drawing in his breath, he sucked in the poor puppet as he would have sucked a hen's egg; and he swallowed him with such violence and avidity that Pinocchio, in falling into the Dog-fish's stomach, received such a blow that he remained unconscious for a quarter of an hour afterwards.

When he came to himself again after the shock he could not in the least imagine in what world he was. All round him it was quite dark, and the darkness was so black and so profound that it seemed to him that he had fallen head downwards in to an inkstand full of ink. He listened, but he could hear no noise; only from time to time great gusts of wind blew in his face. At first he could not understand where the wind came from, but at last he discovered that it came out of the monster's lungs. For you must know that the Dog-fish suffered very much from asthma, and when he breathed it was exactly as if a north wind was blowing: Pinocchio at first tried to keep up his courage; but when he had one proof after another that he was really shut up in the body of this sea-monster he began to cry and scream and to sob out: "Help! help! Oh, how unfortunate I am! Will nobody come to save me?"

"Who do you think could save you, unhappy wretch?..." said a voice in the dark that sounded like a guitar out of tune.

"Who is speaking?" asked Pinocchio, frozen with terror.

"It is I! I am a poor Tunny who was swallowed by the Dog-fish atthe same time that you were. And what fish are you?"

"I have nothing in common with fish. I am a puppet."

"Then if you are not a fish, why did you let yourself be swallowed by the monster?"

"I didn't let myself be swallowed: it was the monster swallowed me! And now, what are we to do here in the dark?"

"Resign ourselves and wait until the Dog-fish has digested us both."

"But I do not want to be digested!" howled Pinocchio, beginning to cry again.

"Neither do I want to be digested, " added the Tunny; "but I am enough of a philosopher to console myself by thinking that when one is born a Tunny it is more dignified to die in the water than in oil."

"That is all nonsense!" cried Pinocchio.

"It is my opinion, " replied the Tunny; and opinions, so say the political Tunnies, ought to be respected.

"To sum it all up…I want to get away from here… I want to escape." "Escape if you are able!…"

"Is this Dog-fish who has swallowed us very big?" asked the puppet.

"Big! Why, only imagine, his body is two miles long without counting his tail."

Whilst they were holding this conversation in the dark, Pinocchio thought that he saw a light a long way off.

"What is that little light I see in the distance?" he asked.

"It is most likely some companion in misfortune who is waiting like us to be digested."

"I will go and find him. Do you not think that it may by chance be some old fish who perhaps could show us how to escape?"

"I hope it may be so with all my heart, dear puppet."

"Good-bye, Tunny."

"Good-bye, puppet, and good fortune attend you."

"Where shall we meet again?..."

"Who can say?...It is better not even to think of it!"

Chapter 35

**Pinocchio finds in the body of the Dog-fish... whom does he find?
Read this chapter and you will know.**

PINOCCHIO, having taken leave of his friend the Tunny, began to grope his way in the dark through the body of the Dog-fish, taking a step at a time in the direction of the light that he saw shining dimly at a great distance.

The farther he advanced the brighter became the light; and he walked and walked until at last he reached it: and when he reached it...what did he find? I will give you a thousand guesses. He found a little table spread out, and on it a lighted candle stuck into a green glass bottle, and seated at the table was a little old man. He was eating some live fish, and they were so very much alive that whilst he was eating them they sometimes even jumped out of his mouth.

At this sight Pinocchio was filled with such great and unexpected joy that he became almost delirious. He wanted to laugh, he wanted to cry, he wanted to say a thousand things, and instead he could only stammer out a few confused and broken words. At last he succeeded in uttering, a cry of joy, and opening his arms he threw them round the little old man's neck, and began to shout: "Oh, my dear papa! I have found you at last! I will never leave you more. never more. never more!"

"Then my eyes tell me true?" said the little old man, rubbing his eyes; "then you are really my dear Pinocchio?"

"Yes, yes, I am Pinocchio, really Pinocchio! And you have quite forgiven me, have you not? Oh, my dear papa, how good you are!...and to think that I, on the contrary...Oh! But if you only knew what misfortunes have been poured on my head, and all that has befallen me! Only imagine, the day that you, poor dear papa, sold your coat to buy me a spelling-book that I might go to school, I escaped to see the puppet-show, and the showman wanted to put me on the fire that I might roast his mutton, and he was the same that afterwards gave me five gold pieces to take them to you, but I met the Fox and the Cat, who took me to the Inn of the Red Crawfish, where they ate like wolves, and I left by myself in the middle of the night, and I encountered assassins who ran after me, and I ran away, and they followed, and I ran, and they always followed me, and I ran, until they hung me to a branch of a Big Oak, and the beautiful Child with blue hair sent a little carriage to fetch me, and the doctors when they saw had seen me said immediately, "If he is not dead, it is a proof that he is still alive"-and then by chance I told a lie, and my nose began to grow until I could no longer get through the door of the room, for which reason I went with the Fox and the Cat to bury the four gold pieces, for one I had spent at the inn, and the Parrot began to laugh, and instead of two thousand gold pieces I found none left, for which reason the judge when he heard that I had been robbed had me immediately put in prison to content the robbers, and then when I was coming away I saw a beautiful bunch of grapes in a field, and I was caught in a trap, and the peasant, who was quite right, put a dog-collar round my neck that I might guard the poultry-yard, and acknowledging my innocence let me go, and the Serpent with the smoking tail began to laugh and broke a blood-vessel in his chest, and so I returned to the house of the beautiful Child who was dead, and the Pigeon, seeing that I was crying, said to me, "I have seen your father who was building a little boat to go in search of you, " and I said to him, "Oh! if I had also wings, " and he said to me, "Do you want to go to your father?" and I said, "Without doubt! but who will take me to him?" and he said to me, "I will take you, " and I said to him, " How?" and he said to me, "Get on my back, " and so we flew all night, and then in the morning all the fishermen who were looking out to sea said to me, "There is a poor man in a boat who is on the point of being drowned, " and I recognised you at once, even at that distance, for my heart told me, and I made signs to you to return to land..."

"I also recognised you, " said Geppetto, "and I would willingly have returned to the shore: but what was I to do! The sea was tremendous, and a great wave upset my boat. Then a horrible Dog-fish who was near, as soon as he saw me in the water, came towards me, and putting out his tongue took hold of me, and swallowed me as if I had been a little Bologna tart."

"And how long have you been shutup here?" asked Pinocchio.

"Since that day-it must be nearly two years ago: two years, my dear Pinocchio, that have seemed to me like two centuries!"

"And how have you managed to live? And where did you get-the candle?

And the matches to light it? Who gave them to you?"

"Stop, and I will tell you everything. You must know, then, that in the same storm in which my boat was upset a merchant vessel foundered. The sailors were all saved, but the vessel went to the bottom, and the Dog-fish, who had that day an excellent appetite, after he had swallowed me, swallowed also the vessel..."

"How?"

"He swallowed it in one mouthful, and the only thing that he spat out was the mainmast, that had stuck between his teeth like a fish-bone. Fortunately for me the vessel was laden with preserved meat in tins, biscuit, bottles of wine, dried raisins, cheese, coffee, sugar, candles, and boxes of wax matches. With this providential supply I have been able to live for two years. But I have arrived at the end of my resources: there is nothing left in the larder, and this candle that you see burning is the last that remains..."

"And after that?"

"After that, dear boy, we shall both remain in the dark."

"Then, dear little papa, " said Pinocchio, "there is no time to lose. We must think of escaping..."

"Of escaping?...and how?"

"We must escape through the mouth of the Dog-fish, throw ourselves into the sea and swim away."

"You talk well: but, dear Pinocchio, I don't know how to swim."

"What does that matter?...I am a good swimmer, and you can get on my shoulders and I will carry you safely to shore."

"All illusions, my boy!" replied Geppetto, shaking his head, with a melancholy smile. "Do you suppose it possible that a puppet like you, scarcely a metre high, could have the strength to swim with me on his shoulders!"

"Try it and you will see!"

Without another word Pinocchio took the candle in his hand, and going in front to light the way, he said to his father: "Follow me, and don't be afraid."

And they walked for some time and traversed the body and the stomach of the Dog-fish. But when they had arrived at the point where the monster's big throat began, they thought it better to stop to give a good look round and to choose the best moment for escaping.

Now I must tell you that the Dog-fish, being very old, and suffering from asthma and palpitation of the heart, was obliged to sleep with his mouth open. Pinocchio, therefore, having approached the entrance to his throat and, looking up, could see beyond the enormous gaping mouth a large piece of starry sky and beautiful moonlight.

"This is the moment to escape, " he whispered, turning to his father; "the Dog-fish is sleeping like a dormouse, the sea is calm, and it is as light as day. Follow me, dear papa, and in a short time we shall be in safety."

They immediately climbed up the throat of the sea-monster, and having reached his immense mouth they began to walk on tiptoe down his tongue.

Before taking the final leap the puppet said to his father: "Get on my shoulders and put your aims tight round my neck. I will take care of the rest."

As soon as Geppetto was firmly settled on his son's shoulders, Pinocchio, feeling sure of himself, threw himself into the water and began to swim. The sea was as smooth as oil, the moon shone brilliantly, and the Dog-fish was sleeping so profoundly that even a cannonade would have failed to wake him.

Chapter 36

Pinocchio at last ceases to be a puppet and becomes a boy.

WHILST Pinocchio was swimming quickly towards the shore he discovered that his father, who was on his shoulders with his legs in the water, was trembling as violently as if the poor man had got an attack of ague fever.

Was he trembling from cold or from fear?... Perhaps a little from both the one and the other. But Pinocchio, thinking that it was from fear, said to comfort him: "Courage, papa! In a few minutes we shall be safely on shore."

"But where is this blessed shore?" asked the little old man, becoming still more frightened, and screwing up his eyes as tailors do when they wish to thread a needle. "I have been looking in every direction and I see nothing but the sky and the sea."

"But I see the shore as well, " said the puppet.

"You must know that I am like a cat: I see better by night than by day."

Poor Pinocchio was making a pretence of being in good spirits, but in reality...in reality he was beginning to feel discouraged: his strength was failing, he was gasping and panting for breath...he could do no more, and the shore was still far off.

He swam until he had no breath left; then he turned his head to Geppetto and said in broken words: "Papa...help me...I am dying!..."

The father and son were on the point of drowning when they heard a voice like a guitar out of tune saying: "Who is it that is dying?"

"It is I, and my poor father!..."

"I know that voice! You are Pinocchio!"

"Precisely: and you?"

"I am the Tunny, your prison companion in the body of the Dog-fish." "And how did you manage to escape?"

"I followed your example. You showed me the road, and I escaped after you."

"Tunny, you have arrived at the right moment! I implore you to help us, or we are lost."

"Willingly and with all my heart. You must, both of you, take hold of my tail and leave me to guide you. I will take you on shore in four minutes."

Geppetto and Pinocchio, as I need not tell you, accepted the offer at once; but instead of holding on by his tail they thought it would be more comfortable to get on the Tunny's back.

Having reached the shore Pinocchio sprang first on land that he might help his father to do the same. He then turned to the Tunny, and said to him in a voice full of emotion: "My friend, you have saved my papa's life. I can find no words with which to thank you properly. Permit me at least to give you a kiss as a sign of my eternal gratitude!..."

The Tunny put his head out of the water, and Pinocchio, kneeling on the ground, kissed him tenderly on the mouth. At this spontaneous proof of warm aifection, the poor Tunny, who was not accustomed to it, felt extremely touched, and ashamed to let himself be seen crying like a child, he plunged under the water and disappeared.

By this time the day had dawned. Pinocchio then offering his arm to Geppetto, who had scarcely breath to stand, said to him: "Lean on my arm, dear papa, and let us go. We will walk very slowly like the ants, and when we are tired we can rest by the wayside."

"And where shall we go?" asked Geppetto.

"In search of some house or cottage, where they will give us for charity a mouthful of bread, and a little straw to serve as a bed."

They had not gone a hundred yards when they saw by the roadside two villainous-looking individuals begging.

They were the Cat and the Fox, but they were scarcely recognisable. Fancy! the Cat had so long feigned blindness that she had become blind in reality and the Fox, old, mangy, and with one side paralysed, had not even his tail left. That sneaking thief having fallen into the most squalid misery, one fine day had found himself obliged to sell his beautiful tail to a travelling pedlar, who bought it to drive away flies.

"Oh, Pinocchio!" cried the Fox, "give a little in charity to two poor infirm people."

"Infirm people, " repeated the Cat.

"Begone, impostors!" answered the puppet." You took me in once, but you will never catch me again."

"Believe me, Pinocchio, we are now poor and unfortunate indeed!"

"If you are poor, you deserve it. Recollect the proverb:"Stolen money never fructifies. "Begone, impostors!"

And thus saying Pinocchio and Geppetto went their way in peace. When they had gone another hundred yards they saw, at the end of a path in the middle of the fields, a nice little straw hut with a roof of tiles and bricks.

"That hut must be inhabited by some one, " said Pinocchio. "Let us go and knock at the door."

They went and knocked.

"Who is there?" said a little voice from within.

"We are a poor father and son without bread and without a roof, " answered the puppet.

"Turn the key and the door will open, " said the same little voice.

Pinocchio turned the key and the door opened. They went in and looked here, there, and everywhere, but could see no one.

"Oh! where is the master of the house?" said Pinocchio, much surprised. "Here I am up here!"

The father and son looked immediately up to the ceiling, and there on a beam they saw the Talking cricket.

"Oh, my dear little Cricket!" said Pinocchio, bowing politely to him.

"Ah! now you call me 'Your dear little Cricket.' But do you remember the time when you threw the handle of a hammer at me, to drive me from your house?..."

"You are right, Cricket! Drive me away also...throw the handle of a hammer at me; but have pity on my poor papa..."

"I will have pity on both father and son, but I wished to remind you of the ill treatment I received from you, to teach you that in this world, when it is possible, we should show courtesy to everybody, if we wish it to be extended to us in our hour of need."

"You are right, Cricket, you are right, and I will bear in mind the lesson you have given me. But tell me how you managed to buy this beautiful hut."

"This hut was given to me yesterday by a goat whose wool was of a beautiful blue colour."

"And where has the goat gone?" asked Pinocchio with lively curiosity "I do not know."

"And when will it come back?..."

"It will never come back. It went away yesterday in great grief and, bleating, it seemed to say: 'Poor Pinocchio...I shall never see him more...by this time the Dog-fish must have devoured him!...'"

"Did it really say that?...Then it was she!...it was she!... it was my dear little Fairy..." exclaimed Pinocchio, crying and sobbing.

When he had cried for some time he dried his eyes, and prepared a comfortable bed of straw for Geppetto to lie down upon. Then he asked the Cricket: "Tell me, little Cricket, where can I find a tumbler of milk for my poor papa?"

"Three fields off from here there lives a gardener called Giangio who keeps cows. Go to him and you will get the milk you are in want of."

Pinocchio ran all the way to Giangio's house; and the gardener asked him: "How much milk do you want?"

"I want a tumblerful."

"A tumbler of milk costs a halfpemly. Begin by giving me the halfpenny."

"I have not even a farthing, " replied Pinocchio, grieved and mortified.

"That is bad, puppet, " answered the gardener. "If you have not even a farthing, I have not even a drop of milk."

"I must have patience!" said Pinocchio, and he turned to go.

"Wait a little, " said Giangio. "We can come to an arrangement together.

Will you undertake to tum the pumping machine?"

"What is the pumping machine?"

"It is a wooden pole which serves to draw up the water from the cistern to water the vegetables."

"You can try me..."

"Well, then, if you will draw a hundred buckets of water, I will give you in compensation a tumbler of milk."

"It is a bargain."

Giango then led Pinocchio to the kitchen garden and taught him how to turn the pumping machine. Pinocchio immediately began to work; but before he had drawn up the hundred buckets of water the perspiration was pouring from his head to his feet. Never before had he undergone such fatigue.

"Up till now, " said the gardener, "the labour of turning the pumping machine was performed by my little donkey; but the poor animal is dying."

"Willy ou take me to see him?" said Pinocchio.

"Willingly."

When Pinocchio went into the stable he saw a beautiful little donkey stretched on the straw, worn out from hunger and overwork. After looking at him earnestly he said to himself, much troubled: "I am sure I know this little donkey! His face is not new to me."

And bending over him he asked him in asinine language: "Who are you?"

At this question the little donkey opened his dying eyes, and answered in broken words in the same language: "I am...Can...dle...wick..."

And having again closed his eyes he expired.

"Oh, poor Candlewick!" said Pinocchio in a low voice; and taking a handful of straw he dried a tear that was rolling down his face.

"Do you grieve for a donkey that cost you nothing?" said the gardener. "What must it be to me who bought him for ready money?"

"I must tell you...he was my friend!"

"Your friend?"

"One of my schoolfellows!..."

"How?" shouted Giangio, laughing loudly. "How? had you donkeys for schoolfellows?...I can imagine what wonderful studies you must have made!..."

The puppet, who felt much mortified at these words, did not answer; but taking his tumbler of milk, still quite warm, he returned to the hut.

And from that day for more than five months he continued to get up at daybreak every morning to go and turn the pumping machine, to earn the tumbler of milk that was of such benefit to his father in his bad state of health. Nor was he satisfied with this; for during the time that he had over he learnt to make hampers and baskets of rushes, and with the money he obtained by selling them he was able with great economy to provide for all the daily expenses. Amongst other things he constructed an elegant little wheelchair, in which he could take his father out on fine days to breathe a mouthful of fresh air.

By his industry, ingenuity, and his anxiety to work and to overcome difficulties, he not only succeeded in maintaining his father, who continued infirm, in comfort, but he also contrived to put aside forty pence to buy himself a new coat.

One morning he said to his father:

"I am going to the neighbouring market to buy myself a jacket, a cap, and a pair of shoes. When I return, " he added, laughing, "I shall be so well dressed that you will take me for a fine gentleman."

And leaving the house he began to run merrily and happily along. All at once he heard himself called by name, and turning round he saw a big Snail crawling out from the hedge.

"Do you not know me?" asked the Snail.

"It seems to me... and yet I am not sure..."

"Do you not remember the Snail who was lady's - maid to the Fairy with blue hair? Do you not remember the time when I came downstairs to let you in, and you were caught by your foot which you had stuck through the house door?"

"I remember it all, "shouted Pinocchio. "Tell me quickly, my beautiful little Snail, where have you left my good Fairy? What is she doing? has she forgiven me? does she still remember me? does she still wish me well? is she far from here? can I go and see her?"

To all these rapid, breathless questions the Snail replied in her usual phlegmatic manner: "My dear Pinocchio, the poor Fairy is lying in bed at the hospital!..."

"At the hospital?..."

"It is only too true. Overtaken by a thousand misfortunes she has fallen seriously ill, and she has not even enough to buy herself a mouthful of bread."

"Is it really so?...Oh, what sorrow you have given me! Oh, poor Fairy-poor Fairy! poor Fairy!...If I had a million I would run and carry it to her... but I have only forty pence...here they are: I was going to buy a new coat. Take them, Snail, and carry them at once to my good Fairy. "

"And your new coat?..."

"What matters my new coat? I would sell even these rags that I have got on to be able to help her. Go, Snail, and be quick; and in two days return to this place, for I hope I shall then be able to give you some more money. Up to this time I have worked to maintain my papa: from today I will work five hours more that I may also maintain my good mamma. Good-bye, Snail, I shall expect you in two days."

The Snail, contrary to her usual habits, began to run like a lizard in a hot August sun.

That evening Pinocchio, instead of going to bed at ten o'clock, sat up till midnight had struck; and instead of making eight baskets of rushes he made sixteen.

Then he went to bed and fell asleep. And whilst he slept he thought that he saw the Fairy smiling and beautiful, who, after having kissed him, said to him: "Well done, Pinocchio! To reward you for your good heart I will forgive you for all that is past. Boys who minister tenderly to their parents, and assist them in their misery and infirmities, are deserving of great praise and affection, even if they cannot be cited as examples of obedience and good behaviour. Try and do better in the future and you will be happy."

At this moment his dream ended, and Pinocchio opened his eyes and awoke.

But imagine his astonishment when upon awakening he discovered that he was no longer a wooden puppet, but that he had become instead a boy, like all other boys. He gave a glance round and saw that the straw walls of the hut had disappeared, and that he was in a pretty little room furnished and arranged with a simplicity that was almost elegance. Jumping out of bed he found a new suit of clothes ready for him, a new cap, and a pair of new leather boots that fitted him beautifully.

He was hardly dressed when he naturally put his hands in his pockets, and pulled out a little ivory purse on which these words were written: "The Fairy with blue hair returns the forty pence to her dear Pinocchio, and thanks him for his good heart." He opened the purse, and instead of forty copper pennies he saw forty shining gold pieces fresh from the mint.

He then went and looked at himself in the glass, and he

The Adventure of Pinocchio

thought he was some one else. For he no longer saw the usual reflection of a wooden puppet; he was greeted instead by the image of a bright intelligent boy with chestnut hair, blue eyes, and looking as happy and joyful as if it were the Easter holidays.

In the midst of all these wonders succeeding each other Pinocchio felt quite bewildered, and he could not tell if he was really awake or if he was dreaming with his eyes open.

"Where can my papa be?" he exclaimed suddenly, and going into the next room he found old Geppetto quite well, lively, and in good humour, just as he had been formerly. He had already resumed his trade of wood-carving, and he was designing a rich and beautiful frame of leaves, flowers, and the heads of animals.

"Satisfy my curiosity, dear papa, " said Pinocchio, throwing his arms round his neck and covering him with kisses; "how can this sudden change be accounted for?"

"This sudden change in our home is all your doing, " answered Geppetto. "How my doing?"

"Because when boys who have behaved badly turn over a new leaf and become good, they have the power of bringing content and happiness to their families."

"And where has the old wooden Pinocchio hidden himself?"

"There he is, " answered Geppetto, and he pointed to a big puppet leaning against a chair, with its head on one side, its arms dangling, and its legs so crossed and bent that it was really a miracle that it remained standing.

國家圖書館出版品預行編目(CIP)資料

皮諾丘奇遇記裡的真相：小木偶教我們的 12 堂誠實人生課 (中英對照)/
卡洛・柯洛迪 (Carlo Collodi) 著；盛世教育譯 . -- 初版 . -- 新北市：笛藤出版，
2025.07
　面；　　公分
譯自：The adventures of Pinocchio
ISBN 978-957-710-997-2(平裝)

877.59　　　　　　114007774

皮諾丘──木偶奇遇記裡的真相
小木偶教我們的 12 堂誠實人生課（中英對照）

2025 年 7 月 28 日　初版第 1 刷　定價 450 元

著　　者	卡洛・柯洛迪（Carlo Collodi）
總 編 輯	洪季楨
美術設計	王舒玗
編輯企劃	笛藤出版
發 行 所	八方出版股份有限公司
發 行 人	林建仲
地　　址	新北市新店區寶橋路 235 巷 6 弄 6 號 4 樓
電　　話	(02) 2777-3682
傳　　真	(02) 2777-3672
總 經 銷	聯合發行股份有限公司
地　　址	新北市新店區寶橋路 235 巷 6 弄 6 號 2 樓
電　　話	(02) 2917-8022・(02) 2917-8042
製 版 廠	造極彩色印刷製版股份有限公司
地　　址	新北市中和區中山路二段 380 巷 7 號 1 樓
電　　話	(02) 2240-0333・(02) 2248-3904
郵撥帳戶	八方出版股份有限公司
郵撥帳號	19809050

●本書經合法授權，請勿翻印●
(本書裝訂如有漏印、缺頁、破損，請寄回更換。)

Pinocchio turned and looked at it; and after he had looked at it for a short time, he said to himself with great complacency: "How ridiculous I was when I was a puppet! and how glad I am that I have become a well-behaved LLTTLE BOY."